First Edition - Skull Cover Edition

Paperback ISBN - 978-1-916531-02-4

Editor - Rumi Khan

Proofreader - Moonlight Author Services

Cover Designer - Pretty In Ink Creations

Formatting - Moonlight Author Services

Contents

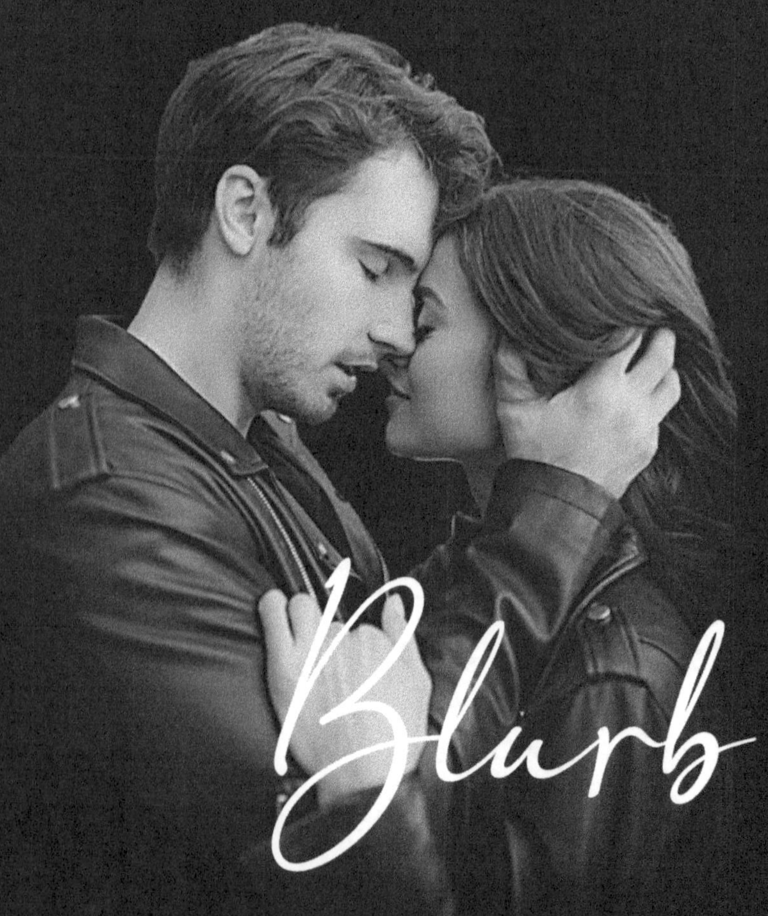

Blurb

Every woman in my life has let me down, hurt me, or abandoned me. Which is why the only female I hold close to my heart is Hallie—my daughter.

But being a single father comes with certain challenges, so I hire a nanny.

Someone who can do her hair, tell her stories, and be the motherly figure she doesn't have.

When Mia starts, I know she'll be perfect, but I have to keep her at arm's length. I tell myself it's because I don't know how to fix her broken soul from the past she's so desperate to hide, but in reality, it's more.

The way I feel about her scares me. She's beautiful, feisty, and so incredibly kind.

Although I try to deny it, I can feel myself falling for her. And when our pasts collide with the present, we have no choice but to face our demons together and fight.

Will I be able to finally put my fears aside and find true happiness?

THE *Beautifully Brutal* SERIES

WELCOME TO THE BEAUTIFULLY BRUTAL SERIES

Trust In Me is a dark mafia romance book that is part of the Beautifully Brutal series. This is Kellan and Mia's story. It follows on from the events of Black Wedding, and so it's advisable that you read that first.

If you want to learn some more about Kellan and his back story, you can read Dangerously Deceptive before starting Trust In Me. It's not necessary to read it in order to follow the main plot of the series, but you may want to learn more about tattooed single dad, Kellan, and how he became so distrusting of women.

The Beautifully Brutal series follows the Doughty's, an Irish mafia family that are fighting to hold onto their power. Each of the main books in the series follows one sibling and the person they fall in love with. So while each couple will get their own HFN ending in their book, you will get more out of the series by reading the others. There are main plots and themes that run through all the main books, and the other characters feature heavily in all the books. So, you will get more out of reading all the books in the series. See end of book for more information.

TO FOLLOW THE MAIN STORY LINE, THIS IS THE RECOMMENDED READING ORDER:

Black Wedding
Trust In Me
Fighting To Be Free
The Time Is Now
The Lies That Shatter
Together We Reign

I hope you enjoy Kellan and Mia's book as much as I enjoyed writing them. Kellan is one of my favourite character to date, and I'm sure you will love him too...

Author Note

Trust in Me is a dark mafia romance and is intended for mature audiences only. It features scenes that may be triggering for some people. For more specific details regarding if your trigger occurs in the book, please email:

emmalunaauthor@gmail.com

Trust in Me is set in both the UK and Ireland, and the story is written in UK English. So, please keep this in mind when reading. If you do think you have seen any spelling errors please contact the email above.

Thanks again for continuing on with the Beautifully Brutal Series. If you want to be kept up to date with all things Emma Luna, please join my newsletter here:

https://www.emmalunaauthor.com

Trust In Me is only intended for mature readers, and features some scenes that may be triggering for people. This list features the main triggers in the book, but is not exhaustive. I acknowledge that some people have triggers that may not be triggers for others. So, if you are worried, please reach out to me. I will respond quickly, and in the strictest of confidences, letting you know if your trigger features in the book or not. Please don't worry about getting in contact with me. Your mental health is important to me, and I don't ever want anyone to be triggered reading my books!

Please note - whilst the world the books are set in is dark, the relationship between the main characters is not. Ultimately it is a love story.

TRIGGERS INCLUDE:

Torture
Violence
Murder
Stalking/Threats
Suicidal Ideation
Drug use/misuse
Sexual Abuse/Non-Consent (not between main characters)
References to childhood abuse (physical and sexual)
Human trafficking
Grooming
Sex auction

Dedication

To My Jamie,
You are my sexy tech geek.
The person who taught me what a real guy should be like.
The person who I want by my side for the rest of my life.

You are my rock, my best friend, and my soul mate.
You showed me that two broken people can become whole.
I would be lost without you.

Always! Truth! And yes, Forever!
Thank you for standing by my side on this crazy journey.
Love You!

KELLAN AND MIA'S STORY

Trust in Me

EMMA LUNA

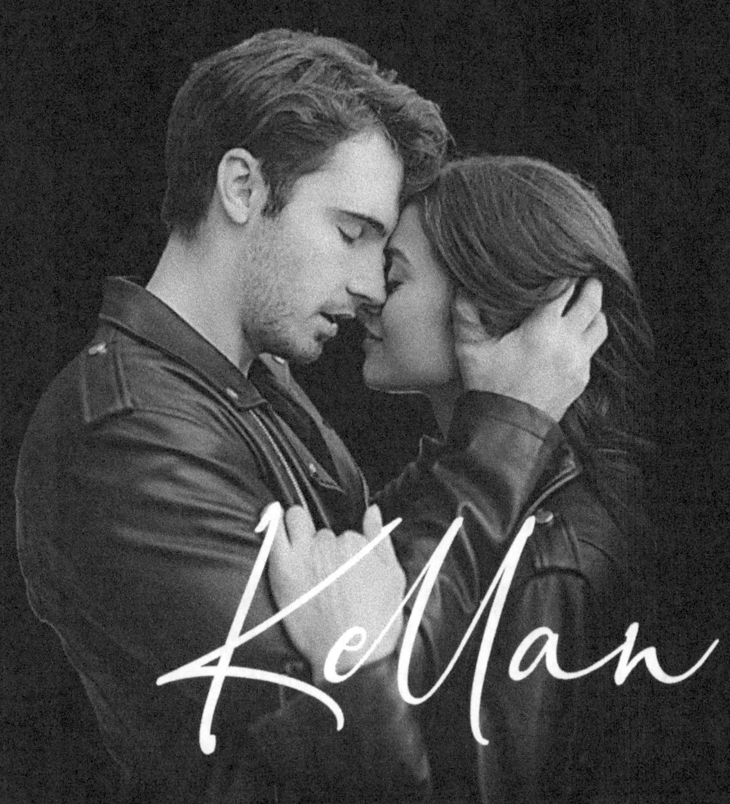

Kellan

"No, Liam. No, no, and no once more. I forbid you to let Mia move in. Whatever romantic hero bullshit you think you are playing here…well, you can think again. I am not interested. Now, pass me those baby wipes before this little monster decides to crawl away again," I whisper-shout at my best friend, as I pin my almost seven-month-old to the floor. Her old nappy is off, which means we are in dangerous territory. This is when she most enjoys running off and basically shitting everywhere. Now that she's mobile, it means I need eyes in the back of my fucking head.

"She is not a monster, don't ever call my beautiful Hallie Bear that," Liam coos, as he hands over the wet wipes.

"She doesn't look so beautiful with shit smeared all over her back and down her legs. Seriously, how does a person so little and cute produce so much shit?" I ask, more to myself than to Liam. I can feel him rolling his eyes at me. Hallie can do no wrong in his book. She could literally take a shit on the kitchen table and he would see the funny side in it.

Liam huffs before responding. "Look, baby shit aside, or actually, this is exactly the main reason why we are letting Mia move in. Firstly, after all the stuff that's been going on with Bree, she wants to have Mia close by. Plus, we have a lot more work coming in. Desmond has pissed someone off. He was working with someone to get financial backing when he was planning to make a move for London, and since he's currently on our side, he decided to cut all ties with this backer. He mentioned something about him being the worst kind of bad guy, which is rich coming from a psychopathic prick like him. Even so, he thinks this guy is playing the long game, and will ultimately want to make a move on us. We need to stop that before it happens. My wife's first year of rule will cement who she wants to be as a leader, and I intend to make sure it's a fucking good first year. So, to do that, we need your help. Which means we need all of you at work, not half of you while the other half is wondering what Hallie is doing. Is she eating something she shouldn't? Has she crawled off somewhere she shouldn't? Is she licking one of your computer wires again?"

"Hey! That was like one time, and I've made sure all the wires are out of the way and that she stays out of my work room from now on," I jump in, defending myself, holding a shit-covered baby wipe out to stop him from talking. Well…it was supposed to be just a hand, the universal sign for someone to stop talking, but I didn't have a free hand. I don't ever have one. I should have known that wouldn't be enough to stop Liam.

He edges closer to where I'm sitting on the floor with Hallie, and he takes one of her little hands in his. Of course she starts giggling and fluttering her eyelashes like the lovesick baby she is, and that arrogant prick just sits and smiles. "That's exactly my point, Kel. You need to work, and you can't worry about her while you do. And quite frankly, we cannot interview another fucking nanny." His deep groan fills my bedroom, and I know exactly what he means. I've lost track of the amount of nannies we've interviewed. I've met young ones, old ones, male ones, even one who looked exactly like Mary freakin' Poppins, but none of them were right.

Releasing the breath I didn't know I was holding, I pull up Hallie's leggings, before pulling the bright pink jumper dress down over her incredibly padded ass. She clutches onto my hair for dear life as she wobbles around, not quite steady on her feet yet. My hiss doesn't bother her, and I gently try to remove her hands from my hair, without it resulting in me having bald spots. As soon as she's free, she falls down onto her padded ass, rolls like she's on a military exercise, before starting to crawl across the room. Thankfully, Liam had the good sense to close the door before he sat down because if not, she would be gone. For a chunky little baby, she moves surprisingly quickly. "None of them have been right. You know it's not as easy as hiring someone who is good with her. We need someone trustworthy. They are going to be around us all the time, and we need to make sure we can trust them not to betray us."

"Okay, so I can't work out if this particular lack of trust issue is because of Her Who Shall Not Be Named, or your mother and the nanny she hired to spy on you," Liam muses, lowering his voice, as though he said something forbidden at the start.

I can't help but chuckle as I reply. "Okay, first of all, she isn't Voldemort, you can say her name. But, if we're using a code name for her, I can think of a few, they just can't be used in front of my daughter. As for the other witch, Marianna, this is exactly what I'm talking about. Trusting anyone is difficult when I know there are people out there like my mum, who, thanks to her ridiculous excuse of a husband, has an unlimited supply of cash, and her only job is to find dirt to ruin me."

We both groan, I don't know which of us hates talking about my mother more. I think it's Liam. If I'd given him permission, he'd have assassinated her years ago. I'm starting to wish I'd let him. "Don't you see why this makes Mia the perfect candidate? She already knows about us and the work we do. Hell, she spent a lot of time here when Bree was taken, and she looked after Hallie so well. They seem to really like each other, Kel. I'm not asking for you to give her blind trust, but some wouldn't hurt," he asks, pleading with me, using those piercing green eyes women seem to love so much.

"Guys, have you lost a baby by any chance?" Bree shouts from somewhere outside the room. We both look over to the door, and as soon as we see it's open, we are up on our feet running towards it at full speed.

"Hallie! Hallie, baby, where are you?" I shout as I begin to panic. I only took my eyes off her for a few seconds, and I thought the door was closed. I didn't think she could get out. I should have been watching her more closely. Anything could happen.

As Liam pulls me towards Bree's voice, at the other end of the corridor where their bedroom is, my heart starts to race. What if she isn't okay?

I know, logically, Bree would've told us if there was something wrong with Hallie, but all I can think of is the dangers she just narrowly avoided. Like the staircases, she missed two of those entrances, and if she opened the gates we have covering them, she could have toppled down the stairs.

I must have been mumbling all of this information to myself as Liam snaps a reply, "Kellan, for fuck's sake. It's a bit different opening a door to opening a child safety gate. I mean, I've seen you climbing over it when you can't get the damn thing open. So if adults can't open the damn thing, then an almost seven-month-old who can't stand up for any longer than a few seconds stands no chance."

I sigh, but not in relief. "All I heard from that sentence is that she could climb over the gate. I'm going to be grey before I turn twenty-five," I moan, rubbing my hands over my tired eyes.

Liam pulls open the door to his bedroom, only to find Bree laying on the bed with her arms above her head, holding my squealing little girl. She loves when people hold her above their heads. I'm sure it's a power thing. Even at just under seven months old, she knows the importance of having power over people. It's something she doesn't even need to try at, she succeeds instantly.

"Hey, you are supposed to be resting, doctor's orders. Holding a baby above your head does not count as resting, Bree," Liam scolds as he makes a move to catch Hallie. But Bree is too quick, and instead she brings Hallie onto her chest for a cuddle, which my baby is only too happy to provide, but only for a second. Then she rolls with expert precision and crawls until she's sitting in Liam's arms.

Bree lets out an exaggerated huff. "What happened to girl loyalty and solidarity?" Of course, Hallie just giggles as she wraps Liam's hair around her finger.

"You will always side with your uncle Liam, won't you, beautiful bear?" Liam whispers affectionately, as he showers Hallie's face with kisses and her loud giggles fill the room.

"Traitor." Bree huffs, and I can't help but laugh.

"How are you feeling, Bree? You're looking better." She really does. I hated seeing how battered and bruised she was when we first rescued her. Even when we visited her in the hospital, I've never seen her looking so small. I mean, don't get me wrong, Bree's not a tall girl, but it's the way she holds herself, and addresses you. Within seconds of meeting her, you can tell she is a leader, and the more I've gotten to know her, the more I know she's a fucking great one. I hate the fact that she is underestimated just because she has a vagina.

She always appears infallible, yet seeing her battered and bruised made her look so fragile. She's been quick to reassert her dominance, and has held many meetings with her associates, reiterating that she's still very much in charge, and that it will take a lot more than a pathetic attempt on her life to force her out.

That doesn't stop Liam from fussing and worrying. He hates thinking of what she went through, and although he saved her, he will always believe he didn't save her in time. If he had, she wouldn't have suffered and they wouldn't have lost their baby.

I still remember how I felt when I learnt about Hallie, and how big a fucking life event it was. I hate they had that moment stolen from them. Having watched them dote on my daughter these last few months, I have no doubt when the time comes, they will be brilliant parents.

These last few months have been tough for us all, specifically the people trying to kill us, my mother plotting to take my baby from me, as well as actually trying to raise said baby. I've barely had a moment to breathe, let alone get any more than three hours of sleep in one go.

So, I get why Liam wants me to get help, I just don't know if I can trust letting someone else into our world.

"Kel, I'm assuming Liam told you about Mia?" she asks, her voice never wavering the way Liam's did. This is why she's a leader. She never questions her decisions, she just rolls with it.

I groan. "Yes, but I already interviewed Mia and she isn't suitable. She has too many secrets, and she's caught up in some criminal enterprise we know nothing about. The last thing I want is to introduce Hallie to people who could be bad influences. So, no. I don't approve of her moving in!" I try to sit up straight at the end of the bed, letting her see I'm sticking to my guns.

Bree just laughs. "Okay, first of all, it's my house, so if I say she's moving in, then she moves in. End of discussion on that one. As for introducing Hallie to bad influences, she already knows and loves Mia, so that's a whole heap of bullshit. As for Mia having secrets, there's no denying she does. But, we talked after that ridiculous excuse of an interview. She's not linked to Kyle Fratacello. Yes, there is a story there, but it's one she isn't ready to share yet. She has been my best friend for years, and she asked me to give her a little trust. It's the least I can do. I'm not asking you to give her all your trust, she is prepared to earn it. But, right now, she needs a helping hand and you need a nanny. Why not give her a trial period?"

This right here is why Bree is in charge, she's an excellent fucking negotiator. But, I've been burned by beautiful women before. There's no denying I grew closer to Mia over the last couple of weeks when Bree was taken. We supported each other, but there were extenuating factors at play. Besides, I'm not going to deny I'm attracted to Mia. I'm also not going to lie and say I don't have an overwhelming urge to fuck her every time she talks back or stands up to me. Nor am I going to hide that seeing her look after my little girl is like the perfect kind of porn. So, yes, I'm desperate for this woman, which is exactly why I need to keep away from her. She is forbidden, and I need to remember that. I'm barely managing to keep him in my pants as it is.

"No. I don't want to discuss it anymore." I don't mean to snap at Bree. I know she is only trying to help both of her friends, but I don't need that type of help. I've made the mistake of trusting a beautiful woman before. She may have left me my most prized possession, but she took everything else I owned, including my last piece of trust. Liam calls her She Who Must Not Be Named, but she does have a name. She's called Shayla, and she broke my heart so badly I don't even recognise myself. Now, everything I do is for Hallie; to protect her, to keep her safe, and to make sure she knows how loved she is by so many people.

"That's fine, Kel. But she is moving in anyway. She is taking the bedroom next door to yours. Don't even think about arguing with me!" Bree snaps and all I can do is groan. So much for keeping her out of my life. I guess, if she isn't Hallie's nanny, there's nothing stopping me from fucking her and getting her out of my system. I may hate women, and have an inability to trust, but a one-night stand that means nothing, that I have no problem with.

Mia

“Are you sure this is a good idea, Bree? I know you said he was pissed about me moving in, but I didn't think that meant he would ignore me for five days, leaving the room whenever I enter. This is your house, I don't want things to be weird for you,” I groan as I flop onto Bree's bed, after yet another awkward breakfast.

Liam's still insisting that Bree remains in bed for as much of the day as possible, but it's driving her crazy. So, for the last few days, I've been coming in and sitting on their bed while she hobbles around the room. I hate seeing how much pain she's in just from moving around, but she is a stubborn bastard and won't be down for any longer than she needs to be. That's why she is secretly training, building up her strength, so that very soon she can get back to running this family.

Ever since people found out about the kidnapping, it's been kind of a free-for-all. Idiots crawling out of the woodwork, demanding raises, or more power, all the things they've been denied before. They knew Vernon and Jimmy were out for good, and they saw it as an opportunity. Although people had heard Bree would be taking over, until the mass meeting the day after she got out of hospital, nobody thought she could come back from her kidnapping. They expected her to crumble, Bree was determined to prove them wrong. It's also the first time I ever got involved in Bree's work.

"Bree, I'm supposed to be looking after you. Liam gave me very strict instructions, and this definitely isn't allowed. Please do not leave," I beg, blocking the doorway with my body. Not like that would work. She's in a wheelchair and can just ram into me, if she can muster the power.

"Look, I'll tell him when I get there, but I have to do this. I have to let them know I'm back, and that nobody will take what's mine ever again. They stole something precious from me, and I sure as fuck am going to make sure they pay." Bree's eyes well up with tears.

Looking at my friend right now, gone is the confident mafia family leader, replaced with a scared young girl who looks battered and broken after everything she's been through. She's only allowing herself this moment of weakness because I'm here, and she knows I won't ever tell anyone she has a secret soft side. I have no idea about what she went through, but there's a lot I can relate to. I, of all people, know what it's like to be a victim, to be hurt by people who should love you the most. That's a type of pain I can relate to. The pain evident in her glassy, silver eyes makes them look almost vacant. Until her eyebrows furrow and her lips purse, as her features morph into anger.

"Bree, I know losing this wedding, and getting betrayed the way you did is unspeakable, but nothing is worth risking your recovery over." I make sure to sound as confident as I can, holding my arm out to stop her from coming any farther.

"They killed my baby." Her words come out as a whisper, but they're more than loud enough to cause my breath to hitch, and I stumble as the anguish she must be feeling hits me. "I didn't even know I was pregnant. I didn't even get to have that moment where I freak out and wonder if I could even be a mother, or where I'm shit scared of telling Liam, only for him to love the idea. Those moments were stolen from me. Replaced by a nurse, trying to keep the sadness from her face, telling me that I had a baby and now I don't. Literally,

I had it for less than a second before it was taken from me. Now I plan to punish the person responsible, and ensure everyone else falls in line. I am done with people thinking I am weak. Nobody is taking any more from me."

My heart aches as Bree explains with tears streaming down her face. Even though she sounds resolute and tough, I know this can't be easy for her. The people responsible, even if they never intended for it to go this far, they're the people who should love you the most. It's the ultimate betrayal, and one I can relate to. I may never have the balls to challenge my monsters, but I sure as fuck can stand by my best friend's side while she slays her demons.

Arriving at a large industrial warehouse, it's not entirely what I expected. Bree, as I predicted, refuses to use her wheelchair, and demands to hold on to me as we walk inside. Luckily, I had already pre-empted this little stunt, which is why I'm not remotely surprised to see a furious Liam practically drag the door of its hinges. I am, however, surprised to see Kellan here with his baby. This is hardly a children's sport.

"Traitor," Bree mumbles in my direction, but thankfully she is cut off by Liam's tirade.

"Don't blame her. I already knew what you were doing once I got the emergency texts. I'm part of the group texts, you know. Why the fuck are you putting your body through this, Princess? You look dead on your feet, and you should be resting!" His voice is more stern than shouting. He knows he's fighting a losing battle, the resolve is not wavering from Bree's face even a little.

"Liam, I am doing this with or without you. So, either grab hold of my arm and help me, or get the fuck out of my way," Bree snaps.

I can see people gathering inside the warehouse, and she obviously doesn't want to appear weak, or like there are fractures in their relationship. "You know I will always stand by your side. I may not be happy about it, but I'll still do it." Liam places a soft kiss onto her lips and I have to look away. Their relationship is so beautiful, even a chaste kiss is fiery. But, as I avert my eyes, I run into a bigger problem. I end up looking directly at Kellan, and there's a fire in his gaze that's honed in on me.

While Bree was kidnapped, and then recovering in the hospital afterwards, I grew close to Kellan. He was there for me while I was scared and panicking. I can deal with my own pain, but seeing someone I love go through that was unbearable. He held me when I cried, and comforted me *when I started to panic. I'm not going to deny that I find him attractive. But, the more time I spent with him, the more I learnt he's next-level messed up. I have no idea what he has been through, but he's a single dad with no trust in women. I don't need that kind of broken in my life, no matter how beautiful the package may be. And it really fucking is gorgeous.*

He is all muscles and tattoos, but personality-wise, he's more of a shy tech geek than a mafia bad boy like Liam. Long and short of it, my lady bits—that I thought had died off far too long ago for a twenty-one-year-old—she wants Kellan. Thankfully, my brain runs this show. So, I avoid his fiery, lust-filled gaze and try to change the subject.

"You brought a baby to a mafia family meeting?" I ask in disbelief, looking down at the sleeping baby who is currently strapped to Kellan's chest in one of those baby carrying harnesses. You get to keep your hands free and your baby close by. They're a great invention, particularly for single dads who refuse to hire a nanny despite desperately needing one. I try to ignore the fact that my ovaries are fucking aching just looking at him.

"We were at the park with Hallie when Liam got the call. What was I going to do, leave her at home by herself?" His sarcastic tone is not lost on me. Normally I would shy away from conflict, I have spent my entire life trying to blend into the shadows and not be noticed. But, with him, it's different. I fucking love challenging him and testing his patience.

Kellan has this amazing ability to rub me up the wrong way. Even though my instincts are screaming at me to back down and cower like I normally do, it feels safe to spar with him. That's part of what I find so thrilling about him. I've never once felt scared to be alone in the room with him, or to let him see the real me. Things most people take for granted, but I've never had that luxury. So, while I can, I see what it's like to banter with him.

"Well, if you pull your head out of your pretentious ass and hire a nanny, that might help. You're worried about me having criminal connections, yet you brought her along to witness what I'm sure will be an assassination." Okay, so I wasn't really expecting to snap quite that much. But, all of what I said—maybe with the exception of calling his ass pretentious—it's all true!

Given his wide eyes and open-mouthed stare, he's shocked I have the balls to say anything. I've spent a long time being quietened, I'm not doing that anymore. Kellan starts to argue back, but Liam shushes us both when a young guy with floppy blond hair bounds towards us.

Holy fuck, what do they put in the water around here? I know I grew up in an all-female boarding school, but I'd still met men before, and none of them looked like these guys. If I thought Kellan and Liam were gorgeous, this guy is like boy band beautiful. Liam has that rugged, bad boy look, despite being one of the nicest guys I know. Kellan has a sexy tech geek vibe that you can't help but lust after, or at least, I can't. But, this guy, this is the one you know is well out of your league. He looks like the type of guy you have a poster of on your wall as a teenage girl, and when he smiles and those dimples appear, that's the panty-melting moment right there.

I feel like I need to fan myself, as the blush creeps up my head and chest, making my temperature rise. He obviously works for Bree, because he heads straight for her. "Hey, boss lady. How are you feeling? You look like shit, are you sure you should be doing this?"

Nope, I was wrong. When he opens his mouth and talks in that sexy Irish drawl with his dimples on display, that right there is the panty-melting moment. Don't get me wrong, he's the obvious kind of gorgeous, the nice to look at kind, but he isn't my type. He's blond and bubbly, whereas I prefer dark and brooding. Probably why I'm so attracted to the asshole standing next to me, giving me an evil glare. Seriously, if looks could kill, I would be six feet under already.

As Bree begins to tell the guy, who she calls Kian, that she is fine, Kellan leans over so that only I can hear, whispering in my ear. "Put your tongue away, Flower. You are drooling."

I try to ignore the feel of his breath as it hits my skin, and the way ripples of desire shoot down my spine. It's like he has a one-way connection to my core, and knows just what to do to heat it up. I didn't think my core was accepting requests, it's never responded before. Then again, after what I've been through, I'm lucky my body responds at all. I thought it was long since dead. Yet, it appears to want to come to life, just for Kellan.

"I'm not drooling! And what have I told you about that damn nickname?" I snap, whilst also trying to discreetly wipe my chin. There's a good chance he may be right. About the drool, I mean, not the nickname. He has been calling me 'Flower' for the last couple of weeks. It may sound sweet, but it's short for wallflower. Apparently, he noticed that I like to fade into the background, to

go unnoticed. But, I have my reasons. "It's really not my fault, he's just so hot." I try to make my voice sound as sultry as possible. Unfortunately, I don't manage it, and instead it comes out so loud that everyone turns around to face me.

Kellan's chuckle does nothing to help the blush that's burning across my face. When I was blonde, you didn't really notice if I was pale, but now I'm back to my natural brunette hair colour, my bright red cheeks stand out like sunburn.

Thankfully, Kian doesn't seem to mind, and he takes a step forward to introduce himself with his arm outstretched. "Well, I will take the compliment coming from a girl as beautiful as you. I'm Kian, Bree's left-hand man."

On autopilot, I clasp to shake his hand, my brow furrowing in confusion over his words. "Don't you mean right-hand man?"

With a laugh that confirms this guy is the whole package, he releases my hand and replies. "No, Liam is her right-hand man. Nobody messes with that. Besides, I'm left-handed, so the analogy fits."

I can't help but smile at his joke, and I don't miss the way Kellan rolls his eyes before snapping at Kian. "What do you want, Kian?"

Kian looks perplexed, clearly unsure as to why Kellan would suddenly snap at him, and I look over at Liam, who up until this point had only been concerned with holding on to his fiancée, but now he's giving Kellan a very apt stare, and shaking his head. I think I may have even caught an eye roll.

"Erm, I was just coming to see if boss lady needs a hand," he replies, in an upbeat way that I'm guessing is the norm for Kian. He seems like one of those generally perky guys. He then turns his attention to Bree, his manner whilst remaining chipper is still confident. "I've gathered everyone like you asked. Most are grumbling since I took their weapons off them. Also, Paddy told me to let you know he personally made sure the package left the country, which is code for he shipped your parents off on a plane yesterday. He says he isn't telling anyone where they've gone, and since your mother has no remaining family, she chose to stay with Vernon. Paddy gave him a small amount of money, but nowhere near enough for him to be comfortable. And thanks to your boy Kellan here, there's no money stashed away."

I catch the cocky grin on Kellan's face when he's given credit for the work he did. There's no denying this guy is good at his job. Liam tells me he can hack anything, even going as far as to contacting police and government *organisations to inform them of breeches in their security software, and telling them how to fix it. He could use his skills for so much evil, but I just don't think he's capable of that. I don't know much about him, but I get the impression he's one of the good guys. Which is music to my ears, since all I've ever met are bad guys.*

Bree ignores the mention of her father, and sets her face into the mask she's known for. "Let's get on with this then, please." I reach out to grab her free arm when I notice she stumbles slightly and turns to address me. "Mia, this is not going to be easy to watch. You might not want to come in."

I release the breath I'm holding, letting out a sigh. "I promised we would do this together. I may not have the courage and the strength you do, but I can stand by your side and give you as much support as you need." I mean it. No matter how much it terrifies me being part of this world—and by going into this warehouse, I really will be part of the world—but I'm not backing out now.

"What about the baby? I was kinda hoping you would look after her, Mia? Then I can go with Bree. I need to film this so we can send it to the people who are absent today," Kellan explains. I cock my hip, placing my hand there in a very obviously pissed off way.

"Well, if only you had a nanny, huh." I'm interrupted by chuckles from Kian, Bree, and Liam, which only seems to frustrate Kellan more. I can see his hands fiddling with the clips of the harness, and he's jigging from one foot to the other. His anxiety is beginning to flare up and I feel for him. I know what it's like to be enslaved by anxiety and panic attacks.

As I look between Kellan and Bree, I'm torn. I want to help Kellan, but I also want him to see how well I get on with Hallie. I'm starting to get desperate for a job. Now I don't have to worry too much about rent, Bree is more reasonable than my previous landlord, and I'm able to concentrate more on my studies. But, if I don't find a nannying job soon, I could fail my studies. As part of my early years childcare degree, I need to get work experience. I can either do a placement at a nursery, or I can make money at the same time as a nanny. I have a supervisor in place who will regularly review my progress, and if Kellan hires me, he will be required to assess me. I haven't told him any of that yet. First things first, get the job.

Just as I am about to relent and say I will stay with Hallie, Kian chips in.

"I don't need my bodyguard, Callum. He's got a couple of kids, so he'll be fine watching her."

Kellan looks unsure, and he twists his gaze to Hallie, looking perplexed, until Liam reassures him. "Kel, we've vetted him, and he's a good guy. If you like, I can leave my phone in the pram next to Hallie. We can call each other and you can wear your ear piece, so you can hear her at all times. What do you think?" Liam asks, and within seconds Kellan is smiling from ear to ear.

"I think that sounds like a plan." Kellan walks over to the car and opens the boot to begin getting the pram out.

I know he's going to struggle with Hallie strapped to him, so I follow behind, offering to help. "Here, let me take Hallie so you can get the pram set up easier."

Holding my arms out, he hesitates slightly before unclasping the harness and handing the sleeping baby to me. I adjust her until she's sleeping peacefully in my arms. Hallie grumbles a bit at being manhandled, but never really wakes up. As soon as she is in the pram, and Liam and Kellan have handed Hallie over to Callum, we are ready to go. Given the way the colour drains from his face, the boys have obviously issued Callum with a threat over Hallie's wellbeing.

The warehouse is a lot bigger than I was expecting, and the main room is almost the size of a big assembly hall in a school. There's a main stage at the front, which is basically some wooden boxes secured together. There are a few seats and tables near the front of the stage, and given the type of people who are occupying the seats, they're obviously the people higher up in the organisation. Everyone else is standing, with the exception of a few people who are sitting on the floor, or the nearest surface they can find.

I notice the people at the tables, most are wearing suits, but some look highly unprofessional in sweatpants, vests, and more gold jewellery than I've ever seen men wear. It's not difficult to see who deals in which bit of the organisation. The ones who look like chavs are clearly the ones who utilise too much of the product they are supposed to be selling.

Just as Liam and I have discreetly helped Bree up onto the stage, a young guy who looks shockingly like Liam, and a bit like Kellan, begins walking onto the stage. He's wearing a suit, so he must be someone important, but his walk lacks the confidence a true boss would have. As he approaches Liam, he hesitates, his face scrunched up as he thinks about what he's going to do. Liam, however, doesn't hesitate and he pulls him in for a hug. At first it seems awkward, as though the guy doesn't know how to respond, but when he finally does put his arms around Liam and shares the hug, everyone seems to relax.

Just as they were about to pull away from each other, Kellan throws himself on top of the duo, so he's hugging them both. "Evan, bro. Nice to see you," Kellan shouts, as their little rabble pulls apart.

Bree, who is still clutching hold of me, leans over so her voice is barely above a whisper, but it's still enough for just me to be able to hear. "That's Evan, Liam's oldest brother. He works for Liam's super crazy father, and he's a bit uptight. They were estranged until Evan and Desmond stepped up and helped to find me. I think Liam is trying to build bridges with his brother, but his dad could be too far gone."

Before I have a chance to reply, Evan approaches Bree. "Hey, Bree. How are you doing? You look a whole lot better than when I last saw you in the hospital." Bree gives him a small smile before pulling him in for a quick hug.

It's clear by the way he reluctantly puts one arm around her, he isn't a hugger. "I'm good, thanks to you. I don't think I've ever really had the chance to thank you and your dad properly for coming to help Liam. It means a lot to us both." I can hear the sincerity in every word. Bree's face is full of gratitude, but I don't think praise is something Evan is used to because he blushes and tries to turn away, but Bree is far too forceful.

"I think the aged bottle of Irish whiskey you sent him went down a treat. He asked me to come today because he's busy with another matter. He didn't want to cause any offence, though, since this is your first big show as leader, as he put it," Evan says to Bree, and her laugh catches everyone's attention.

Okay, so I don't think mafia leaders are supposed to laugh. Now all eyes are on Bree, I guess she decides it's time to get started. There are two seats on either side of the fake stage; Evan takes the farthest on the left, leaving a space near him that I'm assuming Liam will take, as Kellan and I take the ones on the right. Liam seems reluctant to let go of Bree, and I know why. She's still a bit wobbly on her feet, but I don't think she wants to come across as weak, which is why she shoos him off.

The room descends into silence, and I watch as my best friend, despite being battered and bruised, dressed in sweatpants and a vest top, changes in front of my eyes. It's like she holds herself differently, taller almost, and it has *an instant reaction on most of the crowd. There are still a few tittering and talking amongst themselves, and that doesn't go unnoticed.*

Bree appears to take a deep, calming breath before she addresses the room. "Thank you for being here. I know it's not often we have these types of gatherings, and there's a good reason for that. But I feel the need for this far outweighs the risks involved."

Oh shit, does she mean the police? Fuck, I hadn't even thought about what it would do for my career if I got caught. I mean, I'm guessing this is one of the biggest criminal gatherings London has ever seen. I must have physically tensed because Kellan, always so perceptive, takes hold of my hand, clasping our fingers together. I try to ignore the bolt of electricity shooting up my arm, or the way his closeness makes my skin prickle in the best kind of way.

He leans closer, whispering in my ear, and I know he can see my body shudder. "Relax, Flower. I have wiped all records of this meeting. Everyone's phones are scrambled, CCTV has been erased, any form of communication regarding this event has been erased, and if that wasn't enough—which it totally should be—the new police commissioner is on the take. So, we are fine. I promise, and even if you don't trust me, I know you know I would never put Hallie in danger."

As soon as he mentions that his little girl is just in the next room, I know he's serious. We really are safe. I think once I got that straight in my mind, it was easier then for me to really take in what's happening in front of me. The dangerous aspect of it is almost thrilling, and I think the way my heart is racing has everything to do with the situation, and nothing at all to do with the gorgeous man currently squeezing my hand, breathing all over my ear. Seriously, as soon as his breath touches me, it's like he ignites a match that burns straight to my core.

"Now, you all know how very fucking serious I am about running this Family business. I want to set the record straight about some recent events, and get them dealt with officially. I hope this will give you a bit of insight into how I will be running this business. Then, at the end, if you feel you don't want to remain in business with me, that's perfectly fine, just let me know. But let me make one thing very fucking clear, if you walk away from me, you better be walking away from the business in general. Whatever it is you deal in, I am the only Family, the only person running London. You want to go work somewhere else, then go. But, if you stay in London, you are

my competition and that makes you my enemy. You are about to see how I deal with people who become my enemy." Bree's voice has taken on a sharp edge and at the end she almost snarls, and I can tell she's mad. Her lip is curled upwards and her eyes narrow.

Wow, I definitely have never seen this side of Bree before. Just as I was thinking how shit scary my fiery redheaded friend is, Kian, who I hadn't even noticed was missing, comes in through another side door, and has three big, burly men with him, who each have what appears to be prisoners with them.

Kian's men are dragging three people who definitely look like they've seen better days. They're all young men, probably a few years older than me. They have all taken one hell of a beating and have their hands tied together with zip ties, and their eyes are blindfolded with a piece of cloth. Once he has them in position in the centre of the stage, the men holding them let go and all three men fall to their knees next to where Bree is standing. Kian walks over to her side, not because he is needed, but because it's a show of solidarity that the audience seems to understand straight away.

"As you all know, recently I was kidnapped, tortured, and assaulted. Thanks to the amazing friends and family I have by my side, they stopped at nothing to rescue me. These recent events have made me think long and hard, not only about the idea that I need to be very careful about who I keep in my circle and in my employment, but also about how you see me as a boss." Bree does an amazing job of projecting her voice across the room, and it's amazing that a room full of men are just watching, enraptured by every single word.

"When I took over from my father as leader, I met with all your firms individually, discussed with you all whether you wanted to align with me, and you all pledged your allegiance. After that, I didn't think we would have any issues, but apparently there were a few of you that gave me your support, while secretly you were plotting against me. The three men you see behind me are the leaders of these groups. Jedd Sinclair, Matt Hitchins, and Brody Thomas. They each have teams who they rule, but they work for me. Except, it would appear, they were plotting behind my back to overthrow me. Apparently they believe a woman is too weak to rule. Jedd, what do you have to say for yourself?" Bree asks, as she stands in front of the man nearest my side of the stage.

As Kian pulls the blindfold off and Jedd sees the warehouse full of people, he knows he's in trouble. I see the fear flash in his eyes from my position at the side of the makeshift stage. But he tries to hide it, jutting his chin out and holding his head high. Despite the blood pouring down his face from a cut above his eye, he tries to look professional.

"I don't believe you are a suitable leader. My crew will never follow your lead!" shouts Jedd, as he launches himself forward, trying to get to his feet and reach Bree. Kian wastes no time in slamming his fist into his face. The crunch of bone against bone echoes loudly, and I can't help but squirm slightly in my seat.

That's when I feel Kellan's hand squeeze mine, and his breath against my neck. Fuck, I wish he would stop doing that, it's driving me insane, and now I'm squirming for another reason. "Are you okay? If you want to leave, that's fine. Things are about to get a lot worse."

I whisper confirmation that I'm okay, and I see Liam wastes no time jumping to stand by Bree's side, always ready to protect her. I also see, behind their backs, Liam hands Bree a gun and my heart starts to race. Of course I knew what was going to happen here. But knowing it, and then seeing it are two very different things.

"Jedd's crew, please walk to the front of the stage. Now!" Bree yells, and about half a dozen young-looking guys walk forward.

"This is the CRO, they are based in Croydon," Kian explains and Bree gives him a small smile. I suspect she knew that, since they work together so well, almost like two sides of the same coin.

"Which of you would become the leader of CRO if Jedd here was no longer around?" Bree asks the group of men.

All eyes fly to the man standing at the edge of the group. Collectively, there are about twelve men who look to be between the ages of around sixteen and thirty, if that. The group is made up of men from various ethnicities, but the majority are men of colour. They all are wearing tracksuits or sweatpants, vest tops, and far too much gold jewellery. Clearly, these boys thought they were gangsters, a couple even have necklaces and tattoos that say as much.

Without a single shred of solidarity for their friend, Jedd, on the stage, their eyes fly to who looks to be the eldest member of the group. He takes a minor step forward, and pulls his posture higher, jutting out his chin defiantly. I don't miss the way Bree cocks her eyebrow at him, showing she doesn't appreciate his challenging behaviour, something he quickly rectifies.

"I'm Dante, second in command at CRO." Much to my surprise, he sounds more confident than I expected. His Jamaican accent doesn't seem consistent with a kid who was clearly raised in Croydon, as he would need to have been with the gang for a while to reach this leadership role.

"Well, Dante, today you have a big decision to make, and not just for yourself but for the whole of the CROs. By that, I do mean each and every member that isn't here too. As you know, Jedd here has admitted that he doesn't think I am a suitable leader, and that he was plotting my downfall. I know that as soon as he found out I was in hospital, he made plans to move against me. He actually paid someone to come into my hospital room to try and kill me. Only problem is, your fearless leader here isn't all that smart. You see, the best assassin in the world is Liam here, so he knew he couldn't use him. So he asked around for the second best. He made the stupid mistake of not doing any real research on the assassin. It turns out the second best actually trained with Liam, because it's his brother, Evan." She pauses briefly to look over at Evan, and so does Jedd. Evan gives Jedd, followed by everyone else, a slight nod, clearly not a fan of being in the limelight—I don't fucking blame him!—and then all eyes are back on Bree, as Jedd finds his voice.

"You asshole. I thought you wanted her downfall too. You told me you were doing this for your family," he screams, but Bree cuts him off with her laugh. To the rest of the people in the room she looks carefree, but I can see the lies. The beads of sweat collecting along her forehead, thanks to the pain she is no doubt in.

"Shut up, you cuntwaffle. He works with me, which means he told you what you needed to hear. It's not your fault you sang like a canary, and to anyone wondering, he is the reason I have so much information on other groups within this organisation." At this point, there are more boos and hisses from the crowd, and I see the boys in front huddle together as they clearly fear for their lives.

"SILENCE!" Kian's scream attracts everyone's attention, and is more than enough to silence their pantomime theatrics.

"Back to my original point. Dante, there is no saving Jedd. Your friend is gone, that leaves you in charge. I would like to build a relationship with the CRO crew, and specifically with you—as their new leader—but it will not be easy. You will be on probation, and will not have the freedom you had before, not until I trust you properly. I have to be able to trust you as a crew to work

for me, without wanting to stab me in the back. If you decide you wish to continue working with me, and can overlook the fact that I have a vagina, then I will arrange a meeting with you and we can get things officially registered with you as the leader. However, if you decide you don't want to be a leader, you don't want to work with me, or you don't like the fact that I'm imposing restrictions, then this is where we will run into trouble. You need to decide right now. You have the few minutes it takes me to deal with Jedd to come up with a decision. Do you understand or have any questions?" Bree asks, as she circles around so that she's standing in front of Jedd but off to the side slightly. Her body is lined up to face me, but at this angle everyone can see both her face and Jedd's.

Dante is a little scared to speak, but after some cajoling from his group, he does. "I'm sorry, ma'am. Please can I just ask, if we align with you, will the mistakes we made under a different rule go away? And if we don't align with you, what will happen to us? I only ask this because there are a few members who want the whole picture before making a decision."

An evil mask descends across Bree's face. "If you don't align with me, you will be punished along with Jedd," she explains, before turning slightly towards the rest of the room. "You have all heard my evidence. Jedd, do you have anything you would like to say for yourself? One of the things I want to be able to pride myself on during this reign is fairness. If you think you are being treated unfairly, speak up now."

Jedd's face crumples with rage, and hatred spills out. "You're a dumb bitch. My crew will never follow you, no matter what threats you make. They will always follow me beca—"

Before he even gets a chance to finish his sentence, Bree brings the gun out from behind her back, and with Liam holding firmly on to her side, she stabilises herself, before shooting Jedd right between the eyes. His blood splatters all across the stage, and I get hit across my jeans with some residual spray. I can't help the scared little yelp I emit. The very dead man crumples to the floor, and knowing I have blood and brain matter splattered across my trousers more than excuses my girlie screams—in my opinion.

"Now you have your choice to make. Is it true, are you incapable of following my rule, and you're prepared to go down with Jedd? Or, are you with me?" Bree asks a very shocked-looking Dante. All the colour drains from his face, as he looks between his leader's body, and his real leader.

"We would be happy to work with you, ma'am," Dante stutters.

Bree gives him a wide smile before hobbling over to the edge of the stage, nearest where Dante is standing. She reaches over, holding her hand out for him to shake. "I like you, Dante, you seem like a very smart man."

Bang, bang, bang. The men on the stage are taken care of. One by one, the shots ring out, and screams of fear fill the room as Bree doesn't even remotely give them a chance to argue their cases. I guess there's no such thing as second chances in this business. You leave the wrong person alive in this industry, and it could result in your death.

"Thank you so much for bearing with me today. I know some of you may refer to this as a dramatic stunt, or me trying to flop out my dick in a how big is your penis competition, but it really isn't. The reason I'm doing this is to show you that no amount of disloyalty will be tolerated. The men that were on this stage, they had the nerve to dare to speak out against me, but one man went a step further. He plotted, he helped get me kidnapped, and as a result I was physically harmed. So much so, it killed my baby. But the worst part is, this man was part of my inner circle. I would have trusted him above all others, but he betrayed me, and that is unforgivable," Bree explains to the room, and they all know she is talking about Jimmy.

"For those of you who don't know Jimmy, he's my father's right-hand man. He also worked with Vernon to overthrow me. Vernon wished to remain in charge, and didn't respect my grandfather Patrick's decision. So, he tried to get rid of me the only way he knew how, by abusing my connection with this man right here. My grandfather has taken responsibility for Vernon, choosing to abolish him from any country we do business with, which as I'm sure you are aware doesn't leave many. He stripped him of all his money and possessions, all he took with him was my mother, and that was her choice. I asked for permission to deal with Jimmy. I believe that leaders should punish everyone equally, but when it comes to this man, the man who was essentially a father figure to me my entire life, it's hard to judge him on the same lines as the three men who were here before. My reason for this is not because I'm soft or sentimental, it's because in my opinion, the crime is so much worse, the betrayal so much bigger, therefore I will need to ensure the punishment fits the crime. I feel it's my job to tell you why he isn't here now." Bree looks over the crowd, who are all waiting, no doubt wondering what she's about to say.

Kellan squeezes my hand, gently reminding me that he's still there giving me strength.

"My grandfather, Patrick, believes Jimmy has vital information that we need. Therefore, he is being interrogated. This is not me letting him off the hook, or going easy on him. I can assure you, Jimmy will pay for his crimes with his life. This man was the closest thing I had to a father and he betrayed me in the worst possible way. To allow him to live would be a sign of weakness, and I intend to prove to you that I am not weak. I intend to prove to you that no matter how close you are to me, no matter how much you mean to me, if you hurt me, you will pay. This wouldn't have happened if I had a cock. So, this is me proving that just because I have a vagina and ovaries, they won't be my downfall. This is me standing before you, showing you the type of leader I am. And when the time comes that I need to end Jimmy's life, you will each get to stand here while I show you how true I am to my word. This is how I run my business. If you don't like it, you need to get the fuck out of my city, right now," Bree exclaims, her voice never wavering. I can tell she is tired and in pain, and thankfully the crowd have their heads downcast, trying to avoid being noticed.

I think it's finally over. Once Bree has clarified there are no further questions, she tells them all they will be hearing from her soon, and dismisses them. I see her hobble towards the edge of the stage. She bats away Liam's offer of help, and I see the frustration on his face. He only manages to let her take a couple more painful steps before he gently picks her up and carries her off into one of the side rooms.

Before I even know what's happening, Kellan drags me off the stage, clearly wanting to get me out of the room now everyone is mingling. I caught the look on some of those men's faces as they saw me. I've seen those predatory gazes too many times before, and thankfully Kellan didn't want me to remain in their crosshairs.

As soon as the door closes, he slams my back against it and crowds his body against mine. His face is a mix of anger and lust, and I can feel his erection pressing against my body. I yearn for him to slam his mouth against mine, but before he can, he seems to gain some semblance of control. Running his fingers through his black, silky hair, his voice sounds like a growl as he talks. "I don't like the idea of you being at these types of things. You don't belong in this world. Those men are dangerous. They look at you like they're about to consume you."

He doesn't take a step back, continuing to crowd me, as his scent and his presence overwhelm me. "Maybe I want to be consumed."

Fuck, I've never heard my voice sound so raspy and...well, quite frankly... horny. I'm so turned on, I'm not even thinking properly. Instead, I watch as his eyes trace over my face, until they finally stop on my lips. I can't help biting my lower lip, I'm anxious.

One arm remains above my head, caging me in, but the other he brings down and very gently tugs at my lip, removing it from my teeth. The feel of his soft fingers on my mouth has my nerves prickling with excitement. All the air sucks from the room and nothing remains except us and the chemistry crackling around us like lightning.

"This is a bad idea. Particularly if you are going to be my daughter's nanny," Kellan says, as his thumb sweeps across my lower lip, eliciting a moan from me that I definitely didn't mean to give.

"I don't think you have offered me the job. So, you aren't my boss...yet." What the hell? Am I encouraging him now? Hell yes I am. This guy is gorgeous and I can't remember the last time I was kissed with passion, in a way that I wanted and I controlled. That's when it occurs to me, I can control the situation.

Leaning forward, I waste no time capturing his lips with mine. It starts off as just a sweet kiss, but as my lips collide with his, it's like we're electrocuted and we come to life. Our kiss is full of passion, tongues colliding as we both grasp at each other, desperately trying to pull the other closer. I can feel him everywhere, like he's trying to consume me, and if I thought it would feel constrictive after everything I've been through, it doesn't feel that way at all. In fact, I want more...I want him to ravage me.

His hands begin to snake underneath the hem of my top, something I replicate on his body. The feel of his soft skin under my fingers is thrilling, and as I touch every inch of his strong, muscular back, I groan while my fingers trail over his hard ridges. I got so jealous when Bree told me he's covered in tattoos, but now it's my turn to see them.

Knocking on the door startles us both, and we jump apart and away from the door, just in time for Kian to throw it open. His knowing grin tells me our swollen lips, messy hair, and crumpled, half-removed shirts leave nothing to *the imagination. "Sorry to interrupt whatever was, or was not, happening in here. But Hallie is crying. I think she wants food."*

As soon as he hears Hallie's name, Kellan springs into action. We get to Hallie and find Liam has already got to her first, and he's managed to calm her down in that special way that only he can, but you can tell by her grumbles that she's hungry.

"We better get my little Hallie Bear home for some dinner. You'd like that, wouldn't you, beautiful?" Liam coos as he tickles her tummy, making her giggle in delight.

"Liam, can you get her in the car seat?" Kellan asks, and Liam agrees as soon as he sees Kian is helping Bree.

I go to get in the back seat, but Kellan blocks me, leaning in to whisper in my ear. "I don't know what that means. There's a lot of emotions flying around. There's no denying I'm attracted to you, but you have more secrets than I can get behind. You already know I have done a background search on you, and you didn't exist before the age of sixteen. Bree is the only reason I haven't dug further, but her support will only get you so far. I want to believe you are genuine, but I can't. To say I've been burnt before is a massive fucking understatement. So, as much as I want this to continue, and fuck, I really do. I want to kiss you everywhere, to own your body completely, but I can't do that until I trust you, even just a little. I'm sorry." As he pulls away, I feel as though he's ripping my heart out and stomping all over it.

There's a reason I changed my name and hid my background from everyone. It's a past I've wiped from my life because I would rather forget it. I get that he's been burned in the past. Shayla must be a real bitch to have done this much damage to him. He will get no benefits from learning the events of a life I lived a long time ago.

Bree's the only person from my old life that I stayed in contact with, and I only did that because Bree had no idea what was going on in my life back then, she was so caught up in her own family shit. I'm not saying she was a bad friend, more that I was good at hiding it. And it will stay hidden. I like Kellan, and I would love to work with Hallie, but I'm not jumping through hoops for him. Either he likes me or he doesn't.

With a shake of my head, I try to push back the tears as I climb into the car, hating the feel of his body next to mine. I keep my eyes forward, doing my best to ignore Hallie and Kellan, so I don't have to think about what I have just lost because of him and the past I am so desperate to flee from.

I'm pulled from my thoughts as Bree clears her throat to get my attention. I'm still sitting on her bed, lost in my own world as she paces. She starts to get back onto the bed, so I scoot over, making room for her next to me.

"Do you ever think he will stop avoiding me? I know he's mad and wants me to talk about my past, but I don't want to," I snap, and Bree just pulls me against her for a hug.

"Then don't talk about it. The problem is that both you and Kellan are broken. I can't even begin to explain what he has been through, and I think I only know a fraction of your story. Neither of you knows how to trust, yet you desperately want to. Eventually, you are both going to have to go in blind. Learn to trust each other. Trust isn't going to be gained by learning someone's secrets, trust is earned. Show him that you can be trusted, and he will do the same with you. It takes time, it doesn't happen instantly. Just get to know each other. Put up with his brooding bullshit and he will put up with your evasive secretiveness. You both have flaws, you just have to learn to live with them. My advice would be to just be friends. Get to know each other. The rest will follow if it's supposed to."

I can't help but shake my head with a slight giggle. "Okay, okay, oh wise one. I will do as I'm told," I reply, my voice dripping with sarcasm. But the more I think about it, she's got a damn good point!

"**K**ellan, for the love of all that is holy, will you stop jigging that fucking leg. Hallie is with Bree, who she loves very much. Yes, Mia is with her, but they are all still in the same house. I'm not asking you to trust Mia, I'm asking you to trust Bree. Now, please, focus. We need to get this work done so we can start thinking about rebooking the wedding," Liam moans from beside me.

We're both sitting at the desks I set up in my workroom, and Liam's working on the one screen I allow others to touch. We've been doing our background research on some of the newer gang leaders that have emerged after Bree shot the old ones. We're trying to find out, can they get rid of their chauvinistic ideologies and let Bree rule them?

Normally I like this kind of investigative work, I like doing deep dives on who they are, and reading all their social media and texts. It's kinda like having an insight into someone's life that you shouldn't be allowed to have, it's addictive. I can tell early on whether I would work with the person or not, and Liam often takes my advice into account when he's thinking about taking a job. Those jobs are few and far between compared to before we met Bree. Keeping her alive and in power is turning into a full-time job. One that pays nicely, but I would do for free if I could afford to.

Despite never saying this to Liam in the early days, mainly because I thought their plan was fucking moronic, I actually liked Bree. Now that I've really got to know her, I like her even more. She may be feisty with balls of steel, but she knows how to leave all that psycho bullshit at the door and just be a fun, kind person. I thought when she first got home from the hospital she might struggle with having me and Hallie in her space. Seeing my baby looking so happy and healthy when theirs wasn't even given a chance must be hard to deal with. But, if it did bother her, she never let me, and especially not Hallie, see it. Then again, they live in a completely different wing of the house, and this place, since Bree had the extension built, could probably house another ten people. I think secretly that's what she wants. All the people she loves under one roof. That way she can protect us all.

"This Dante guy, whilst being a bit of a tool, he looks genuine. We might need to have a word with him regarding the way he treats women, though. From my last count he currently has two pregnant, one fiancée, a girlfriend, and two fuck buddies. I'm guessing that's one for every night of the week, and a day off to get over all that bullshit. But, seriously, he seems to be running CR0 with an iron fist, and the couple of anti-Bree supporters he identified, they were dealt with. So, I think it's safe to continue working with him."

Before Liam has a chance to answer, the theme tune from *Jaws* begins to ring out from his phone and as Liam groans, it doesn't take me a second guess to work out who he could possibly have assigned that tune to. Who in his life does he see as an impending threat? His father. The one bad thing that has come out of his relationship with Bree is needing to allow that piece of shit back into his life.

Answering, he puts it on loudspeaker so I can hear too. "Hey, son," Desmond answers cheerfully, as soon as Liam acknowledges he's at least picked up the phone to him.

"Don't call me that," Liam grinds out before snapping at Desmond. "What do you want?"

With a scoff, I can hear the playfulness in Desmond's voice, and I know he is trying to wind Liam up. "Can't a father ring up for a social chat with his favourite son?"

Now it's Liam's turn to sneer. I'm even trying hard not to laugh at that comment. "We both know you don't like any of your kids enough to play favourites, and if you did, it would be Evan. Now, what did you ring for?" Liam's voice is beginning to sound forced, and I can tell he's struggling to be pleasant. Since Desmond officially joined on as part of the business, Liam tries to deal with him like any other business partner, but it's so much harder. Then again, Desmond knows all the right buttons to press to wind Liam up.

"I have a bit of a problem, and I need some help. I've started working with this man who has a penchant for underage girls. He has a lot of money, and seems to think he can get whatever he wants. And what he wants is to use my club to sell under-aged girls as sex workers. I tried to tell him that it's against your policies, but he just said he doesn't work for you. In the end, he agreed to allow us to part ways, but only if I pay him a severance package. What he wants is something I can't afford." Whoever this guy is, Desmond actually sounds scared of him, I can hear the quiver in his voice.

Liam and I look at each other, suspicious over why Desmond says he can't afford the payment, since we both know he has a small fortune stashed away. "What does he want that you don't have?" Liam asks through gritted teeth.

"He wants fifty non-marked, untraceable AK-47s, and he wants them by next week." As soon as the words leave Desmond's lips, a string of expletives erupt from Liam's mouth, as he calls his father all sorts of names under the sun for getting himself into this position.

"How do we know that if we give him the guns that he isn't going to use them against us? What the fuck do you think you were doing being so reckless? You know we don't work with anyone who hasn't been vetted yet. Have we done a full background check on him?" Liam's questions fire out in rapid succession. We already know the answers.

Desmond groans, as he realises his son has caught him out. He shouldn't be doing business with anyone we haven't authorised. "Erm, so…no. But, in my defence, I was working with him before I allied myself with you, son. I knew he was a bit dodgy, but I didn't really realise he dealt in underage kids and girls until it was too late."

"That is not a defence!" Liam shouts, his tolerance wearing thin. He runs his fingers through his hair, tugging on the ends in despair. "When do you need to make the drop by?"

We can hear Desmond on the other end of the phone, shuffling bits of paper around, no doubt trying to find his diary. To normal people, the day you're supposed to arm a potential threat should stick in your heads, but not Desmond. His brain works differently, and I'm not sure any of us will ever grasp it. "Ten days," Des finally replies.

"Okay, here's what you are going to do. Text me all the information you have on this guy. If you have a picture of his face, that would really help a lot. Give me all the information you have, and I want it in the next hour. Obviously I don't want you working with someone like that, but at the same time, someone wanting that much firepower isn't a good thing. Do you have any idea what he wants them for? Any of his known associates that could want them?" Liam asks, trying to get as much information out of Des as possible.

"Honestly, I have an idea, but I really hope I'm wrong. I think the Celtic Reapers might be getting ready to go to war. As for who, or why, I have no idea. But tensions have been strained the last few months, and I think things aren't all sunshine and rainbows at the compound. I have a girl who works for me, she is a Sweetbutt with the MC, but given I'm the one who pays her, her loyalties lie with me. She keeps me updated on all the gossip, and apparently everyone is on edge. Someone is threatening to tear the Reapers down, but they have no idea who it is. I'm thinking the guy wants to arm the Reapers."

As soon as I hear the word Reapers, my ears start to ring, and spots cloud my vision. I can hear my heart racing, like a pulsing sound in my head, and I feel myself start to hyperventilate. Liam looks torn between dealing with his father and helping me. I can't listen to it anymore. I run out of the room, gasping for air, as I slide down my bedroom wall, the nearest place since my work room is adjoined to my room.

Placing my head between my legs, I try to focus on breathing, but it isn't easy. That's a name I thought I'd never hear again. We are in London, the Reapers are a Limerick-based MC, and even if they were branching out, they would never leave Ireland. I hate the idea they might, somehow, worm their way back into my life. I need to make sure that doesn't happen. Not just for my own sanity, but for Hallie too.

I send Liam a quick message telling him I need a break, and not to worry about me, before I drag my ass off the floor and head down to the main part of the house. Ever since hearing the word Reapers, I've had this overwhelming need to cuddle my little girl. Everything I do is to keep her safe and give her the best life. She can't have the best life if the Reapers, or Shayla, are part of it.

As I look around all the main rooms of the house, I can't find Hallie or Bree, and I start to panic. Bree wouldn't have taken her out without letting me know. Just as I'm about to run back upstairs and check Bree and Liam's bedroom suites, I hear laughter coming from the backyard.

Walking towards the backyard, I see both Bree and Mia are in the pool playing with Hallie. When I found out Bree had an outdoor pool, I was initially sceptical as to how practical that was. I mean, we live in London, for Christ's sake. You can count on one hand the amount of truly hot weeks we have. But, this pool is not only covered over by a large gazebo, complete with side walls to protect you from the elements, it's also heated. So, it's more like an indoor pool, and I suspect once Bree is granted the planning permission from the local council to extend further, she will build a permanent structure for it to be inside, and that will give us a bit more living room upstairs too. Even with a large swimming pool nearest the house, there's still a massive garden beyond that.

More giggling pulls me back to the here and now, and I look over just in time to see Hallie splashing the water with her hands, laughing hysterically while Mia tries to keep hold of her, getting soaked in the process. But she doesn't get mad, instead she blows raspberries on Hallie's chest, causing her to laugh even more.

I stay there for a bit, just leaning against the door jamb, watching Mia play with Hallie. Bree joins in every so often, but the rest of the time she swims laps. Mia holds Hallie up, like she's standing outside, on the edge of the pool. Then, very loudly and dramatically, she starts a countdown, which Bree joins in for, even while swimming her laps. Once they get to one, Mia lifts Hallie off the side of the swimming pool and jumps up in the air with her, making Hallie feel like she's flying, before they land back down in the water. My gorgeous little girl screams and giggles, her little hands clapping together as she coos in her own little baby language.

I try to focus on Hallie, the way her smile lights up her chubby little face, or the fact that she's actually having fun and clearly likes being with Mia. But that just brings me back to thinking about Mia, looking at her, which is dangerous. She's wearing the most ridiculous black bikini. Strings tie around her neck, and at the back of the stupid triangular-shaped top of the bikini. The bottoms tie on either side of her hips, with barely enough fabric to actually cover the gorgeous swells of her ass. It's the perfect bikini for if you want to take advantage and ravage someone. Which is most definitely not something I should be thinking about.

After that day at the warehouse, I know I can't let anything happen between us. Hallie is the most important person in my world, which means, if she likes Mia, which she clearly does, then I can't fuck with that. I can't have her liking someone, who I then screw and hurt, only for that person to walk away, like Hallie didn't even exist in the first place. I don't give a shit if she hurts or leaves me, but nobody is abandoning my little girl, not again.

I must have been so distracted thinking about that damned bikini, I miss them getting out of the pool. Bree's on a sun lounger, wrapped in a towel as she wraps a grumbly Hallie in one too. Clearly my little monster didn't want to get out of the pool, and her grumbles soon turn to screams. Just as I'm considering going to her, I see Mia, her towel wrapped around like a sinfully short skirt, walking towards me. There's nowhere to hide, and given the little smirk on her face, she knows I've been here for a while. Watching them. Well, fuck, I guess I look like a creepy stalker now.

I try not to stare but her hips sway while she walks towards me, hypnotically, and it's almost impossible. I find myself praying that the damn towel will fall down, but alas, I'm not that lucky. As she reaches me, she pulls the door open, giving me that small, shy smile that I can't help but like. She looks fucking adorable, a blush spreading across her cheeks as she realises I'm obviously checking her out. I don't think this girl knows how fucking beautiful she is. If I thought she looked good when I first met her and she had that platinum blonde hair, now she has gone back to her natural brunette colour, she looks perfect.

Off-limits, Kellan. Keep repeating that. I mentally chastise myself, but sometimes the sight of her in a bikini and the memory of her lips against mine is too much to ignore. My dick certainly can't forget. He's standing to attention, desperately trying to break free from my boxers and ripped jeans at the mere memory of her.

"Hey, what are you doing here? You are supposed to be working hard. We're just stopping for a food break. Which is code for Hallie is hungry. Do you want to come and have a drink with us?" she asks, as she strolls past me towards the kitchen.

I don't even think about it, I just follow her, my feet taking on a life of their own. Standing beside the island in the middle of the kitchen, I watch as she clicks the kettle on, and then out of the blue she removes the towel that was protecting her modesty. Or stopping me from perving on her seems more accurate. She's far too close, showing far too much skin, it leaves me mesmerised. The curves of her breasts that are only just being held in by the black triangular patches that just about cover her nipples. The creamy white of her soft skin that is stretched taut across her stomach. As soon as I catch sight of the glistening jewel in her belly button, I realise it's pierced, and I know my cock will never come down now.

I want to keep looking, to explore every aspect of her skin, but before I have a chance, she grabs a big T-shirt off the side and pulls it over her head. It's not until she gets it on, do I realise it's one of my T-shirts. Fuck, that's even worse than the bikini. I'm getting caveman-like thoughts about owning her, and claiming her as mine while she's wearing my stuff.

We stand there in silence as she makes up a bottle for Hallie, and makes a few sandwiches, before she turns to face me. "What do you want to drink? I've made enough so you and Liam can join us, when he's not busy, I mean." Her voice is like music to my ears, and my cock. Fuck, what the hell is wrong with me? So, I'm attracted to her. I've been attracted to lots of girls and managed to not sleep with them. Since Hallie's birth, I've had no choice but to change my ways. As much as I would love to fuck around, Hallie comes first.

"He will be down soon, he's just on the phone." I go to try and help her pick up some of the plates and drinks to carry outside, but she stops and turns to look at me.

"Are you okay? I don't know, your voice sounds kinda strained," she asks with a small smile, as she shuffles around nervously trying to avoid meeting my gaze.

Taking a step closer, I reach out and place my hand on her chin, lifting her gaze until she has no choice but to meet mine. "I'm okay, just dealing with some ghosts, that's all. Why can't you look at me?" My voice comes out as a gruff drawl, full of lust and insinuations.

"Because every time I do, I think about that day at the warehouse, and I can't keep torturing myself like that."

Before I have a chance to reply, Liam comes bounding down the stairs, taking them two at a time. Mia and I spring apart, like we're fucking teenagers caught doing something we shouldn't. Even though my fingers are no longer touching her silky, smooth skin, it's like I can still feel her under my skin.

"Hey, where's Bree?" Liam asks, as he reaches the island in the kitchen, looking between the two of us with his disapproving stare.

"She's by the pool. We're just about to have some lunch. I made enough for you too. Kellan, could you grab the drinks please," she asks innocently, as though she didn't just cause my heart and my cock to ache for her.

I do as I'm told, and when we reach the table, Hallie is really screaming for her food. I notice Bree has changed her out of her swimming stuff, which means I've missed out on her pre-food nappy change. Bonus!

"Aww what's wrong with my beautiful girl. Are you hungry? Come and give Daddy a cuddle," I say, as I put the drinks down and free up my arms to take my baby girl. But instead of holding her arms out for me, as soon as she spots Liam, she reaches for him. I should have fucking known, this girl idolises him.

"Looks like someone wants Uncle Liam to feed them," Bree says as she hands Hallie over to Liam with a smile.

"Oh yeah, it's like I don't even exist!" I moan, only half joking. I love the fact that she loves her uncle so much, I just wish she showed me that much love some days.

Doubt creeps in, and I try to hide it from everyone, but I worry she somehow knows what happened before she was born. That, for the shortest amount of time, I wasn't sure I wanted to be a father, or if Hallie was even my biological daughter. Hallie came with so much baggage, namely Shayla and the Reapers, but I can't change that. No matter how much I may want to. I worry that's why she doesn't show me as much affection at times.

Pushing those dark thoughts aside, we sit together, joking and just talking about nothing as we eat the lunch Mia made for us. Liam updates Bree about Desmond, but he doesn't mention to her that we're familiar with the Reapers. He glosses over them, which I'm grateful for. I have a sneaky suspicion he'll tell Bree everything later, but Mia doesn't need to know. Not unless I choose to tell her.

"So, I'm treating Bree to a special date night tonight since she's been moaning like hell about getting out of the house. You two, or should I say three, will have the house to yourselves. Since I'm feeling extra kind, why don't you get a takeaway on me," Liam says, with that cocky grin of his as he looks between us.

Mia drops her gaze, a blush spreading across her cheeks, and that's when Bree chips in. "It will be good for you guys to hang out, as friends. Since we're all going to be living together, getting to know each other, and becoming friends, it will be good for everyone." I don't know if I'm the only one who picked up on it, but the way she emphasises the word *friends*, it feels like a warning. Mia is off-limits.

Mia doesn't look like she's going to be the first to speak, her head is firmly down, trying to avoid everyone's gaze. So, I take pity on her and reply. "Well, I'm not going to turn down free food and the chance to avoid cooking. We could always watch a movie together, if you like, Mia? I should be able to get Hallie asleep by seven, and then we can get food and a movie in before she wakes up for her next bottle. What do you say, fancy keeping me company, and eating food we didn't pay for?" I ask, and as she lifts her head and our eyes meet, my heart begins to race, and it's as though she sees into my soul. Her stunning chocolate eyes glow, and there's a fire there that seems to set my body alight.

"On one condition, we don't have to wash up either," she jokes, and Liam laughs, telling her they have a deal. I don't know if my meddling best friend has just done me a favour or not. I know Liam wants me to get to know her so I'll keep her as my nanny, but what he doesn't realise is that pushing us to spend more time together before we decide if anything is going to happen between us is a mistake. It's like we're in a pressure cooker, and the more our emotions bubble and boil, the sooner it will explode. I promised him a few weeks ago that I wouldn't shit where I eat, and I know he meant that I wasn't allowed to fuck Mia. I just don't know if I can stick to that.

I can, however, spend the evening with her, getting to know her. That I can agree to. Whatever else happens, we will just have to see.

It's not a date. It's not a date. Maybe if I repeat it in my head a few more times, I will start to believe it. I know Liam and Bree want this to be two roommates getting to know each other, a way for us to become friends, and hopefully secure my job as Hallie's nanny. If only they knew about the kiss, and about the burning ache I feel for him. They would know that we can't just be friends. It feels like something could happen with Kellan, and every logical part of me is telling me to walk away.

In truth, I need this job more than anything. Besides, living with a guy after a one-night fling would be super awkward. But, that's all that could ever happen between us, one night, and even then I'm not sure I'm ready for that. Part of me wants to run away from Kellan and his wandering penis, but the other part of me actually craves him. It feels wrong to want sex when I've spent my whole life detesting it.

I try to block those thoughts from my mind, focusing instead on how I look in the mirror in front of me. You have no idea how hard it is to get dressed up, but make it look like I'm not dressing up and that I didn't try. It even took me close to thirty minutes to make my bun sufficiently messy enough. Clearly I'm going insane. I suspected as much when I put make-up on, but tried to make it look like I wasn't wearing any. After trying on numerous outfits, I settled on some skinny jeans and a strappy vest top. I look like I'm just chilling out, but underneath, I'm ashamed to admit I have on my best pair of black lace matching lingerie.

Yeah, I've definitely gone insane!

Looking down at my watch, I see it's five minutes before seven, which is the time we arranged to meet. I bet he is still putting Hallie down, so I decide to head down to the living room. Why do I feel so awkward wandering around my own home all of a sudden?

Walking down the stairs as quietly as I can, I genuinely feel like I've gone crazy. I just need a few minutes of deep breaths before I jump into this. I know this isn't a date, my head has repeated it enough times, but the truth is, I've never been on a date. Like, never. And yes, I'm a twenty-one year old girl who has no idea what a date even looks like. Is it any wonder I'm freaking out?!

As I reach the living room, I hear a soft tune that becomes more obvious the closer I get. As soon as I realise it's Kellan singing, I'm hooked. I'm not saying he is going to win a Grammy anytime soon, but the guy can hold a tune. What really has me laughing is the fact that he's clearly singing "Let it Go" from the *Frozen* movie that Hallie absolutely adores, but he's changing up the lyrics, using it as a way to tell Hallie to let go of her tiredness and to go to sleep so he can watch a movie that doesn't rot his brain.

I slowly peer around the entryway to the open-plan living room and kitchen. I was hoping to catch sight of him without him realising I'm here, and thankfully he has his back to me. He is pacing at the back of the sofa and as he turns around to head back the other way, I catch sight of him and he takes my breath away. This gorgeous man is singing while swaying his daughter in his arms, but it's painfully obvious Hallie is not ready to go to bed just yet. She isn't grumbling or anything, she is literally just laying there in his arms, her big, bright blue eyes staring up at her daddy, like he's the greatest guy in the world. Obviously, this look alone is enough to make my ovaries explode, but then I get a chance to look the rest of him over and see he too has made slightly more of an effort than usual.

Typically, given Hallie's ability to throw up on anything, Kellan tends to just wear sweat pants and plain T-shirts around the house. I've seen him get dressed properly when he goes out on jobs with Liam, and he rocks the dark jeans look. But this is a whole new side to him. His dark blue jeans are faded and ripped in all the right places, and whenever he turns so he isn't looking at me, I get a very delicious view of his tight ass in those jeans. He looks to have paired it with a T-shirt, and a dark blue shirt over the top of it. The sleeves of the shirt are rolled up, revealing the tattoos he has across his forearms, giving me the slight hint of what Bree told me is underneath. Apparently before I started living here, and Kellan was trying to wind up Liam, he would constantly walk around topless. Personally, I would've had no issues with that game continuing. I'm desperate to see what's underneath. Believe me, I've fantasised about it enough.

Kellan's hair is still a little wet from the shower, but running his baby-free hand through the strands leaves it floppy and styled in just the right way. He's gorgeous, and I can't fucking wait to spend the evening getting to know him, because that's where our problems lies. Maybe when he gets to know the real me, not the broken kid I used to be, he will stop searching for answers in a past that doesn't exist anymore.

"Please, Hallie, baby girl. Just close your eyes. Daddy needs to have a little bit of grown-up time before his head explodes. You would probably think that was funny, wouldn't you, my beautiful little weirdo?" Kellan coos before kissing Hallie on the cheek. Her resounding giggle makes me laugh, giving away my hiding space.

I address Kellan, since I'm sure he knows I'm here. "Problems with the baby?"

Kellan's responding laugh is a mixture of desperation and despair, and this time when I look into his eyes, I can see how tired he really is. He has dark circles under his eyes, and one is starting to look a little bloodshot. Even his rugged stubble looks like it's probably not supposed to be there. It doesn't detract from how handsome he is, but it reminds me this guy is a single dad doing it all alone. He gets up in the middle of the night with Hallie, and then looks after her all day when he isn't working. Other than the small amount of time he lets either Liam or Bree look after her, he does everything, and it shows.

"I wouldn't say it's a problem. This is a regular occurrence at the moment sadly. She just hates sleep, or me, I haven't decided which yet. Once I get her down, she wakes up a couple of hours later for food, and we go through it all again. The health visitor I saw said she's going through a growth spurt, and this type of behaviour is very normal. But, she isn't the one getting around three hours of sleep a day." I can't help but giggle as his ramble continues. I love the fact that he was so worried he asked a health visitor for help. He strikes me as the type of guy who isn't big on admitting when he's struggling, or asking for help of any kind.

"Why don't you let me have a cuddle for five minutes while you order us some food? We can even put a child-friendly movie on, if you like?" I ask and his eyes go wide as saucers.

"For the love of God, no more cartoons. These bloody films are driving me crazy. I'm also not convinced those movies give off good messages, but since she's only seven months old, I'm choosing to let it pass. Well...when I say choosing, I don't really have a choice. When you find something that makes the screaming stop, you do what needs to be done. When she was a baby, like a tiny newborn, I couldn't get her to sleep then either. The only time she ever stopped screaming enough to consider sleeping is when the Hoover was on. Once I discovered her love of the Hoover, I kept it plugged in and switched on for hours at a time, all while I desperately grabbed a bit of sleep."

As I sit down on the couch, he walks towards me, and I realise he's actually going to do what I suggested. He gets her settled in my arms and breathes a sigh of relief when she doesn't start screaming. So, I continue our conversation. "There's a lot of research to show that babies like white noise because it reminds them of the sounds they hear in the womb. But I think it's more of a comfort to them. Like just now when you were singing. Hallie was looking at you like you're a rock star, and I've only ever seen her do that with her uncle Liam." I try not to sound overly technical, but I do also want to impress him a little. We never got a chance to have a real job interview, so he doesn't know I have a lot of experience in this field. If I had the money, I'd have gone to college full-time, and would have already graduated. But, as it is, I'm doing a part-time online course and should hopefully be able to finish next year. I've worked hard and gone through the course quicker than I needed to. The only thing outstanding is the placement experience hours that I need to qualify, and my final dissertation.

"Ha, you must have caught her during a moment of gassiness. She only looks at me lovingly when she wants food, or when she knows she's doing something she shouldn't. She is so close to being able to pull herself up now. It won't be long until she's walking. She's growing up way too fast, and I feel like I'm barely holding on," Kellan groans, as he flops onto the sofa beside us. He's sitting so close, I can feel the heat from his arm next to mine. "So, what do you want?"

My eyes fly to his, and I could get lost in the bright, crystal blue eyes that he currently has aimed at me. I expect to see the cocky smile I'm becoming used to, but his smile is just normal. Like he didn't just ask me a loaded question. "Erm...yeah, but..." My voice trails off as my brain struggles to think of the correct words. What *do* I want?

My brain feels like a scattering of thoughts, as each possibility flicks through my mind. I want him to kiss me like he did the day at the warehouse. I want him to do unspeakable things to my body, when I'm ready for that. I want him to get to know the real me and forget about the past. But, mostly, I want to feel his warmth as he cuddles up beside me, to fall asleep on his chest, and have him hold me. I want it all, and I know I can't have it. Even though that thought annoys me, the bit that really shocks me is how strongly I feel about Kellan. I didn't think I was capable of liking a guy, or having these types of yearning. I thought they were long gone, scared away by the ghosts of my past.

Kellan's chuckle pulls me out of my thoughts, and as Hallie replicates her daddy's laugh, I can't help but join in. "Relax, Flower. I meant what do you want to eat, so I know what type of food to order. Chinese? Pizza? Indian? Italian?" he asks, scrolling through his phone, and what I'm guessing is a food delivery website, as he reads out all the options.

Well, that could have been a whole lot more embarrassing than I thought. Thank fuck I didn't actually answer him out loud like I was contemplating doing. I do my best to cover it up, making it sound like I was umming and ahhing about the food choices, rather than how much of my soul I was about to bare to this guy. "I'm fairly easy-going, what do you want?"

With his signature cocky smirk, he replies in that gravelly tone that sets my insides alight. "Good to know that you are...easy."

Seriously, if I'd been taking a drink, I would've spluttered it everywhere. Instead, I settle for choking on my own saliva, or maybe it's just thin air. Either way, I'm coughing and spluttering, all whilst trying to make sure I don't disturb the baby in my arms, and that I cover my mouth with my free arm. Kellan's laugh fills the room, and I really fucking want to hurt him right now.

"God...you are the worst. Is there ever a time you don't flirt?" I cough and splutter at the end, my body only just getting used to breathing normally again. Hallie starts to grumble, presumably annoyed at being shaken whilst in my arms, and I'm worried she's seconds away from crying. Well, that is until the cutest little laugh erupts from her body.

"Oh my God...is she laughing? She never laughs at me. Only Liam has ever been able to get her to laugh, and I've never seen it so I keep telling myself it's gas, or that he's messing with me. But that was a real honest to God laugh, wasn't it?" he enquires, as he leans forward and starts to tickle Hallie's tummy, which earns him some more laughs. The smile on his face is blinding. I've never seen him look so happy, and I'm glad I got to be a small part of it.

"Yeah, it's definitely a laugh. I know you have been freaking out about Hallie hitting milestones at the right times, and things like that, but you really don't need to worry. Hallie will do it in her own time." I lay my hand on the top of his. It's supposed to be for reassurance, but as soon as my skin touches his, it's like I'm electrocuted. A strong current heats its way up the nerves in my arm. It burns as it goes, until finally settling in my core. Fuck, this guy must have magical powers that directly link to my most intimate places.

"I know, that's what the health visitor said. There's definitely some areas where she's more advanced, but there's also some areas that I know she should be excelling in and she isn't. I just worry, given her history, how broken she really could be." His voice breaks as I think he's just confessed something that's been worrying him for a long time. I don't want to pry, or make him feel like he has to tell me anything. But at the same time, I want him to know he can talk to me.

How fucking ironic is that? I'm desperate for him to open up and talk to me so I can learn more about him, yet that's the one thing I told him was off-limits for me. How can I ask him to do something I'm not willing to do?

"Look at this beautiful little girl, there's no way in hell she's broken. What would make you think that? You know you can talk to me, and it will remain just between us. You will always have my word on that." I try to make it seem like I'm not desperate for any morsel of information that he's willing to throw my way. Given the way his face, that was so beautifully happy just a second ago, is now contorted with anguish, I want him to talk not just for me, but because it looks like he needs to.

"Thanks, that means a lot. Let's get some food ordered, get this bottle in her, and then we can talk." His face wears the briefest of smiles that doesn't even reach his eyes.

I watch as he tests the bottle on his forearm before handing it over to me. As I place it into Hallie's mouth, she begins to suck as though she hasn't been fed in ages. I know Kellan probably gave her a bottle about an hour ago, when he was trying to get her ready for bed. This is another last-ditch attempt to get her to fall asleep.

"Okay, so shall we go with a pizza or Chinese? Those are the two I'm feeling most, but you can overrule me if you like," I say, a slight blush spreading to my cheeks. I know he sees it because he looks confused as to why I would be blushing over something as trivial as this. But, the truth is, I'm not used to being the one making the first move, or making decisions. All my life I've had people choose for me. Ever since I left my family and became independent, as soon as I'm with another person, that indoctrination kicks in. I tell myself the other person knows what's best for me, just like I was always told. But with Kellan, I don't think that, and more importantly, I know he doesn't think that. He always asks for my opinion, or gives me choices. He's never forced me into anything.

"I like both, but let's go with pizza. What's your topping of choice?" he asks, as he pulls out his phone and begins scrolling through, no doubt bringing the menu up on his phone. But I don't need a menu where pizza is concerned.

"Well, I'm pretty easy-going and like most toppings, but I love garlic bread with cheese. Maybe we could share a pizza and a garlic bread with cheese? I can eat a fair bit, but there's no way I can eat a whole pizza by myself and then some garlic bread." Kellan laughs at my words, and I look over at him to see what he finds so funny.

"Flower, you are so small, you're almost see-through. When you say you can eat a fair bit, I think that's an overstatement."

I sit with my mouth open, not quite believing what I'm hearing. Is he really body shaming me for being too thin? "Are you kidding me? Why is the fact that I'm petite such a problem?"

Kellan looks shocked and holds his hands up, like he's telling me he's not a threat. I know my body's ugly. I'm very aware I have no curves and am painfully thin, but I'm working on it. I've been trying to eat and put on weight for the last few months, desperately chasing the womanly figure with curves that every girl dreams about. But, I was never allowed to look like that. I needed to look as young as I could, for as long as possible. As a result, puberty never quite hit me properly. Causing me to loathe my body so much more. I just never thought Kellan, of all people, would shame me about it.

"No, I think what I said came out the wrong way. What I mean is you are very thin…not that there's anything wrong with that, though. It's just, when someone says they eat a lot, I imagine them not being as thin as you. I realise now that talking about a girl's weight is a minefield of a subject, and I in no way wanted to offend you. But, I'm not going to lie. You are petite. You have a beautiful, yet small, body. Not that you need my opinion, but if I'm giving you it, I think you would look a lot healthier if you were to put on a little more weight.

That is all I meant by it. I wasn't meaning to offend or hurt you," Kellan stutters, and it looks like he is going to continue with his mumbling, probably until he thinks I understand him. I get what he's saying, and I agree with him, it's just hard hearing it from another person. Particularly someone who I desperately want to like my body.

"I understand. I know I don't talk about my past, but the one thing you should know is that I didn't have a good childhood. I wasn't raised well. I suffered a lot, in ways you can't even imagine. I'm as thin as I am because I had to be, not because I ever wanted to be. I'm trying to put weight on, to grow some curves. I want my body to be desirable. But habits you've had drilled into you your whole life are hard to get past." I look down at Hallie the whole time I talk, grateful I have something keeping my hands occupied while I talk about things I've stayed silent about my whole life. Not even Bree knows. I told her a little after the disastrous interview, and elements of my life were exposed, but she doesn't know any of the main stuff, not the full extent.

"Mia, you are beautiful just the way you are, and nobody should ever tell you how your body should look. But, if *you* want to be more curvy, then make that decision for you. If you need someone to eat junk food with, I'm your guy. Now I have a daughter, I need to work on my dad bod anyway. Apparently women prefer single dads with a bit of meat, rather than abs. Who knew?" Kellan laughs, and I can't help but laugh along with him.

"Whoever told you that is lying. Women love abs, and that V. That's the money-maker right there," I joke, and although Kellan is smiling, I can see a sadness in his eyes. I wait for him to speak, begging him with my eyes, but when he doesn't, I decide to ask, "What is it?"

"This conversation just got me thinking. I'm not really sure I even want a girlfriend, or am capable of being in a relationship. Even if I decide I do want to, it won't be for a hell of a long time. Hallie will always come first. It was hard for me to see myself as a catch before Hallie was born, but now it will be even harder. I have so much frickin' baggage, nobody is going to want to get anywhere near."

Hallie starts to grumble, drawing my attention away from her dad.

She spits the bottle out, and I hand it over to Kellan, who already has his arm outstretched to get it. I lay Hallie over my shoulder and stroke her back, trying to wind her for a bit, while I stare at the beautiful, broken boy in front of me. Maybe this is why I get on with him so well, why our souls seem to connect. We both recognise brokenness when we see it. Our broken souls speak to each other.

"Okay, I have so much to say about that, but right now we need to order that damn pizza because I can hear my belly rumbling and it's not a good look."

Kellan's smile brightens and this time when it reaches his bright blue eyes, my stomach does a little somersault. I don't know why I want to make him happy, but I really do.

"How about we both say what type of pizza we usually order, and then we can work out how to combine it, or get a half and half pizza. So, I usually order ham and chicken with extra cheese. I'm a big fan of extra cheese," he laughs and I can't help but agree with him.

"Everything's better with extra cheese. I usually go with BBQ chicken, which is a BBQ sauce base with chicken, mushroom, and red onions. But I'm definitely a fan of ham, so we can go with your order."

Before Kellan gets the chance to reply, Hallie lets out the biggest belch I've ever heard, followed closely by a giggle. As I pull her away from my shoulder, I'm glad I put the muslin cloth there, as that small amount of baby vomit would now be dripping down my back. I put her on my knee, and her little face crinkles. Her big blue eyes, that look so much like her daddy's, are wide open, and as her mouth opens in a yawn, I notice her eyes are starting to sag. She looks so peaceful, but determined to fight the sleep. So I curl her up into my arms and start to rock her.

"Are you okay with her?" Kellan whispers, knowing this is the crucial time when you don't want to alert her in any way. If she sees people and things going on around her, she will fight more to stay awake. As it is, her little eyelids keep fluttering closed, and it's clear she can't fight it for much longer.

"I'm fine, you order."

"I like the BBQ base idea, but the vegetables I just can't get on board with. So we will do chicken and ham, and if they will let us, I will get mushrooms and onions on your side. I will also get us a cheesy garlic bread pizza. Want to share a double chocolate cookie dough for dessert?" I'm sure I'm physically drooling. Not just at the food either, this guy is almost too perfect. I agree and he starts typing on his phone, while I continue to rock Hallie until her eyes eventually flutter closed.

"Where do you want her? Upstairs in the cot?" I ask, and Kellan's face whitens, like all the blood has drained from him.

I look down at the perfect sleeping baby, expecting to see that I've done something wrong, or missed something, but I can't see anything.

"I know this is going to sound crazy, but I can't let her sleep in a different room just yet. So, normally I would put her to sleep in the Moses basket down here, and then when I'm ready for bed, move her to the cot I have attached to the side of my bed. I know she should be in her own cot in her room. Hell, it took me and Liam so fucking long to build it, she should be sleeping in it for that reason alone, but I can't." His voice breaks.

I lay Hallie down in the Moses basket that lives here by the sofa, and put her little blanket lightly over her body and smile as she coos. Once I'm sure she's settled, I turn to address Kellan, who walks to the other side of the cot and mumbles his goodnights to his daughter. It's so fucking cute, I literally have to turn my eyes or risk losing an ovary. I mean, this guy sets my body on fire under normal circumstances, but this is so much more.

"I don't think there's anything wrong with that, with wanting to be close to watch over her. She's lucky to have a dad as great as you. I know you think having Hallie means you bring a lot of baggage into any potential relationship, and I'm not going to lie to you, for some people that will be true. But, believe me when I say this, we all have issues and baggage. The main thing is finding a girl who doesn't see Hallie as baggage, and who learns to love her as much as she loves you. Never settle for anyone who doesn't put that beautiful little girl first. Okay?" I exclaim as I flop back down onto the sofa, after getting Hallie settled, while Kellan heads towards the kitchen.

"Thanks, I need to remember that! Beer or Diet Coke?" he asks, holding one of each up to help me decide. I opt for the beer. I don't often drink. Well…I don't often drink anymore. When I first found my freedom, I partied a lot. Bree was by my side for a lot of it, but she was also battling her own family crap, so there were times I partied without her. Those were usually the nights I made the most stupid decisions.

Kellan flops down right beside me, ignoring the entire side of the sofa I left him, and he's sitting so close I can feel his body against mine. He seems to take a deep breath, like he's worried about saying something, or like he's plucking up the courage. I hold my breath in anticipation, and as he starts to speak, I slowly start to breathe again. "I can't tell you the whole story, only Liam knows it all, but I will tell you some. The pregnancy with Hallie was filled with so much turbulence, I can't even begin to explain it. We were together for a while, then she had to go back to her family due to a family commitment, and when she returned, that's when she told me she was pregnant. But, I wasn't the only guy in the running for being the dad. When the test came back to say Hallie was mine, we moved ahead quickly. I had never been in a relationship before, and I knew absolutely nothing about being in love. All I knew was that I felt more for her than I ever had before, and I mistook that for love. She moved in, and we became the proper, ideal couple, getting ready to raise a baby together. Then the day Hallie was born, it was the best and worst day of my life, all in one go."

Giving me a sad smile that makes my heart break, I want to speak, he's giving me the option to, but I know there's more. So I wait. I take a long swig from my beer bottle and then point the bottle neck towards him, indicating he should carry on talking, the ghost of a smile getting a tiny bit brighter as he does.

"The moment I held Hallie, I realised I knew what love was. I mean, I'm sure it feels slightly different when there's a romantic connection, but I knew the love I felt for Hallie in no way matched what I felt for Shayla. To me, that didn't matter, I was still all in. I wanted us to be a family. We had a house, a nursery, a trust fund set up. I had spent eight months preparing to be the perfect parent that I never had. And all that went to shit when Hallie was just five hours old. Shayla left the hospital, leaving behind a letter and a stack of legal documents. She signed all her parental rights away, stating I'm Hallie's only parent now by law. Then, as an added bonus, she sold my dream house that I had made into the perfect house for Hallie. She stole all my assets, and all my money. The only thing she left me with is that little girl, a stack of legal papers, and a half-assed apology." Kellan gets more angry the more he talks, and I don't fucking blame him. Obviously I know Shayla is no longer in Kellan's and Hallie's lives, but I had no idea things had gone down like that.

I don't have a violent side, never had, but the overwhelming urge to punch Shayla should I ever meet her is so strong. Normally, I accept that there are two sides to every story, and try to play devil's advocate. I've spent most of my life presenting an image to the world that in no way represents my life behind closed doors, and I know people have secrets. Maybe Shayla has a good reason for what she did, but my brain can't come up with one right now. In fact, I'm shaking my head in disbelief, causing Kellan to ask me what's wrong.

"I just can't believe she would do that. I know everyone has secrets and I want to believe she had a really good reason, but it doesn't really matter if she has the best excuse in the world, what she did is still unforgivable. I'm so sorry you had to go through that, but you are capable of loving again. I promise you, one day a girl will come along that will blow you out of the water," I say, very fucking hopeful that one day that's me.

That cheeky chappie smile I like so much is back. He starts to talk, but the ringing doorbell interrupts him. He goes to the door to collect the pizza, and I pull my phone out to see what's going on. I can feel it vibrating incessantly in my pocket. But it shouldn't be. Only a few people have this number and they are either on a date or sat with me. There are a few texts and calls from an unknown number.

UNKNOWN

Mia, you can't run away forever. I know you are mad at me, but we need to talk. You have family obligations that you committed to. Do not let your mother down. I have given you this time, but you have almost graduated, which means your time is up. Get in contact with us. Now!

Mia, so help me God, if I have to track you down and drag you back by your hair, I will.

Did you really think changing your last name would be enough for me to leave you alone? Of course I know where you are, with that O'Keenan bitch. I know who she is, and I know you are getting involved in stuff you have no business being involved in. So, get your ass back home and I won't hurt each and every person in that house. Last chance, Mia!

I swear, Mia. I will get what is rightfully mine. You don't get to walk away from familial obligation. You are engaged and it's expected you should return to him. You dishonoured me by not texting me back or picking up any of my calls. So I have shared your location with him. Maybe now you will think twice before rejecting my polite messages and calls. If you had, I would have allowed you the rest of the time I promised you. Since you didn't, time is up!

KYLE

Hey, Little Bunny. Keep hopping and bopping as much as you like, but the rabbit always gets caught in the end. I have my traps, and you are in my sight. If you don't come home willingly, Little Bunny, then I sure as fuck will drag you home. Not to mention, I will burn down the house you currently call home, with all the people inside. You are supposed to be my wife, Little Bunny, and that isn't changing anytime soon. Time is up. Run, run, Little Bunny, as fast as you can. You can run, you can hide, but I'm coming for you, and I always win.

Fuck! This is not good. I start to panic, looking around the room, frantically trying to think of what to do next. I always knew changing my name was never enough, but I wasn't prepared to disappear completely. I had just been accepted to university, I had a life all planned out, and I couldn't leave Bree. So, I changed my last name, and I even dyed my hair blonde for a bit, before going back to my natural brunette colour. I hoped it would be enough. I should have known it wouldn't be. I should have known he would find me.

Kellan walks back, carrying the pizzas with a bright smile on his face, and all that does is cause me to hyperventilate further. My heart feels as though it's going to beat right out of my chest and my palms are so sweaty. Pain radiates through my body as each breath I take burns. I can hear Kellan talking, but it feels as though I have cotton wool stuck in my ears, and I can't quite hear what he's saying.

His cold yet soft hands cup my cheeks, and the sensation of his skin against mine is at least enough to bring back my attention, and I can finally hear what he's saying. "Hey, Flower. You need to breathe, okay. Mia, just listen to my voice and do exactly as I tell you. We are going to breathe together," he states, his beautiful, crystal blue eyes honing into mine.

I follow each and every instruction he gives until I'm back to breathing normally. Kellan doesn't move, he just lets me sit there, with his thumbs gently stroking across my cheeks until I calm down. He's not looking at me like I'm a crazy person who just had a panic attack for no apparent reason. Instead, he looks concerned, like he really wants to help me but he just doesn't know how. If only he knew that just him being here, giving me space whilst holding me tight is exactly what I need.

I'm not sure how much time passes, but it feels like far too long. It's not until he is certain I'm not going to freak out again does Kellan start to speak. "How are you feeling? Do you have panic attacks often?" he asks tentatively, as he gently removes his hands from my face so that he can settle back onto the sofa. I hate how cold and lonely my face feels without his touch.

"I'm okay now, thank you. Erm…yeah, I-I have panic attacks regularly, but I usually try to hide them. That's the worst I've had in a while." My voice is strained, and as I settle back onto the sofa, Kellan hands over my beer bottle.

With a smile, I take a long gulp of my drink, loving that sweet burn that travels down my throat to settle in my stomach. Kellan reaches over, opens the pizza box, and grabs the most delicious-looking slice of garlic pizza bread. I know he can see my eyes light up, and he hands me the slice. I take it with thanks, and as the deliciousness hits my taste buds, I can't help but moan. Great, now I'm the girl who makes sex noises when she eats pizza. Could I get any more socially awkward if I tried?

"Do you want to tell me what your freak-out was about?" he asks, in between bites of pizza. He has now moved onto the BBQ chicken and ham, which looks and smells amazing. I can't wait to dive in. In fact, diving into the pizza would be the perfect way to avoid answering his question. It's what I would normally do, but he's opened up to me so much tonight, I feel like I owe him, even just a little bit.

Taking a deep breath I start to explain parts of my life that I've never told anyone about, not even Bree. "I can't tell you the whole story, not yet. But I can tell you bits, as long as you promise to keep it to yourself. It's not something everyone knows, including Bree."

"Anything you say to me will always be confidential, I promise you that," Kellan says, as he takes hold of one of my hands with his, and the feel of his touch is electrifying. It gives me a confidence I didn't have before.

"Do you remember when we had the interview to be Hallie's nanny, and you said there were a lot of blanks about my life that you weren't happy about? Well...they are blank for a reason. I wouldn't say I'm in hiding, or have run away, or anything like that, but I left a toxic lifestyle, and I made it clear I won't ever be returning. But, some people are not happy about that. One of those people is Kyle Fratacello. I was supposed to marry him a few years ago, which is the marriage certificate that you found. I obviously didn't go through with it, and that started the events that led to me essentially leaving and never speaking to my family ever again." My voice is barely above a whisper, and each word feels as though I'm going to choke on it. There's a reason I don't talk about these things with people, not just because I find it difficult to trust, but also because it's heartbreakingly painful to bring up a time I would much rather forget ever happened. Yet Kellan doesn't judge, he just holds my hand in his, stroking his thumbs over the back of my hands, waiting for me to finish.

When I finally look up at him, I don't see the pity I expect to see, his gaze is burning furiously. "The marriage licence was drawn up a few years ago, and at the time that never really registered with me. I was more pissed you didn't tell me you were going to marry that Italian idiot. But, now you mention it, the date on the certificate was over five years ago, if I remember correctly. Yet, you have only just turned twenty-one. Am I wrong?" Kellan seems to speak through gritted teeth, like he hates the idea of saying the words, but says them anyway.

I can't help but avert my eyes to the floor, shame rippling across my skin as thoughts of those traumatic times spring right back into my memory. I try to pull my hand away, and when he lets me, my heart sinks. I really thought Kellan would be the type of guy to hold on, to fight to help you. I guess I was wrong.

Except, he proves me wrong straight away, by instead gripping his hands around my cheeks, moving my head until I have no choice but to face him. Tears blur my vision, as I begin to regret confiding in Kellan at all. Until he opens his mouth, and I can't help but swoon over him. "Mia, I need you to tell me the truth right now. I know you think I will think differently of you, but I won't. You will just have to trust me on this one, because I can only show you. But if you don't tell me, I am more likely to hunt down Kyle Fratacello and blow his head off. Which is usually something I don't do…that's kinda Liam's part of the business." I can't help but giggle at his babbling. That's one of the many endearing things I've discovered about Kellan, when he's nervous, he babbles and talks about all sorts of random things, and it's hard to get him to shut up. Not that I want him to. I love the fact that he isn't afraid to show he isn't perfect. He gets nervous, he has anxiety, and he suffers with mental ill health from time to time. He has never hid any of that stuff away. I know some men think that's the most unmanly thing you can possibly do, to show this softer side, but Kellan proves that's complete bullshit. He's never looked more attractive or more real to me.

"I was fifteen when Kyle drew up the licence. My father agreed to sign it as a sixteenth birthday gift for me. That's when I decided to escape. It wasn't easy, and I did some stuff I'm not entirely proud of, but I won't ever regret running away. God knows where I would be if I hadn't."

"So, if all this is well in the past, why did it give you a panic attack just now?" he asks, and I almost forgot, or should I say, I hoped he realised why I was bringing all this shit up again in the first place.

"My father just made contact. He made a big fuss when I left, for the first two years, about how he would force me to return, to fulfil my familial responsibilities. That he was giving me time to get my qualification, but then I had to return. Then all communication stopped. I haven't heard from him in around three years. Then a few months ago, he started calling and texting again. Letting me know that as I was near the end of my university course, our agreement was also drawing to a close. I would have to return and fulfil my commitments. That means getting married. He obviously didn't like me ignoring him, and he just texted to let me know he's shared my number and location with Kyle. Who promptly messaged to say he is coming for me, and will take me by force if necessary." As soon as the words leave my lips, I break down, sobbing hysterically. "I'm so sorry, Kellan. I never meant for this to happen. I honestly didn't know you or Hallie would be placed in harm's way. I would never do that to you."

I genuinely mean every word that rips out of me alongside the cries of pain. I'm finally building a life for myself. I think Bree moved me in because she wants to protect me, but that was never why I agreed to move in here. I never intended for any of my shit to follow me here.

I wait for Kellan to push me away, to get mad at me, but it never comes. Instead, he pulls me against his chest until I'm almost curled up in a ball on his lap. His arms wrap around my body protectively. One hand strokes my back in a soothing motion that replicates what his other hand is doing with my hair. He wipes it out of my eyes, tucking it behind my ears, before wiping away the tears that are now collecting on his shirt.

Thank fuck this isn't a date because this is not how dates should go.

"Mia, let me be very fucking clear about this," Kellan states, as he tilts my chin, forcing me to look at him. Although there's fire in his eyes, and the way his brow furrows suggests he is still angry, the look he gives me is anything but. "I'm not even remotely concerned about Hallie's, or my own, safety here in this house. The security in this house is top of the range, there are security guards manning the external perimeter, and don't even get me started on what would happen if they do manage to get inside. I may not look it, but I'm not a bad fighter, and I sure as fuck learnt to fire a gun at a young enough age. You don't grow up living with Desmond Doughty and not learn to fight or fire a gun. But, even if I was a shit shot—which I definitely am not—they will still have to get past Liam, who is the best hitman in the world for a reason. Even then, I think the one this Kyle guy should really fear is Bree. That fiery redhead would cut his bollocks off and feed them to him if he took even a step into this house, and that's just what she would be able to do while still recovering. I promise you, Mia, this house is safe, and we will all look after you."

The tears are falling again, if they ever really stopped. His words are exactly what I want—no, need—to hear, so why does it scare me so much? Maybe it's the fact that I don't want these people I care about so much to have to put their lives on the line for me? This is why I've always been alone. I can recover from any pain that is inflicted on me, I've been doing that since I was a child, but to witness someone else experience a pain that was meant for you, that I can't handle.

"You shouldn't have to look after me. I don't want anyone to have to fight for me. I just want to get on with my life. I thought when I turned twenty-one I would have no more value to my father. I was much more valuable in a younger age bracket. When I turned eighteen, that's when he stopped contacting me, and I thought that was why," I muse aloud, trying to work out what the hell my messed-up family is up to.

"Okay, I know you said you don't want to talk about your family, and I respect that. Before today, I wouldn't have even known you had a father, you've never spoken about him. It means the world to me that you feel you can tell me this stuff, and so don't be offended when

I tell you this," he says, taking a giant deep breath before continuing. "Your dad, he sounds like a massive twatwaffle."

I release the breath I don't even know I'm holding, and burst out laughing. Kellan has the most serious expression on his face, and I think he actually may have been worried about saying something bad about my father to me. But, that just makes the whole thing more hilarious. When Kellan realises I'm giggling hysterically, as in, I'm seconds away from losing the plot completely, a smile crosses his face, lighting up all his features. Fuck, he really is so gorgeous, I just want to reach out and touch him. I mean, I'm currently curled up in a ball on his lap, and have just flipped from sobbing hysterically to laughing like a maniac. I think it's safe to say I have pushed all normal boundaries as it is. But, touching him while we are so close like this, it feels like something I shouldn't do, which naturally makes it more appealing to me. Fuck, I'm not a child with a shiny new toy. I have self-control, even if my very wet panties disagree.

"He really is. I'm sorry to have unloaded all this onto you. This should have been a fun night together," I say, averting my eyes again, only for him to waste no time pulling my gaze back.

"Mia! Not only did I get to eat some amazing pizza and drink some beer with you, I also managed to make you laugh, and get you to tell me some of your past. Plus, I have you curled up on my lap, which is so much more than I expected. I've had dates that haven't been as good a night as this, and the night is still young. We still have a movie to watch and popcorn to devour." Kellan's tone has a playful edge that's like music to my ears, and I can't help but banter back with him.

"Wow, these dates must have been really bad if me sobbing hysterically is better." I wipe a stray tear off my cheek, not sure if it's from crying or laughing.

With a laugh that causes my insides to flip, Kellan replies. "Oh, Flower. You wouldn't believe the amount of disastrous dates I've had. This doesn't even come close."

I freeze. Did he just say this is a date?

He begins to chuckle again and I can't stop the flush from spreading to my cheeks as I realise I just said that out loud. I don't know what to say. Should I backtrack? Say something to cover up with massively embarrassing word vomit? Or maybe I should just shut the hell up and hope he glosses over it?

Fuck, this is Kellan, and sarcasm drips off every other word he uses. I should have known he wouldn't let it drop. I feel his hands grip my hips, and before I even realise what he's doing, he readjusts me so that I am no longer curled up on his chest. Instead, I'm straddling him, with my knees either side of his thighs, and I can feel his hard cock through my jeans.

Fuck, this just got really good really fast.

"Now it feels like a date," Kellan says, his voice husky and full of promise.

I sit there on his lap, frozen, loving the feel of his hardness beneath my body. My hands rest on his shoulders, but that's only because I've yet to decide what to do with them. Do I want to do anything?

Images of the way he kissed me that day at the warehouse flood back into my mind, and I can't help but squirm. Only that was completely the wrong thing to do. His cock just grinds harder against my denim-covered clit, dragging guttural moans from both of us.

"Wow, you don't waste any time at all on your dates, do you?" I joke, trying to cover up the chemistry that is practically sizzling in the air around us.

"Only when they are as beautiful as you." His gaze roams over my face, then my chest, making me feel naked. I watch as he takes in the swells of my breasts, and he licks his tongue over his lower lip, like I'm a delicacy he can't wait to taste.

Fuck, now I'm squirming again, and his cock grinds against my clit in that beautiful way. As I moan, my back arches and my chest is thrust into Kellan's hungry gaze. Shit, things are going to move very quickly if I don't stop it.

Wait, do I want to stop things?

"If you want to stop, Flower, you are going to have to climb off my cock because if you grind against it one more time, I'm going to lose the little control I have left." Kellan sounds as though he's talking through gritted teeth, like it's actually painful for him to say the words. I should be mortified that I spoke the words from my head aloud again, but I'm too busy melting in this gorgeous man's arms.

He is giving me the choice, and I couldn't be more grateful. There's no denying I want this man. Fuck, I really, really want him. But, I know I'm not ready. I'm not the kind of girl who has random sex. I didn't even know I was capable of enjoying sex, and whilst I'm enjoying this with Kellan, right now, that might change when things get hotter and more hands on. I know I'm broken. I know I might never be capable of having a normal sexual experience, but these little interactions with Kellan give me hope. It's a hope I'm not ready to lose just yet.

"I'm going to climb off, not because I want to, but because I'm not ready to take things further. I like these moments we keep having. I know we shouldn't have them. Yet, it still doesn't change how much I like them. For now, can we settle on just watching a movie?" I ask, hoping like hell Kellan won't see this as a rejection. It isn't a rejection. I really wish I was the type of girl who could have sex with the hot guy and not have to worry about him seeing how much of a freak I really am.

I should have known Kellan wouldn't take it badly. His genuine smile warms my heart, and does nothing to help me actually get up off his lap. I know I said I wanted to, and he said I should get off his cock, but we both seem to be frozen. The only parts of our body that are moving are our heads as we slowly drift closer together. He's so close now, all I have to do is lean forward slightly and my lips will press against his. It's so tempting. I'm intoxicated by his scent, a mix of coffee, peppermint, and the coconut shampoo he uses. It would be so easy. Just one little kiss, but we both know it wouldn't just be one kiss. Not while I'm straddling his cock.

"You have no idea how much I want you to kiss me right now. But, I can't go any further than that, and it isn't fair on you. So, when I get the strength to pull away, please remember it's not a rejection. This is all on me, and my issues. Okay?" I whisper against his lips, making sure to hold eye contact—even though it goes against every natural instinct I have—to let Kellan know how serious I am.

Tilting his head slightly, he closes the gap so that our cheeks are touching and he's able to speak into my ear. Even though our cheeks are barely connected, it's like there's an electric current running over that spot, heating me up from the inside. I want to squirm, but I hold still, waiting to hear what he's about to say. "Who says I won't be happy with just a kiss? Don't make decisions on my behalf, Flower. If it's your choice then absolutely you can do that and I will respect your wishes. But, you can't say what's best for me."

His warm breath hitting my sensitive neck sends shivers down my spine, heating my core further. Whilst that feeling is intoxicating, it's his words that cause my body to tremble. I want to believe that it will be enough, but for guys like Kellan, sex is important. I know I shouldn't pre-judge him. But, I've heard Liam talking. Before Hallie came along, Kellan was a giant manwhore, sleeping with anyone he pleased. I'm not even going to pretend that knowledge didn't make me jealous because it did. That's how I know a guy like Kellan won't be satisfied with just a kiss.

Just as I'm about to tell him that, I feel him lightly press his lips against my neck, just below my ear. It's a light, chaste kiss that is over before it's even begun. The spot that just a second before was burning hot, now feels cold and lonely, but I don't have a chance to focus on that, as his lips hit another spot on my neck, just a little higher than the last. He continues this process, kissing his way around my neck, across my collarbone and up the other side of my neck. He uses one hand, fisted gently into my hair to guide my head into whatever position he requires, and the other hand holds my hip in place to make sure I don't grind on his cock. Believe me, I want to. If I wasn't so caught up in the overwhelming sensations, I would feel embarrassed by the moans he's pulling from my body. Instead, I fist my hands into his hair, and just hold on. Letting him take whatever he wants.

Actually, that's not at all correct. He isn't taking what he wants from me, I'm giving him it. I know what it feels like to have people take things from you, to steal what you never wanted to give in the first place, and it's nothing like this. This may be Kellan taking what he needs, but I am giving it to him willingly, and I know if I ask him to stop, he will.

After it feels as though he's kissed every part of my neck, he pulls my head back slightly so I can look into his eyes. His normally crystal blue eyes are almost black, the pupils so dilated with lust. His beautiful red lips look plump and swollen, and so fucking inviting. His eyes rake over my lips, and I can see he's asking for permission with his eyes. Leaning forward, I close the gap, and press my lips against his. I only meant for it to be a sweet kiss, but as soon as I feel his lips against mine, it's like I'm brought to life. I can't control myself. I push my mouth against his, swiping my tongue across his lower lip, demanding access. At first he seems frozen, unsure of what he should be doing, but I don't give him a choice. He deepens the kiss as our tongues mingle together, and I crash my body against his. His cock grinds against my denim-covered pussy, and I groan appreciatively.

Suddenly, it all stops. Kellan lifts me up and sits me down on the sofa next to him, as we both pant, desperate to catch our breaths. "You can't make noises like that. It makes me want to do dirty, dirty things to you," Kellan groans, running his hands through his hair, sounding as though he's in pain.

"Sorry," I mumble, although I'm not really sure what I'm apologising for. I barely even realised I was moaning like a porn star. It's just the way he makes me feel.

His slight laugh sounds a little more sarcastic than anything. "You really don't have to be sorry, Flower. That was so fucking hot. But if I don't stop now, I'm not sure I'll be able to. Maybe we really should just watch a movie?"

I release the breath I didn't know I was holding, grateful he hasn't taken any of this the wrong way. Even though he hasn't known me for a long time, it's like he gets me. He knows my limitations, and when I've reached them. It's something I never thought I would have with another person, even Bree can't do it. She pushes me too far sometimes, even though she doesn't mean to.

"We definitely should."

"I'm not saying this because I want to get you in my bed, although after that I really fucking would like to. But, Hallie is likely to wake up for a feed anytime around now, and then I like to get her into her cot. She settles better in there, and I will be able to get a bit more sleep. She's a grumpy bear if you wake her up. So, would it be okay if we watch the film in my room?" Kellan almost looks embarrassed to ask, and since he has done a great job of making me feel less of a freak, I reassure him.

"Of course, anything for Hallie. This isn't me judging, just asking. Is there a reason you can't put her in her cot and then come downstairs with the baby monitor?" I ask tentatively, not wanting him to think I'm judging his parenting at all.

"It's a long story. I know you know a little about Shayla, Hallie's birth mother—and I call her that simply because there's no other name for someone who simply pushed my baby out of her vagina. She is by no means a mother. She left Hallie, lying in a hospital cot, all alone at just five hours old. She abandoned her, and even though when I found Hallie she was still asleep, I don't ever want her to feel abandoned."

"I'm so sorry, Kellan." I don't really know what else to say. There's an element of sadness in his voice that makes my rage for Shayla grow. She left Kellan too. They made a baby together, so feelings must have been involved, and the way Kellan explains it, she didn't just abandon Hallie, she abandoned him too. I love that he wants to protect his daughter from that pain, but who is protecting him? I can't even imagine how painful it must have been to go into the hospital as a couple, and come home as a single dad.

"Don't apologise. We are better off without her. I just don't ever want Hallie to feel like she is anything less than loved with my whole heart."

"Kellan, you are without a doubt one of the nicest guys I have ever met, with the biggest heart. Anyone loved by you should be honoured and cherish it. Hallie will know that, and Shayla should regret losing that. Nobody will ever question how much you love your daughter. Do you want to take her upstairs and get her ready for bed while I tidy up down here and make her bottle?" I mean every word I say. I want to touch him. To let this beautiful man know how amazing he is. But I don't, hoping my words are good enough.

"Why don't you take her? I can do the cleaning," he says with a genuine smile on his face.

Fuck, I think we really have made progress today. He normally doesn't let me look after, or even change Hallie by myself. Now he is offering for me to carry her up the stairs, and get her ready for bed, all while he will be downstairs. This really is progress, one I'm not going to scoff at. "Thank you."

With a giant smile on his face, Kellan jumps to his feet and pulls me up from the sofa. He has that cheeky, cocky grin back on his face, and I just know he is going to say something inappropriate, but I've come to enjoy this playful side to him. "I will meet you in my bed then," he says with a wink, and I hear him chuckle as he walks away to the kitchen.

Cocky fucker. Why does he have to be so fucking hot? I'm so screwed!

Kellan

"ARGH! No, please don't. Please."

I wake up with a start, as the loud screams puncture my sleep, forcing me out of my very pleasant dream. Instantly, my eyes go over to the cot I have connected onto the side of my bed. Hallie's asleep, exactly where I left her. Cuddled up with her beautiful elephant teddy that I bought her when she was born. The tag on the elephant says Hallie, which is why I bought it for her. Obviously for child safety I had to remove the tag, which was a good move considering she's constantly putting it in her mouth. Even now while she sleeps she is sucking on the elephant's ear. She looks so adorable, the way her little face looks so serene, and her plump, pink baby lips look almost like pouts in between sucking on the elephant.

"Fuck! No, please don't hurt me. I will do anything."

Shit, as I listen to the terrified cries, I realise Mia is still in the bed with me. We must have fallen asleep watching the movie. We're both dressed exactly how we were the night before. Only now she's curled up next to my body, her back plastered against my side, with the duvet cover pulled up over us both. She isn't cuddling me, but where our bodies touch, I can feel heat passing between us.

Changing my attention over to Mia, she looks the opposite of Hallie. I've never seen someone look so scared while asleep. Her face is a crumpled mess of pain and anguish, as her body appears to lightly shake, as though she's genuinely terrified. In between screams, she babbles almost incoherently about needing to be left alone, begging for something to stop.

My instinct is to shake her and wake her up, but I was always told that you should never wake someone from a nightmare. I know it's probably an old wives' tale, one my mother believed in and no doubt tried to pass along to me during one of the rare episodes where she tried to raise me. Well…that was before she gave up on me and ditched me completely when I was just six years old.

I try to pull Mia into the crook of my shoulder, wrapping my arm around her lightly. I want to keep her close, to let her know I'm here without actually waking her. I pull her close and simply stroke her hair, hoping that it's enough to quieten whatever is haunting her.

Her screams continue, and after two more loud screams, I decide I have to do something. Not only because her noises are starting to wake up Hallie, which would not be good because I would never get my little monster back to bed, but also because I hate seeing Mia in pain. Some of the things coming out of her mouth are horrific, and it doesn't take much to work out she's reliving a trauma from her past. She said she wants to forget the Mia she was before, and now I think I can guess why. But, she can't run from it, not when it's keeping her awake and pulling her back into her nightmares any chance it gets. Part of me thinks that if I keep listening, I will get a glance into Mia's world, the one she hides from everyone, but that isn't what she wants. She would never want me to see her like this, and to be honest, I don't think I can watch her pain any longer.

Turning over until I'm sitting up in the bed, I gently place both hands on either shoulder and lightly shake her. At first there's no response, so I push a little harder. Her eyes fly open, but I can tell she is still asleep. She thrashes violently against my hands, trying to push me away from her. She looks like a psychopathic zombie, so I pull my hands away from her instantly, letting her go. Thankfully, that is enough for her eyes to close and her to settle a little.

Sitting there, listening to Mia's light whimpering, I give myself a mental pep talk. I need to do this. I know it will be hard, she looks so small and terrified, her face drained of colour, and simply replaced with fear. Her teeth chatter together, as her body shakes vigorously, and I can tell she is gearing up for another shouting meltdown. Not only can I not let her put her body through any more, I don't want to hear it, and I sure as fuck don't want Hallie to wake up.

This time when I grab hold of her shoulders, I don't hesitate, and I'm not gentle. I shake her roughly, my fingers pressing into her, as I pull her head towards my face. Trying to be as loud as possible, without waking the baby, I call to Mia in her sleep. "Mia, Flower, please can you wake up? Listen to the sound of my voice. It's Kellan. You have to wake up now, okay. Wake up!"

This time when her eyes fling open, I can tell she isn't stuck in her dream, I finally manage to bring her out of it. Mia's eyes glance around rapidly, while she tries to work out exactly where she is. Luckily, before we fell asleep last night, I left the bedside lamp on. So the light from the lamp floods the key area of the room, around the bed, but it's still not enough for Mia. I can tell she still isn't sure of where she is.

Approaching her like she's a startled doe, one that is going to spook and run off at any second, I squeeze her shoulder—lighter than I normally would—trying to grab her attention. It works, and she turns her frightened gaze on me. The look I see reflected back hurts me like I've been stabbed in the chest.

Her body trembles, as any remaining colour she had in her face drains out. Her eyes look as though they are popping out of her skull, as she stares straight at me, without even really knowing I'm here. Her chest rises and falls rapidly as she desperately gasps for breath, a light sheen of sweat coating her furrowed brow.

"Mia, baby, look at me. It's me Kellan. I'm here and I've got you.

Nobody is going to hurt you again, I promise." I don't even really know what I'm saying, I just want her to look a little less terrified.

Upon hearing my voice, her shoulders physically start to sag, and she looks like she's about to collapse back onto the pillow, so I gently wrap my arm around her. I'm torn between not wanting to touch her in case it freaks her out even more, and wrapping my arms around her to hold her so tight, protecting her and comforting her until I never see this look on her face again. So, I settle for middle ground.

At first I feel her muscles go rigid under my touch, so I keep talking to her, letting her know I'm here, and that nobody will harm her while I'm here. I make sure not to overwhelm her, to remain consistent, just holding her with one arm and using the other to sweep the hair off her face. As I tuck the loose strand of hair behind her ear, I keep my eyes trained on her face. Before she was looking but not really seeing, and now she's staring right back at me.

Her eyes glass over as tears fill them to the brim. Her breath hitches as she tries to get control of the sniffling and panting from her terror, but as the new tears begin, it feels like an impossible task. Without even thinking about it, I pull her onto my lap, resting her head against my chest and holding her tight. Sobs rack her tiny body, and as I hold her tight, I can't get over how small she looks wrapped up in my arms. I'm not a big, burly guy, but this beauty looks so small and fragile, and I can't help but want to protect her.

I hold her until the tears stop and she finally pulls herself out of a ball and sits next to me on the bed. Her face is red and swollen from the tears that've been falling for far too long. But, it's her vacant expression that wounds me the most. I like to see the fire in her eyes, and the sparkle on her face.

"Do you need anything? A cup of tea? Alcohol?" I ask, grasping at straws. I have no fucking idea what to do in situations like this. As I look at my watch, seeing it's not even four in the morning yet, I realise most of those options probably aren't suitable, but I have to say something.

"Maybe just some of that water," she says, pointing to the bottle of water I keep beside the bed.

I hand it over and she takes several large gulps before breathing a sigh of relief. It's like she uses the water to cleanse herself of her nightmares, and it seems to work. Her eyes look downcast as a blush spreads across her cheeks. Shy Mia is back, at least that I can work with.

"How are you feeling? Don't get me wrong, I like having you curled up in my lap, but maybe without the tears next time. Or maybe without your clothes?" I joke, hoping she will take my pathetic attempt at humour in the right way.

Her little tinkle of laughter is like music to my ears, and when she looks up with a small smile on her face, I know she is slowly coming back to me. "What, so girls with puffy red faces and snot and tears dripping everywhere, they do nothing for you?"

Now it's my turn to smile. I can see the pain is still there, it hasn't gone away, and given the nightmare I just witnessed, I would guess that her ghosts never fully go away. But she's trying, which is what spurs me on. This girl is a fighter. She may look shy and timid, but I think that's just what she wants you to see. There's a courage and a power in her that she doesn't let anyone see. Someone might have tried to knock her down in the past, but that's not going to happen again. Even if nothing at all happens between me and Mia, I will make sure that she's supported and never has to hide who she really is again.

"I might make an exception for you." I wink, amping up the flirting on purpose. She shakes her head but the laughter continues. "Seriously, though. I won't ever force you to talk, but I want you to know, if you ever need to talk to someone, I'm a good listener."

With a sigh, she appears to deflate and I feel a sting in my heart, like it physically pains me that she looks so downcast again. But then I realise she's taking a deep breath, most likely to gather the courage needed to speak. "I've had nightmares since I was eight years old. That's when my life turned into a living nightmare. I don't want to talk about it, but maybe I will one day. This particular nightmare is from when I was fifteen and I was made to spend the summer with the Fratacello family. Kyle was their only son, the heir to take over their drugs business. They operate out of Liverpool because Bree's family didn't want them near London. They still work under Bree's rule, but are separate. They're a powerful family, with some very important ties."

Her voice sounds different, almost like she's reciting the most boring poem. There's no emotion there, and that worries me. If she's angry or sad at what she's lived through, that I can understand, but indifference is harder to manage.

"Kyle was twenty-three when I met him, which doesn't sound like much, but I was only fifteen. My father wanted a connection to the Fratacellos, probably so he could manipulate them in some way, or use their connections. My father is an asshole, for want of a better word. He thought that if I married Kyle, it would give him that bit more power and reach. Kyle's aim was to utilise my father's money, and make a bid for London. He didn't care when he met me that I was underage, in fact, he commented that he liked that I looked younger," she spat in disgust, and I'm not surprised. I can already tell what type of a guy Kyle is, and it's not one that I like. He's also the type of guy Liam and I prefer not to keep using up all the quality air that should be for good people, not perverts like him. We may have to rectify that problem, and soon!

"I can't believe your father would put you in that position. I'm so sorry, Mia." I don't even know if they're the right words.

Reaching out, I take her hand in mine. It's not much, but it's the only thing I can think to do to reassure her. As our fingers clasp together, I feel her gripping me tightly, and I welcome it. She can take as much from me, whatever she needs.

"My father is not a good guy. That's why I don't talk about him. To the world he's this perfect businessman and family man, but if you truly get to know him, you will see how poisonous he is. I think it must have been the texts that put Kyle in my head. I try not to think about him, and I usually take medication to try and control the nightmares, but since I fell asleep in here, I obviously didn't take them. I'm so sorry for waking you. I didn't wake Hallie, did I?" she asks, a look of regret and shame flashing across her face.

Squeezing her hand tighter, I shake my head. "That little monster could sleep through a fucking earthquake. But once she is awake, that's it then, there's no going back. Look…" I point over to the cot to the side of me, and she leans over to look into it. "See, I told you, she's sleeping like a baby."

Mia laughs gently at my joke, before giving me a small smile. "She looks so peaceful when she's fast asleep."

Now it's my turn to laugh. "She is. It's when she wakes up that she's a fucking monster," I joke, hoping Mia knows I'm only joking. Hallie might be a handful, and I may never have expected to be doing all this by myself, but I wouldn't change it for the world.

"Maybe she just feels safe sleeping next to you. I like the side cot idea," Mia says, pointing at the special cot I bought. I know it's intended to be used for mums who are breastfeeding, so they can feed and put the baby down without getting out of bed. But, I'm a tired single dad with abandonment issues. I want to be able to see Hallie at all times, to know she is safe and loved. The cot helps me to do that.

"Maybe now you know where you are, and that I'm here watching over you, do you think you can go back to sleep for an hour or two? That's all I've got until this one wakes up." I hate how shy and shaky my voice has gone all of a sudden.

I know I like Mia. I know I'm attracted to her. But, I also know I don't trust her yet. I like that she is starting to open up, and I'm starting to trust her more, but we still have a long way to go. She thinks she's the broken one, but what she doesn't realise is that I'm equally as broken. I'm held together with sticky tape, just enough for me to function and be a dad for Hallie. But as each day passes, the tape gets a little weaker, the burdens get a little heavier, and it won't be too long before I smash completely. I don't know if I can hold myself together, let alone her too, but I sure as fuck am going to try.

"Are you sure?" she asks through hooded eyes.

Fuck, this is not the time for her to start looking sexy. It's hard enough to get my cock under control when I'm around her at the best of times, and now really is not the time. So, as I pull us both down so that we're lying on the bed, Mia nestled in the crook of my shoulder with her head on my chest and her body beside mine, I try to think of anything to get this fucking erection to go down.

She falls asleep fairly quickly, and as she makes these delicate little snores, I'm pleased to see the serene look on her face. Looking between the two beautiful girls at either side of me, both softly snoring in tandem, like they have been doing it forever, my heart soars. It's the strangest feeling, one I've never really felt before. It's almost like serenity, if that's the right word. I could stay engulfed in this forever.

Like clockwork, as soon as the clock turns to six in the morning, Hallie begins to cry. I reach over to settle her, to bring her over to lie on my chest the way I do every morning. Only this morning it's harder for me to grab Hallie as my other arm is occupied. Mia is sleeping peacefully by my side, and I'm torn between pulling my arm out from under her, which could wake her up, and doing it slowly so as not to jostle her, but that leaves Hallie screaming the house down for longer.

I make the decision to pull off the plaster, quick and painless. I yank my arm out from under Mia, trying as hard as possible to let her just roll to the side, but not too far away. Then, I quickly grab Hallie, and lay her on my chest. It's enough to stop her griping, for now. She wakes up instantly, there's no transition period with this kid. Her head is up, her bright blue eyes that match mine are wide open, looking around at everything. She reaches out with both of her hands, grasping onto my lip with one hand and my hair with another.

"Hello, my beautiful bear. How are you this morning? You slept so well for Daddy. Yes you did," I coo, as quietly as possible, in the most unmanly baby voice possible. I just can't help it when I'm with Hallie. I don't give a shit how many man points I lose. If talking like an idiot earns me a smile, or on a really good day a laugh, I will act like the biggest joker in the world. That's what being a dad is all about. I live for her little giggles.

We sit there just playing peek-a-boo or chatting away in her own little baby language for a little while. I try to be quiet, to not disturb the beauty I pulled back into my arms, but if Hallie wants to screech when I tickle her, then she will.

Sure enough, that wakes Mia up. I know she's awake because her soft little snores stop and she suddenly feels rigid beside me. I pretend I don't know she's awake, and just carry on playing with Hallie until Mia starts to relax.

"All right, my pretty lady, you are starting to smell. You have ruined the party for everyone. So we better get you changed and get you some breakfast because I'm sure you are hungry," I say to Hallie, and I know she doesn't really understand me, yet she reaches out like I'm offering her food right now.

"You better be talking to Hallie. It's not nice to tell a girl she smells," Mia jokes, lifting her head slightly so she can see me. I flash her my best smile, one she happily returns.

"Don't worry, I wasn't talking about you. But, I'm not going to lie to her. This girl has a talent when she fills her nappy," I joke, although it's all true. I've never seen so much shit come out of such a little person. For the first few days, before I learnt that yellow runny shit is normal for a baby, I was convinced there was something wrong with her. That's the sort of thing they don't teach you in the baby books. And don't even get me started on the black tar they first shit out. I nearly called an ambulance!

I'm proud to say I've become a much better dad. Now when I think she's doing something weird or alien-like, I consult the internet. If there's nobody else with the same issue, then I worry. It's basically freestyle parenting, but it's working so far.

"You are not wrong there. Do you want me to change her while you do the breakfast?" Mia asks, and I can't help but smile. I've never had anyone to share the responsibilities with before. It feels kinda nice, but I'm not quite there yet.

"Would it be okay if you got the breakfast ready? I'm gonna go get Uncle Liam on changing duty. Then maybe we can have a chat about you being Hallie's nanny. It will have to be for a trial initially, but we can go over the details at breakfast. When I say trial, it's not because I don't think you're good enough, or anything like that," I mumble, and Mia reaches her hand out, putting her finger over my lips to stop me from speaking.

"A trial would be perfect. Hallie's your baby, and you have a rough past. I, of all people, can understand struggling to trust other people. I'm honoured you want to give me a chance." Her voice is bright and airy, to match her smile. Hallie obviously likes what Mia just said as she starts to giggle, before reaching out to grab Mia's finger that's covering my mouth. Mia lets her take it and giggles when Hallie tries to put the finger in her mouth.

We stay like that for a few minutes, me just laying there while Hallie and Mia play together, both lying on my chest. That strange somersault feeling in my stomach returns. It feels so alien, but I quite like it. Only when Hallie starts to grumble do I quickly get up.

"I'm gonna go get Liam. Can you hold her a second while I grab the stuff I need?" I ask, and before I can answer she pulls Hallie over onto her chest. She then stretches her arms out above her body so Hallie is floating above her. They make aeroplane noises and every so often Mia will drop her arms quickly, making Hallie feel like she is being dropped, even though she isn't, and my little girl's laughter rings out around the room.

I should be grabbing what I need to change Hallie and get her ready for the day, but instead, I'm mesmerised, watching Mia play with Hallie. I've seen her pressed against a wall, panting my name, and writhing around whilst straddling me, and she looked fucking hot each time, but never has she looked as beautiful as she does when she is laughing with my little Hallie Bear.

Once I've grabbed everything I need, I throw it into the changing bag, and throw it over my shoulder. I reach over to pick up Hallie, who grumbles at being taken away from Mia, which is obviously a good sign. She clearly likes her. Then, it's like my body has a mind of its own, and I lean over to press my lips to Mia's. It may have been short, but it's deep and intense, just the way a good morning kiss should be. The only problem is, good morning kisses are for girlfriends, or people you are dating, not for your newly hired nanny who accidentally fell asleep in your bed.

Mia's just as shocked by the kiss as me, her fingers touch her lips, feeling where mine just were. She looks stunned, like she wants to say something but is lost for words. It was a fucking great kiss!

No, focus. No more kissing! Now she is my nanny, she is even more off-limits. Besides, I'm far too broken to give Mia what she deserves. She deserves someone who can give her the world, and I am barely keeping my head above water with life. We don't belong together, no matter how much my heart burns for her.

"See you at breakfast in about ten minutes," I shout over my shoulder as I head out of the door.

I run down the corridor, trying not to question what the hell just happened. Holding Hallie in one arm, her changing bag over the other shoulder, I make my way through the house, towards Liam and Bree's room. I know I should knock. They're an engaged couple who went on a date last night, and are probably enjoying a lie-in together. Probably some sexy time. But I don't care. From the moment Mia woke me up in the middle of the night, I have only had one thing on my mind. Well…two things, but I'm trying not to think about the overwhelming desire I have to fuck Mia, instead concentrating on the second thing.

I burst through the door, and luckily they are both asleep. The noise from the door opening wakes them up. To make sure they are fully awake, I flick on the light, causing them both to groan. That should do it! I stride towards them, ignoring their complaints and Liam's extreme curse words. They both sit up in bed, and I'm pleased to see Bree is wearing Liam's T-shirt.

While he's still half asleep, I hand Hallie over to a stunned-looking Liam, and she squeals with excitement, while I climb over his legs to sit in between them in the middle of the bed. Liam's face softens as he looks at my daughter, who wraps him around her little finger in an instant. Bree, on the other hand, looks at me with fire in her eyes that's as bright as her red hair. "Kellan. Why the hell am I awake at six in the morning?" Bree groans, as Liam hits me around the back of the head.

"We were supposed to be having a lie-in. Date night, remember?" Liam groans at me, before turning to face Hallie. "Not that I mind seeing your gorgeous face, though, Hallie Bear. Although Uncle Liam would love you even more if you smelled less." I can't help but laugh as Liam practically sings to Hallie. She giggles and coo's like he's her shiny new toy.

"Yeah, well, this is important. You can change her while I talk. I have a job for us. I need your help to kill someone." My voice doesn't waver, and Liam looks at me, his brow furrowed with concern. I've never asked him to kill anyone for me. Not when Shayla and Whiskey screwed me over, not any of the Reapers who ruined my life, not even my fucking mother who is still a pain in my ass. I've never asked him for this, which is why he looks so concerned.

"I will change Hallie, you two talk." Bree hops out of the bed, and I avert my eyes just in case. She comes around to Liam's side of the bed and has already pulled some sweatpants on, much to my relief. She grabs the changing mat they keep in here—it's not the first time I've come into their room for help with Hallie.

"Actually, Bree, we probably need you in on this," I say, as Bree lays down the changing mat on the bed in front of Liam, and he lays Hallie on it. They don't need words, they just seem to know what the other person is going to do. They're the perfect couple, just totally in sync with each other.

"Why? Who is it?" Liam asks, scepticism dripping from every word. He doesn't think I'm serious. He thinks I'm having one of my anxiety meltdowns and that I'm just pissed at someone. That I will get over it, but not this time.

"Kyle Fratacello." Disgust ripples off my tongue as I say his name, and it tastes like ash on my tongue. Just the idea of him repulses me.

Liam looks lost, the name means nothing to him, but Bree knows. I see the look of recognition on her face, followed by the mutual hatred we share.

"Is he as bad as my imagination is making out? I don't know the full story, but the bits I know are bad," Bree says, and I know what she means. Mia isn't good at opening up, so Bree probably knows even less than me. But together, I think we have enough evidence to make a case to Liam.

"It's bad. She has nightmares about him nearly every night, and last night he made contact saying he wants her back. I'm not going to let that happen." My voice is stern, making it very fucking clear I will not waver in the slightest.

"No, it fucking is not. I will get Kian to bring him to the warehouse. I think me and my knife need to have a little chat with Kyle. He needs to learn that people do not belong to him. Mia is not an object. She is under my protection, and the sooner he learns that the better." Gone is the Bree that was here just a second ago. This Bree is harsher, and more ruthless. This is the girl tough enough to bring an army to their knees, to rule as the first female mafia family leader. This is the girl I want on my side.

Liam, however, doesn't know any of the backstory and needs a little more convincing. "Okay, back up for a second before we slaughter someone and no doubt start a war. Tell me everything. Then we can have him come to the warehouse, and decide what to do. As much fun as it is assassinating people who deserve it, I may not know who Kyle Fratacello is, but I've heard that name before. They're a big family up north. We are not starting a war unless it's justified. Understood?" Liam states firmly, and Bree turns to him with a fierce look on her face.

"We will talk to him at the warehouse, but if I don't hear what I want to hear, I will kill him, Liam. Consequences be damned. I'm the leader of this family, and I make the decisions. He is a pervert and a psychopath, and if he poses a danger to someone I love, then I will take him out. I do not need your permission." I can't help but sit there with my mouth wide open. I don't know whether to be shocked she has the balls to say that, or proud as hell. She's becoming quite the feisty little leader. Nobody should ever doubt Bree is capable of leading this family, she's a force to be reckoned with.

"Relax, Princess. I'm not challenging your leadership. I'm just stopping us from starting a war. But, if he genuinely is a threat to Mia, I will happily take him out. So, let's get him to the warehouse and get this sorted, shall we?"

As they finish changing Hallie together, I do subtly mention something I may have forgotten. "Oh, and can we not say anything to Mia? She's downstairs making us all breakfast. I'm not sure she would approve of us interfering, but I really don't give a shit. I need to make sure she's safe." I ignore the looks they give me. I know what they are thinking, why do I care so much? I keep asking myself the same question. I think my shy little wallflower has crawled under my skin, when I wasn't expecting her to, and I'm not sure I can let her go.

The next week passes by in a torturous blur. When I woke Bree and Liam up that morning almost a week ago, demanding the assassination of Kyle Fratacello, I meant it that day. But, of course, Liam and his big fucking conscience had to stick his nose in. Bree and I were all ready to storm Kyle's house and murder him in his fucking sleep, which is really unlike me. I'm the guy who stays back and does the mission from behind the screen. Not because I'm a coward or because I'm not able to run into the fray, because I will. I'm just better at running surveillance.

When Bree was taken, I was the first to say I wanted to run into the thick of it, that's what you do for the people you care about. Bree, though I've only known her a small amount of time, she's family to me. I can see the way Liam loves her, but more importantly, I can see how much she loves Liam. She's taken him in, and by extension me and the rest of the crazy family, never once complaining. So, of course I would throw myself into the mix for her.

I'm telling myself the reason I would do that for Mia is because she is family to Bree, but we all know it's more than that. For some reason, I want to protect this beautiful, broken girl.

Not so long ago, there was another beautifully broken girl who needed my help, and I gave it without a second thought. I not only gave her access to all my money—with the exception of the hidden off-shore secret account, thankfully—I let her into my home, and I gave her a chance with my heart. She stole them all, claiming she was doing the right thing and that I'd understand one day. I don't, and I hope I never see her again and have to find out.

What happened with Shayla, it ruined me, and it means that I'm not capable of being the person Mia needs me to be. Whenever she tells me stories about her past, and about how broken she is, I'm looking for the inconsistencies. I'm questioning which bit is the lie, or what her ulterior motive is. I don't trust her completely, and even though every fibre of my being tells me this girl is nothing like Shayla, I can't get rid of the nagging feeling in the pit of my stomach. I can't allow myself to be distracted by love, or lust, again.

So, as I pace up and down my office, waiting for Liam to finish reading the document he has in front of him, I try to convince myself that I'm doing all of this because she's like family. But, every time I'm in the same room as her, I have to give myself a mental pep talk that this girl is now my nanny. Hallie's bonding with her, and that means my daughter should always come first. I can't have my daughter bonding with another woman who abandons her.

Mia's been working as Hallie's nanny for the last week, and she's doing a great job. She's more than qualified, but I knew that after the shitshow of an interview. I know that by hiring her as my nanny, I have to assess her as part of her university course, which means allowing a strange person to observe how she interacts with my child. I may not like the idea, but Mia deserves her qualification. She loves her work, and the more I watch her with Hallie, I can see how good she is at her job. Hallie adores her, and it's beautiful to witness.

"Liam, for the love of God, are you finished reading?" I snap, losing my patience, as I have done every fucking day for the last week. It feels like Liam is purposefully dragging his heels, and I haven't worked out why yet.

"If you stop pacing, I might be able to concentrate." Even without looking at him, I know he's rolling his eyes right now.

Liam's always been the level-headed part of our duo, but despite knowing this, it's still winding me up. I've avoided calling him out over the last week, but my patience is waning thin. I know this is his business, and I have to respect his process, but that doesn't mean I have to like it, and I'm not entirely sure Bree does either.

I hear a knock on the door before it swings open, the person on the other side not bothering to wait for a reply. Since it's her house, I don't blame her. Bree storms into the room, her face a mask of determination. This is the ruthless mafia leader, not the sweet friend I live with. She looks murderous, and quite frankly I'm glad her cold, focused eyes are trained on Liam and not me. Her left-hand man—as Kian named himself—trails behind her, looking slightly uncomfortable. He's still relatively new to the family, and is not entirely used to Bree yet.

"Liam, what the hell is going on? Kian has just informed me that Kyle Fratacello now wishes to pledge his allegiance to me, as the new leader, in person. What the fuck happened to the plan we had to shoot him? If he aligns with us, I can't shoot him!" Bree shouts, stabbing her finger into Liam's chest to make her feelings perfectly clear. Fury practically vibrates off her, and I notice Kian takes a healthy step away from them at the same time I do.

Instead of getting mad, or yelling back at Bree, Liam just gives her a small smile. "This is perfect, Bree. We need to get him here if we're going to interrogate him. As much as I would love to kidnap him, his family runs a lot of our drugs trade up north. His father worked for yours, so they've always been on our list of families that need to pledge allegiance to you. Doing it this way, he won't see us coming. When we interrogate him, he will think it's his interview to remain affiliated with us. Despite being one of the biggest families in the north, Kyle and his father know that without your blessing, without your seal of approval to work with them, they would lose everything.

We can just as easily give the business to another up-and-coming family in that area, and they know it. So, if we do things my way, we can make them seem like the bad guys. If he doesn't give us the answers we want to hear, we can get rid of him and claim he didn't wish to remain loyal to you. People will see it as us teaching him a lesson, as opposed to us just outright killing him, and starting a war with the north."

Fuck! The more I listen to Liam, the more I know he's right, and I really fucking hate to admit it. I watch as Bree starts to deflate, obviously reaching the same realisation as me, and hating it too. Liam's about thirty seconds from his smug, cocky gloating, and we both know it.

Kian, who hasn't yet learnt to leave Bree and Liam when they're in the middle of this kind of argument, adds in his opinion. "That's actually a good idea. For the last few days, I've been thinking of ways to kidnap him without starting a war, and I couldn't think of anything. This is a really good plan. We can test their loyalty and ensure he stays as far away from Mia as possible. Two birds, one stone. Perfect!"

All eyes turn to Kian, and his usual grin doesn't leave his face. This guy is just one of those people that is happy and outgoing all of the time. The more time I spend with him, the more I like him. But my darkness is not a fan of all his light and bubbliness. I think we get along so well because we're cut from the same cloth. I deal with my pain through an unhealthy mix of anxiety and obsessive tendencies, whereas Kian smiles with his boy band good looks, and then beats the shit out of people in underground cage fights. We all have demons. I wear mine on my face, whereas Kian wears a smile and lets his rage consume him in organised bursts of anger. Essentially, we get along because we are the same. Two lost boys, desperately craving the family we never had, clinging to the hope that one day we will find the happiness we don't even know if we deserve.

"Kian, I'm trying to bollock Liam for going over my head, and you're not helping." Bree's voice is strong and authoritative, but it's softened a lot since she first stormed into my office. Kian looks a tad uneasy, like he wasn't too happy about being reprimanded. He said exactly what we're all thinking, but I've learnt not to get in the middle of these two when they're having one of their stupid tiffs that are usually as a result of Liam being an overprotective ass.

"Sorry," Kian grumbles, and I have to cough to hide my chuckle. Although, it isn't all that funny when Bree turns her death stare on me.

"I don't give a shit if it's the right thing to do or not. Liam, you went over my head. You should have talked to me." Bree takes a seat in my computer chair, next to Liam, and as they stare at each other, their stances soften. They never can stay mad at each other for long.

"Look, Bree. From the minute Kellan asked me to assassinate Kyle, it became my business. I don't kill unless I have to. I know all the facts, and believe me, after what I've learnt, he's lucky to still be alive. If it was just me, running my own business, I probably would have done the job already. But, I have so much more to take into consideration now. You are still not healed from the last fucking hospital trip. I would like to keep you alive long enough to actually marry you this time. So, yes, I contacted the Fratacellos to try and do this diplomatically. It goes against all my instincts, of course it does. But, we do not need another enemy or another war right now. My thinking was we could bring him here under false pretences and make our feelings perfectly clear. If he refuses to follow your orders then we will have undeniable proof, and we can kill him without any blowback on us. I'm sorry if you think I went over your head, but it was all for you. You are not strong enough for another fight, and I'm not strong enough to see you lying in a hospital bed again."

The more Liam talks, the more Bree softens. I have to admit, it's hard not to. He really has brought out all the big guns for this speech, and Bree swoons. I always knew when Liam fell in love for real that it would be big. He has a lot of heart, he just closed it off for a long time. But, I knew as soon as he gave his heart to someone, it would be an epic love. Yes, he is jealous, and overly protective, not to mention a cocky asshole, but having Liam Doughty by your side is worth it. Nobody will fight harder, or love you more than he will. I'm just glad Bree is able to replicate that and give Liam the love he's never experienced before.

"Liam, what happened to me, it was terrible and scary, but I'm not going to let that influence my future actions. I can't live life scared I'm going to be kidnapped. Of course we will have enemies, probably a fucking lot of them, but that won't scare me. I am a leader and I won't cower. I know you don't want to lose me, I don't want to lose anyone. But, you have to let me do my job, the way I trust you to do yours. I agree with your decision, but we should have talked about it. We are a team and without good communication, we're at risk. So, from now on, we will talk about everything, okay?" She may direct the question at Liam, but she looks at us all.

Kian, who's now learnt there are certain times when he shouldn't speak, simply nods his head in confirmation, and I can't help but smile. The guy is a cage fighter, yet he's terrified of this tiny redhead.

"I'm all for us not going to war, believe me. I have a very beautiful face and I intend to keep it that way, but I want this guy to pay. This guy is the reason Mia wakes up in the middle of the night screaming and crying, terrified by her nightmare. We have to help her, to make her safe," I explain, wanting them to know how serious this matter really is. If talking will work, I'm all for that, but this guy is a disgusting excuse for a human being, and he needs to be punished.

"How do you know what she does at night?" Kian asks, with his big, cocky grin and a suggestive wiggle of his eyebrows. If Liam and Bree weren't looking at us with a mix of anger and outrage, I probably would have laughed at him. But this guy really needs to learn to read the room quickly, or he is going to get me killed.

"Not that it's anyone's business," I reply looking poignantly at Bree and Liam who continue to glare at me. "Mia fell asleep while we were watching a movie the other night. She woke up having a nightmare. That's when she told me about Kyle. I've never seen her look so terrified. She was shaking and sobbing, and I had no idea how to help her. Other than this, making him pay...that I can do. So we will!"

"Kel, I'm not saying this guy isn't going to pay. We're just going to do it in such a way that doesn't get us all on a shit list. I made you a promise that I would help, and I will. Mia should feel safe, and by the end of the day tomorrow, I hope we can say that to her," Liam says, and I can tell by the fire in his eyes and the confidence in his voice, he has a plan. Which is exactly what I've been pushing for all week. So why does the idea of Liam being the one to save Mia cause my chest to ache?

"Okay then, we will meet at the warehouse tomorrow, shall we say around ten in the morning?" Kian asks, as everyone confirms the time, he nods before turning to leave. That is, until Bree stops him.

"Kian, before you go, I have to talk to you all about something," Bree says, looking shy all of a sudden. A blush spreads to her cheeks as she lowers her eyes to the floor, trying to avoid all of our gazes.

"What's the matter, Princess? Remember the lecture you just gave us a few minutes ago about good communication," Liam asks, and I can't help but chuckle. He has her on that one.

"As you all know, me and Liam are going to give this wedding thing another shot in less than a month's time. I know Gramps and Kian are organising all the security for the event, so I'm not worried about that. But, I've just had a message off Ryleigh this morning, and it would appear the girls feel I should have a hen night." Bree's face scrunches up as she cringes at the idea, which causes both Kian and me to burst out laughing.

"So, basically, you let a girl who has just turned eighteen talk you into taking her on a night out?" I ask in between laughs.

Bree begins to reply, but Liam, who doesn't find this funny at all, interrupts. "Hell no. Ryleigh is far too young for that, and she would probably be a bad influence on the rest of you. There's no way we can keep you safe on a night out."

Bree's face shifts from embarrassed to pissed instantly. When will this guy learn that the more he tells Bree she can't do something, the more she wants to? She didn't even sound like she wanted a hen night a few minutes ago. Now it's obvious she's going to argue she wants one, just to piss Liam off. Luckily, Kian steps in.

"How about I come on the night out with you? Not as your bodyguard or anything like that, just as your friend. That way you don't feel like you have security there, but Liam is reassured that you do."

They both stare at him, like they are unsure if they should compromise or not. In true Kellan style, I decide to add a bit of humour in the hope it breaks the tension. "Will you be going dressed as one of the girls? Or will you be the evening's entertainment?"

Three sets of eyes swing my way and unfortunately not one of them looks happy. Oops, it would appear my attempt at humour just fell flat on its ass.

"Why can't we just have a joint hen and stag do?" Liam asks, looking at Bree with big doe eyes in the hope she caves. Unfortunately, he's throwing his eyes in the wrong direction. I grew up around his younger sister. Ryleigh is a force to be reckoned with, and if she's decided they are throwing Bree a hen party, then you can be damned fucking sure it will happen.

"I think Kian's compromise is a good one. You can enjoy your stag night and I can enjoy my hen party. I promise I will be safe," Bree reassures Liam, before reaching over and swinging her arms around his neck. She pulls him in for a kiss, and both Kian and I look away.

"We need to have the hen and stag parties on different nights, though," Liam adds when they finally pull away, drawing my attention back to the conversation.

"Why?" Bree asks, her brows scrunched in confusion.

"Well, first of all, Kian is invited to mine as a guest, not just as a bodyguard," Liam explains, as he looks at Kian with a smile.

Kian seems genuinely shocked that he would be invited, but he is family now, so of course Liam would invite him. "Thanks, man," Kian replies with his signature dimpled smile, although this time it looks a lot more genuine, more humbled. I prefer this version.

"Also, I can't be responsible for looking after your drunk ass while I'm drunk. And if we have it on the same night, someone will have to miss out to look after Hallie. I don't think either the best man or the maid of honour should miss the party. So, we have to do it on separate days," Liam explains, and now it's my turn to sound stupid.

"Shit, I forgot we would need someone to watch Hallie." I say it out loud before I think it, and Kian starts to chuckle.

"Did you just admit you forgot about your daughter?"

With a very swift, but hard punch to the shoulder, I remind Kian of what being in this family means. "Fuck off, man. I meant that there is always someone around to help me with her. It's rare we are all out together without her."

Kian rubs his arm, which I'm sure is hurting, if the pain ricocheting through my hand is anything to go by. I don't often punch people, and even though it wasn't a real punch, with very little force behind it, Kian's obviously a lot more ripped than I thought. His arm is like hitting fucking stone.

"Okay, let's agree to both having parties but on separate days. Since the girls aren't here for long, you can do it the week before the wedding, and we can do it the weekend before that. Does that sound okay?" Liam asks, and everyone replies with confirmatory nods or chants of agreement.

With everything organised, and nothing further to discuss, we all agree to meet up again tomorrow morning at the warehouse to deal with Kyle. Everyone parts ways, but I stay in my office for a little longer, making sure I have gone through every last bit of information regarding Kyle and his family. I want to know all his secrets, and I intend to use every last one of them against him tomorrow. This time, I'm not waiting behind, staying in my office to watch the drama unfold on my screens. This time I intend on being there, and I won't be leaving until I'm sure Mia is safe. I need her to be able to sleep soundly at night. I really hope it's just the damsel in distress part that calls to me, and once she is safe, and I've played the hero, I can go back to being the villain we both know I am. We both know I can never give her the happy ending that she craves.

B ree and Liam have been spending a lot of time up in Kellan's office over the last week. I know I'm not part of the business, and since Kellan officially hired me as his nanny, the whole point is that I'm supposed to free them up to work. But, each time they go off into his office, leaving me with Hallie, I can't help but feel like I'm missing out. I know I'm probably being super paranoid, and the reason they always clam up whenever I walk into the room is because they don't want me to be involved in the business, but I hate it. I feel like an outsider.

Still, I've been making the most of my time with Hallie. She may only be seven months old, but the little monster is determined to be able to do everything. From the second I put her down, she is off. Her favourite thing to do is to simply roll around everywhere. So you lay her down to change her nappy and she turns her body, rolling away before you even have a chance to get her. Sometimes the only reason I even know she has moved is when I hear the cute little giggle getting farther away. She can crawl, she just prefers to log roll.

Recently she has been getting better at sitting up straight, and she keeps pulling on the furniture, determined to stand up. I don't think it will be long before this little monster is walking, talking, and terrorising us all. But, I wouldn't change it even for a second. Although, this morning, as I stand here covered in the mushed-up banana that she literally just threw all over me, my patience is being tested.

Laying Hallie down in her playpen with some toys, I know she is safe for a few minutes while I get myself cleaned up. She has only just started eating proper mushy food, and one of her favourite things to do is to throw it everywhere. But, before I can begin cleaning all the banana-covered worktops, I'm distracted by a buzzing on my phone.

Dread settles in the pit of my stomach, and I feel my breakfast beginning to slowly creep back up as the nausea overwhelms me. I can feel my body beginning to shake of its own accord, fear rippling through every piece of me. My hand trembles as I try to focus on the message and I mentally chastise myself. I've been like this every time my phone so much as beeps for the last week. Ever since that night, when I told Kellan about Kyle, he has continued to message me.

I know Kellan knows about my nightmares and my anxiety. He checks on me frequently, and has repeatedly asked if Kyle has texted again. And for some fucked-up reason, each and every time I tell him no.

I don't even know why. I think maybe it's because if I tell him about this piece of the puzzle, there's nowhere else left to go. I would have to tell him about the rest of the sordid tale and I'm not ready for that. I don't know if I ever will be. At the moment Kellan looks at me with lust in his eyes, and since he found out about Kyle, it hasn't changed all that much, but I can tell he sees me as a little more fragile, and I don't want that. I don't need that. Besides, what happened with Kyle is like dropping a stone in the ocean. The rest of my past is what led to Kyle, that's the real story, and I know as soon as Kellan finds out about that, he will never look at me the same way again.

Looking down at the phone, as suspected, it's another message from Kyle.

KYLE

> Little Rabbit, I don't like waiting. You better find your way home to me, or I guarantee I will hunt you down and slaughter anyone and everyone who dares to keep you from me. I will find you. However you are hiding your location from me, it won't last. I'm hiring the best hacker in the country to find you! If you come willingly, I will make your punishment light, if I have to track you down, everyone will pay, and your punishment will be severe.

Thankfully, Kellan was able to hack Kyle's phone and scramble the location data my father sent him. He isn't able to find out where I am, and knowing that helps me feel a little safer, for now. I just hope Kellan can keep preventing him from finding my location.

I also notice I have two messages from earlier on, but I must have missed them when I was playing with Hallie. They are from an anonymous number, but we both know it's from my father.

UNKNOWN

> Mia, I am not happy with your behaviour. I have left you alone these last few years, giving you the space you needed to complete your education, as you requested. But I am done waiting. You are a member of this family, and you will fulfil your familial responsibilities. You will marry the Fratacello boy. We need to align with his family. You will report back home immediately, or you will regret it.

> I know at school you had ties to Brianna O'Keenan. She is the first place I will look for you, Mia. I will use every resource at my disposal and you will not like my methods.

The phone crashes to the floor once I finish reading, bouncing off the carpet and hopefully not breaking. Although, if it does break, it won't be the end of the world. Then I wouldn't have to hear from them ever again.

The words repeat constantly, over and over in my head as I just stand there frozen, staring down at the phone that was once laid in my hands. What the fuck am I going to do? These are not men that should ever be messed with, and I have always known that the reason my father hasn't found me over the last five years isn't because I did a fucking great job at hiding, it's because he didn't need to find me. But, now he does. He already knows Bree's the most likely person to help me, but I don't know if he knows how much of a badass Bree is now. Either way, I need to think up a plan fast. I can't let them come here. I can't put Kellan and Hallie in danger.

A loud squeal erupts from the play pen, and my nerves are so fried and on edge that I can't help but scream.

Once my heart starts to return to normal, and I stop hyperventilating, I begin to remember where I am. As I look over at Hallie, I realise her high-pitched noise is actually a squeal of delight. Liam had obviously walked into the room and of course that made the little girl scream louder than a hen party at a Magic Mike show when the guy rips off his trousers. She idolises this guy, and the look on his face tells me it's very much reciprocated.

"Hello, my gorgeous Hallie Bear. What are you doing? Are you being a good girl for Mia?" Liam asks as he bounces the girl up and down in his arms. She just holds on to his big, strong muscles and giggles with each bounce.

I love the fact that a girl so small is able to turn the world's best assassin into a cooing, baby-talking, softie just by staring at him with those big, doe-eyed baby blues. If she keeps this up, she will get away with murder where her uncle Liam and Dad are concerned. I think even Bree may be coming around to it, and I don't blame her. Hallie is easy to love, which is why I know that I can't be the one responsible if anything happens to her.

"Are you okay, Mia? You screamed and look like you've seen a ghost!" Liam's voice is dripping with concern, as he stares at me. I hate when he does that. Liam is the type of person that cares about people so much, and when he looks at you, it really does feel as though he is trying to peer into your soul. He makes me want to spill my deep, dark secrets to those pretty emerald eyes. These boys are all too pretty for their own good.

"Erm…no. I mean yes…no. Wait I—" Words stumble out of my mouth until Liam places a gentle hand on my arm to calm me down. The only problem is that I never saw his hand coming and couldn't help but scream as he startles me.

My terrified screech of surprise echoes around the room, and Liam takes a giant step back, holding his arm outstretched and his palms out, showing me he's not a threat. He looks around tentatively, and that's when he sees my phone on the floor. Luckily, it's only the tempered glass screen that's broken.

Liam reaches down to pick up the phone, and even though I don't think he would read it, I'm pleased the screen is locked and he can't get into it without a passcode. "Looks like it got damaged when you dropped it. What has made you even more skittish than usual, Mia?" Liam asks, his eyes and his voice a lot gentler than you would expect when you look at him. Liam may have been raised by shitty parents, taught to murder at a young age, to turn his emotions on and off as needed, but in spite of all that, Liam is actually an emotionally well-balanced guy. He's also one of the nicest guys I've ever met, with a morality streak and a hero complex. I have no idea if he's secretly screwed up on the inside. I think I secretly hope he is because the idea that it really is possible to survive a shit childhood pisses me off. Then again, to the outside world I had the perfect life. Sometimes scars aren't visible but they burn deep into our soul. It's the type of pain that intrinsically alters a person so they're never the same again.

"Oh erm, nothing. But thanks for picking my phone up." I reach out and take the phone out of his hand, quickly putting it into my back pocket while Liam stares at me. He's looking at me, assessing my body to try and find out if I'm hiding something. I used to be good at hiding my secrets, schooling my face so that nobody would know I was different. But, the more time I spend with Kellan, Bree, and Liam, the more human I feel. I've spent the last five years getting comfortable, and now my father has pulled the rug out from under me, terrorising me all over again.

Fuck, maybe that is why he let me run?

When I first ran away from my family, and the obligations that came with it, I was shocked that he didn't drag me back. I changed my last name legally, but that didn't mean, with his connections, he couldn't easily track me. Yet, he never did. Now I'm wondering if he let me go because I'd become immune to his bullshit. For years I cried, I fought back, I lost sleep as the terror and pain spread through my body, causing me to feel ill constantly. This went on for years, until I realised that instilling the fear in me, and seeing the terrified expression on my face, that was all part of the game to him. Part of the abuse, and he got off on it. When I finally realised that, I learnt to school my face, to pretend that the horrendous shit he put me through each and every day wasn't too bad, and with each day that passed, I could see his annoyance grow.

When I finally stopped caring, that's when he grew bored with me and I saw my opportunity to run. But, now that I've tasted freedom, I have a lot more to lose.

Liam clears his throat to get my attention, and I realise he just said something that I missed entirely. I mutter an apology, but he repeats his question anyway. "I know you aren't as close to me as you are Kellan and Bree, but I want you to know there's nothing you can't tell me. I consider you like family now, and I protect my family. I can tell I walked in on something here, but I completely understand if you aren't ready to talk about it. However, I need to know that the rest of my family is safe too. Has Kyle Fratacello been in touch again since the other day that Kellan told us about?"

Releasing the breath I didn't realise I was holding, I wait for him to say something. For him to realise that me being here is a danger for not only him but the people we both care a lot about. Even though the idea of leaving Kellan, Hallie, and Bree causes a deep ache in my chest, I also know it's probably for the best. They are better off without the shit I bring with me. I keep thinking Liam will tell me to leave, but he doesn't say anything.

"Yes," I whisper, not bothering to lie anymore. What's the point?

I'm going to be in danger regardless, and maybe this way Liam can keep the people I care about safe.

Liam uses his free hand to lead me over to the sofa, Hallie sits peacefully on Liam's knee, as she strokes his face and pulls on his hair. Every time he gives her even the smallest smile, she chuckles and giggles like a lovesick school girl.

"Why didn't you tell any of us?" Liam asks, and I avert my eyes from his piercing green gaze.

Taking a deep breath, I try to school my nerves so I can reply as honestly as possible. "I was afraid. Not of them, but of you guys. When it was just me, I had nothing left to lose. But, now that I have all of you, I have so much more to lose. I can't let any of you get hurt because of me. These are dangerous psychopaths, and I don't want any of you anywhere near them."

I see the moment my words register with Liam, and it's like a red mist descends across his face. Fury etched there for all to see. Fuck, looks like I better get my shit packed. But, as he opens his mouth to speak, I'm stunned by what he says. "What do you mean by *them*? Is Kyle not the only person threatening you, Mia?"

Oops! I obviously didn't tell him about my father's involvement.

"My father has been in touch with me. He is the one who made it very clear that my familial obligations are to marry Kyle. I ran away from them both five years ago, but with the exception of changing my name and trying to keep off social media, I didn't exactly hide. My father left me alone to complete my course, but he's always made it clear that when I finish, I have to return home. Now my course is almost finished, he wants me to come home and plan my wedding to Kyle. I don't think he knows exactly where I am. Kellan has been working on hiding my location, but he has a good idea I'm with Bree. I know I shouldn't have brought this shit to your door, and I can only apologise." My words rush out and I can't hold back the sob that racks my body at the end. Tears I didn't even realise had formed begin to stroll down my cheeks.

"Listen, Mia. Am I happy you brought this shit to our door? No. But I also acknowledge that it isn't your fault. Besides, we all bring a fair share of baggage to this house, but we get through it all as a family. You don't have to go back to them, Mia. Talk to Kellan and have him block the numbers. Okay?" he asks, as he very tentatively lays his hand on my shoulder. He obviously remembers from before that touch isn't something I'm used to or comfortable with. Strangely, the sensation of having his firm hand on my T-shirt-covered arm isn't startling this time because I know it's coming, and I'm not as repulsed by him as I am with strangers. I think it's because I don't fear him.

I whisper words of thanks, which Hallie finds hilarious and she giggles for no reason, lightening the mood around us. But, Liam still has that no-nonsense look on his face, and I realise he isn't finished. "Mia, we have respected your wishes so far, and we haven't told Kellan the details of who your father is. Bree hasn't even told me his name, only that he's a bad guy. The type of guy that has his sticky fingers in a lot of pots, but never gets caught. He is the type who is quick to push others under the bus to save himself. If he's a danger to us, all I ask is that you divulge who he is, so we can do our research and get properly prepared. We will go to bat for you, but we can only do that if we know the enemy we are fighting against." His words are stern but honest, and I know he's right. The longer I keep them in the dark about my father, the more risk I put them in. But, I am also worried about the danger they will walk into if they do start looking into who my father is. To say he is a bad guy is a massive fucking understatement. Even I don't know the true extent of his evil, but I know what he did to me. If he's capable of inflicting such horror on his only daughter, then in my opinion his evil knows no bounds.

"When the time is right and we have no other alternatives, I will tell you everything. It's a lot to deal with, and I don't want you all to see me differently if you don't have to," I mutter, averting my eyes from his penetrating gaze. I can tell he isn't happy with my response, but I think he understands. This is more than me just being ashamed of my background. Thankfully he nods understandingly. Even if he isn't happy, or doesn't agree with my choice, he respects it. I like Liam.

"You know, Kellan won't ever trust you completely until you open up. I'm not telling you this to talk you into telling us, that is your own decision and I respect that. I'm not stupid, I can see that you like Kellan, and he likes you. I think that's why you scare him so much. He will kill me for saying this to you, so please don't ever repeat it. I'm not going to tell you the whole story, because it's not mine to tell. But before Hallie, he had never had a girlfriend. He was quite happy sleeping around and not forming any real commitments. His mum abandoned him at just six years old. He bounced around to several foster homes before I eventually brought him home with me, and my parents adopted him. He had severe abandonment issues before Hallie came into his life. The woman who carried Hallie for nine months doesn't deserve the title of Mum. She steamrolled through Kellan's life, and when she fell pregnant, Kellan knew he had to settle down. I think he really thought he had feelings for this girl. I don't believe he did, but the point is, he did. Then she did the worst thing imaginable, she abandoned him and Hallie, only further adding to his already harmful abandonment issues. So he closed himself off, and he vowed never to let anyone else in. That Hallie would be his priority, and I believe she always will be. Then you come along, and you make him feel, which is what scares him. He will push you away, that's what he does. If you like him, you have to let him push you away until you are strong enough to trust him implicitly. Until you are strong enough to hold on and fight for him, you need to let him go."

Fuck. Liam isn't telling me anything I didn't already know, but hearing him say the words out loud, warning me off Kel, it makes me feel like shit. The sinking feeling in my stomach seems to grow, and it feels like a black hole's opening up inside my chest, and I'm about to sink into it. I already know I'm not good enough for a guy like Kellan. He's smart, funny, kind, caring, and unbelievably hot. He's the type of guy that girls like me fantasise over. He isn't the type of guy we ever get to take home, no matter how much we fucking desperately want to.

"I know I'm no good for him. I've made that very clear to him. Besides, whatever happened before is in the past. He's my boss now. I can promise you, I won't risk my career for any guy," I say passionately, and I mean it. The only difference is that, where Kellan is concerned, I know I don't even have to consider risking my career. Guys like him don't end up with girls like me. He may enjoy flirting with me, and the thrill of the chase, but we both know that between us we barely make up one whole person. Two people as broken as us can never work together.

Before Liam has a chance to reply, Bree comes bouncing down the stairs, her eyes wide with a look of shock and terror etched across her face. She's holding her phone out in front of her, and it looks as though she is on a video call. Whatever the other person is saying has obviously scared the shit out of her. As soon as she reaches the living room, she leans down as though she's about to kiss Liam, but places her lips on Hallie's forehead. It's such a sweet gesture, yet Liam looks hurt that he missed out, and Hallie is obviously a jealous baby because she whacks Bree around the face with her little chubby hand. Apparently Hallie feels threatened by Bree, and is determined she won't stand between her and Liam. I can't help but chuckle as they both stare at a giggling Hallie like they can't quite believe she just did that. This girl is going to be a fucking nightmare when she's a teenager!

An indistinct, muffled voice escapes from Bree's held out phone, and that's when Bree looks at me with fear in her eyes. "Ryleigh is on the phone. She wants to know about the hen party. Apparently she wants to organise a stripper. Help me," Bree pleads, a comedic look of fear spread across her face.

I hear a giggling from the comfy chair in the corner of the room and look over to see Kian has joined us. I know that it's the guy's job to be Bree's bodyguard, and that covert behaviour is a skill in his world, but if that boy jumps out at me one more time, I'm going to smack him around his head. My heart stops beating every time he shows up unexpectedly, and it's frying my bloody nerves to shreds.

"I don't know what you are laughing at, Kian. You are going to be at this bloody event, and you are damn sure going to be by my side every fucking second. So if some muscular guy, covered in baby oil, with a thong shoved up his ass starts thrusting in my face, your face better be fucking millimetres away too. What I endure, so do you!" she shouts, but Kian just laughs harder, as he almost creases in half on the chair.

Liam, who clearly has no sense of personal safety, starts to laugh too, and the evil gaze that Bree throws this way is enough to kill.

Before she has a chance to throw down with Liam, and it's very fucking clear she's willing to tear him a new asshole for laughing and not helping her, Ryleigh's voice echoes through the speaker. "There isn't supposed to be any boys at a hen party, other than very naked strippers," Ryleigh moans like the spoiled little baby of the family that she is. I may have only known her a few months, but I know that everyone sees her as the baby of the family, and they wrap her in cotton wool to protect her. As a result, she rebels. That's why she currently has her hair dyed a bright purple colour, she wears very provocative clothing, flirts with anyone who moves, and isn't above doing things just to shock her family. This is the only version of Ryleigh I've ever got to know, but there will be a real version in there, the one hidden beneath all the bravado and teenage angst.

"Wait, does that mean I'm not invited?" shouts a male voice over the phone. Bree's face lights up into a smile and it's clear the person just became visible on her phone screen. I recognise the voice as Vinnie Marcushio, or Shane as he is now known. He's the reason Bree is here, alive.

After the dust settled, the Marcushios wanted revenge for what happened, hating the idea their name was dragged through the mud. Half of them blamed Vinnie, and wanted his head on a platter, the others still acknowledged him as their leader. But, Vinnie is just a terrified kid who was put in a shit position, he was manipulated by Vernon after his dad's death. He's far too young to be involved in our world. So, Liam enrolled him in Ryleigh's boarding school, and now they are doing their final year together. They are the best of friends, but it's obvious to everyone except Liam and Vinnie—shit, I need to remember to call him Shane now—it's obvious to all except them that they are head over heels in love with each other.

"You are invited to my stag do the week before, Shane," calls Liam from beside me on the couch.

"Sweet, thanks for that, Liam. God, you aren't letting Kellan organise it, are you?" Shane shouts with a groan. Kellan appears out of nowhere, bouncing down the stairs just in time to hear his name being mentioned.

Once he reaches the living room, he leans down to kiss his

daughter—who responds with a giggle before she pushes him away with her fist—then leans over Bree, so that his head is in line with the camera phone. He probably looks like his head is on its side given the angle he is leaning at, but he doesn't seem to care.

"What the hell makes you think I can't plan a bachelor party?" Kellan shrieks, clearly insulted by Shane's comment.

"Erm...well, it's just that you...erm. You don't really go out that much," Shane babbles, seemingly frightened of voicing his opinion now Kellan is in the room. Both Liam and Kian continue to chuckle as Kellan's cheeks flush under his five o'clock shadow.

Fuck, why is my heart getting all fluttery at the sight of his blush? So what if the guy has a sensitive side, even one that he tries to hide. I need to think of this guy as my boss or my friend. I can't keep looking at him like I'm wondering what he has on under those sinfully tight dark jeans.

I need to focus on the conversation, and not on Kellan.

"You listen here, you little punk. I may not be as hardcore as I was before I had Hallie, but before I became a dad, I knew how to party. I knew how to find the best clubs, and pick up the best pussy. So don't even question my ability to throw a good party. There will be plenty of booze and pussy, just like a good bachelor party should have," Kellan shouts down the phone. This is clearly one of the occasions where he should listen to what he's about to say in his head before saying it aloud. It takes less than a second before the room erupts into chaos.

Bree begins shouting about how there will be no pussy, and if there is then Liam isn't allowed a bachelor party. Liam, who had begun to tell Kel that he didn't want that kind of party, heard what Bree said, and then starts shouting about how she can't tell him what type of party he could have. That she should trust him. Shane yells through the phone, confirming his earlier statement that this is proof Kellan should not be planning the bachelor party. Kian, in the meantime, keeps whooping and hollering, almost as though he's watching a pantomime.

The noise and the arguments are just too much for me. Out of nowhere, I gather confidence and begin to shout. "Shut up! All of you, shut the fuck up!" Clearly that's exactly what was needed, as they all stop mid-sentence, their gazes turning to me in clear bewilderment. Even Bree who has known me the longest has never heard my voice go up that loud.

Shit, now they're all looking at me, I'm going to have to say something now. "Look, Bree, you can't tell Liam what type of bachelor party he can have. You just have to trust that even if there's a thousand pussies there that all want him, he will still choose you. And you, Liam, you need to reassure your fiancée that you will always choose her. Have the party you want, just don't choose a big elaborate event because Bree tells you that you can't have it. That's stupid and pig-headed, something I would never have associated with you. You, however, Kellan, are an idiot. Stop trying to prove you are young and carefree. You may have known how to party a few years ago but that changed when you got Hallie. Organise the best party, let your hair down, but remember no matter how much Jager you drink to reminisce and remember your youth, your baby will still wake up at five in the morning demanding her dad. And as for you, Shane, you have plenty of time to get drunk and watch strippers. You do not want to do it with these fossils."

"We are not fossils. I'm not even twenty-fucking-five yet," shouts Kian, and I turn my attention to the blond-haired cocky guy who missed out on my last rant, but now he's earnt one of his own.

"Yes, you are compared to him. We may not be ancient, but we sure as fuck don't recover from hangovers like we did in our teens. You, pretty boy, you need to stop leading them astray and make sure they don't get themselves into any trouble. Because I guarantee, if you let anything happen to the groom a week before the wedding, you won't know what wrath is until you meet Bree." Kian's face drains of colour as Bree begins to chuckle. "So, can we all agree to just have nice, quiet nights? Nobody gets so wrecked they have to have their stomach pumped, and nobody comes home covered in stripper body oil. Yes?"

Agreements ring around the room, until Ryleigh's voice echoes through the speaker. "How about we compromise on a 'watch but don't touch' stripper experience? Since it's already paid for."

"Ryleigh!"

The same shout in various different tones fills the room. Liam is pissed, Bree sounds desperate, whereas Kellan and Kian seem to find it funny. Liam, however, doesn't just stop at shouting her name. "Ry, not only do I hate the idea of my fiancée watching some big dick flapping about in her face, I hate the idea even less knowing my two baby sisters will be there too. Have you told Freya about this?" Liam asks, and before Ryleigh even has a chance to reply, Kian draws our attention.

"Oh yeah, she will hate this," he says, like he knows her personally. Both Bree and Liam focus their eyes on him with laser precision, and he looks to be shuffling under their fierce gazes.

Thankfully, Ryleigh can't see what is going on in the room, only what is in front of her on the screen, so she's oblivious to the tension and continues to reply to Liam. "No, she doesn't know yet, and obviously she will be pissed and moan about not wanting to go. But, we never got a chance to throw Bree a hen party last time, and I want this wedding to be special and memorable, so it makes all the memories of the last one fade away. It has to be really good to do that. So, please let me try and organise it. I know I'm not the maid of honour, and I don't want to take over from Mia, I just want to help." Her voice sounds so lost, and she may have glossed over it briefly, but she hit the nail on the head. The reason she wants a big, elaborate event is so that everyone will talk about the scandalous hen party, rather than the time we did the whole wedding thing already and the bride never showed. Ryleigh doesn't want to be sitting there at the wedding venue thinking about the last wedding, and I don't blame her.

"We can plan the party together, Ryleigh. How does that sound?" I shout to her.

All eyes shift to gaze at me, but I don't care. Bree should have a hen party, it's the right thing to do, and we all know that when Ry sets her mind to something, she goes with it. So, why not go with it under my watchful eye. I can rein her in without her even realising it. Cries of *yes* and *thank you* ring out from the phone, and everyone else seems a little pissed.

"Fine, but no strip clubs." Bree sounds as though she is grinding that out reluctantly through gritted teeth. "And we stick to one or two clubs only, no walking as it brings out evil Mia."

Everyone looks to Bree as she explains the night out we went on. "The club had to unexpectedly close and there were no taxis, so we walked to the next one. Mia's feet were killing her by the time we arrived at the club and it was packed. We saw only one chair available at the bar, and Mia practically ran towards it. But a woman cut in front of her, and started to sit in the chair, and that's when Mia lost the plot, the alcohol in her system not helping things. She told the woman about how much pain she was in and began to do her word vomit thing. The woman dismissed her, claiming she got there first and that Mia should leave. In response, Mia removed one of her shoes and threatened to use the torture device on this woman, indicating she planned to stab the stiletto into her eye. The woman moved pretty quickly after that and Mia got her chair."

All eyes look at me like they're just seeing me for the first time, and Liam and Kian look quite impressed. Kellan, on the other hand, looks unsure. His face is scrunched up like he's trying to solve a really hard maths question, but his eyes are ablaze with the fire that calls to me. All my nerve endings feel like they're on fire, and I can feel a delicious prickling beneath the surface.

Despite being in a room full of people, as our gaze connects, and the sensations rippling across my skin makes me feel as though I'm really alive. I ache to reach over, to touch him, but I know I can't. Not just because all our friends are here, but because I can't risk my job.

It pleases me when I see Kellan squirming as much as I am. I feel like the air is suffocating as sexual tension floats around, making the atmosphere almost dense, as though you could cut through it with a knife. But nobody else seems to notice.

"I like this plan. Mia, I will be in touch soon to get some more details. Bree, please can you pass my number along to her so we can discuss things. Also, when we come over for the wedding, can we talk about maybe coming there to spend Christmas with you?" Ryleigh asks, her voice echoing through the phone pulls me from the fantasy my brain was just starting to engage in.

Liam perks up, clearly liking the idea that his sisters want to visit and spend some time here. I know he misses them. "Of course we can talk about it. You are always welcome."

"Maybe I can come the week before with Shane, and we can both stay for the week. It's half-term anyway." I don't know why but it sounds as though Ryleigh is trying to say something, but not say it. Liam obviously knows what she's not so subtly hinting at, because there's a big smile on his face.

Kellan begins to speak, and I realise he must be in on it too, because his grin matches Liam's. "You wouldn't be hinting that you want to celebrate your eighteenth birthday, would you, Ry?"

That seems to open the flood gates, and just before Ryleigh begins talking a mile a minute, I hear a very loud groan from Shane through the phone. Apparently we just opened Pandora's box. "Yes, of course I am. I want to celebrate with my family. We are doing some stuff here on the day, and Freya is coming to spend the day with me. But I want to celebrate with you guys too. I don't want to take away from your big day, though." The last sentence is added on so quickly, it's almost an afterthought, but we all knew Ryleigh means it. Although she can come across as a stroppy teenager at times, because she is one, she's also incredibly kind and loyal. She's a lot fiercer than people think, and she's severely underestimated every time.

"I will get in touch with Finn and Evan, they can come too. We will have a little mini party here one night while you are over. It will be a movie and takeout night, it will not be a getting shitfaced event that results in me cleaning up vomit. Agreed?" Liam asks, his voice taking on that stern, father figure tone he seems to have for everyone, it's just worse for Ryleigh.

"Fine, but you have to get some champagne. I promise, no excessive drinking, but we have to celebrate," Ryleigh counters, and I can see Kellan's face twist into a big, cocky grin as he watches Liam's face fall. It's very obvious to all involved that Liam has lost this round, as we all know Ry has him wrapped around her little finger. It might look like a negotiation, but it's most definitely not!

After that's all been agreed, we all part ways for the evening. I ask Kellan if he needs any help with Hallie tonight, unsure what I want his answer to be. Part of me would give anything for more time alone with him, but we both know I have an essay due soon that I've barely made a start on. He reminds me how important it is that I keep my grades up.

I go towards my room and Kellan goes to his, where he has already laid Hallie to sleep, and we stand in the hallway, ready to say goodnight to each other.

Standing with my back against the wall outside of my bedroom, trying to keep the pout off my face at the fact that he told me to go to my room to do my school work. I've never felt so juvenile around him before. Then again, I don't think the pouting and sulking is helping to change his mind either.

He begins striding towards me before placing his hands flat against the wall, caging me in as he closes the distance between us. His body is mere millimetres away from touching mine, I feel the heat radiating off him, and it warms me. As he leans closer to my ear, his five o'clock shadow brushes against the side of my face and as his breath hits my ear, a shudder rips through my body.

"If you want to come and watch a movie in about an hour or two, after you have done your essay, then my door is always open." His voice is husky and full of desire.

Fuck, this is a bad idea. What happened to maintaining our distance, and to him just being my boss and friend? Then again, what he's really offering me is so much more than a lust-filled night of me pining for him. This isn't the first time he has invited me into his bed. Ever since the night of the nightmare, he has made excuses for me to fall asleep in his bed. Nothing ever happens between us, except he holds me as we sleep. And every night that he holds me, is a night I get to sleep without any nightmares. He makes me feel safe.

"I would love to," I reply, before casting my gaze away from him. I don't want to look at him as I ask him the next part. "Isn't it hard for you?"

He chuckles, his breath hitting my cheek, and the deep rumble of his chest vibrates against mine. As I look up through my hooded lashes, his face is spread into a cocky grin.

"Oh, Flower, it is very hard for me," he says, grinding his hardness against my stomach for effect.

As soon as his erection touches me, a deep moan escapes my body as all the pent-up sexual tension returns. That is so not what I meant, and he knows it. Fuck, I should really think through what I say when I'm with Kellan. "That's not what I meant and you know it."

I place my hands gently onto his chest and give him a small push. It moves him back by just a couple of centimetres, but that's enough space for me to breathe a bit of air that isn't filled with Kellan, and my brain begins to clear of the constant sex fog I seem to be in whenever I'm around him.

"I know it's not what you meant, but the answer is still yes. It's excruciatingly painful to lie next to you every night, to hold you in my arms and know I'm not allowed to touch you in all the ways I want. But, I'm also not an idiot. I know you have experienced trauma, and you need time to heal. If I can help you even just a little by holding you all night, then I will put up with blue balls for as long as it is necessary. I care about you, Mia. Probably too much, but that means I have to look after you. Do I think we would have a fucking phenomenal time if we did fuck? Of fucking course we would. It would be mind-blowing. But neither of us is in a position to have a relationship. What we feel is lust, and I'm not prepared to lose a friend, or let Hallie lose her nanny just because my cock is hungry for your tight pussy."

Fuck, it really doesn't help when I can feel his cock straining through his trousers, desperate to get to me. But it's true. We are both far too fucking broken to ever make good partners in a relationship.

Although, the more I think about having a relationship with Kellan, the more it appeals to me. He would make a good boyfriend; kind, caring, considerate, and don't even get me started on how hot the sex would be. But he has demons, ones left behind when he was abandoned by his ex.

I can't fight against demons of the past, all I can do is keep showing him that I couldn't be more different from her, and that I will always be there for him. Maybe then, one day in the future, when we both have our shit together, we can finally give this a chance to see where it goes. But, until then, this is the most we can offer each other. Friendship. And maybe a bit of flirting.

"Well, he will have to settle for spending the night nestled in between my ass cheeks while we sleep. Sadly, that's the most action he will get," I joke and Kellan's face blushes red beneath his stubble.

"I think we will enjoy that. Come in whenever you are ready," he whispers in my ear before beginning to pull away.

Using the hand that was resting on his chest, I quickly fist his T-shirt and pull him back so his body's flush against mine. Without even thinking about what I'm going to do, I stand up on my tiptoes and press my lips against his. The kiss is firm and demanding, which is very unlike me.

Kellan seems frozen, clearly not expecting me to kiss him, but as soon as my tongue swipes across his lip before tangling with his, it's like a bolt of electricity wakes him up. His hands that were on the wall, now waste no time sliding over my body, cupping under my ass. I follow his lead and allow him to pick me up easily. He slams my back firmly against the wall as I wrap my legs around his back, his cock rubbing against my fabric-covered clit. But it was more than enough contact to make me moan.

The sound of my moan seems to wake us both up from the lust-filled haze we are both in, and our lips pull apart. His crystal blue eyes gaze into mine, and fuck does my stomach do those little flips and my heart seems to skip a beat. Our breathing is almost synchronised as we pant. The lust-filled silence is deafening, and I have to break it.

"Thanks," I mumble, which earns me a chuckle from Kellan. One that vibrates through our still connected bodies.

It's at this point that Kel seems to realise he's still holding me in his arms, and he slowly lowers me to the ground. "What are you thanking me for? Not that I'm complaining, you can thank me like that anytime you want, Flower," Kellan jokes, and I playfully smack his bicep.

"For letting me stay with you. We both know it helps with my nightmares. I know I haven't talked about it, and you haven't brought it up, but I want you to know that it means a lot, you wanting to look after me."

He gives me a big, genuine smile, and fuck if it's not even hotter than the cocky smirk. "Always."

With that we reluctantly part ways, and the whole time I'm doing my coursework, all I keep thinking about is how long I have until I can go next door and curl up in his arms.

I think it's safe to say, I like this guy a lot more than I should. I'm so fucking screwed.

Kellan

Waking up tangled in Mia, her limbs, her hair, and her scent envelops me. I feel warm, but it's not just from the heat of her body, it's from her. It's like she lights up my soul, and it scares the shit out of me. Laying there and watching her chest rise and fall, the urge to touch her, to claim her and make her mine becomes overwhelming. But, we were right when we talked about it last night. We are both far too damaged to ever be capable of having a real relationship, and that's exactly what she deserves. She deserves flowers, chocolates, and romance with all the bells and whistles on. I'm not that type of guy. She deserves better than me.

My little princess grumbles from the cot attached to my side of the bed. In a routine we have perfected, I slide my arm out from underneath Mia, and quickly grab Hallie before she screams and wakes up the whole house.

As I lay her with her belly against my chest, and she holds her head up to look at me as her hands reach out to grasp at whatever they can reach—my lips, my hair, my arm. As long as she has something fisted in her hands, she is happy. I can't believe my baby girl, who not so long ago laid on my chest after she had just been born, is now over seven months old. She's crawling about, eating actual food, or should I say throwing food all around the kitchen with her spoon, before scooping it up and licking it from her fingers. My little girl is growing up and it's scaring the shit out of me.

Holding her above my head, the same way I watched Mia do the other morning, we pretend Hallie is my little comet and I tell her all about how she flies around the moon before dropping her back down to earth. Then I remind her that I love her to the moon and back. I feel a twinge of sadness in my chest whenever I use that saying, same as when I hear Liam call her his Hallie Bear. My heart breaks for the girl who will have to grow up without a mother.

If someone had told me at the time that none of it was real, I would never have believed them. She called her our little gummy bear. She is the one who kept telling her the entire time that we would love her to the moon and back. I look back now and it all makes much more sense. She spent most of her time teaching me how to be a parent, getting me to bond with her bump, as opposed to doing it herself. I think that was her way of teaching me, getting me ready to be a single dad.

Part of me wants to believe she cared, that she was making sure I would be a good enough dad for Hallie, but her actions speak louder. If she cared she would never—could never—have left.

"Morning, baby girl, aren't you beautiful this morning," Mia coos as she rolls over and takes Hallie's outstretched hand into her own. She grips her tightly, and even as we pretend to fly about in the sky, she never lets go of Mia's hand, which does crazy things in my chest. My heart feels like it's fluttering, and it's not a nice feeling— okay, so it's fucking amazing—but what I mean is, it can't be good. After that soul-destroying kiss last night, I'm not even ashamed to admit I had to blow my load not once but twice in the shower. There was no way in this world that I would've been able to lie next to her the entire night with my cock as hard as he was and not want to ravish her completely. It's getting harder and harder—pun intended—to be close to her and still have nothing happen between us.

"I don't know if I mentioned it yesterday, but I'm going to be out of the house for most of the morning with Bree and Liam. They need me for an on-site job they are doing. Will you be okay with Hallie while we are gone?" I ask, hoping she doesn't ask too many questions. I really don't want to have to lie to her. If I want her to trust me, I need to be trustworthy and lying about where I'm going or what I'm doing definitely doesn't count towards that.

"Yeah of course. I was going to take her to this new baby group they have at the library. I know she is too young to fully interact with other babies, but they say the music, sounds, and playing with things really help their development. But if you'd rather we didn't, that's okay. I also planned to take her to the park, or go swimming. It's whatever you think," Mia mutters quickly, like she's worried she may be overstepping with her suggestions. I don't know why she feels like that. I know I'm supposed to be her boss, but the way we are with each other has never been all that formal. I try to keep it casual, so I don't know why she is acting weird with me.

"Relax, Flower. I think it's a great idea, and I think Hallie would love it. I like the idea of her interacting with other kids her age. We don't really know anyone with kids, and I don't need to put her into a nursery, but I know that having her interact with other children is essential. It wasn't something I was worrying about just yet, but no reason not to start her early. So, yes to that, and the park and swimming. You are her nanny, and as long as you let me know where you are going, I have no problem with it." I mean every word I say, with the exception of the worrying part, because all I ever seem to do at the moment is worry. I worry I'm doing things wrong, or that the choices I make now will shape Hallie's future. That's a massive fucking responsibility for one person, who just a year ago could barely look after myself. I have gone over and over in my head the pros and cons of putting Hallie in a nursery, and I know that in a year or two, I will have to. Not because I want her to, but because she needs to. Until then, I want to keep her close by, and Mia's the perfect person to help me do that.

As Hallie begins her usual morning babbling, which usually means she is done playing and having cuddles with her daddy, she wants to get up, get a nappy change, and get some food before playing in her playpen for a bit. The girl has a lot of energy first thing in the morning, and she is a creature of habit. She hates it if you change her routine in any way.

Mia takes her from me to allow me to get up. In a routine we have perfected over the last week, we go about our morning, working completely in sync as we get Hallie ready and keep her occupied while the other person gets ready to start their day. It's not even something we talked about, it's just like this dance we do together, without even talking about it. We move around each other with ease, almost like we know what the other person is going to do next, and it doesn't even require thought. We rarely talk, but Mia seems to know that I'm not much of a morning person. I'm the type of guy that doesn't get going properly until I've had my first cup of coffee. So, as I jump in the shower, I know Mia will get Hallie changed and dressed for the day and then we will swap over. I will take Hallie for her breakfast while Mia showers.

As I climb into the shower, all I can think about is the beauty that will be climbing in after me. As the water cascades over my head and down my body, I imagine what her soft, silky skin would feel like under my touch. I've had a very small taster, and it's nowhere near enough. Her pale, ivory skin seems to glow whenever I'm near, and I can just imagine watching the blush spread from her cheeks down over her chest and to her breasts.

Mia has the perfect body; she's starting to get curves in all the right places, her tits are just enough of a handful, as is her ass. I can tell she carries a lot of insecurity, but she doesn't need to. She is one of the most beautiful girls I have ever seen, and I feel like I'm driving myself crazy thinking about what is underneath her clothes.

I want to be the person that makes her nipples tweak into perfect buds after I suck and pull on them, electrifying them. I want to tease my finger through her perfect pussy, dragging it through the slit to see how wet she gets just for me. I want to rub the pad of my thumb across her sensitive clit until she is writhing around and begging for more. Before I drop to my knees and use my tongue. I want to taste her pussy, to dive into the sweet nectar I already know will be there. Then, when I finally have her writhing, moaning, pleading with me, and begging me, that's when I will give her my cock. The thought of her falling apart on my cock, screaming my name, it's too much for me. My cock stands tall, straining and angry. I can't resist wrapping my hand around the shaft.

In slow practised movements, I fist my hand up and down the shaft, making sure to catch the pre-cum from the tip and spread it out to act as a lubricant. Not that I need it, the water is doing an amazing job, but it's just the way I've always done it. I don't even think, I just do what feels right.

As thoughts of pounding into Mia, harder and faster, flood through my brain, my hand works harder, matching the speed. My hand feels nowhere near as good as how it would feel buried to the hilt in Mia's sweet cunt, but for now this will have to do, and fuck me is it working. I can feel my balls begin to tighten, and my hand movements become more frantic. My body starts to tense, and I use my free hand to lean against the wall for support. My legs begin to quiver, and I feel the muscles in my lower abdomen tighten. I let the fantasy fill my mind, and it's almost like I can really hear Mia screaming my name, telling me she is going to come on my cock.

The fantasy overwhelms me, and seconds later my cock explodes. Rows and rows of cum shoot out of my dick, as my pleasure-filled groans echo around the shower room. Cum plasters across my hand and the wall, as my body quivers. I lean against the wall to try and catch my breath. Fuck, that was hot. But it's nothing like the real thing. Even just thinking that makes my cock twitch, and there's no way he's ready to go again that quickly. That's what Mia does to me, she makes me feel things I know I shouldn't. That's why I allow myself this time. Just a few minutes each day in the shower to live out the fantasy, but as soon as I'm done, the shower washes away all evidence, and any other thoughts I might be having get washed away too. Until tomorrow morning, and we get to do it all again.

I'm so fucking screwed. I know most people would argue this is a very unhealthy way of dealing with the attraction I have for my nanny, but I'm not fucking her and I don't have blue balls. It's the best-case scenario, in my opinion. Well, second best. Actually fucking her out of my system would be the best-case scenario, but since that is off-limits, second best—my hand in the shower—will have to do.

As I walk out of the shower, I realise I've forgotten to bring my sweatpants in with me. I usually bring them in so I don't have to walk out there in a towel and get changed in front of Mia. But, now that I think about it, maybe this is my chance to torture her as much as she does me. I know she doesn't do it intentionally, but when she comes to sleep in bed with me wearing tiny little shorts that barely cover her ass, and a tight vest top that shows off the swells of her tits, and a patch of skin below the T-shirt, exposing her pierced navel. She drives me fucking mad, and this is my chance to get a little bit of revenge.

Wrapping the towel around my waist, I walk out of the shower and find Mia sitting on the end of the bed, holding Hallie out at arm's length like she is trying to get her attention to talk to her. Whatever she's saying is keeping Hallie amused because I can hear her giggling as soon as I open the door. I watch Mia's face, waiting for the moment she realises I'm wearing just a towel, and I wish I had a camera to record it.

Her mouth physically drops open as her eyes widen before flaming with desire. Her hands judder and for a second I worry she is going to drop Hallie, but she quickly recovers and places her safely so she is sitting on her knee. Never once does she take her eyes off me. Her fiery gaze trails over my dripping wet, black hair, down over my inked chest and across my abs. She bites her lower lip when her gaze reaches the top of the towel. I know the exact moment she hits the V I have swooping from my hips, down below the towel, because I can feel her heated gaze. It's like she leaves a trail of fire across my skin.

My dick responds instantly, standing to attention like it didn't just have the best orgasm in a long time just five minutes ago. Mia notices my growing erection too, as I can see her neck bulge as she gulps nervously. I walk closer to her, and it's like everything is moving in slow motion.

Fuck, this was supposed to be to torture Mia, yet I'm the one standing here with a fucking painful erection and an irrational desire to tear her clothes off. It's like I don't even see my baby sitting on her knee. It's not until Hallie starts to cry that we both seem to snap out of our lust-filled haze. As soon as we break eye contact, we both start seeing sense again. Mia starts to soothe Hallie while I head towards my chest of drawers, mumbling something about forgetting to take my trousers in with me.

"I'm just going to put Hallie in her crib for a minute, then you can take her down for breakfast. When you have finished changing, I will be back in to jump in the shower, if that's okay? If you need any help with breakfast you can wait for me, I won't be too long." Mia talks so fast I can barely keep up with her. But, I agreed anyway, and as soon as she puts Hallie in the crib, she hightails it out of my room and into her own.

Fuck, I don't know how much longer I can want that girl without having her.

Once we are down in the kitchen, I settle her into the high chair, making sure to tie her in properly as the little devil will try to throw herself out if she feels like it. As I mix together the Weetabix, milk, and mashed bananas, I can't help but think about Mia climbing into my shower. What the fuck is wrong with me? I thought I literally just gave myself that lecture, the one about not daydreaming about my daughter's nanny!

Hallie's screams let me know she's not willing to wait while I fantasise, which is probably a good thing. I hand her the bowl of mush and get the baby spoon for her. She tries to grasp the spoon, but can only just manage it, so I try to help her. I scoop up some of the hideous-looking slop—that my daughter loves, by the way, and eats every morning—and we make little aeroplane noises as we pretend the spoon is delivering her food. She munches on the spoon, and that's when I remember what the health visitor suggested. Apparently, for baby-led weaning, I'm not supposed to be helping her, she should be doing it herself. So, I take a step back, leaving her with the bowl and spoon, and head towards the coffee machine.

As soon as I turn my back, I feel something hit me on the back of the neck, and it feels icky. Reaching up, as soon as my fingers make contact, I know it's Hallie's breakfast. Her cute little giggle should have given her away really. I should tell her off, but I'm really not ready for that so early on. So, instead I get my cup of coffee ready.

In the space of time it takes for me to make the pot of coffee, she pelts me on the back at least four times, and that's not to mention the amount of times it hits the various kitchen work surfaces. I take a big gulp of coffee, ready to pluck up the courage to tell off my little devil child, but the more I drink the coffee, the more I want. I gulp it down in between yawns as more splashes sound out around the kitchen. As soon as I finish the first cup, and pour myself a second, I pluck up enough energy to challenge her. Besides, she must be low on food by now, given the amount she's thrown.

I turn around, but she must have been waiting with a supply in her hands, as with expert precision she launches two tiny fistfuls of food straight into my face. Without even thinking it through I drop to the floor, hiding behind the island in the middle of the kitchen. Hallie giggles as I let out a sigh. It's times like this I realise what a fucked-up parent I am.

I sit, cowering behind the kitchen island, drinking my coffee for far longer than I should, until I hear light footsteps drifting down the stairs. I slowly raise my head to see Mia entering the kitchen wearing tight ripped denim jeans, and an off-the-shoulder baggy black jumper. Her hair is pulled up into a messy bun, with brown strands breaking free and framing her beautiful face. When I first met Mia, she was a blonde, but since then she has gone back to what she informs me is her natural brunette colour, and she looks classically beautiful. It suits her so much more.

Sadly her beautiful, yet understated look doesn't last long, as the moment she's in range, Hallie fires at her. Giggles erupt from Hallie as she hits her target with a precision I can't help but be proud of. The girl has got a good arm!

"No, Hallie. You are supposed to eat your food, not throw it. Stop! Or I will take it off—"

Before Mia even gets the chance to finish the sentence I hear Hallie release what can only be described as a battle cry, and Mia drops down behind the island beside me. She looks shocked to see me, and I hold out a cloth in one hand and my coffee in the other. "Coffee?" I ask, and she takes it with an exhausted laugh.

"Hallie's still playing with her food instead of eating it, I see," Mia adds sarcastically as she takes a few sips out of my coffee. The appreciative moan that escapes from her lips does stupid things to my insides, and my cock.

"That's not completely fair. She is eating too," I add, feeling the need to defend my little monster. Although, I'm not sure she has earned my defence on this occasion.

"I'm sorry. I've been trying to teach her what to do, but she is being a bit stubborn. I guess I could look at trying a new technique. I can do some research today, and I promise I will make sure to get the kitchen cleaned," Mia mumbles a mile a minute and I struggle to keep up with her. I don't know why she is apologising. I'm the one who gave Hallie her breakfast and ended up hiding under the counter first.

"Relax, Flower. I have absolutely no doubt that Hallie is fine. After several panicked visits to the health visitor, worried about her feeding, growth, and development, I have been told repeatedly that she will grow and develop when she is ready. I can't control it, I just have to come along for the ride. So, I have stopped worrying. I have far too many other things I need to worry about with her. I literally have nightmares about what she'll be like as a teenager if she's this stroppy now! Besides, I got her breakfast, and I could have tried to stop her instead of hiding behind the counter. There's just only so much I can handle before my coffee kicks in." I am very aware of how fast I'm talking, but the more I talk, the more it occurs to me that I'm panicking, even if I tell her I'm not. I'm thinking about how stressed I'm going to be when Hallie's a teenager. Then I remind myself that's a worry for another day and I just have to focus on keeping her alive long enough to reach her teens.

Besides, I'll just let Mia deal with all the puberty related bullshit. There's no way my nerves can handle shopping for bras or talking about periods. That thought hits me like a tonne of bricks. Do I really still see Mia standing by my side, helping me to raise Hallie when she's a teenager? I think you're only supposed to hire nannies for the first year or two, until the child goes to nursery. But Mia is more than just the nanny, and I know it.

Fuck, I can't handle these big life conundrums so early on in the morning. Particularly when I'm hiding in the kitchen whilst under attack from a hostile baby throwing food at me. What the hell has my life become?

Mia and I sit there for a while, leaning against each other, and I try not to think about how nice it is being close to her. Even if we are cowering on the kitchen floor. We share the coffee until we run out and Mia takes some big, deep breaths before whispering in my ear, "I'm going up for more coffee. Surely she'll have run out of food soon. By the sounds of it, she's eating some of it."

Before I have a chance to reply, she stands up and quickly reaches for the coffee, but sadly Hallie is quicker. She must have had missiles in both hands, and with an aim that can only be described as fucking impressive for a seven-month-old, she manages to hit Mia with two blobs of banana before she has a chance to duck down again. Thankfully, she managed to get the coffee.

"Your daughter has impeccable aim," Mia mutters before taking a big mouthful of steaming hot coffee and offering it to me. I can't help but laugh as I take the coffee and drink a big gulp, the delicious burn tickling my mouth.

"So, I guess we should be proud of her then."

Before Mia has a chance to reply, we hear footsteps running into the kitchen. Mia and I look at each other frantically, wondering if we should get up and warn the person, or if we should stand up and look like we're actually trying to do the parenting thing. As opposed to letting Hallie just run riot.

Before we even have a chance to move, a high-pitched yelp fills the kitchen and I move quickly. Handing my coffee over to Mia, I quickly jump up to find Bree standing there with banana mush smeared across her face. Hallie's giggling and getting ready to throw again as she fills both hands with more food. Thankfully, she moves one hand to her mouth, tasting more of the banana and giving me the opening I need. I quickly pour a cup of coffee from the machine for Bree, before pulling on her sleeve and yanking her down to hide with Mia and me.

As soon as we are all crouched down again, Hallie's giggles fill the room, and Mia hands Bree a towel so she can clean the banana off her face. She looks like she's still in shock, like she can't quite believe what's happening.

"What the fuck is happening? Why are we allowing a baby to terrorise us in my own kitchen?" Bree yells in the quietest voice she possibly can. She may be pissed but she knows not to shout and anger Hallie even more.

"Look, we are trying a weaning technique that the health visitor suggested. We're supposed to let her feel the food, as she's more likely to want to eat it. And to be fair, she's putting it in her mouth occasionally." The explanation sounds pathetic even to my own ears, but I can't help the small amount of pride in my voice when I say she's eating something. Hallie's a very fussy eater and it's something I've been frantic about for the last few weeks, ever since the health visitor said I should be weaning her. I will admit, it's not quite going to plan, but my life never does. I can't help but laugh.

"Kellan, there is banana all over my kitchen, and all over us. We are having to hide from a fucking baby," she yells, as she smacks me around the head with her hand.

"Ouch. Look, she's just in a bit of a bad mood, that's all. She's not a morning baby, she's—"

Before I have a chance to finish my sentence, we hear footsteps entering the kitchen. If we didn't know it was Liam—since everyone else is currently already here hiding behind the kitchen counter—Hallie's girly high-pitched squeal would have definitely given the game away.

"Good morning, my little gorgeous Hallie Bear. Where is everyone? And why does it look like a banana bomb exploded all over you and the kitchen?" Liam says as Hallie just continues to squeal and giggle.

As if like something out of a cartoon, Mia, Bree, and I all pop our heads up to find Hallie sat there, munching on the banana in her hand whilst giving Liam the biggest smile she can. Once she has cleaned her hands, she holds them out for Liam, making the clutching motion with her fists, which is her way of asking for him to pick her up. All thoughts of throwing food are long forgotten, and she actually sits there like a perfect angel while Liam gets the baby wipes and cleans all the food off her.

"Son of a bitch," I mutter, although why I'm whispering is a mystery to me. Hallie clearly has something better to do now than throw crap at us.

"Is there a reason why three fully grown adults are hiding behind the kitchen counter covered in bananas?" Liam asks sarcastically while picking Hallie up out of her high chair. He walks into the adjoining dining room, and places her in her playpen, surrounded by her toys. Hallie rolls over and starts playing with the toys around her.

We slowly stand up, and I can't help the sarcastic response I give Liam. "Well, we were going to have a dirty orgy, covered in food, but then Hallie and you interrupted us. Guess we will have to do it another time." What can I say, I'm jealous. I hate how good Liam is with Hallie. More than that, I hate how good she is for Liam. She looks at him like he literally hung the moon, and I just wish she looked at me like that.

"Get this place cleaned up, Kellan. We are leaving in twenty minutes." Liam stomps, clearly not finding my orgy reference very funny.

"I will get everything cleaned up once you leave. Go and get changed, I will make some toast for everyone. It will be ready when you come back down. Go." Mia points between Bree and me before pointing to the stairs. She then instructs Liam to play with Hallie while she makes us all some toast. I'm pleased she offered to make food. I'm not sure I can face today on an empty stomach.

My stomach flips at the thought of getting to interrogate Kyle. This is not normally what I do, normally I stay behind the screens, but not this time. This time I want—no, I need—answers. More than that, I need to know that this asshole will no longer have power over Mia, that he will never be the cause of another nightmare ever again.

The car ride to the warehouse seems to take forever. Liam's driving, with Bree sitting next to him. They're talking—or should I say arguing—about how this is going to go down. Liam wants to interrogate, while making sure the guy walks away with all his limbs intact and without starting a war. Bree, on the other hand, is shrouded in blood lust, and she's brought her favourite carving knife.

It's the knife Jimmy bought her as a teen, and it's the same knife I plan on using to kill him, when the time is right after Paddy finishes interrogating him. Apparently, Vernon was being bankrolled by someone, but Jimmy's yet to divulge who. He's also sure that even in exile, Vernon won't stop his vendetta. He will always be our enemy, and we need to watch our backs. In the meantime, we need to find this bankroller. But for me to find him, I need to have a rough idea of where to start, if not I'm literally looking for a needle in a haystack, without even being sure I'm in the right haystack. Until Jimmy gives us more, we're fucked.

Bree has made it clear that if Paddy doesn't get answers soon, she will step in and interrogate him herself. Paddy and Liam don't want her to, they think she will get too emotional and kill him without meaning to. Or they think it will be too much for her. While Bree may look healed physically, the mental scars are on a whole other level. Bree was betrayed by the person she trusted the most, which is something I can relate to. That betrayal cuts deeper than any knife. Bree went through a great deal of trauma when she was held captive, and she may never get over that experience.

Maybe that's why Bree wants to interrogate Kyle, why she brought the knife that reminds her of that pain. It also reminds her of who she is. She's strong and nobody is exempt from her wrath.

"Rather than continue with this tedious argument, can we all just agree that Kyle is a douchecanoe, and as long as Bree promises not to kill him, she can interrogate him however she wants?" I groan, trying to get them to stop their incessant bickering. It's not like proper arguing, more like being in the car with an old married couple. He's being overprotective, and she is rebelling. They both care about each other so much, it's leading to them squabbling. If they listened to each other, they would realise they both want the same outcome.

"I've already said I won't kill him…unless he deserves it." As soon as Bree adds the last part, I can't help but sigh. I can almost feel Liam rolling his eyes from here.

Liam, despite being a world-class assassin, happens to be one of the most logical, mild-tempered people that I know. If he kills someone, they deserve to be dead. He never rushes in, and needs a mountain of evidence before even considering it, which is what he's doing with Kyle. The Fratacellos are an influential family, and we really don't want to go to war right now.

"Liam, we already know this guy's a pervert who wanted to marry Mia when she was underage. That's good enough information for me. But, I hear what you're saying about not starting a war, I've had the same lecture off Gramps too. I will show restraint, unless he won't listen to us." Bree clearly means what she says, her family—us—are the most important factors to consider in any decision she makes. She won't do anything that poses a risk to us.

"There's no way this guy can be allowed to walk out of here still thinking he's going to marry Mia. We need to make damn sure this guy knows she's off-limits. If you aren't prepared to do that, I will." My voice is snappy, and a lot harsher than I intended, but the fact that Mia even exists to this guy is driving me crazy.

Liam begins to reply, and I'm only half listening as he waffles on about how much we need to follow the rule and be patient. It's a speech I've heard too many times before, and focuses on how reckless and impulsive I am. The more he speaks, the more I drown it out. I'm distracted by my phone buzzing, it's a text from Mia.

MIA

Look at this little angel. All dressed up in her winter coat ready to go to the library.

Attached to the text is a picture of my daughter wearing this massively padded winter romper suit that Bree bought her. This suit is so big and thick she literally looks like she can't bend her limbs. She's in a starfish position, lying on the bed in the picture, and it looks like Mia will have trouble even sitting her up in the pram.

I can't help but laugh. She looks so adorable. Apparently, Liam was in the middle of saying something important and didn't like being interrupted. "Why are you laughing? What did I say that was so funny?" His voice is snappy, but I just ignore him and address Bree.

"Look, Mia just sent me this photo." I hand the phone over to Bree and she starts to laugh too. That just winds up Liam even more, who demands to be included. I show him the photo, but tell him to concentrate on the road too. He quickly glances at it before turning his attention back to driving, although I can see in the rear-view mirror that his facial expressions have changed. He's more relaxed, his brow is no longer furrowed, and he actually appears to be smiling. I know how he feels, she has that effect on me.

I shoot a quick text back to Mia as I listen to Bree talk about how gorgeous she looks.

KELLAN

She looks like a beautiful little marshmallow. Hope you have an amazing time. Thanks for keeping me in the loop.

I really mean it. I'm starting to trust her with my child, but that doesn't mean my irrational fears concerning Hallie have just gone away. I still worry about her, and knowing she's out and about without me or any real protection is killing me. In fact, the idea that Mia doesn't know how to protect herself is now scaring the shit out of me too. Why didn't I teach her about self-defence? Why didn't I make sure she was armed before she left the house with my baby? Probably because normal people don't do that sort of thing.

There's a war going on inside my head. I want to protect them both, to know they are safe. But I also know it's not normal to arm your nanny. Besides, I think if I try, she may run, and that's the last fucking thing I want.

"Should we have armed Mia, or at least taught her to fight? I don't know why it didn't occur to me until now, but I can't have my girls going off on their own unprotected. I need to make sure they are okay. Fuck! Why didn't I think of this before now?" I can't sit still. All my muscles are starting to coil as fear and anxiety grips hold of my body. I can feel myself rocking back and forward, my right leg jiggling up and down of its own accord. I'm very aware I look like a crazy person. But the more I think about how much danger they could be in, the more it terrifies me. My breathing speeds up until I'm panting, feeling like I can't quite get enough oxygen into my lungs. I gasp for air and my heart races as a fine layer of sweat covers my body. Fuck!

"Breathe, Kellan," shouts Liam from the driver's seat of the car.

I feel someone touch my hand, but my vision is starting to blur so I can't work out who it is. "Kellan, listen to me. Take my hand and listen to my voice. You need to slow your breathing down. Mia and Hallie are safe, I promise you. Can you hear what I'm saying? They are safe." Despite the loud ringing in my ears, I hear Bree say the words *they are safe,* and that's all I need to hear.

I try to get control of my breathing, listening fully to Bree as she talks me out of the full-blown panic attack. I don't know what came over me, I just started thinking of all the worst-case scenarios and my world felt like it was caving in. I'm going to subtly swerve around the fact that I called them *my* girls. I have no idea where that came from, and I'm definitely choosing not to think about it.

A blush spreads across my cheeks as the car grinds to a halt in front of the warehouse. Bree is still holding my hand but hasn't said a word. She's just giving me time to calm down. Embarrassment consumes me as I think about Bree knowing I have an anxiety disorder. Liam obviously knows, he's been dealing with my freak-outs for as long as I can remember. I hate feeling anxious, and I hate the panic attacks even more. They've become a lot worse since Hallie was born. I realise my thoughts are irrational, but that doesn't mean I can stop them.

"Bro, are you feeling okay now?" Liam asks, as he turns in the driver's seat to face me.

I give him a small nod and Bree squeezes my hand. I mumble an apology for overreacting and as Bree gives me a little laugh, I look up in confusion. She might not know how anxiety works, but surely she knows not to laugh at a man in crisis. I fix her an angry glare, my eyebrows furrow in a silent question, asking her what is so funny.

"I'm not laughing at you, Kel. I'm laughing because if you think you're overreacting or being paranoid, I must be even worse. I hired four plainclothes bodyguards who are fully trained and fully armed just for them. If Mia and Hallie even step foot outside the house, they will be monitored at all times. Mia doesn't know, as she probably would say she doesn't need or want them. So I figured doing it in secret's the safest way to keep everyone happy, and more importantly, safe."

Shit, now I feel like a proper asshole for yelling at her. "Thank you. You have no idea how much this means to me," I exclaim, squeezing Bree's hand and giving her a very genuine smile that I hope speaks volumes.

"Hallie means the world to me, Kel, and Mia is my best friend. Of course I'm going to make sure they are protected. I have no idea who our enemies are at the moment. Things have been too...I'm going to say stable because using the Q word would be a death sentence," Bree whispers just as Kian knocks on the passenger-side window.

We get out of the car and welcome Kian, but I'm keen to get things started. "I'm assuming Kyle is ready for us?"

With a nod of her head, Bree begins walking towards the warehouse, and we all follow as Kian explains the set-up. "Yeah, I have him. He thinks he's here for his loyalty review, which to be fair is sort of what we are doing. To make him think we are doing things right, I have the room set up like a conference room. You should note, he has four guards with him, but I have them sat in the waiting room. I have guns aimed at them, all I need is the word from you and no help will be coming for him. I have a full team set up around the perimeter and inside, as always, but you won't have to worry about them. I will be liaising with them. Just so you know, Kyle's been here waiting for around an hour. I figured he could stew a little, but it's got him all riled up, so apologies for that."

"You don't have to apologise to me. If he's angry and irritable, that will give me an easy opening to shoot him in the head," I reply before Kian even gets a chance to continue speaking.

Liam groans, drawing all our attention to him, and we freeze just outside the warehouse's main door. "There will be no shooting. In fact, maybe you should stay in the other room with the security team and monitor things from there."

I glance up towards Liam, catching Bree's eye as I do, and I watch as she grits her teeth and her eyes narrow. She appears to be wincing, and she should. Her fiancé just walked into a steaming pile of bullshit. "Are you fucking kidding me? There's no way you are benching me. I'll sit there and behave while you put on this fucking ridiculous show, but if I suspect, even for a moment, that he's not willing to let Mia go, I will end him." I grind each word out, letting him know I'm very fucking serious. I may not be a fighter, and I'm certainly not the first to run into a fucking gun fight, but on this occasion, I want to be... No, scratch that, I need to be!

"Kellan," Liam groans, but before he has a chance to say anything further, Bree puts on her boss voice and takes over the situation.

"Enough, both of you. Kellan, you can be in the room, but you will not go rogue. Nobody in that room cares for Mia as much as I do, so you are going to have to trust that I will make the right decision. And if the time comes that he needs shooting, you will get the first offering. Now, Liam, I have listened to everything you've said, because I know you're only trying to do what's best for me, but this is about what's best for the business. Of course I don't want another war, but there will be more wars. There always is in this business. But, the one thing that means more to me than anything is the people I love. Mia is one of those people, she is family. I would start a war for any family member. So, you have to trust I can do this, but you also have to stop being afraid for me."

Bree gently strokes his cheek and I watch as my hard-ass friend melts into a puddle beneath her fingertips. I'm so stupid for not realising that's what this was about with him. I thought he didn't want to start a war, since we've only just got out of one battle and aren't ready for another yet. I should have known this is more about Bree and keeping her safe.

Just a couple of months ago, he was getting ready for the happiest day of his life, and it was all ruined. They may not have started in a conventional way, but there's no denying how much he loves Bree. Until that day, I'd never seen him be afraid of anything, but he was scared of losing the woman he loves. Growing up, I was terrified by the slightest of things, but Liam never made me feel stupid. He would just sit with me and give me some of his strength. Now it's my turn to help him.

"We will do everything to avoid a war. Now, can we go inside cos I swear my left bollock is starting to freeze to death," I joke, and thankfully Liam starts to smile. Pleased the attention is no longer on him.

Kian jumps in then with his cocky smirk. "What, just your left bollock? Why is your right one okay?"

"Because your mum's holding it, keeping it warm for me." It was supposed to be a joke, but as that dimpled smile falls off his face, I realise I've crossed a line. I don't know anything about this kid, and I, of all people, know you shouldn't pull mum jokes unless you are sure they will be well received.

As soon as he catches us staring, he schools his face, that grin returning, only this time the smile doesn't quite reach his eyes. "Joke's on you, my mum's dead. So, if her hand is on your ball, it's probably frozen to death already." His voice sounds jovial, but I can hear the edge there. Hell, I've used that tone myself. When it's easier to joke about your pain than face it. I know Liam has been there too. And given Bree was just nearly killed on the instruction of her father, we all know what it's like to be angry and resentful over your family situation.

Fuck, until this moment, I hadn't quite realised we're all so messed up by our parents, or lack of in some cases.

"Shall we go in?" Bree says, as she gestures to the door, slicing through the awkward silence that's begun to descend.

Walking into the warehouse, I recognise some of it, but there are a lot of rooms darting off the main corridor that I've never been in. This place is a maze. We pass a couple of doors; one is where we had the big meeting the other week, the other I know they use for generally torturing people. I also recognise the main security room, as I've been in there a few times. There are some rooms set up like normal interrogation rooms and some jail type rooms, one of which will be housing Jimmy, amongst others. As for what the other rooms hold, I've no idea.

We follow Kian until he stops in front of a room labelled *Boardroom*, which seems a little suspicious given it's the only door with a label on it. Either this Kyle guy really is an idiot, or he knows he's being played and can't do anything about it.

As Kian throws the door open, and we all pile into the room, a tall man with broad shoulders is pacing on the opposite side of the room. It really is set up like a boardroom, with a large oval wooden table taking up most of the room. There are four chairs on one side of the table, and one opposite. There's a carafe filled with water on our side of the table, alongside four upside down cups. At the other end, there looks to be a plastic cup filled with water. Obviously an attempt to make sure he doesn't have any kind of weapon available to him, which is why there's no glass in the room, just plastic cups.

Looking over at the man who stops his pacing as soon as we enter the room, I'm shocked to see he's better-looking than I was expecting. I don't know why but I had built him up in my head as a loser. Someone who offers to marry a teenage girl, he must only be doing that because he isn't capable of getting girls the old-fashioned way. Obviously that isn't true. This guy is tall with broad shoulders, and his black shirt is stretched tight across his muscular chest. His clipped short brown hair, and matching beard are all perfectly manicured, and he looks like one of those guys who takes a lot of pride in his appearance. He looks smart in his perfectly pressed suit, and as I round the table, I notice the light glistening off his overly polished shoes. I hate this douchecanoe even more now!

"Miss O'Keenan, or should I call you Mrs. Doughty, how lovely to meet you," Kyle addresses Bree with his arm outstretched as he walks towards us.

He doesn't get far before both Kian and Liam fix him with the same stare, reminding him that he shouldn't get too close without Bree's permission. She doesn't move, or give him permission. Instead, she leans forward with her hand outstretched just enough so that Kyle could reach her if he leans forward. Their hands clasped together for only a few seconds, but I still hate that we're pretending to be nice to this guy.

Bree takes her seat, and we all follow, but it's not until Kyle takes his seat that Bree begins to talk. "We're not technically married yet, which is good since we have never really talked about what my name will be. So, for now, we can stick with Miss O'Keenan. Although, I suspect I will change it to O'Keenan-Doughty," Bree muses, and I catch Liam's cocky grin.

"That suits you, Miss O'Keenan. I hope you don't mind me asking this, or see it as me speaking out of turn, but your assistant over there said you wanted to discuss my loyalty to your family. Shouldn't that be a conversation for you to have with my father, since he still runs my family? I'm just in the background learning the ropes," Kyle explains, and Bree looks towards Liam for answers. Luckily, he seems to have them.

"We know your father is the current ruler of the Fratacello family, and we will be having a conversation with him at a later date, but we're more concerned with the future. Your father cannot lead forever, and he's made it abundantly clear that you will be taking over. So, we've brought you here to vet how good a decision that is. If we decide to continue doing business with your family, we have to know it's a long-term investment. As I'm sure you are aware, there are plenty of loyal families ready and willing to step into your place. We need to know that when you step up to the mark, you aren't going to suddenly shift loyalties or fuck us over in any way." As Liam speaks, I notice Kyle appears to be gritting his teeth, as his nose twitches in disgust. It's almost like he is happy to talk to Bree, as she's the leader, but talking to anyone else is below him. Kyle's starting to show his true colours, and I'm suddenly enjoying this a little more. I suspect if we give him the tiniest bit of rope, he's going to hang himself with it. As I cast glances to the people sitting beside me, I can tell they all see it too.

"So, what are you saying? That if I don't pledge my loyalty to you today, my family will lose the deals we currently have with you?" Kyle asks, but before anyone gets the chance to reply, he continues to speak. Only this time, his face is starting to tinge red with anger and I can see him balling his hands into fists. "I don't think you realise how powerful my family is, or the reach we have. Even if we part ways with you, our connections are still strong enough that we could continue operating and ruling the north." Kyle's brow furrows and his face transforms into a scowl. Clearly, he doesn't like being challenged, but neither does Bree.

"Kyle, let me be very clear when I say this. I may rule London predominantly, but we all know my reach extends to the whole of the UK. If I cut ties with you, I will ensure you and your entire family are blacklisted. Nobody will deal with you, or sell for you, in the entire country. Don't even bother testing to see if I'm that powerful, I am. So, do you want to challenge me? Do you want to see what I am capable of?" Bree's voice is confident and strong. She doesn't shout or get angry, but the unwavering determination in her voice, and the harsh tone she uses, almost makes it chilling. This is why such a small girl has gained the support of nearly every male-run criminal enterprise she's ever dealt with. Bree is always underestimated at first, but she never fails to show them what she is capable of.

Kyle appears visibly shocked by Bree's comments, and he holds his arms out indicating caution. "There will be no need for that, Miss O'Keenan. My family has, and always will be, loyal to you." He sounds like he is just reciting the party line through gritted teeth.

"That's good to hear. Now, let's find out a little bit more about you, shall we?" Bree continues, ignoring the fact that he's obviously talking rubbish. We already know Kyle isn't loyal, but his father is.

"I'm an open book, ask away." Kyle's voice has a cocky edge as he reaches out to the cup of water in front of him and takes a large gulp.

"That's good to know. So, are you married?" Bree asks, making it sound as though she's asking the most boring question she can think of.

"No, I'm not, but I am engaged." I clench my fists and my jaw, trying to stop myself from laying into this guy. Knowing he's thinking about Mia while he talks is enough to make me want to kill him.

"That's so great, who is the lucky lady?" Bree asks, as I take a gulp of my own water, desperately trying to calm my nerves. It feels like a million ants are crawling underneath my skin, and I want to scratch at them. As all eyes draw to me, I realise I'm squirming around in my seat.

Kyle looks down his nose at me as his eyes zero in on mine. He just has one of those rich, posh boy faces that you can't help but want to punch. His reply to Bree sounds forced. "You don't know her. She isn't part of our world."

"Does she have anything to do with the marriage licence you requested a few years ago?" I ask, and his dark eyes flick straight over to me. If looks could kill, I would be dead now.

"How do you know about that?" he snaps, not able to control his emotions anymore.

"It's our job to know everything about you. We have world-class hackers that work for us, and it's their responsibility to assess anyone and everyone that is part of our business. There's a lot at stake in our world, and we can't have it going all to shit because of some girl you fell for," Liam steps in to explain, as he places his hand on my knee under the table, squeezing slightly. It's his subtle way of telling me to calm down. But the more I think about this piss-poor excuse for a human touching Mia, the more I want to slaughter him.

"It is the same girl. Her father and I struck a deal a few years ago. He promised me his daughter's hand in marriage, in exchange for my family's loyalty."

I look over at my friends, wondering which one of us should speak next. The conversation has flown naturally up until now, but with the mention of Mia's father being involved, it's like all the air has been sucked out of the room, and we all look to Bree for guidance. But instead of replying, she grabs her cup of water and begins to take a few small sips. It feels like it is taking her forever, and the silence is deafening.

"I don't often discuss this, but our marriage is derived from one of convenience, but it was something we chose. I wasn't told who to marry by my father. So, I'm not all too happy about arranged marriages happening in my territory."

With a scowl on his face, Kyle is quick to reply. "Believe me, Mia wants this wedding just as much as I do. We have been engaged for a long time."

"That's not what I heard," Kian chips in, his face not wavering from his usual cheeky dimpled smile. It's enough to wind anyone up, and given the growl leaving Kyle's mouth, he's unhappy too.

"What is that supposed to mean?"

"Well...I mean, I've seen the marriage certificate that was requested five years ago, and that would have made your bride-to-be just fifteen at the time. Yet, we are five years down the line, and you still aren't married. I heard that you aren't even in touch with Mia anymore," Kian explains, trying to sound as though he has no idea what he's talking about, just that he's relaying information he's heard. He plays his part well. He's one of those people that people underestimate because of his boy band good looks, and dimpled smile, he doesn't look like a threat. They couldn't be more wrong. Kyle has fallen for Kian's trap, hook, line, and sinker. He doesn't even realise he is being played.

"That's not true. Mia has had some time away from the family to go to college and get her degree, but now that's over, she will be moving back home to be with me. The fact that she was only fifteen when we first agreed to get married is irrelevant. We planned to marry after she turned sixteen, which, with her father's permission, is legal, but we decided to wait for her to finish school." Kyle's words are short and sharp, the defensive tone in his voice now plain for all to see. Kian doesn't hesitate as he winds him up further.

"So, she didn't leave you and run away then?"

Kyle's cheeks flush red as his dark eyes glare at Kian. Running his fingers through his greasy-looking dark hair, he snaps back. "Who told you that? She didn't run away. We let her go, but she knows she's coming back to me so we can be married. Her father has assured me of that, and he's not someone who should be trifled with."

I wait for Bree to speak, but she doesn't. As I look over at her, I notice she appears frozen at the mention of Mia's father. Who the fuck is this guy? Why can't I remember his name? Fuck, I'm starting to regret not digging deep into Mia's past.

"Look, it's irrelevant who Mia's father is. She will not be marrying you," says Liam, as he looks over at Bree, concern moulding his facial features, as he reaches out and takes her hand in his. That's enough to snap her out of her stupor, just in time, too, because Kyle doesn't seem to like the way the conversation is going.

"No offence to you, Miss O'Keenan, but my loyalty to your family doesn't extend that far. You have no right to say who I can and who I can't marry." His voice is raised far more than it should be, and the tension begins to crackle away in the air around us.

I feel the phone in my hand buzzing, and as discreetly as I can, I read the text from Kian. Looking up at him, he gives me a small wink, and I can already tell I'm not going to like this.

KIAN

Play along. This is the best way to get the info out of him, and get him away from Mia. It will put a target on your back, but I've got you.

Oh fuck, what is this crazy asshole up to now?

"Actually, we do have a right. The reason we have brought this up is because Mia is no longer available, therefore her father should never have promised her to you. She's already living with another man," Kian explains, a lot more fucking smugly than was probably necessary, but I have to admit, I'm enjoying the look of disgust and anger rippling across Kyle's face.

"What the fuck? How do you know she's with another man?" His face is now a burgundy colour, and his hand is shaking uncontrollably. The last of his control is quickly slipping away.

Liam is shaking his head, making his feelings on this perfectly clear, but Kian ignores him, and flicks his eyes to Bree. She looks to Liam first and then to me, and when I give her a slight nod, I see the sharp intake of breath before she starts to speak. "Mia is my best friend. So, I know. She and her boyfriend live with me, which means they are both under my protection. Even though you are aligned with me, and therefore have my support, let me be very clear when I say, they are family. I will always back them first before anyone else. So, as far as I'm concerned, this discussion is over."

Kyle obviously has a different idea, as he pushes himself up from the table so roughly that the chair flies backwards. Kian's hand automatically travels to the gun that I know he has holstered to his side, but Bree reaches her hand over, indicating for Kian to stop. We just wait and watch as Kyle paces like a mad man, his hands scraping through his greasy hair.

"I don't believe you. I only spoke to her father a couple of days ago and he said nothing," Kyle spits, as he continues to pace at the opposite end of the table.

Kian, obviously trying to rile him up even more, leans backwards in his chair like he's the most relaxed in the world, which could be true for this cocky fucker. He's so relaxed he's almost horizontal. "Her father obviously doesn't know shit. He hasn't seen her for years. She's very loved up, isn't that right, Kellan?"

All eyes are on me, and I can see Liam out of the corner of my eye shaking his head and giving Kian his best death stare. I don't even need to look at Kyle to know he, too, is staring at me, he even stops pacing while he takes me in. I don't bother looking at him, instead I look at Bree. I don't want to do anything that will cause more trouble in this business. But, at the same time, I hate the idea that this fucker thinks he can stake a claim against Mia, particularly without her consent.

Bree gives me a small smile, and I know she's telling me that it's up to me. It's my choice whether I play along with Kian or not, my risk to take. But the thing is, it's not even something I really have to think about. It may have been Kian's plan, but I was on board instantly. Anything to show this guy we mean business.

"Yes, that's right. Mia's with me, we live together, and I have no intention of letting her go. So, you should forget all about whatever her father promised you," I say, my voice holding a confidence I didn't know I had. Although I try not to show it, my heart is racing, my palms are sweaty, and I'm having to mentally remind myself to breathe. I'm not scared, I just don't like these kinds of confrontations, the ones where you have no idea what the outcome will be. They make me anxious as fuck, but with Bree, Liam, and Kian by my side, I know I'm fine.

"You! There's no fucking way my beautiful girl is marrying you. What the fuck do you have to offer her compared to me? You are a nobody," Kyle shouts, and I can see both Liam and Bree getting ready to pounce on my behalf, but I don't let them. I can do this myself.

"I'm not a nobody to Mia. We are a family, and that's the end of this discussion. So, I would strongly advise you to let this go. Make sure you delete Mia's number. I'm deadly fucking serious when I say this to you, if you make any form of contact with Mia again, they will need to use DNA to identify your body because all other markers will be obliterated. I don't think I can make that any clearer." I hear a chuckle coming from my right, and I look over at Kian who hasn't changed from his laid-back position, only now he is laughing at the ridiculous, shocked expression plastered across Kyle's face.

I reach over to take a sip of my water. It looks like I'm as laid-back as Kian, but I'm fucking not. I need to replace the fluid in my body because I'm sweating in places I didn't know I could sweat from. There's a reason I sit behind a computer screen. I get far too fucking anxious for these types of interactions. I could have walked in and shot him, but mind games are not my thing.

Kyle pulls his phone out of his pocket and starts playing with it. Instantly, that pulls Kian out of his relaxed position. He has his finger pressed to his ear with one hand, while the other is tapping away on his phone. He's obviously warning the security staff that the threat level is rising. For all we know, Kyle could be calling for his security, planning to slaughter us all. What we didn't expect is for him to put the phone on speaker, and as he pulls his chair back up to the table, taking a seat again in front of us, he places the phone on the table as it rings.

After a couple of rings, an older, somewhat familiar, posh British male voice answers, and as soon as I realise where I've heard his voice before, my blood runs cold. "Hello, Whitlock speaking."

I can tell both Liam and Kian have no idea who is on the other end of the phone, but Bree does. Her face isn't giving anything away, but she doesn't look confused like the guys do, or shocked like I do. Of course she knows who Mia's dad is, but does she know who he really is?

"Sorry to bother you, Mr. Whitlock. I'm here with Miss O'Keenan and some of her associates. One of them is claiming that he and your daughter, Mia, are an item. I was very much hoping you would correct them and kindly confirm that I indeed will be marrying Mia very soon," Kyle explains, although he doesn't sound anywhere near as cocky talking to Whitlock as he did us. You can tell by the little quiver in his voice that he's afraid of Whitlock, and I don't blame him.

"Miss O'Keenan, how lovely to finally get the chance to speak with you. I was sure we would have met sooner, given I had strong ties with your father. I am awfully sorry about that terrible ordeal, but rest assured, my loyalty lies firmly with you now you have taken over as leader," Whitlock replies, directing his attention to Bree in the poshest voice I've ever heard.

We both look towards Bree, waiting for her to speak. She appears to be taking several deep breaths, her eyes scrunched together as she focuses on her breathing. I don't know if she's trying to calm herself because she's nervous, or angry. But, whatever the reason, when she opens her eyes, there's a fire there that matches her bright red hair. "Nice to speak to you too, Mr. Whitlock. Your loyalty is much appreciated. We have met before on several occasions, but I would only have been present as either Mia's friend, or my father's daughter, so it makes sense you wouldn't remember." Bree sounds pissed, and Liam grips hold of her hand tightly, no doubt giving her some of his strength. I just wish I could tell her how bad this is, how much of a bad guy this man really is.

"Yes, well...it's still been a long time. Look, I know my Mia is living with you. I'm assuming this boyfriend that Kyle is speaking about is your other lodger, Mr. Kellan Burke?" he asks, using my full name to show us just how much he truly knows about us.

"Yes, that's correct," Bree replies quickly, her voice not even wavering in the slightest. There would be no point arguing because I'm the only person other than Liam living at the address. Besides, we already told Kyle it was me, he would have told him even if Bree kept quiet.

"If that's the case then I'm going to have to insist Mia come home at once. I was under the impression she moved in to work for Mr. Burke as his nanny, not to keep his bed warm. Mia was promised to Kyle years ago, it was a business deal made long ago, and she agreed to it. I gave her time to complete her studies and gain work experience, but apparently she's no longer doing that." Mortimer no longer sounds as posh as he did before, instead venom drips from his tongue as he talks about Mia letting him down and jumping into bed with me.

I already know I shouldn't do it, but I can't seem to stop myself. My voice is harsh as I snap. "No way. There is no fucking way she's moving out or marrying this cuntwaffle. Mia is staying with me, and this is not open for discussion." My voice echoes loudly around the warehouse, as the phone crackles, waiting for him to speak. Silence fills the air, and the tension starts to feel almost claustrophobic.

I look to my right and Kian is back to his relaxed posture and cheesy grin, like me snapping at Whitlock is the most entertainment he's seen in a long time. Bree and Liam, on the other hand, both look nervous as they hold each other's hand and look across at me. Kyle looks furious. His face is turning purple and he's actually biting his lip to stop himself from speaking. We all know that if he were to interrupt Whitlock after he rang him for help, it would be suicide. So he's keeping quiet, and we're all staring at the phone, just waiting for something to be said.

"Do not use that kind of language in front of me. I don't care what *fun* you think you are having with my daughter, it ends now. She has commitments," Whitlock finally snaps, and I can hear the fury lacing his words. I would love to see what his face looks like right now.

I get ready to reply, but before I can, Bree interrupts me. "Mr. Whitlock, I'm sorry you feel this way about Mia and Kellan's relationship. I completely understand why you would be upset if she made a commitment. But, as is my understanding, you made a commitment too. You promised Mia the time to finish her qualification, did you not?"

"Yes, bu—"

Before Whitlock can finish his sentence, Bree interrupts him. "Well, Mia is in her final module. They anticipate she has around two to three months left, and then she will graduate. Surely you are honourable enough to allow her the time you promised her." Bree isn't just challenging him, she is challenging his honour, which, for a man like Whitlock, is everything.

"Of course I'm honourable enough to do that. But let me make this very clear for all parties involved, Miss O'Keenan, and that means you, Mr. Burke. When Mia's school work is finished, and she graduates from university, there will be no more excuses. She will return home and do her duty to this family by marrying Mr. Fratacello, as agreed. Do I make myself perfectly clear?" I'm not sure who he is addressing the most, but as I see the smug smile spread across Kyle's slimy face, I want to scream and shout. I want to tell them all they can fuck off. I want to tell him that she is *my* Mia, and if he calls her his ever again I will cut his bollocks off with gardening shears.

But, instead, I obey the silent gesture Bree is giving me. Her head is shaking vigorously and it couldn't be any clearer that she is telling me not to respond. So I concentrate on breathing, hoping to regain some control over my anger, as Bree replies. "I completely understand. If that is the agreement that Mia made, then when the time comes she will need to honour that. But, until then, she can do as she pleases. And I hope I don't have to remind you all that she is under my protection. If either of you attempt to make contact before the agreed time, you will have me to answer to. I'm only saying this so that it's acknowledged. I trust you are both clever enough to know not to mess with me and my people." As Bree speaks it sends shivers down my spine, the threat in her voice plain as day.

Kyle puts his fist into his mouth to prevent himself from speaking. He was obviously raised well, and is honouring the hierarchy rules that have been drilled into him regarding being around high society members. Bree may not be high society, but she is the top of the totem pole with regards to power, and everyone knows it.

Whitlock replies. "Of course, Mia will receive no trouble from me. I trust Mr. Fratacello will agree to this too. For me, business will always come first. As I said at the beginning of this call, it's important that I maintain a good working relationship with you, Miss O'Keenan. As far as I'm concerned, this is a family business that you should never have been dragged into and I can only apologise for that. Thank you for looking after Mia, but please remind her when you speak to her of the terms of our arrangement. She must return at the end of her training, and she must marry Kyle. These things are non-negotiable, no matter how much Mr. Burke may wish they were."

Bree holds her arm out, palm facing me, the typical stop hand gesture. It's her way of telling me not to say a word, and so I don't, despite really fucking wanting to.

"Will do. Glad we got that all sorted. I will be in touch soon, Mr. Whitlock. I have you on my list of people to discuss the business side of things with. But for now I will say goodbye, and, Kian, if you can escort Mr. Fratacello out, as I believe we are done speaking to him. That is all."

With that, Bree reaches over the table, her ass leaving the seat, so she can reach Kyle's phone to end the call. She then hands the phone to Kian, who is now by Kyle's side.

"Wait," Kyle shouts as Kian slides the phone into the pocket of Kyle's suit jacket. "What about the loyalty test?"

Kian chuckles and Kyle shoots him an evil grin that doesn't hold any power now. After we watch him quivering in his boots at the mere sound of Whitlock's voice, Kyle has no power over us, not that he had much to start with. Liam replies to Kyle's question. "As far as we're concerned, your true loyalty test starts now. We are instructing you to cut all contact with Mia. You will not talk to her, text her, or threaten her in any way. If you do, we will kill you." Liam stands, Bree's hand in his, and I follow suit.

"But, you heard Mr. Whitlock. I will marry Mia."

"We did hear that, but until that time comes, you will leave her alone. If you make contact with her in any way, you will be responsible for forfeiting the arrangement, and Whitlock will be informed of that. Do we make ourselves clear on this?" Liam's voice takes on that deep, gravelly threatening tone that I know he hates to use. But there's no denying it's fucking effective. Kyle looks like he's about to piss his pants.

"I understand," Kyle says, and before he has a chance to say anything more, Kian grabs hold of the side of his arm and pulls him out of the room, slamming the door behind him.

Bree, Liam, and I stand there, staring at each other, not really knowing what to say. But the tension is too much for me, so I speak first. "You knew Whitlock was Mia's father, why didn't you tell me?" I ask Bree.

"Because I didn't know you would even know or care about Whitlock and who he is. He was one of my father's many money men. He's like a gazillionaire, and is obsessed with becoming the most popular rich kid on the playground, but that's about it. He wants his family name, his legacy to live on, which is why he wants Mia to marry into a good family. Why are you looking at me like that?" Bree asks, as my face morphs into confusion. Does she honestly not know who Whitlock really is?

"Bree, Whitlock isn't just a money man. He's a big player, if not the top player. He has his fingers in a lot of pies, and he plays both sides off against each other. He's a master manipulator, who wants a hell of a lot more than power. He thinks he's God. His little Black Book is basically a who's who of the criminal underground, and he knows it all. But, putting all the power play bullshit to one side, he's also a fucking disgusting excuse for a human being. He is into kids, and makes a lot of money buying and selling them as sex slaves. He's the worst type of person, and now I know Mia grew up with him as a father, it tells me far more than I ever wanted to know. If you get into bed with this asshole, Bree, I promise you will regret it. He wouldn't know loyalty if it bit him in the ass," I explain, and I can see the colour draining from both Bree's and Liam's faces. I know they are putting together the pieces the same way I am.

Obviously I won't know for sure unless I talk directly with Mia, but I don't think she could possibly have grown up in his household and not know what he's like. It's bad enough that Whitlock likes children, but the thought he may have abused his own daughter causes my stomach to flip as nausea grips hold of me. I don't want to believe it, but I know Mia experienced a trauma she won't talk about. Something so bad she can't even say it aloud. I just never guessed she had been sexually abused by her own father.

No! Do not jump to that assumption. I could be adding two and two together to make five. I could be getting it all wrong. I don't want to push Mia into feeling like she has to talk to me, but for the sake of my own mental health, I have to know the truth. I'm hoping what I'm imagining is the worst-case scenario.

"How the hell do you know all of this? I've heard of a Black Book, but I had no idea it was Whitlock's," Bree asks, musing aloud about the elusive Black Book.

"I know because I have the Black Book. A little over a year ago, I did a job with a woman, she was working for the Celtic Reapers. They wanted the Black Book and tasked her with getting it. We got it, and even though I handed some data over to the Reapers, I didn't give them everything. I couldn't. I didn't want to give them any more power. Which turned out to be a great move, given they were playing me the entire time. She made me think we were a team, until she stole everything I had and left me holding a baby."

"Are you saying..." Bree's words trail off as her eyes widen. Liam's, on the other hand, are narrowed into a glare and he says the word I've tried not to say for the last few months.

"Shayla?" Liam asks, his voice lifting at the end, turning her name into a question, but he already knows the answer. He lived it with me.

"Yes. Shayla. The woman who gave birth to Hallie before abandoning her at five hours old and taking everything I owned. If I never hear that bitch's name again, I will die a happy man. I will give you everything I have on the heist we did, and the Black Book. But, if this leads back to her or the Reapers, you have to know I'm out. I don't want my daughter anywhere near her or them. Okay?" I state, trying to hide the shake in my voice.

I hate that I can't say her name without my voice quivering like a little girl. I may not feel anything for her except pure, unadulterated hatred, but I despise that she once had my heart. I'd only ever trusted one person with it, and the whole time her and Whiskey were playing me. She took my heart and stomped all over it. Yeah, I'm bitter and angry, but there's also a small part of me that's grateful. Hallie's the most important person in my world, and without Shayla, she wouldn't exist. Hallie's the only reason Liam and I didn't wipe out the Reapers entirely. One day, when Hallie asks about her mother, I want to know this was all Shayla, that she's the one who walked away. I will be the one to ensure she stays away. Shayla isn't capable of loving anyone else, and I will do whatever I can to protect my girl.

"Okay, we'll have a meeting tomorrow with Kian to go over all this. But I promise you this, Kel, I love Hallie like she's family, because you are my family now. I hate the idea that anyone wouldn't want that gorgeous little girl, so I can promise you, no matter what happens, Shayla will not come back into our lives. Now, let's go home, shall we?" Bree says everything I want to hear, and I can't help but smile. I see her as family too.

Mia

I've had such an amazing day playing with Hallie, and I know it is, but it really doesn't feel like a job. It's just like hanging out with a very bossy friend, who can barely speak and loves to throw food at my head. The more time I spend with Hallie, the more I get to know her and her quirky traits. I know which cry is because she's hungry, and which means she needs a nappy change. The more I look at her, the more I see Kellan. She has his eyes, and her cute button nose is just like his, but when she smiles, that's not Kellan's smile. That must be from her mum.

Obviously I know Hallie has something missing from her life, but you would never know it. I know I don't know this woman, but I don't think I'll ever get my head around her leaving her baby and Kellan. Why anyone would leave such a gorgeous, sweet, and unbelievably caring person is baffling to me, but to leave Hallie… that's just unimaginable.

Kellan doesn't talk about it, and I've learnt not to bring it up, but that doesn't stop me from wondering. Is Hallie going to grow up to look like her mother? Will Kellan hate the face of his daughter if she grows up to look like her mother? I don't know why I think that, I know Kellan could never dislike anything about Hallie.

Looking over at the clock, I'm shocked to find they aren't here. I know they had a big job going on today, and it must be big if they needed Kellan on site. I think maybe that's part of the reason I went out all day. I deliberately didn't want to be stuck at home, worrying about what they could be up to. For other jobs, I've always rested a little easier knowing Kellan is safe behind his computer. This is a feeling I've never experienced before. I'm actually fucking terrified I might lose him, but he shouldn't mean that much to me.

Hallie's laying on her play mat, giggling at the mobile hanging above her head as she repeatedly swats it. The more she giggles, the more it makes me smile. There's something infectious about this little girl…and her dad, for that matter. The doorbell rings and I scoop Hallie into my arms to answer the door. Shuffling her until she's sitting in the crook of my left arm, her legs wrapped around my side while her hand grabs at my hair.

Using my only free hand, I fling the door open with a little more vigour than normal, but Hallie chooses that exact moment to tug at my scalp. I chastise her, which causes her to wrinkle her adorable nose into a frown.

Someone coughs, clearing their throat in an obvious way to get my attention. I look up and take in the woman standing on the other side of the threshold, but I don't recognise her. Her face tries to wrinkle, but it looks like years of Botox abuse has made her skin so paper-thin it barely moves. Her thinning brunette locks are pulled back with a tight clip at the nape of her neck. Her face is covered with far too much make-up and the bright red lipstick she wears makes her lips look thin and pursed. Her nose is pointed and turned up in the air, like she's smelt something really bad. I'm tempted to sniff Hallie's nappy, worried I may have missed something. But, as I take in the woman's tight Gucci suit jacket, silk shirt, and above-the-knee matching skirt, I realise her nose is turned up at me.

Everything about this woman exudes money, from the pearls around her neck, to the fancy manicure on her nails, and the Louis Vuitton heels she is wearing. I know branded clothes when I see them, and I'm painfully reminded that this woman looks exactly like my mum, and how I will be expected to look one day. I hated even thinking about becoming anything like my mother. She's so down-trodden and controlled that she stood by and just watched as her only daughter went through hell. In my opinion, that makes her as bad as my abusers. I was her little girl, and she should have protected me.

She ignored the bruises and the cuts, she ignored the tears and told me to put more make-up on. She had the maid's change the bloody bedsheets, telling them I'd unexpectedly started my period. She covered for him, for all of them, and she watched as her beautiful daughter withered away. So, seeing this woman standing before me, I can already tell she's everything I hate.

Whilst I'm assessing this woman, her gaze roams over me too. She sees my baggy sweatpants, and tight black vest top that's covered in drool, thanks to the beauty on my hip. I'm in my lounging clothes as I didn't expect to see anyone other than my roommates, and they've all seen me looking worse than this. Granted, as this posh snob is judging me, I wish I'd opted to wear a bra, so my boobs wouldn't look like they're trying to burst free from my vest, and I'm sure she can see my nipples pebbling through the thin material.

I don't know why I care. I don't even know this woman, and yet I hate being judged by her. Hallie's squeal as she tugs on another strand of my hair grabs both of our attention.

"Hi, can I help you?" I ask, and her face shifts even further into a scowl.

"Yes, I am here to see my granddaughter and my son. Now, do you want me to stand out here in the cold until I freeze to death, or are you going to find some manners and invite me inside?" she seethes, her words sounding like acid dripping off her tongue.

Fuck, if I didn't like this woman before, I hate her now.

"Well, Kellan actually isn't in at the moment. He didn't tell me that you would be coming. Did you arrange a visit with him?" I ask, mentally chastising Kellan if he forgot to tell me.

"He's my son, I don't need to schedule an appointment with him. Now, kindly move out of the way, I will come in and wait for him. No doubt he will be home very soon." She doesn't even give me time to say a word, she simply begins striding into the house. I don't have time to move for her, so she barges against my baby-free shoulder, as she pushes her way into the house.

She walks down the hallway, her head turning rapidly from side to side, and it becomes painfully obvious this woman has never been here before. As she makes it into the living room, which has Hallie's toys dotted all around the floor, along with her playpen, baby mat, and a little ball pool in the corner of the room that she loves to sit in. Yes, the room looks messy, but to me it's homely and well lived-in. The way this woman looks at the room, her nose upturned and her face scrunched in a mixture of disgust and a scowl, I instantly hate this woman.

I don't know what it is, but there's something inside of me screaming, telling me I need to keep Hallie away from this woman. It may be unfounded, but if it is I will apologise. As the saying goes, it's better to be safe than sorry.

"Well, don't just stand there, young lady. Give me my granddaughter, and make me some tea. What kind of help has my son employed? You should be in a proper uniform. Set better standards than…this." I don't know what's worse, her acid tongue or the way she glares at me like I'm dog shit on the bottom of her shoe.

"I'm not the maid. I'm a family friend who Kellan employed to be his nanny, but I also live here. I don't know you, and I haven't had any kind of heads-up from Kellan telling me you were coming, or that it's okay for you to play with Hallie. So, I apologise if this causes any offence, but my job is to keep her safe. I can get you some tea, and I will call Kellan while I do that. If you would like to have a seat, please do." I try to keep my voice as neutral and polite as I can. This is Kellan's mother, after all, I don't want to offend her any further.

"You may not want to cause offence, but you have. She is my granddaughter, and you are keeping me from her. Don't think I am so naive as to see what is really going on here. If you really were the nanny, you would be in a professional uniform, the house would be spotless, and my granddaughter wouldn't look like she's being raised by wolves. It's clear you have something going on with my son. But, let me make this perfectly clear, young lady, that little girl has had enough women in her life that have let her down and abandoned her. I will not allow my son to be led by his penis on this one. You are not a replacement mother. She needs real parents, people who can care for her properly, and give her everything she needs. We both know that when you grow bored of my son, you will be out of here so fast. I will not allow my granddaughter to be put through that." Her voice gets more and more animated the more she rips into me, and I honestly don't know what to say. This woman has taken one look at me and judged me. No matter how much I argue with her, she will never see reason. I need to leave this for Kellan to deal with.

Clearly my fish-like expression, with my mouth bobbing open and closed while I think about what to say next, is too much for this woman. She rolls her eyes at me and perches on the edge of the sofa, her ass more off it than on. Seriously, she looks like she thinks she'll catch some kind of disease if she sits on it properly.

Looking up at me, before I even get a chance to defend myself, her face becomes stern. "Make yourself useful. Fetch me some tea. Milk, sugar, and in a proper teapot. That is…if you have one," she demands, her voice sounding every bit as snarky as her face looks.

I don't even bother to answer, I just walk over to the kitchen. Sadly, because of the open-plan layout, there's no reprieve from her watchful eye. I quickly place Hallie into her high chair, which we have positioned next to the stools around the kitchen island. I hand her some of her baby biscuits and she immediately shoves far too many in her mouth and begins to chew on them with her gums, squeals of excitement spitting bits of biscuit everywhere.

"Aww, pretty girl. Are you enjoying that?" I coo, as I rush over and fill the kettle.

Hallie's responding shriek tells me everything I need to know, and I ignore the bits of soggy biscuit that flies out of her mouth. She is too sweet, and I can clean up afterwards. Besides, right now I have to find a fucking teapot…and no, I have no idea if we even own one.

I take this opportunity to pull my phone out of my pocket and quickly send a text to Kellan. I can't exactly ring him with his mother right there, and I don't want to freak him out if he's working.

MIA

Hey, do you know what time you will be home?

His response is almost immediate, and I let out the breath I didn't realise I was holding.

KELLAN

We are less than five mins away. Everything okay?

Oh, thank fuck for that. I'm about to text him back when the kettle starts making that whistling noise indicating it's nearly boiled, and I still have no idea where the fucking teapot is. I don't even know if we have a posh cup I can give her. All our mugs are proper mugs, with funny sayings or our favourite characters on. Somehow I don't think this woman will appreciate that. I realise I don't have time to mess about, so I just start opening all the cupboards in the kitchen, even ones I've never bothered to look in before. I can hear her tutting, and can feel her eyes roll from the other side of the room, but I don't care.

Jackpot! There, at the very back of the cupboard, is a full china tea set. It's obvious Bree was either given this as a gift that she's never used, or it was left over from when her grandfather used this house for his holidays. The pretty pastel flower design doesn't exactly scream Bree's or Liam's tastes. Besides, the amount of dust scattered over the surface tells me this has most definitely not been used in a long time. So, I waste no time in getting it clean. Placing the teabags in, I pour in the streaming hot water, and while the tea is brewing I pour some sugar into the matching sugar bowl, and milk into the milk jug. I even dust off the matching tray and place the now clean teacups and saucers on it. I have no idea if this tea service is going to win me any points with Kellan's mum—shit, I didn't even ask her name—but I really hope so. This woman makes me so nervous, I can feel myself sweating in areas I didn't even know were capable of sweating.

Carrying the tray over to the coffee table, I place it down and look over at the woman who I can feel glaring at me. I'm guessing she isn't the sort of woman who pours her own tea, not when there's help like me around to do it for her. Stuck up bitch!

"How do you take your tea, Mrs. Burke…?" I ask, deciding to call her by Kellan's last name, since that's all I know about her. Given the way her eyes glare and her nostrils flare, I really shouldn't have bothered.

"My name is Mrs. Mattherson. I haven't been Mrs. Burke for over twenty years, since Kellan's father was murdered. So, thank you for bringing up that horrific memory. I take my tea with just a dash of milk and two sugars. Are you capable of that?" Her voice is nasally and ripples down my spine, prickling at my nerves. This woman is quite literally driving me mad.

"Erm…I-I didn't know t-that. Sorry. I mean, I knew Kellan's dad had passed away, but I didn't know what your new name was. I didn't know what to call you. Sorry." Fuck, could I sound any more like a bumbling idiot than I do right now?

I distract myself by pouring the tea for her, to her exact specifications, and try to ignore the way my hand shakes as I pick up the teapot. If I don't get control, the tea is going to go all over the place. I take deep breaths, managing to pour the drink successfully, and I hand it over to her. I pour one for myself, and although I would much prefer a coffee, anything to keep my hands busy will do right now.

Placing my cup on the table nearest the free end of the sofa, I run and grab Hallie from her high chair. She has biscuit all over her face and hands, but she looks happy. I don't even think she realised I'd left the room, she's too busy chomping on her biscuits. I grab some wet wipes off the side and start wiping down her face and hands, much to her annoyance. Her squeals are really not helping this whole situation. But, she will have to put up with it for a second because I can't bring her to her snobby grandmother with chewed-up biscuits in her jet-black ringlet hair.

As soon as I've managed to get the majority off her, and she stops shrieking like a banshee, I pick her up and take her through into the living room. I know Mrs. Mattherson has been taking this time to glare at me, and take in the general mess that is the house. But I don't give a shit.

I stare at this woman, wondering what the hell I'm supposed to say to her, and I can see she's doing the same. I pray to whatever deity is listening that she keeps her acid tongue to herself and we can just sit in companionable silence until Kellan gets here. Didn't he say he was only five minutes away? This is the longest fucking five minutes in the history of the world. I take a mouthful of my tea, careful not to get it anywhere near the handsy baby on my lap. Naturally, she tries to reach for it, and I tell her not to because it's hot.

"You do realise she's a baby and has absolutely no concept of what hot or cold is, nor does she understand what is right or wrong? They learn through doing. So, if she were to burn herself, she would know that was bad. Or if you smacked her bum every time she did something wrong, she would learn a lot quicker than this namby-pamby approach you appear to be using." I sit there with my jaw open wide. Did this woman really just advise me that the best way to teach a child is to harm them?

"I'm very aware how old she is, she isn't even one years old yet. But studies have shown that if you talk to them, they can take in your tone and your body language. The kind of punishment you're talking about isn't encouraged, and it's certainly not a method Kellan wishes to adopt. If he did, there's no way I would be working for him," I state firmly, holding Hallie a little closer, my protective nature towards her kicking in at just the thought of her being harmed by someone else.

Her gaze narrows and her glare turns evil. She doesn't like me talking back to her. It's probably not something that people do around her. I can tell she's about to shout at me when the front door bursts open. Kellan and Liam come through the door, into the open-plan room. They are both on edge, looking around for the danger, and that's when I realise I never texted Kellan back. I got so caught up in the teapot crisis. Oops.

"Mia, is everything okay? Is Hallie okay?" Kellan yells before he's fully through the door.

Once they're both standing in the living area, taking in the sight before them, I see them both physically deflate. They obviously built the situation up in their heads and thought we were in danger. When they see Mrs. Matterson, Kellan looks on edge and Liam looks repulsed.

"Mother, what are you doing here? How did you know where to find me?" Kellan asks, before striding towards me, completely ignoring his mother while he speaks.

As soon as he reaches my side, he crouches down and leans forward to give Hallie a kiss on the cheek, before whispering in my ear. "Are you okay? Did she do anything to you?"

I shake my head saying no, letting him know we're both okay, and the last bit of tension leaves his body. Hallie reaches for him, grasping onto his jet-black hair that matches her own and giggles when she manages to get a few strands in her fist. I prise open her hands to free his hair, as his mother answers his question.

"I hired a professional to find you. I needed to know your address for the legal paperwork. Kellan, Hallie is my granddaughter and I wanted to see her," she states, and both Kellan and I look at each other at the mention of a legal document. I can tell by the pain in his eyes, he knows what she's talking about, and I hate the dejected look on his face. How this woman is able to have power over a guy like Kellan truly pisses me off.

Liam is clearly not happy with her, and he snaps at her, anger vibrating from him. "Well, now you've seen her, maybe you could kindly fuck off and we can get on with burning the couch you are sat on. It's hard to get the stench of bitch out of the fabric." Bree comes through to stand by his side. She has her phone in her hand, no doubt letting Kian or security know there's no real danger.

Kellan and I both look at each other and let out small chuckles at Liam's blatant hatred for the woman sitting next to us. Her face ripples in disgust as she glares at Liam, the feeling clearly mutual. "I have always hated you, Liam. You are just like your father, he's a menace too."

"I'm nothing like my father," Liam grinds out, both him and Bree wearing matching angry expressions, though her hand on his seems to calm them both down.

"Mother, you can't come into my house and start insulting my friends...actually, they are my family. So, why don't you say what you came here to say, and then you can be on your way," Kellan states firmly. Although he sounds confident, I can see the hand he's holding on to Hallie's with is shaking slightly. Without thinking, I press my hand over both Kellan's and Hallie's, hoping my touch will be enough to soothe his nerves.

His desperate, lost eyes meet mine, and he looks like a sad little boy being told off by his mother. I want to hold him, to make his pain disappear. His small smile lets me know my touch is helping. I'm hardly an expert when it comes to dealing with shit family members, all I've ever done is run from mine, but I'm happy to help Kellan take a stand.

"Fine, have it your way. I told you before you moved to London how I felt. I don't believe you are capable of looking after this girl on your own. I can give her a much better life than you can ever dream of. I submitted papers to the courts this morning, I'm here to give you your copy. I'm petitioning for full custody, and my case will be heard. Jasper's hired the best family solicitor in the country and we will win. So, save yourself some money and sign the papers now. You can voluntarily hand her over and we won't drag you through a messy court case." With each word that comes out of this evil witch's mouth, the silence in the room becomes heavier. Kellan becomes heavier.

I watch as the beautiful, strong, sarcastic man in front of me shrinks away, looking completely dejected, like he's actually considering giving this bitch what she wants. The problem is, she's just voicing Kellan's worst fears. I've heard his off-the-cuff comments before. He worries he won't ever be enough for Hallie, but you only have to take one look at them together to know they're all each other will ever need.

Kellan doesn't look like he's going to find the words to reply, so I look over at Liam. His face is turning a violent shade of purple, and the fire in his eyes matches Bree's, but I see her silently telling Liam this isn't his fight. I know she thinks this is Kellan's fight, his family, but fuck that. Kellan can do this—and the whole parenting thing—by himself, but that doesn't mean he should have to.

Squeezing Kellan's and Hallie's hands, I give them both a small smile, letting them know I'm here for them. I found a strength I didn't know I had to address Mrs. Mattherson. "How fucking dare you?! You have no idea what kind of an excellent dad Kellan is. Look at her. Look how well she looks, and how happy she looks. That is one hundred percent because of Kellan." I point to Hallie as proof, and thankfully the little beauty gives me a chuckle at just the right time.

Kellan's mother begins to talk, but I hold my hand out to interrupt her, letting her know I haven't finished speaking. "I'm not finished. You may not think Kellan is capable of raising this little girl, but I'm willing to bet that anyone who spends even ten minutes with these two will see what utter bullshit that is. Besides, Kellan may be able to do this alone, but he won't ever have to. He has me, and he has Liam and Bree. When you abandoned him at six years old, he found a new family with the Doughtys. You may not like them, but they have supported your son through everything. They are his family, and if Kellan ever needs any help with Hallie, each one of his brothers and sisters would volunteer. They're his family, and so am I. You've spent ten minutes with me and judged that I'm not good enough to look after Hallie. You think I'm a commoner, but I'm not. I was raised by a mother just like you, and a father who believes money can buy him everything and for a fucking long time, it did. I can assure you, that isn't how you raise a child. The fact that Hallie is happy, beautiful, and filled with love and laughter, that's more than enough."

Oh fuck, I just can't stop talking. I keep telling myself, with each point that I make, that it's okay to stop now. That I've made my point and I'm very fucking done, yet more just keeps on coming. Mrs. Mattherson's eyes are as wide as saucers and her mouth bobs open and closed.

I wait for someone, anyone, else to speak, and that's when all eyes fall on Kellan. I expect him to be glaring at his mother, like he was a moment ago, but instead his gaze is latched onto me, and there's a fire in his crystal blue eyes that lights my soul ablaze.

Liam decides to step in again for Kellan. "I think we can all agree that what Mia said is correct. Kellan can do this alone, but he doesn't have to. He will have every member of the Doughty family by his side, not to mention Bree and all the people that work for her. Did I mention that my fiancée's last name is O'Keenan? Or did Mia tell you her last name? She isn't kidding around when she talks about coming from high society. In fact, she comes from the highest. She's a Whitlock." As soon as the words leave Liam's mouth, shock-filled gasps echo around the room, each for a different reason.

Kellan seems shocked Liam would say that out loud, and Bree seems to agree with him. I, on the other hand, am shocked they know my last name. I didn't tell them, and I trusted that Bree wouldn't ever tell them. As for Mrs. Mattherson, her shocked expression tells me she not only knows exactly who my father is, but she knows to fear him. I guess if ever there was a time to capitalise on having such a fucked-up family, this would be it.

"Do you think that scares me? Your father is pathetic, and that means you are too," she snaps at Liam, before turning to Bree and me. "As for these two, being an O'Keenan or a Whitlock, that means nothing to me. We both know that women are nobody in this line of work. Besides, you've just confirmed that my son is cavorting with known criminals, and is most likely engaging in some severely illegal activities. If you think flashing some surnames will work on me, you are wrong." Her words may say one thing, but the quiver in her voice says something completely different. She is scared, and she has every right to be.

Bree's obviously had enough of standing on the sidelines, or she's worried Liam's anger will get us into more trouble. "Let me be very clear, Mrs. Mattherson. I'm not just any O'Keenan, I am the ruler of our family. Historically, women haven't had positions of power and were content to sit in the shadows of men, I'm not that type of woman, and neither is Mia. When Kellan needs us, we will be there to help him raise Mia, to teach her to be as resilient as we are. I don't know if you think what you're doing is helping, but it isn't. You aren't thinking about what is best for Hallie, you're thinking about yourself, and that's why we won't let this happen. You can hire as many people as you want, but I assure you, you will not win. We will do *whatever* it takes to make sure that doesn't happen. Understand?" Bree's voice remains calm and professional, but the snappy way she delivers the words indicates she's pissed.

Hearing everyone else stick up for him and Hallie, it seems to be enough to pull Kellan out of the trance he is in. He lets go of Hallie's hand and laces our fingers together, giving my palm a gentle squeeze. I'm not sure if it's for reassurance or if he is trying to pull more confidence from me. Either way, I give him a squeeze back to let him know I'm still here, and I always will be.

"I think that answers your question, Mother. No, I will not be handing my child over to you...today or any other day. You're not capable of raising a child, you couldn't even raise me. So no, you will not be going anywhere near Hallie. She has all the family she will ever need right here. You want to go to court, bring it on. Now, get the fuck out of our house," Kellan shouts, as he angrily points towards the door, making his point very clear.

The cheeky girl on my knee squeals with delight at just the right time, making it sound like she's cheering her dad on. You gotta love this beautiful girl.

"How dare yo—"

Before Mrs. Mattherson even gets the chance to finish her sentence, Liam cuts her off. "Well, as lovely as this has been, Marianna, it's time for you to get the fuck out of our house. And next time you decide you want to visit, please do give us a bit of extra warning. That way I can go and boil my head in a bucket of piss, because even that would be more fun than seeing your ugly face. Let me show you to the door," Liam says snarkily, as he jumps up and makes a big, grand gesture towards the door.

Marianna stands, gathering her big designer bag onto her shoulder, before opening it and pulling out a Manila envelope. She places it on the coffee table and heads towards the door. Just when I think she's about to leave quietly, she turns her head and glances at Kellan with a sadistic grin. "I want that baby, and I always get what I want, Kellan. Read the papers. You will see you have already lost."

"That's enough out of you," Liam says, as he places his hand against her back and practically pushes her out of the open-plan living room, into the corridor, and towards the front door. We all listen as the door opens and then slams shut only moments later. Just before Liam pushes her out of the house, we can hear him whispering to her, but it's impossible to understand what he may have said. Although, I'm pretty sure I can guess.

As Liam walks back into the room, the silence is almost deafening. We all seem to be staring at the envelope she left here, and even though we just spoke a good fight, we don't actually know what we're doing. Bree, ever the leader, takes charge.

"Liam and I are going to go and get changed. We will do some research into the best family solicitors we can find, and we will cover it. You don't have to worry about anything, we have got this. Shall we bathe this little lady since we are going up anyway? That way you two can get changed as well. We can meet back down here in like an hour and I will order us some takeout. How does that sound?" Bree asks, and honestly, it sounds amazing, but this is all on Kellan. I don't know if he has any idea how he wants to fight his mother, but he sure as fuck isn't doing it alone.

"Yeah, that sounds perfect, thank you. And you better be talking about Chinese?" Kellan asks. He still hasn't got over the last time Bree was allowed to pick the takeout and she ordered Thai food. Apparently, Kellan is not a lover of spicy foods, nor is his sensitive stomach.

"Don't worry, bro. Your asshole is safe with Chinese," Liam jokes as he reaches down to take Hallie from my knee. Naturally, she reaches up for him, clutching onto him like a spider monkey and squawking with glee. There's no denying he is her favourite person. Well…after her daddy…I think.

As soon as Bree, Liam, and Hallie have left the room, I feel Kellan physically flop next to me. He sits on the floor in front of the sofa with his back against it, but he doesn't drop my hand, our fingers remain laced together. His head falls into his one remaining hand, and I feel him trying to get control of his breathing.

"Come on, let's go and get you showered and changed," I say, as I stand up. If I don't get him moving, he's just going to wallow here in his own self-pity.

As I get to my feet, I gently tug Kellan until he takes the hint and stands up. I lead him in silence up to his room. I don't know when it happens, when the air around us starts to crackle from the chemistry.

One minute it's innocent, and I'm just helping my friend up the stairs, then it all changes. My heart starts to race, and my breathing speeds up as I try desperately to get control over my feelings. I know he can feel how clammy my hands are becoming, but I don't care. It's like our bodies are reacting of their own accord. I can hear his breathing become hitched, and it's clear that his body thinks the same as mine. Blood is rushing to my lady parts, and she's taking the lead.

As soon as I get him into his bedroom, I lead him over to the bed, pushing him to sit down on the edge and reluctantly our hands let go. I stand there, completely frozen over what to do next. If I listen to my pussy, who really fucking wants to run this show, then I should climb into his lap and devour him in every possible way. But, if I listen to my brain, the more logical side, I should walk away and let him have some time alone.

Luckily, Kellan makes the decision for me. He pulls me until my body is standing in between his legs. From his position sitting on the edge of his bed, his head only just reaches my belly. He snakes his arms around me, one hand resting on my lower back, the other on my ass, and he presses his cheek against my stomach. He lets out a deep sigh and it feels like he's holding on for dear life. Then, so quietly I almost miss it, he speaks in a whisper. "Thank you."

I remove my arms from around his neck until I'm cradling his cheeks and I pull his head up so that his gaze meets mine. I could get lost in the crystal blue orbs that are glistening slightly with unshed tears, making them look like a bottomless ocean. I want him to see the fire reflected in mine, so he knows I mean each and every word I'm about to say. "You don't ever have to thank me. What you need to do is believe in yourself. That little girl couldn't ask for a better father, and you sure as shit are not letting that asshole raise her. I was raised by a woman just like her, and I will not let that happen to Hallie."

He looks at me with genuine warmth in his eyes and I can feel it heating my core. Having him so close is driving me fucking crazy. I've never felt like this before. Sex has never been a positive experience for me, nor have I ever found pleasure in it. Over the last couple of years, after a lot of therapy, I tried to experience sex under normal circumstances. I picked a guy up at a bar, I went on dates with a guy I met at the library, I even tried internet dating. But each and every time, sex just felt like a chore. I never got turned on or felt pleasure. My therapist always talked about passion and how I would feel it with the right guy. I laughed and told her that's impossible, and that I'm broken.

Throughout my teens, I trained myself to view sex as something evil, and my brain became hardwired that way. I don't think it's possible to change how my brain's intrinsically wired. My therapist would laugh and tell me one day I would feel it, I guess I owe her an apology now because I do feel. I feel everything with this man, and for the first time ever, I actually want more.

Without even thinking about what I'm doing, I act. Using my hands against his chest, I push him so that he shuffles back on the bed and I crawl until I'm straddling him. My knees on either side of his muscular thighs, and his hands instantly grab my ass, pulling us closer. We both still have our clothes on, but I can feel his hard cock pressing against my sensitive clit, and the sensations overwhelm me. A deep groan rips from my lips and fisting my hands in his hair, I waste no more time, slamming my lips against his.

As soon as his soft lips crash against mine, it's like the electricity in the room starts to coarse straight through our bodies and our movements become frantic. He nibbles on my lower lip, demanding I give his tongue access. I don't hesitate and as I taste his tongue against mine, another soft moan escapes, vibrating into his mouth. My hands clutch desperately at his hair, and I'm sure I must be causing him pain each time I tug on it, but he doesn't seem to care.

One of his hands leaves my ass before travelling up my side, under my T-shirt before scraping along the edge of my boob. Fuck, it's so surreal having the overwhelming urge to have someone touch my most intimate places. Yet it feels so right.

My nipples harden into pebbles, almost like they're anticipating his touch, but something seems to be holding him back. So I decide to show him just how much I want this. I place my hand over his and guide him to my nipple. As he gently rubs his thumb over my nipple, a shudder ripples through my body and I slam my pussy onto his denim-covered cock. It's just enough sensation to cause matching moans of pleasure to escape.

Kellan pulls away, his hand leaving my nipple so that both his hands can firmly grip my hips, preventing me from grinding against him any further.

"Why are you stopping? Please don't stop," I beg, trying not to sound too desperate and failing miserably.

"Mia, believe me when I say I don't want to stop, but—"

"Then don't!" I interrupt him, but as he lays his cheek against mine, I know he has more to say.

"I found out who your father is today. Whitlock…that's your real last name, isn't it?" he asks nervously. Way to fucking kill the mood. I try to shuffle off his knee, to get as far away from this conversation as possible, but he holds on tight, refusing to let me go.

"Let me go, now. That's fucking great news for you, now you know my last name and can do a proper search into my history," I shout, and a grim expression crosses his face as he no doubt remembers that shitshow of an interview back when we first met. It feels like forever ago now, rather than just a couple of months.

"Mia, I promised you I wouldn't search you, and I stick to my word. But that doesn't change the fact that I already knew who your father was. I was involved in a job that included him. I know a lot of his deep, dark secrets, and the kind of man he is. I'm not going to jump to conclusions about what your childhood may have been like. You know you can talk to me whenever you want, or not at all, if that's easier for you. But, if you suffered the way I think you have, then my first time with you isn't going to be a quickie, hoping we don't get interrupted by Bree, Liam, and Hallie. I want to take my time with you, to show you what it can really be like." His words echo to the deepest part of my heart, the part I thought was hollow and incapable of feeling anything. Except, Kellan seems to be working his way in, beneath the walls I built, and setting up home. It's like my heart was made for him.

"What if I just want one moment, right now? One that's based just on how we feel. One moment where I forget about my shitshow of a past, and I just enjoy feeling. Can you do that?" I ask, trying to flutter my eyes enough to stop the tears from falling. I hate that he knows, or he thinks he knows. In truth, there's no way he can truly know the horrors I went through until I tell him, but I know when I do, he'll never look at me the same. I just want one experience, I want to feel just once before it all changes.

"I think I can manage that."

Kellan

Fuck, I've never been more in awe of this woman than I am right now. The way she stood up to my mother, the way she went to bat for me, I've only ever had Liam do that. I've never had anyone in my corner other than him. She did it, even though I know it terrified her. Just like her making the first move now.

I may have only known Mia for a short period of time, but I've come to know her, especially all the things she says without words. The fear on her face she tries to hide as she crawls into my lap. The slight moment of hesitation as she presses her beautiful body against my straining cock. I know the hesitation isn't because she doesn't want this, it's because she really fucking does and that terrifies her.

I'm very aware my timing couldn't have been more sucky. I don't know if I did the right thing by telling her that I know about her dad, and that I'd jumped to conclusions about her past. But, if I'm right, I don't want her to feel she has to be intimate with me before she's ready. I want her to know I'm different from any other sick fucking pervert that's touched her before.

The thought of anyone even placing a hand on my beautiful flower's creamy white skin has my blood boiling. I hate seeing the vulnerability in her eyes, which is why I try to mask my features as much as I can. I don't want her to think I pity her, and thankfully she didn't. Instead, she did one of the hardest things anyone can ever do, she asks me to see beyond what I think I know, to ignore her past, and to just be here in the moment.

If she wants just one moment where she can forget everything, then I think I owe her that. Besides, I don't think I could walk away from her if I wanted to.

Without even a moment's hesitation, I cup my hands under her ass and I lift her off my cock, ignoring the groan that leaves her mouth and the throbbing desire I feel in my jeans at the displeasure of being separated. That doesn't last long, as I lift Mia and roll her so that her body is on the bed, and I'm lying on top of her. My arms press hers above her head and my knees are on either side of her thighs, caging her in. My cock's pressed against her stomach, and he desperately wants to be pulled out so he can indulge his desires, but this isn't for me.

Leaning down, I capture Mia's lips with mine, managing to swallow her startled gasp as my hand slowly slides under her vest top. Her fucking fantastic pebbled nipples are right there, but I take my time. My kisses are slow, deep, but passionate, as my hand explores her silky smooth skin. Every time my finger lightly sweeps over her hard nipple, her back arches and a delicate whimper escapes into my mouth. After a few teasing sweeps, my movements become more deliberate as I tweak her nipples, quickly finding that line between pleasure and pain.

As I continue to play with one of her nipples, I pepper kisses along her jaw and over her neck. As I lay my lips over her pulse, I can feel her heart racing beneath my lips and my heart soars at the idea that I'm able to make Mia feel this good.

Sucking and nibbling on her pulse point as she moans with delight, I quickly sweep my tongue over it, to help dull down the pain.

As I reach her collarbone, I look up into her eyes, so I can see if she has even the slightest bit of hesitation. Her beautiful brown eyes glisten and look hazy—appearing almost love-drunk—and it makes me feel fucking ten feet tall to see her looking so fucking delectable.

Silently asking her with my eyes, I begin pulling her vest up slowly, gently exposing the skin around her belly button piercing. As it reaches just below the swells of her tits, I stop, looking at her for instruction. Her enthusiastic nod in confirmation is all I need, so I rapidly pull the shirt off, throwing it onto my bedroom floor, which is where all her clothes should be whenever she is in this room. Having Mia naked in my bedroom should be a new house rule!

As soon as her round tits are exposed, I'm surprised by how big they are. Her T-shirts clearly do a very good job of hiding the amazing curves she has underneath. I choose to ignore why she would hide her curves, and instead I seal my mouth over her nipple, lapping my tongue over it and sucking. Her squeals of delight let me know she likes what I'm doing, which is always a good start.

I continue alternating my mouth between both nipples, using my fingers to tweak the one not getting all the attention from my lips. With my other free hand, I explore every patch of skin I can find, sweeping over and along the hem of her sweatpants. I test the waters on a couple of occasions by pushing my hand inside them, without ever touching anything other than the smooth skin of her stomach.

Her back arches and her moans become more desperate as she wordlessly pleads with me for more, but there'll be no ambiguity with me.

"Tell me what you want, Flower. Use your words," I growl into her ear.

Her eyes become fiery with lust, and I can see her almost shy away from it, but I won't let her escape. I have her in my clutches and now she can't ever run from me.

"I-I...want...erm, you. Touch me, Kellan."

By the time she finds her voice enough at the end, it's already more than enough for me. Almost as though it has a mind of its own, my hand swoops below the elastic of her pants, going down until I find my intended target. I can't hold back the moan of delight that rips through me when my fingers make contact with the smooth surface of her bare pussy. Not only is my flower bare and ready for me, the naughty vixen isn't wearing any underwear. Just the thought that this sexy little siren was sitting in front of my prim and proper mother, fighting my corner for me, all whilst going commando, it's too much for my poor dick to bear. I can feel him straining, bobbing painfully against the fabric of my boxers, desperate to break free and join in the fun. But, right now it isn't about me. I will have to have a cold shower with my right hand when we are finished, because I have no intention of setting my dick free. I don't have long before Bree and Liam will call us for dinner, and I will need to check on Hallie. So, with the time I do have, I intend to spend it all on her. Showing her how beautiful she is, and how much I can make her body sing.

Gently, I lower my finger so that I'm able to use just the tip to swipe through her slit. An appreciative groan leaves my mouth and echoes around the nipple I have in there, as I take in how wet my flower is for me. I repeat the same gesture again, only this time I use two fingers and use slightly more of my fingers. It's just a quick swipe through her slit, and once I have enough of her juices collected on my fingertips, I carefully pull them out of her pants before holding my fingers between our faces. I make sure to keep eye contact the entire time, so I can see the look on her face when she sees how turned on she really is.

She looks over at my glistening fingers and a war of emotions spread across her face; lust, heat, confusion, and shame. Sadly, the latter seems to win as she averts her gaze and begins to pull her arms over her body in a desperate attempt to cover up her naked body. But, using my free hand, I stop her before she has the chance.

"Don't ever hide from me, Flower. You are gorgeous, and the fact that your tight little pussy gets this wet just for me is all kinds of hot." My voice is deep and raspy, lust evident in the gravelly tone that is all for her. Without taking my eyes off her, I watch her beautiful chocolate eyes widen as I move my fingers into my mouth. I let her see my tongue lick the wetness from my glistening digits. Her eyes start to widen before her pupils dilate with lust, and without even thinking about it, she squirms about beneath me, no doubt desperately trying to quench the thirst that's building. But, I'm here to take care of that.

"You taste so fucking delicious, but that's nowhere near enough for me." As I speak I slowly slide down her body, pressing a trail of kisses down her body as I make my way towards my destination.

As I start to pull down her trousers, she grips onto them tightly, and I look up at her straight away, worried I have gone too far. "You don't have to do this, Kellan. I know I said I don't want to talk about it, and I really fucking don't, but as soon as you lower my trousers, my past will be very fucking evident. So, you don't have to do this." Her voice quivers and I can see the shame as tears begin to fill her eyes. As a rogue one escapes before she can blink it away, I use the pad of my thumb to wipe it from her cheek.

"If you want me to stop, I will. But if you want this as much as I think you do, then I will make you a promise. When I take down your sweatpants, I promise to only see you, not your past. You know you can always say stop with me. Then, another day, another time, when you are ready, we can talk about your past. But not right now." I don't know how to make my voice seem any more sincere, and if she doesn't trust the words, hopefully she can see it in my eyes.

Her gaze deepens, almost like she's trying to see into my soul, but I realise this is her moment. The moment where she decides if she can put her trust in me, or not. I don't envy her. I haven't exactly been open and honest with her about Shayla, although I think she knows enough to put the pieces together. Maybe this is the moment for us both. If Mia, who has clearly been through so much more than I can even imagine, is capable of trust, then I will have to put my trust in her too.

"Are you sure?" she asks, and I can tell she wants this, it's just fear holding her back.

"Pinkie promise," I say, holding my pinkie out for her to shake, like I used to do with Liam growing up. When we were kids this was the equivalent of an unbreakable vow.

At first she looks at my outstretched little finger, before giving a light chuckle and linking her finger with mine. "Make me feel, please," she begs, her voice raspy and guttural.

Fuck, I almost came in my pants just hearing her say that. After pressing my lips against hers for a quick but passionate kiss, I waste no time pulling her sweatpants down. For a second, I allow myself to see what Mia had so desperately been trying to hide, but I quickly school my face and continue like I promised I would. I don't know what I was expecting to see, her skin everywhere else is almost perfect, but as soon as her trousers come down it's a different story.

All the way across her pubic mound, along her inner thighs, and no doubt travelling over her ass cheeks, are scars. Lots of different shapes, sizes, and colours. There are some that look like cuts, others that look like welt marks, and some that are very obviously cigarette burns. Most are a silvery translucent colour, indicating they are old wounds, but some are still in the angry red, purple phase, indicating they didn't happen all that long ago.

How could I have not seen this? I have slept with her when she has been in her underwear, and I've seen her in a bikini. I guess because the majority can be hidden by the way her legs touch, or covered with fabric. I hate seeing it, but I made her a promise and I intend to fucking keep my promise. We will talk about this, but right now I'm going to give her exactly what she asked for. I'm going to make her feel things that I imagine nobody else ever has. That thought alone makes my heart soar. For once, I'm not the villain in this situation, I don't want to be. I don't want to tell this beautiful girl, my beautiful flower, that I can't promise her tomorrow because the truth is, I can and I would. If I was braver, I would give her everything I could.

Things with Shayla were different, I didn't know how I felt or what I wanted. I didn't want to promise her tomorrow as she deserved more than someone who wasn't sure how I felt. I wanted to love her, particularly after she got pregnant, and I would have made it work, but it would have been the wrong choice. I feel more for Mia, from the moment I met her, than I ever have with anyone else. She makes me feel and I want to be better, to be exactly what she needs. It's like I was made just for her and I didn't start really living until I met her. I don't give a shit how soppy I sound, or how many fucking reasons there are not to date Mia, I want her. And now that I've had a taste, I can't ever let her go.

Before Mia has a chance to notice my moment's hesitation, I use one hand to spread open her pretty pink lips, exposing her dripping wet cunt, and with the tip of my tongue, I slowly drag it through her slit, making sure to circle the clit as I reach it. Mia's back arches up off the bed, and I snake my free hand around her body so that I can use my strength to keep her pressed onto the bed.

I don't waste any more time, diving into her pussy with my tongue, feasting on her delicious juices. The more I circle and flick her clit, the more wanton Mia gets. At first she seems almost shy, trying not to make any noise or move, but after I tell her it's okay, and to just listen to how her body feels, she does and it's fucking amazing. Her moans are like music to my ears. Her little pants as she begs me for more has my cock so hard I don't even want to imagine how purple the head must be right now. I do contemplate pulling my cock out. A few strokes with my hand and he will be blowing his load for sure. But, I don't want to scare Mia off. She is like a timid little animal, experiencing life for the first time. I'm worried that if I startle her, she will run and never look back. I need to take my time with her, to cherish her and make her feel more than she ever has before.

I can feel her orgasm building. It's harder to keep her pinned to the bed as her hips continue bucking up to meet the wet edge of my tongue. Gently, I slip a fingertip into her dripping pussy. I'm not even up to the second knuckle and I can already feel how tight she is. Her throaty moan fills the room. "More," she begs, and so I do as I'm told.

Pushing my first finger all the way into her hot pussy, I pause to give her time to adjust, continuing my assault on her clit with my tongue. She rocks her hips, fucking my finger to chase the pleasure she so desperately craves. I can't keep the shit-eating grin off my face. I'm able to make this shy, broken girl, who only half an hour ago was too shy to show me her naked body, cry out in ecstasy. Now she is fucking my hand and chasing the pleasure she knows she deserves, and I love that I did that. I want to see her fall apart, and I know she's close.

Without any further hesitation, I pull out my finger and this time when I push back in, I add a second finger too. Fuck does her pussy feel tight. So fucking tight. I give her a few seconds to adjust again, but as she starts bucking her hips, I decide to show her who is really in charge.

"No, Flower. If you want to come, I will be the one to make you. All you have to do is ask," I say sweetly, as I move my fingers in and out of her pussy at a torturously slow rate. My breath as I speak flutters over her clit and I see her quiver.

"Do it," she whispers, but I don't take orders from her. I slow my fingers down even more, almost to the stage where they aren't moving at all. I hope she gets on board with this very soon because it's just as torturous for me as it is her. Okay, so maybe she has it worse, but I'm the one walking away from this with blue balls, I deserve to have a little fun.

"Oh, Flower. I don't take orders in the bedroom, I give them. Now, ask nicely, or better yet, beg me. Then you can have whatever you want," I reply gruffly, sounding extremely fucking horny. I can't wait until we've done all the talking and we finally get to the stage where I can plunge my cock into this gorgeous fucking pussy. Because we will get to that stage, and very fucking soon if I have my way.

"Please can you move your fingers?" she mumbles so quietly I can barely hear her. I want her to be confident, and to take the pleasure she deserves. This may look like me trying to exert my dominance, and in a way it is, but it's also teaching her to listen to her own body. To know what she wants and to not be afraid to ask for it or to take it.

"My fingers are moving, Flower. Tell me *exactly* what you want." I do speed my fingers up ever so slightly, since she was a good girl and did what I asked, but I still want more. I want to hear her shout from the rooftops.

"I want you to fuck me with your fingers. I want to feel your lips against my clit. I want to fall apart in your arms, knowing you will catch me. Happy now?" she yells, sitting up slightly so she can look at me while she shouts, and her face gets angrier as she sees my cocky grin getting bigger.

"I'm very fucking happy. That is exactly what I wanted to hear." As soon as I finish the words, I dive in like a starving man eating his first meal. My tongue lapping at her clit, as my fingers piston in and out of her tight, wet pussy with reckless abandon. She meets every one of my thrusts and begs for more. This beautiful woman is killing me, and that's just while I'm using my fingers, I don't even want to imagine how good her cunt will feel wrapped around my dick, like a glove made just for me. I can only imagine how fucking amazing she will feel. If only I could feel her now.

Fuck that, Burke! You have restraint, so use it, I mentally chastise myself. But the problem is, that's the logical side of my brain talking. The side that gets pushed to one side when the blood flows south. So, now a very different head is running the show and he wants more. He doesn't want to walk away with blue balls. He wants to sink balls deep into the fucking hot girl who is currently writhing around on my fingers.

No matter how much my dick may want that—and trust me, he wants it really fucking bad—I'm not breaking my promise to Mia. She deserves more than that. She deserves to know that sex can just be for her.

I see the exact moment when Mia starts to lose control, but it doesn't quite go the way I hoped. Her legs begin to tense, and I can feel the muscles underneath where my hand is resting on her lower stomach, they are all clenching together. Her pussy feels like it's getting impossibly wetter, and her walls are clamping down on my fingers, making it difficult to move them as much as I would like, but I do what I can. Her back is arched off the bed, tits pushed out above her and it's such a fucking gorgeous sight. Arms splayed on either side as she clutches onto the bedsheets and I can see some of her knuckles turning white from how tight she has them gripped. It's not until I look up at her, and notice her wide, open eyes, do I see the fear reflected back.

Fuck, I don't know what to do. That's when it dawns on me, she probably doesn't like the feeling of losing control. More than that, she may never have had an orgasm before, so it's my job to reassure her.

"Relax, Flower. I've got you. Just listen to your body, and let yourself feel. It feels like you are losing control, but I promise you that you aren't. I will be here with you. Now, take some big, deep breaths," I instruct, and thankfully she begins to breathe. I notice her body respond, as she seems to deflate and relax. Now I just need to capitalise while she's at her most relaxed and push her over the edge.

Increasing the speed of my fingers again, I use my thumb to press against her clit instead of my tongue this time. I need to keep her eyes on mine, to know I'm here with her, holding her every step of the way. No matter her much it kills me to stop tasting her, I know this will not be the last time. This is just the beginning, and for once, I plan on fighting for what I want.

"Oh, fuck. Kellan…what…fuck…I don't—" Her mumbles come out fragmented and almost incoherent, but I can tell what she's asking with her eyes. She doesn't know what to do or if this is normal. She's scared, but that's no longer the primary emotion on her face. Fear was replaced by lust a while ago, so I know she is safe.

"Shush, Mia. It will feel like your body is climbing to the tallest peak and it's hard and almost painful. Your muscles are tense and coiled, breathing is hard and you'll feel like you aren't getting enough oxygen. Your eyes will have floating dots and you'll question if you might pass out. It all feels scary as fuck. But, once you get to the top of that climb and you freefall off the edge, all you will feel is relief and bliss. It's an indescribable feeling, and you are so close. All you have to do is let go. Come for me, Mia. I want to see you fall apart on my fingers. Come for me, right now." As soon as the instructions are out of my mouth, it's like she allows herself to listen and to trust in not just me but the whole scenario.

When she's at her most relaxed, I increase my efforts. Hooking my fingers slightly as they hit the deepest part of her pussy. It takes me a couple of tries, but as the tips of my fingers scrape across the right spot, it's clear I found what I was looking for.

With each thrust hitting her G-spot, and my thumb giving her clit the attention she so deserves, it's not long before her body starts to shake, her legs become loose, and her cries of pleasure echo around the room. Keeping my eyes on her fucking sexy expression, I want to keep this memory of her falling apart just for me in my mind, but I also need to taste her. Without breaking eye contact, I lower my head and begin tasting her again. Her pussy is flooded with her juices, and I fucking love the taste that is all Mia.

As she lowers her back to the bed, and unclenches her death grip on the sheets, I watch as she relaxes into the blissed-out state that I warned her about. She pants, desperately trying to take in as much oxygen as she can, but as her eyes roll, I can tell her dizzy feeling is still there. I no longer need to hold her down onto the bed, so I release one hand, before slowly pulling my fingers from her sore, red, yet sopping wet pussy. Her groan is like music to my ears and using the flat part of my tongue, I lick as much of her pussy as I can. Her eyes bugged out as she watches and feels me tasting her. This isn't about me trying to make her feel, because I already know her clit is at its most sensitive. This is all for me.

Once I have tasted her, it's physically painful to pull away, but I know she isn't ready for more. I'm not even sure if I pushed her too far this time. I really fucking hope not, but I could see how afraid she was, and it still wasn't enough for her to stop. I just never imagined I would be her first orgasm.

Picking her up by her hips, ignoring her squeals of surprise, I drag her backwards until I have my head on the pillow at the top of the bed, and she is laying plastered against my side with her head on my chest. Her cheek no doubt feels the pounding of my racing heart, but I want her to know how much she affects me. I wrap my arms around her and pull her into my body, loving the way her naked skin feels against mine. I still have my jeans on, but I'm able to wiggle them off without disturbing our hug too much.

Within seconds of my jeans coming off she tucks her leg over mine, and I hear a small sigh. I'm getting ready to talk to her, to ask her how she's feeling, when I hear very small snores coming from her. I look down, gently stroking her hair away so I have access to her face. Her mouth is open slightly as she lets out the softest snore, and I can't get over how serene she looks. Like a little angel lying on my chest, one that turns into a sexy vixen when you open her legs.

Reaching over onto the cabinet next to the bed, I pick my phone up with one hand, trying carefully not to wake up Mia. I shoot a quick text to Liam asking him if he can do me a favour.

His reply is almost instant, and I don't need to read it to know he will have my back. He always has, and that's why he asked me to move in here. He is the support system my mother so delightfully informed me I didn't have. Only now it has expanded to include a feisty redhead with an unusual taste for violence, and a sweet but strong beauty who is somehow able to knock down each and every wall I put up.

I groan as I take in his message. Trust Liam to go all dad-like and give me advice around half an hour too late. He is fucking right, though, she's more fragile than she lets people believe. And she is part of the family now, which means I can't mess this up. I don't know at what point I made the decision that I wanted more from Mia. It's not like it was ever really a conscious decision. Just the more I thought about her, the more I knew I needed her. The longer I tried not to let anything happen between us, the more I wanted it to. When I'm not near her, I crave her. I have no fucking idea how this is going to turn out, I don't even know if she is interested in more, but I intend to find out.

Should we have talked before we had any sexy time? Yes, probably, but it's too late for that now. I need to stop being a pussy. Of course the idea of opening up to another woman scares the shit out of me, but I need to do this. I quickly reply to Liam, carefully avoiding any landmine conversations, so I can just enjoy being here, snuggled up with Mia beside me.

Before I know it my phone beeps not once but several times, and as I open my phone, I find a group chat has been created. Or should I say, I have been added to an already existing one. I look at who is in the group; Bree, Liam, Mia, Kian, Freya, Ryleigh, Evan, and Finn. It's the Doughty extended family chat, and at first I'm a little pissed I wasn't added to it straight away, but then I see Liam's individual message come through, for my eyes only.

I open up the group chat, and I try scrolling back, but it looks like this chat has been going for a while and there's no way I can catch up right now, but I read the newest messages since I was added to the group.

LIAM

Adding Kel to the group, he's finally realised he's part of the family. His mother served him custody documents today. It's time to move forward with our plan.

BREE

Better late than never, Kellan. I will call Gramps and set up a meeting with the solicitor we vetted.

FREYA

Yeah, from the research I did, Julliett & Lawson are the second-best firm in the country. Packard, Kingston & Miller are obviously the best, but she has them. Welcome, Kel!

FINN

I have an appointment with Packard tomorrow, I will see what I can find out. We need to know what that bitch is using against him.

RYLEIGH

Hey, Kellan. We have got this. Hallie Bear is going nowhere, we promise.

EVAN

Don't make promises you can't keep. We will try our best, but we can't promise.

RYLEIGH

Like hell we can't. That little girl is going nowhere. Get on board, Evan, or get out of the chat.

EVAN

I never said I'm not on board. I will fight like hell, just like I said I would, but we can't make any promises. She has a lot of fucking money, and we have no idea what she has on Kellan. There's no way the big fancy lawyer is taking her case, unless he thinks he has a chance of winning. No matter how much money Daddy Money Bags throws at him, it's his career. Packard has a perfect record, he's never lost a family law case, and he isn't going to fucking start now just because he plays golf with her husband!

KIAN

Remind me again why we can't just shoot this woman?

BREE

It's actually not a bad idea, but my fiancé and his conscience won't allow it.

FREYA

Trust you, Kian, to want to turn to violence. Stop being an ape and use your brain for once.

LIAM

I'm actually starting to reconsider my stance on not killing the bitch.

RYLEIGH

That would be an easier plan. Finn wouldn't need to go undercover then.

FREYA

We are not killing Kellan's mother. Yes, she is a first-class bitch, but we are not killing her.

KIAN

Stop being such a prude, Frey. You need to let loose more.

FREYA

Screw you, Caveman. You know nothing about me. I'm hardly a prude just because I don't think killing someone is our best choice.

EVAN

Why don't we agree that we will try the talking plan first, but if that doesn't work and we become absolutely desperate, then we kill her?

KELLAN

I don't think this is how family group chats are supposed to go, guys? I don't think there is supposed to be a debate on whether we should kill my mother or not.

BREE

We are just coming up with options.

LIAM

We need to make sure our Hallie Bear stays with you…with us!

KELLAN

I know, and to be honest, at this moment in time, I am definitely on Team Kill The Bitch. But in the morning when I'm not as angry I will most likely have changed my mind. So go with your original plan. Have Finn find out everything he can, and we can come up with a proper plan after that.

FINN

I got you, bro. You know that.

RYLEIGH

We have all got your back. We love you, Kel. You are family and always have been.

KELLAN

Thanks, guys, I love you all.

I close the phone, and decide to turn off my notifications, as I can hear their messages still coming through. Looks like I'm going to have to mute the Doughty chat. Too many people in one place, all thinking they know best. I should have known they would all have my back. I may never have officially belonged in their family, but I lived with them for longer than I lived with my own mother. They are my family, and no matter how crazy they are, I still love them like hell. It literally warms my heart that they want to fight for my daughter just as much as I do.

Pushing all that aside, I decide that is a worry for another day. Tonight I need to spend time with Mia in my arms. I know when she wakes up we will need to talk, we both have a lot we need to say, even if we may not want to. Once all the serious shit is out of the way, I need to tell her how I feel. I need to know if she feels the same way. I know we are both broken, and embarking on a relationship will never be a smooth road, but I want to try, and I need her to try too. Or, at least, I need to know she wants to.

Mia

Waking up beside Kellan feels so natural now, we've got into the routine of making sure we fall asleep in each other's arms. It's the only way I can even think about going the full night without a nightmare. I don't know what it is about being encased in his strong arms, but it's like my body knows I'm protected. That there's no point even trying to hurt me because just being in his arms, having him near, keeps me safe.

Though, when I woke up this morning, something felt different. Maybe it's the fact that a screaming baby didn't wake me? I blink a few times, waiting for my eyes to adjust, and I can't help but take some deep breaths because I can't get over how hot I am. I mean, Kellan always runs a little warm, he's like my own mini heater, but today it's so much worse than normal. As my eyes return to normal, I suddenly realise why.

Holy fuck, we're naked.

The room is darker than I expected, and when I raise my head slightly to see the clock on the opposite wall, I realise it's only one in the morning. We must have fallen straight to sleep after that fucking mind-altering experience. I've never been more attracted to anyone than I am with Kellan. He's just something else. So when the option for more presented itself, I quite literally jumped on it. But what surprised me most is he never tried to take things too far. He always listened to how I felt and what I wanted. Kellan made sure last night was all about me, and I loved it.

Even the moment when I started spiralling, he grounded me. I know it sounds stupid, but any orgasm that I was able to give myself— and they were very few and far between—they never felt anything like that. I've always heard people talk about fireworks going off, their bodies shaking, legs going limp, but I've never had that before. They were more like a limp rocket; lacking in impact, and over very quickly. But with Kellan, it was like a fucking firework display taking place in the middle of an earthquake. To say he rocked my world would be a massive fucking understatement.

I try not to do that girly thing, where I lay here wondering what this all means. I know I asked him to put a stopper on my past, that I would talk to him about it when the time is right, but I know as soon as he finds out everything, he won't want me anymore. Why would he? He can do so much better than some abused, broken victim. Yet, he's never once made me feel like a victim. Even when he brought up the fact that he knows who my dad is, he still didn't push me to talk. He let me have this moment, our moment together.

"If you keep wiggling underneath me like that, I can't be held responsible for what I do next," Kellan growls from underneath me, and I can't help the gasp that leaves my mouth.

Turning my head slightly, I look up at Kellan and the small slither of light brightens his far too pretty face. Fuck, he looks even better than he normally does. As I stare at him, I feel his hand that was previously pressed flat against my lower back, moving lower. Slowly, he slides the palm of his hand until he's cupping my ass cheek, and before I know it, almost like I weigh nothing at all, he moves me until

I am sitting on top of him, straddling him. My knees are on either side of his hips, and my very naked pussy is pressing against his hard abs as my tits hang freely. Don't even get me started on the rock-hard length I can feel hitting my ass cheeks. If I was sitting just a few centimetres lower, I would have landed on his cock. I try not to squirm at the thought, but there's no way for me to quench the indescribable feeling between my thighs.

His hands grip my hips, holding me in place, preventing me from moving about any more. As I look down, the way this gorgeous, tattoo-covered man is looking at me makes me feel like the most beautiful princess in the world. I bite my lip, to prevent me from saying something stupid. Currently, the only thing running through my mind is, *Please can I swivel on your pole?* And I would really rather not say that out loud, or I feel it may be the last time I ever see his fucking pole again!

"You look so fucking sexy like this. You have no idea how much I want to watch my cock sink inside you from this angle. But, I said last night was just about you, showing you pleasure, and I meant it," Kellan groans, as his hands lightly trace up and down my thighs. The action itself is maddening. I've never felt this overwhelming urge to have a man's hands all over me, but with Kellan, I want to feel him everywhere.

"Technically, it's tomorrow now," I reply, trying to sound as seductive out loud as I do in my head. Fuck, I'm not good at this. The whole flirting thing is new to me.

"We said tomorrow is for talking, and as much as I want to lose myself in you, we need to talk a bit before we do." I can't help but bring my hands that were resting on his chest up to cover my tits. I don't think I can have any kind of conversation with him while I'm naked.

Before my hands even reach their destination, he takes hold of my wrists, encasing them with his big hands, before pulling them back to his chest. His eyes lock with mine, and I couldn't avert my gaze even if I wanted to. His expression is fierce, and his normally bright blue eyes now almost look black as he sets my skin alight with one look.

"Don't ever feel like you have to hide any piece of yourself from me, Mia. No matter what we talk about, no matter what you say, it will never change how I feel. I've had a taste of you now, and I will always want more. I know we have talked time and time again about how we can't do this, and about how wrong it is. But I no longer give a fuck. I want you, and I very much plan on fucking having you." His voice is just as fierce as his gaze, and it melts me. My stomach flips at hearing the words I have literally been fantasising about hearing from this man. But my life is so much worse than he can ever imagine. I find it very difficult to believe he will want me when he hears what I have to say.

"Don't make promises you can't keep, Kellan. I know you think you know what my secrets are, but you don't. I will tell you because I think we've reached the stage where I have to, you have to know, but don't promise how you will react because you don't know. There's a million reasons why you shouldn't get involved with me, where've they all gone?" I ask aloud, while internally I'm shouting at myself to shut the fuck up. He's finally saying the words we've dreamed of him saying, and I'm literally blowing it. Why am I pushing him away?

"Mia, I know I've been a dick about this and made excuses, I don't even really know how to apologise for that. I could stand here and blame it all on Shayla, tell you all about how she messed me up and left me the asshole I am now, and to a degree that would be right. But, the truth is, I was a mess before I even met Shayla. Before her, I'd never had a real relationship, and I'm not entirely sure I would have had one with Shay, if it hadn't been for her getting pregnant with Hallie. I have major abandonment issues, and as a result, I push people away before they get a chance to ditch me. Before I held Hallie in my arms, I was convinced I didn't know what love was. I knew I felt something for Shay, and I called it love. I definitely felt more for her than I did for anyone else." Kellan takes a deep breath and he looks like his mind is somewhere else for a moment. I try to hide how fucking horrible it is hearing him talk about loving someone else, even though she's Hallie's mum.

His gaze finally reconnects with mine before he continues. "I didn't really love her. I think I wanted to love the mother of my child, and I really did try the entire time we were together. But the moment

Hallie was born and I held her, I knew what love really felt like. My heart doubled in size, and I knew beyond all doubt how I felt, and I wasn't *in* love with Shay."

Thank fuck for that, I think, but as Kellan starts to chuckle, I realise I just said that out loud. My cheeks flame as embarrassment spreads over my cheeks.

Kellan takes one of my hands and holds it in his, our fingers clasped tightly together, and he gently strokes his thumb over the back of my hand. It's such an innocent gesture, but I feel as though he's leaving a burning trail over my skin. My stomach is doing somersaults, and I feel like every time I breathe I'm trying to gasp for air. I'm almost light-headed as this man consumes me.

"When I first met you, I was terrified. I knew you made me feel things I never had before. Not just the sexual chemistry, because of course I would want to fuck you. Any living man with a dick can see how gorgeous and sexy you are, but it's more than that. I wanted to know you, and when I found out you were keeping things from me, I couldn't cope. It brought back all the feelings I had about Shayla. I know I'm a hypocrite because I've never really told you what happened, and why should I ask you to place all your trust in me when I can't reciprocate? But, all that is changing today. I'm willing to tell you everything, if you are. I know I can't promise what the outcome will be after all this, but I can promise you that this is the best way to try. I want you, Mia. I want all of you. I can't promise you the world, but I can promise that if you put your trust in me, I won't ever break it. Surely that's a good place to start?" Kellan looks hopeful, his crystal blue eyes sparkling as that cocky grin I love so much spreads across his face.

I reach up and swipe a rogue piece of hair off his forehead, before running my fingers through his silky smooth black hair. His deep rumbling moan causes his stomach to vibrate, and fuck can I feel it ricocheting through my pussy. I didn't know just touching his hair could be a sexual move, but apparently it is. I can't resist any more. If having this gorgeous man laying naked underneath me wasn't enough, he then goes and literally says everything a girl could want to hear.

Leaning down, I grip his hair with one hand, and use the fingers of my free hand to trail over his tattoos, before I lightly press my lips against his. It was meant to just be a sweet kiss, but as soon as I feel his mouth under mine, I lose all control. My lips crush against his, and I swipe my tongue across his lower lip, desperate to demand access. Kellan wastes no time in responding, his hands grip my hips, pulling me down harder until my clit is scraping across his abs. I groan into his lips, but I don't stop my tongue from mingling with his.

When we finally pull away, we are both desperately gasping for breath and my whole body feels as though it is on fire. My clit feels like it is throbbing, in desperate need of more attention. All my nerve endings are sizzling, and I can still feel the ghost of his touch against my skin. I almost feel lost without his lips on mine. But I know we need to talk first.

"That's the perfect place to start. I want you to know, Kel, that nobody has ever made me feel even a fraction of what you do. I know there is great potential here for me to get hurt, and I know there are a million reasons why I shouldn't be here in your bed, but I don't care. I like you, as in I like you a lot. I have never done this with another person, I have never put my trust in anyone. Even Bree only knows bits, and she is legit my only friend. So, even if you want to walk away when this is out there, please promise me that you won't hurt me. Please promise that no matter how this evolves, I'll always be Hallie's nanny. I don't want to lose what I have. I know there's potential for me to get everything I've ever wanted, which is why I'm willing to make this blind leap, all I ask is that you will catch me when I jump." I try to look away, not wanting him to be able to see my vulnerability, but in the end there's no point. I'm sitting here naked, baring my soul to him. I've already taken that leap, now it's all on him.

His cocky smile tells me he has no doubts that he will be there to catch me. "Mia, you will always be Bree's friend, and you will continue to live here. I don't even feel I need to say this because it won't happen, but I know you need to hear it. So, here it is. If anything happens between us, and I suddenly become an asshole who doesn't realise how fucking amazing you are and we break up, I guarantee you can stay on as Hallie's nanny. Unless you do anything crazy illegal, or anything to put my daughter's life at risk, then there's no reason for you not to stay on as her nanny. You love her, and she loves you. Besides, finding a nanny who is okay with our family business and doesn't want to report us to the police is not easy," Kellan jokes, and I can't help but chuckle. Growing up the way I did, being around criminals is the norm for me. But, when we are all at home, it doesn't feel like I live with some of the most dangerous people in the world. They are my friends, and what they do for a living barely even registers with me.

Jokingly, I reply, "I promise to not call the police on you in a fit of jealous rage."

Kellan's responding chuckle does dangerous things to my insides. "Okay, then I guess I should start." He takes a big gulp, before reaching for the bottle of water on the side of the bed. He shuffles me slightly so he is sitting up more, his back against the headboard of the bed. This new position has his cock nestled between my folds, and it feels fucking amazing. I try not to move, as just a slight tilt of my pelvis would have allowed the tip to enter me easily. I'm so distracted, I almost miss Kellan beginning to talk when he has finished with his water.

"Hallie's birth mother, Shayla, is part of the Celtic Reapers MC. I was hired by her to pull off a job, and if she successfully completed the job she earned her freedom from the Reapers. The Reapers are evil men, who have absolutely no respect for women. Shayla was their princess, her father is the president, but that didn't keep her safe. I got a call to say she'd been taken to hospital, and they had beaten the shit out of her for staying too late at her meeting with me. After that, we bonded while I visited her in hospital. No matter how much of a front she put on, I knew she was terrified. So I agreed to help her. She stayed with me while we planned the job. We pulled it off successfully and Shay earned her freedom, but she had to return to them for a month; they called it giving her notice on the MC.

"When I met back up with her, and her friend, Jamieson, came with her, I knew there was something wrong. She was clearly on drugs, and not the Shayla I left. She finally confessed that she was pregnant, and I could be the father. But, so could fifteen other

Reapers, as she was gang-raped around the time she fell pregnant. We organised a foetal DNA test and it confirmed that I was the father. After that, Shay came to live with me. We left the Reapers behind, or so I thought.

"I spent months preparing for Hallie's birth, building a home with her, and I thought we would be happy. Looking back now, there are obvious signs. She spent more time preparing me to be a father than she did anything else. She didn't want to name her, or bond with her in any way. The day of the birth came, and even when Hallie was born, I adored her, but she never did. She wouldn't even look at her, let alone hold her. Then, around five hours after the birth, she asked me to get her a sandwich from the local deli she likes, and since she had just pushed a baby out of her vagina with no pain relief, it was the least I could do. That's when Shay decided to leave. She left my baby in one of those glass fishbowl cots, and abandoned us.

"I watched the CCTV and her friend Whiskey came to collect her. That's when I did my research and found out she actually married Whiskey the day before she came to live with me, saying she wanted to build a life with me. She stole all of my money, had me legally sign over everything I own to her. I was left with no house, no money, and a newborn baby to raise all by myself. The local authorities informed me they would be doing a spot check of my place within the first week, just to make sure I was a suitable single parent. If I was, they would close the case and accept that Shay abdicated all her parental rights, leaving me a single parent. But they could take her from me if I didn't pass the checks. So, with the help of Liam and his family, I got myself a shitty apartment, and made it the best little home it could be. I passed the inspection and that was it. Until fatherhood beat me. I just couldn't cope by myself, and so when Bree offered to let me live here, I jumped at the chance. My life has never been better."

He seems to speak forever, but I don't ever want him to stop. I'm captivated by each and every word that leaves his mouth. I wanted to hate Shayla, and fuck there's a part of me that really fucking does hate her. I mean, who abandons their baby while they are still in hospital? That on its own is unforgivable, but the way she hurt Kellan, it's no wonder he's broken. He believes their entire relationship was built on lies, and so even if it actually did mean something to her, he will never believe that, and I don't blame him.

"Kellan, I don't even know what…" I tail off, not entirely sure what the fuck I should say to this. How do I tell him that I understand, that I feel for him? But more importantly, how do I tell him that I won't hurt him like she did? I won't just leave, and our relationship won't be built on lies.

"It's okay, Mia. I know you aren't like Shayla," he says, but there's a sadness in his eyes that I hate to see. Without even thinking, I press my lips against his. It's hard, bruising, and over before it ever really begins. But it's enough to tell him how I feel.

"Too fucking right I'm not Shayla. I would never leave you or Hallie like that. Even if things break down between us, I would always say goodbye. I can't promise to never hurt you, but I can promise to try. I will be open and honest with you, I will put my trust in you, and I will let you see a side of me that I've spent the last five years keeping hidden. I know you want me to promise to hold your heart in my hand and to never break it, but I ask the same of you," I say, hoping it's enough for him to put the hurt he feels behind him. Are my words enough to make him forget about Shayla, and to take a chance on me?

"I promise to hold your heart in my hand and cherish it. You can trust me, Mia." Any hint of sadness is long forgotten, and the smile on his face seems to be the one he uses just for me. I match his smile and before I can speak, he continues to talk. "When I was telling you about the job I did with Shayla, I missed an important part out, but not intentionally. I didn't realise it was important until yesterday. I need to tell you where I was yesterday, and I need to ask for your forgiveness."

The way he looks at me, I want to forgive him without even knowing what he's talking about, but years of behaviour can't be undone in just one moment. "I need you to explain." I don't know what else to say, so I wait and hope that I can forgive him for what comes next.

Mia's big brown eyes stare up at me as I ask her to forgive me. I have no idea how I'm going to explain yesterday, but I also know that if we stand any chance at a relationship, honesty is the foundation. Although, as she wiggles around, my hard cock nestled between her warm pussy lips, concentrating becomes almost as hard as my shaft.

"Yesterday, Bree, Liam, Kian, and I attended a meeting, but I set it up. After you told me about Kyle, I knew how terrified you were. So, I did a bit of digging, and his family works with Bree. So, we arranged a meeting with Kyle under the pretence of a loyalty meeting. He thought we were testing his loyalty to Bree. Naturally, while we were quizzing him, the subject of his future wife came up. We made it very clear that you were already spoken for and would never be his wife. He didn't take it well, and called your father to check with him. Long story short, both Kyle and your father know you're spoken for. I know

I shouldn't have told them that without speaking to you first, but I needed to keep them away from you. Your father argued that you have an obligation that you agreed to, and that Whitlocks keep their word. Bree countered, reminding your father that he promised you could graduate first, which you haven't yet. Is all that true so far?" I ask, wanting to check I have all the second-hand facts correct. That is what Bree and Whitlock said, but it doesn't mean it's true.

Tears fill Mia's eyes and my heart breaks that I'm the reason they are there. Sadly, things will get worse before they get better. We need to get it all out in the open, no matter how much it hurts. "I mean, it's kinda true. He said I had to marry, and I said I wanted to get a qualification. He agreed I could graduate first. But then I ran away. I thought he just never chased me. I didn't realise he was simply giving me the time he'd promised, and now he expects me back. It makes sense, it sounds like something he would do."

"Mia, listen to me," I say, as I take her hand in mine while the other sweeps a lock of hair behind her ear, cupping her silky, soft cheek. "I made it very clear that you're with me, and nothing will change that. In the end, Bree agreed that when you graduate, you would honour your commitment, but that will never happen. We only said that to buy us time. We wanted you to have a couple of months with no contact from them, and if either does reach out to you, tell us straight away please. It will forfeit the deal and you can walk away. I think that's what Bree is hoping they will do, but if that doesn't happen, we have a few months to come up with a plan."

Mia simply nods her head, as a gentle stream of tears strolls down her cheek. Fuck, I hate that this isn't over yet. "Mia, there's more." Her eyes widen, and I see the sharp intake of breath she takes before she fixes her resolve, her back a little straighter. My girl is showing how strong she can be.

"Just tell me," she says, as she wipes a stray tear from her cheek.

"Remember I told you about the job I did with Shayla? Well, the person we pulled the job on was Mortimer Whitlock. I did all my research on him. I knew he had a daughter, but that she was estranged, so I didn't look further. Everything I know about you, I learnt in person, and I promise you that. But, I do know who your father is. I know the type of public figure he is, but I also know what the real Whitlock is like. What he gets up to in his spare time, and the type of things he likes to do for fun. I didn't associate him with you until today. That's when it clicked into place. You should know, I told Kyle and your father that you are mine, and I made the decision to pursue this thing with you before I connected you to him. I can't deny my jealousy was overwhelming, and the idea of you being with anyone else was driving me crazy, and that's when I realised I feel that way because I want you to be with me." I mean every single word I say, and I want her to know that I'm not just saying it because I feel sorry for her.

My hands cradle her face, as I use my thumbs to wipe away the tears that are falling. Her eyes look hollow, and I've never seen Mia look in so much pain. When she starts to speak, there's a quiver in her voice that I hate to hear. "You know, don't you? I don't even need to tell you, you've worked it out. How can you still want me?" I pull her into a hug as sobs rack her body and my heart breaks.

Cradling Mia against my chest, I wait for the sobs to die down before I talk. "Yes, I know what your father's secrets are, and I might be able to guess what yours are, but I don't want to do that. I want you to be the one to tell me. I don't want to cast aspersions that may be incorrect. I want you to trust me enough to tell me your story. As for asking me how I can still want you, you have to be fucking joking! Mia, you are the most beautiful woman I've ever met. Yes, you have scars and I want to be with you because of those scars. They make you stronger, they make you the person you are today. You've grown so much just over the last few months. I've watched you cuddle and laugh with my daughter. I've held you while you've cried and helped you feel safe. I have yet to see a part of you I don't like. I don't say this lightly, but I know falling for you will be easy. I was scared to give it a chance before, but now I'm not. I want us to be brave together."

Her tears stop, and as she raises her head to face me with a smile on her face, my heart soars that this girl could feel the same as I do. "Please don't think less of me when you hear my story," she mutters, before taking a big, deep breath. She tries to hold herself taller, her back straighter, as her gaze meets mine. I give her a smile, but don't say anything. I can tell her a million times that I won't leave or see her differently, but these are things I will need to prove over time. It must be enough as she starts her story.

"I've been abused one way or another my entire life, I can't even pinpoint when it started. To the outside world, I was the posh little rich girl—Daddy's princess—but that was all for show. It started as neglect. My mother doesn't know how to care for another human, I think she only had a baby because my father made her. I was four years old when I burnt myself for the first time trying to make toast. I was taken to hospital, but Father didn't like all the questions and how it reflected badly on him. It's the first time I was properly punished. I was bent over my father's desk while he beat me with his belt until the pain from the burn melted to nothing. After that, the beatings became fairly regular."

My hands ball into fists as I listen to Mia tell me the worst parts of her life. My thoughts go to my little Hallie, and no matter how pissed I am with her, I could never treat her like that. I don't know which parent I'm most mad at. Her dad for being an abusive asshole, or her mother for allowing it. She should be the one to protect Mia, but then again, I know all about mothers who don't have an ounce of maternal instinct in their bodies.

Taking a few deep breaths, Mia seems to find her courage to continue. "The cycle of neglect and abuse continued for a few years. My father perfected beating me in places that couldn't be seen, and I became good at hiding it. Some days the pain was so bad, I physically struggled to walk to school, but I knew I had to hide it. If anyone at school suspected, it would taint the perfect picture my family portrays to the outside world, which would result in me being in even more trouble. So, I learnt to push on. Until one day, the school called them anyway. I thought I'd done a good job of hiding the bruises, and I always did all my school work.

"My heart raced as I waited to find out what I'd done wrong. It turns out the teacher wanted to let them know I was working to a more advanced level and they were considering putting me forward to a higher learning group. I thought this was a good thing, living up to my family name. It was all good until right at the end, when my teacher made an off-hand comment that I was quiet and she'd like to see me make friends with other kids. I was seven years old and had no friends. I didn't even realise that was abnormal. I was just so focused on doing what was expected of me, I didn't have time to laugh and joke with the other children. I also didn't have the energy to run around the playground, I was in too much pain trying to walk.

"Naturally, my father latched onto the negative comment, and punished me. As he beat me, he told me the importance of manipulating people to my own benefit. That real relationships are pointless, that you should always benefit from a relationship in some way. He told me he's always the most popular person in the room and has everyone's trust. My father loves to be the puppetmaster, pulling everyone's strings, manipulating them for his own gain, and now he wants me to do the same thing."

I don't mean to gasp as I'm enthralled by Mia's story, but I think I may have just connected all the puzzle pieces together without even realising it. Her eyebrows raise and she questions me with her eyes.

"Sorry, I didn't mean to interrupt your story, but I've been trying to learn things about your father, and I think you may have just connected the pieces. I couldn't understand why he seems to be friendly with everyone, with no real agenda, but that's just how it looks. He has a goal, we just don't know what it is exactly. He appears non-threatening to them, so he can manipulate them. I'm guessing, if a time comes where we decide to cut ties with him, your father will use what he knows to either change our minds, or create a force to challenge Bree's leadership. He has an extensive Black Book, so that every move he ever needs to make, will be covered. That's why he needs you to lock down the Fratacellos. They're probably the biggest family, after the Doughtys, who are capable of making a move against Bree. With Desmond temporarily aligned with Bree, I'm guessing your father realises he won't be able to use that angle, which makes your alliance with Kyle all the more important," I explain, and Mia's chocolate brown eyes widen in shock.

"Is he working with Desmond?" Mia asks, and I can't help but chuckle.

"Yeah, he has been for a while. Sometime last year, before Bree took over as leader, everyone was speculating who would take over from Vernon, and some saw that as their prime opportunity to move on London, overthrowing the O'Keenans in a moment of weakness. Around that time, Desmond got an influx of cash and weapons, readying himself to move. Liam doesn't know this, but I was keeping an eye on Des. I wanted to ensure he wasn't going to get my family killed. I was going to look into who was backing him when Liam went and kidnapped Bree. Thankfully, Des supported their partnership, but it was around that time that I became a dad, and looking into Desmond fell to the bottom of my to-do list." My words tumble out far quicker than I intended, but I can't help it. When I finally crack a puzzle that's been irritating me for a while, the excitement is overwhelming. I understand our target a little more now, which gives me the upper hand.

I'm brought back to the moment by a gentle squeeze of my hand, making me remember what we were talking about originally. Fuck, I got so distracted, my brain ran off on a tangent. Mia gives me a small smile, ready to continue her story.

"I was just eight years old when the abuse reached its worst. Eight years old when my father raped me for the first time. It took you a while to figure out who my father really is, but I always knew. His business associates would bring children over to the house, and at first I thought it was so I could have a friend, but I was very wrong. He abused them in the worst ways possible, and I had to help them get cleaned up afterwards. I had to warn them to never utter a word of the horrors they experienced in my house. I was responsible for silencing them. Then, one day, the girl he'd bought didn't show up, she was ill, but that didn't make my father any less horny. His exact words were, 'I don't know why I'm bothering to order takeout, when the exact food I crave is right here.'" Mia shudders as the memory consumes her. My stomach rolls, and if I'd eaten anything last night, it'd be threatening to make a reappearance right about now.

I knew Whitlock was bad, but I never suspected he was capable of this. It's fucking sick that he does this to other kids, but to his own is reprehensible. I worry day and night about keeping Hallie safe from monsters, so the fact that Mia's supposed protector was her monster is awful. She had nobody on her side.

Taking a deep breath, her voice thick with emotion, she continues, "The abuse just got worse after that. If he wasn't raping me, he was pimping me out to his friends for them to rape me. When I became a teenager, he started selling me in sex clubs, making money from my pain and misery. I was fifteen when I met Kyle, he was twenty-three. I thought he was just another asshole who'd bought me for the weekend. But, Kyle hadn't bought me as such, he'd demanded my hand in marriage, in exchange for his family connecting with mine. After that, I was made to spend every other weekend with him. At first I looked forward to them, they were a chance to get away from the assholes my father sold me to, or my father himself.

"To start with, Kyle was kind, and we simply got to know each other. I had my own room, he fed me, and gave me books because he knew I enjoyed reading. That only lasted a couple of months. He was buttering me up before the training started. I spent my weekends training to be the perfect, obedient little housewife. They taught me how to run a household, during the day, but at night I was taught to put my own feelings aside and simply pleasure my husband. I was fifteen and I was taught about orgasm denial, anal, and so much more. I was taught to accept the pain, as long as it gave my husband pleasure."

Mia tries to fight back the tears filling her eyes. My heart breaks for her, and I know my eyes are filled with unshed tears too. I hate that my beautiful, fragile Mia has seen more horrors than anyone ever should, let alone a child.

Reaching up, using the pad of her thumb, she swipes away a rogue tear I hadn't meant to allow to fall. Just when I think she is going to continue speaking, she bends down and places a quick but firm kiss on my lips. It may be short, but it's bruising and memorable. Why is she the one supporting me? Fuck, if I didn't know how strong this fucking woman was before, I do now.

"I hate that you went through all that, Mia." I don't know what else to say. She doesn't need my apologies or my pity, nor will she get them. But she will get my unyielding support.

"Thank you. As I'm sure you've worked out, it caused me unimaginable pain and suffering. So, when I met Bree at the debutante training, I was pretty much living a lie. We became friends very quickly, but we both had secrets. I was never available on weekends, and Bree knew not to ask questions. If she heard all this now, she'd be so pissed she didn't do or say something, but we were just kids. There's nothing we could have done."

"How did you get away?" I ask, not really sure what else to say.

"One weekend, after my father beat and raped me while I was barely conscious, I made the decision that I needed to leave. If I didn't at least try, I'd die there. I set off for school like I always do, only that day my bag was packed with whatever I could carry. I'd been hiding stuff in a locker at the station for around a week, including whatever money I could get my hands on. My father's so rich he didn't even notice me taking the odd twenty-pound-note from him every so often. Once I was sure I had enough, I made my move. I'd managed to steal a few thousand, which I knew would keep me going for a while, and after grabbing my things I bought a train ticket and just kept moving. I hopped from trains to buses, trying not to get caught. I hid in crappy motels for months, checking in under a false name.

"One day, I came back to the motel after my shift—I'd started working in a local cafe for money—there was an envelope on the bed. I don't know how he found me, but he did. It basically said he was pissed at me, and that I would be punished for this. Apparently, my age, and the fact that I now have a woman's body, meant I wasn't worth as much to him anymore, which is why he hasn't wasted too much effort trying to find me. He said that since he's a fair man, he will allow me to finish my studies, but then I need to return to marry Kyle. I didn't think too much of it, and I just started living my life. I tried to tell myself he would forget all about me, but I've always known there's a hammer above my head just waiting to fall."

I see the lost look in her eyes, and my heart breaks for this beautiful girl. I don't even know how to explain it, but I feel like my heart is growing to make room for her. I'd already decided I want to give us a chance, to see where this might lead, but as I stare into the eyes of a girl who has been through more pain and heartbreak than any person ever should, I have an overwhelming urge to not only protect her, but to also show her that there's good in this world. All she's ever known is pain and suffering, and men who are more interested in their own pleasure than her. I want her to know there are men who treat women like the queens they really are. I need to do this, not just because Mia deserves it, but for Hallie. I need to know I'm not raising my daughter in a world filled with assholes. I want her to look at the way I treat Mia, and Liam treats Bree, and know that's what she should aim for. She should never settle for any man who is less than we are.

"I wish I could tell you that we've sorted all your problems, but that doesn't mean we won't. We have a plan, Mia, we just need more time. Getting them to back off for a couple of months gives us time, and I promise you, we will come up with a plan. If it was as easy as killing Kyle, I would have done it this morning for you, but now we know your father is clearly planning something, taking out the Fratacellos wouldn't make a difference. Your father is power mad, and you're a resource he needs."

I run my fingers lightly down Mia's back to comfort her, loving the way she shivers beneath my touch. "Now you know everything. Why aren't you looking at me differently?" she mutters, barely above a whisper as a blush spreads across her cheeks.

"What?" I ask, unsure of how exactly I'm supposed to look. I didn't think she would want me to feel sorry for her, or pity her—which I don't, so I keep those emotions off my face. Of course I feel her pain, how could I not. I also feel rage, and if it wasn't for the beautiful, naked girl sitting on top of me, I'd be pacing, trying not to punch something. I know when I truly allow myself to think about the horrors Mia's endured, I'll become consumed by blinding rage, so I'm trying to keep that out of my head and off my face.

"Kellan, I've liked you since the first time I met you. Or should I say, I've been attracted to you since then. I didn't like you because you were an asshole," she adds with a chuckle, and I roll my eyes at the memories. I was insanely attracted to her too, more than I'd ever been with any other woman, and that scared the shit out of me. I know now why she kept secrets from me, this isn't the sort of thing you tell just anyone, but that doesn't mean I wasn't affected by the secrets.

Before I get a chance to cut in with my own comments, she places a finger against my lips and continues. "The more I get to know you, the more I like you. You are kind, caring, insanely sexy, and I swear to God my ovaries explode every time I see you playing with Hallie. I've watched you change the way you are with me. I've seen it become harder and harder for you to come up with reasons why we can't be together. I've been right there with you, and I'm over the fucking moon that you want to be with me. But I've always been terrified that when I tell you the truth, you'll look at me differently. Who wants a girlfriend that lost her virginity to her father at eight years old? Or one whose sexual experience only includes being raped? I don't even know if I can. You make me feel things I didn't think were possible, and last night was hands down the most amazing experience of my life, but I don't know if I can ever give you more." The tears she managed to keep at bay earlier flow freely now, and it hurts me so much that she finds talking about this more painful than talking about what her father put her through.

I cup my hands over her cheeks, making sure to wipe away the tears with the pads of my thumbs before I pull her gaze to meet mine. "Listen to me very carefully, Mia. Knowing all of this, it doesn't change a single thing. I like you, all of you. Of course I think sex is important, I'm still a guy, after all. But, it's not the only part of a relationship. I would wait an eternity if that's what it takes for you to feel comfortable enough for me to show you what sex should be like. I want to show you that sex isn't about what someone can take from you. All those men ever did is take what they needed from you, and fuck the consequences. That's not how it should be. I want to show you how much you should get out of sex. How every touch, every kiss, every movement, they should all be aimed at giving you what you need. But, if we never get there, and you don't ever feel like you can have sex, then that's okay too." I watch as she rolls her eyes and it makes me chuckle. Even in the midst of the most serious conversation we've ever had, she still finds something to disagree with me over.

"There's no fucking way you would give up sex." Her voice is strained and she tries to laugh at the end, making out she's joking, but I can see it in her eyes. She means every word, and it hurts. I'd hoped she knew me better than that.

"Mia, for you I would. But I don't think we will need to. As far as I'm concerned, you are a virgin. Until you have given it up willingly, it's still there. I plan on being your first, and hopefully your last. I want to show you how to feel, and how to love sex, and I'm willing to wait until the time is right," I explain, as I pepper little kisses across her jaw and neck. I genuinely mean it when I say I would live my life without sex, as long as I know she's safe. Obviously, I'd prefer teaching her to enjoy sex.

"Kel, I feel things with you that scare the shit out of me. I trust you in ways I've never trusted anyone. The problem is, I don't trust myself. I know more than most people that my body can betray me, and lie to me. I remember one time when I was around thirteen, I was an expert at sex by that point. Fuck, it hurts me to even say that, but it's true. I'd done more things sexually at that age than most people experiment in their whole lives. But, I swear to you, I've never enjoyed it the way I just did with you. Thirteen was when I started getting periods, and essentially becoming hormonal. That's when my body began betraying me. My head was repulsed, but if the man knew what he was doing, he could drag an orgasm out of me, even if I didn't want him to. I stopped listening to my body because it lies."

Fuck. I have no idea what to say to that, or how to help her. Her eyes look so vacant, they almost appear lost, and she's staring at me like I might have the answers she craves. "Mia, the sensations I made you feel, did you experience anything like that with them?" I ask, and her eyes snap up to mine.

Shaking her head, she mutters, "No, nothing like that."

"How were they different?" I ask, hoping that her answers will give us both some direction. It's not like there's a handbook to teach me how to deal with this shit.

"I don't really know. With them, my body clenched a little, like my muscles were coiling without my permission. But with you, I still felt the coiling sensation, but it was so much more. I felt like tingles were spreading all over my skin, my heart was racing, and I couldn't catch my breath. It was like this overwhelming sensation of needing more from you, and when you gave it to me I felt like I was falling apart in your arms. Like fireworks exploding in my brain." I can't stop the shit-eating grin from spreading across my face, hearing how I affect her.

"Don't you see how different they are?" I ask, tilting her chin up so that her eyes meet mine. "What you experienced before was probably just your body responding, not even a full orgasm. I gave you your first, and nobody can ever take that from you. I'm not an expert, and I sure as fuck am not a psychologist, but just hearing you describe them, it's obvious how different they are. I'm not asking for anything from you. We move at your speed with this one, and we can go as slow or as fast as you want. Even if we get caught up in the moment, like we did tonight, all you have to do is tell me to stop and I will, in a heartbeat. No questions asked. Okay?"

She nods her head, and leans down to place a kiss on my lips. I try to hold back, but just like every other time that her lips met mine, it feels as though it activates something primal, deep, within and I can't help it, I'm desperate for more. I deepen the kiss, our lips bruising as my tongue sweeps across her bottom lip, begging for permission. She opens, and I can't hold back the groan of pleasure I feel when our tongues meet. She tastes so sweet, and I can't get enough.

My cock starts to harden underneath her as soon as Mia starts to wiggle around. The beautiful moan I hear is like music to my ears, but I know we need to hold off. We literally just talked about this.

Pulling back, we both gasp for breath, and Mia's hands claw at the back of my head as she frantically tries to pull me back into the kiss. Fuck, I want to do it. I want it all with this girl, but I have to do it right. Even though it pains me, I pull my hands away from her silky skin, and reach around to grab hers. "Mia, I'm not going anywhere. We have all the time in the world to do this right. I'm going to take you on dates and show you what it means to be cared for. I will kiss you whenever you ask. I will do a whole fucking lot more if you ask me to. But tonight has been a long night, and our emotions are running high. I don't ever want you to regret anything that happens between us. So, tonight we sleep. Tomorrow we can see how we feel. Okay?"

She smiles the biggest smile I think I've ever seen, and with a cheeky glint in her eye she leans down and steals a quick but incredibly sexy kiss. My dick's screaming at me, telling me what an asshole I am, but I know I'm doing the right thing.

"A date, you say? Now I am intrigued," she says, biting her bottom lip in a way that makes my cock twitch. Fuck, I may actually die from blue balls if I have to hold off from this girl for too long. Shit, I need to stop thinking with my dick, and start planning a fucking date. It needs to be romantic yet magical. This is not my strong suit. I have no fucking idea what makes a good date, but I know a hopeless romantic who will be able to help me. Well, I'm hoping he holds off on killing me long enough to give me advice. Liam specifically told me not to start anything with Mia, so he probably won't be happy when I tell him. But, I don't give a shit. I like this girl and I'm done denying it. So, Liam better get on board quickly because I have no fucking clue how to be romantic.

The next few days pass by so quickly, Kellan and I have got into a routine together. We'd sort of established one before, an unofficial version, but now it's very much official, and it involves a lot of kissing. We go to bed together every evening, and we wake up together every morning. Then we start our routine of looking after Hallie, and swapping off until the other person is showered and dressed. We move around each other, sharing the responsibilities like we're a well-oiled machine. Kellan goes to work, or works in his office, while I spend time with Hallie. Sometimes if Liam or Bree is free, they will be there too. Sometimes they take her so I can finish any assignments I have.

I used to do my university work after Hallie went to bed, but that's proving a lot more difficult now that I spend every evening with Kellan. Sometimes we laze around and watch a film with Liam and Bree, but the majority of the time has been spent in Kellan's bed. With each night that passes, the more we kiss, the more I want him. I've spent my whole life terrified that my body betrayed me, but it didn't. Yes, I felt things, but I know I couldn't help it. What I felt back then is merely a fraction of what my body is truly capable of. And each night we've explored together.

His kisses are intoxicating, and every night I push him to give me more, but he refuses. Insisting he wants to show me this is more than just sex for him. Instead, he explores my body, finding all my sweet spots. There's not an inch of skin his lips haven't explored, well… except my pussy. He's learning to play my body the way a musician learns to play an instrument; with patience and practice. And I'm so fucking here for it, but I want more.

Last night, I decided I was done being worshipped—temporarily— and I wanted to take a bit of control. The more Kellan worships my body like I'm the only God he prays to, it gives me confidence. I feel like a queen and now it's my turn to learn his body. I want to devour, kiss, and inspect every curl of ink that adorns his gorgeous skin. I want to give him the pleasure he shows me. The only way to do that is to experiment.

Kellan was only too willing to give up the control for a little while. I found sweet spots that caused him to groan under my touch, and fuck did that turn me on. Ever since, I can't stop thinking about how far I want to take things tonight. I want to touch him more, but if I'm being honest, his cock kinda scares me.

The problem is, I was taught how to be a good little cocksucker early on. I know all the tricks of the trade to get a guy going. I learnt how to suppress my gag reflex, and to breathe as and when I can, while allowing the guy to face-fuck me as he desires. I know all that, but I don't want to just go through the motions with Kellan. I don't want to use all the techniques I was taught, only for it to result in flashbacks that ruin the moment. I want it to be different with him, but I'm not sure how. I'm worried that as soon as I touch his cock, I'll turn into the girl they made me. The good little cocksucking whore.

"Mia, are you okay?" Bree asks, as she waves her hand in front of my face.

Looking around I realise I'm standing in front of the coffee pot, that's clearly been ready for a while, but I still haven't poured my coffee. I obviously got lost in my own head. Frantically, I turn around to find Hallie safely in her high chair where I left her. Admittedly, she is covered in banana, and it's all over the kitchen, but at least she is happy and safe.

Fuck, I can't blank out like that while I'm looking after Hallie. My heart races and my palms start to sweat at the thought of all the things that could have happened to her while I'm supposed to be looking after her. After I've fully checked her over from head to toe, and helped to wipe all the excess banana off her, I place her back into the high chair and turn to my friend, who thankfully gave me a few minutes to compose myself and made the coffee.

"I'm fine, honestly," I lie, not entirely sure how to find the correct words to describe what's really going on.

I think Liam and Bree have worked out there's something going on between us, but we decided not to tell them officially yet. They're our best friends, and they only want the best for us, but we don't want to deal with the pressure of them knowing. They'll worry about what will happen if our relationship doesn't work out, and if they'll have to choose sides. That puts a burden on our relationship, having so much riding on us having to stay together, it's a lot to deal with so early on. But, the problem with not telling my best friend everything is that when I have freak-outs like this, I don't have anyone to talk to.

"Look, Mia, we haven't talked much over the last couple of days, and it kinda feels like you've been ignoring me. I know Kellan told you about what happened with Kyle, and I'm sorry if you're mad at me about that, or feel like I overstepped," Bree mutters as I gulp down the hot coffee much quicker than I probably should have.

Bree fiddles with her cup as she looks and waits for me to answer. With everything going on, I'd almost forgotten about the horrendous day that started it all. Why she would think I'm mad is baffling as hell, which I tell her. "Why would you say that? I'm not mad at you. I'm so fucking grateful you've been able to help, even if it's just a little. I promise, I've just got some other stuff going on."

"Let me guess. You don't want to talk about it?" Bree asks, with a small smile, and though her words seem kind, there's a definite element of sarcasm in her tone.

"What's that supposed to mean?" I didn't really intend on it coming out as snappy as it did, but there was something about the way she spoke just then that caused my hackles to rise.

"I just mean that you are an expert at keeping things to yourself. I know for a long time, you've needed to, but now you don't. I'm supposed to be your best friend, Mia, and you don't trust me enough to talk to me. I had to find out about that asshole Kyle from Kellan, for fuck's sake. You trust him more than you do me." Her voice is strangled, almost like she's struggling to hold it together. I want to shout, to remind her that she isn't all that fucking great at communicating either, but the truth is, she's right. I should've trusted her. We aren't scared little teenagers anymore. Fuck, Bree runs the London criminal underworld, and she's scarily fucking good at it. I should've known she could help me.

"I'm sorry. You're right. I should've known you could help me, but it has fuck all to do with trust. Kellan and I have spent a lot of time talking, learning to trust each other, not for me, but because he needs it. He needs to know he can trust me with Hallie. It makes perfect sense that I would learn to trust him in return. As for Kyle, the only reason Kellan knew first is that he was here when I got the texts. I know you're a badass now who can help me, but it's hard to not see us as scared kids trying to learn to be fucking debutants despite not having an inch of class between us."

Bree laughs. "Speak for your fucking self. I'm very classy, I will have you know."

Now it's my turn to laugh along with her. "I hate that people know my secrets, particularly you. But not for the reasons you think. You care so much, Bree. I knew when you found out about my father, you would feel guilty for not being able to save me back then. We were just kids. Even if I'd told you, there's nothing we could have done. But, for those moments that I hung out with you, it gave me a chance to be a normal kid for a while, something I'd never experienced before. I'm lucky to have you, Bree. Don't ever question our friendship."

Her breath catches and as I look into my beautiful, fiery friend's eyes, I'm shocked to find they are filled with tears. I can count on one hand the amount of times I've seen this strong, stubborn woman cry, and to see her shedding a tear for me breaks my heart.

"Just so you know, I'm very much considering taking out Whitlock. I just need to find out what he's planning before I do." I nod my head, not entirely sure what to say to that. I know it's something Kellan's talked about, but I've never really thought about how I feel.

There's no love lost between my father and I. I don't view him as a dad, and I would most definitely go as far as to say I fucking hate him. So, why do my insides do crazy flips to the point of nausea at the thought of them killing him? My father's the cause of all my nightmares, and he's the reason I'm struggling to have even the most basic of relationships with Kellan, yet killing him doesn't sit right with me and I don't know why. It doesn't seem enough. I had to live through years of abuse, yet he's able to just stop existing. That doesn't feel like a punishment, and I want him to be punished.

I don't answer, I just let the silence fill the room, until Hallie's giggling cuts through it like a knife. "What are you up to this morning?" Bree asks, as I pick Hallie up when I've cleaned up even more banana off her. How the hell does this girl have so much of the stuff left over? I thought I got it all before, but it appears she had some stashed away. I think she's going to need a full outfit change before we head out.

"I was just going to take her to the park this morning. Kellan is around this afternoon. He asked me to be back by lunchtime so we could all go somewhere together. I have no idea where, though." My brain has been running over all the possibilities since he told me yesterday. At first I thought this was our date, but he informed me that we wouldn't be taking Hallie on our date. Not that I mind, but he keeps joking that typically a date just involves two people, and no babies.

"Would you mind if I tag along with you to the park? It's the wedding in a couple of weeks and if I'm being totally honest, I'm trying not to think about it. Every time Ryleigh or Freya ring me to plan something, I freak out. My heart races and I feel physically sick. I want to marry Liam, of course I do. I'm just terrified of something going wrong again," she explains, her voice sounding strained. If Bree's admitting that she's scared, then she must be fucking terrified.

"Of course. You really don't have anything to stress over, Bree. You know as well as I do that Liam, Kellan, Kian, and your Gramps plan on making sure that the wedding will be one hundred percent safe. No expense will be spared on security, you know that. And Ryleigh was given strict instructions to dial it back." Bree's eyes practically shoot out of her head. Ever since Ry was given permission to plan the party, Bree's been freaked out over what it's going to be like.

"I know that, but it doesn't stop me from having flashbacks. I think that because I haven't dealt with Jimmy yet, it's not helping. Gramps thinks he's got important information, and that's the only reason he's still alive. I was never close to Vernon, and honestly wasn't shocked he put himself first, but I never saw Jimmy's betrayal coming," Bree explains, while I place Hallie on the living room floor to start getting her changed.

Bree hands over the changing bag and gathers the clothes off the side to help me get her ready to go out. I give Bree a small smile. I, of all people, know exactly how she feels. "I know what it's like to be betrayed by the person who's supposed to love you. Take it from me, however you deal with him, it won't help how you feel. Everyone deals with things differently, but doing nothing will be worse. Don't ever forget you're a badass!"

Hallie giggles as I finish my sentence, making it sound like she's joining in our conversation. Once she's ready and secured into her pram, we head towards the park. I love being able to spend time with my friend, talking to her about the wedding, and hopefully helping to calm her down a bit. Although we live together, we don't often spend much time as just the two of us. It's actually quite refreshing getting to gossip like we used to.

The more she talks, I can see she's getting calmer. They love each other so much, and I hate that their special day is tainted by their previous attempt. They deserve to have such a special day.

We reach the park, and even though Hallie isn't even one yet, this park is equipped for younger babies. There are some baby swings, little rocking ducks, and even a sandpit for her to play in. Hallie's squeals when she realises where we are lets us know how much she enjoys it here.

We put her in the sandpit to start with, and we both sit with her to make sure she doesn't eat the sand. Hallie's current phase means anything and everything goes into her mouth. I think it's because she's teething. It's hard enough getting the sand out of her nappy, I don't need it in her mouth as well.

We play in the sandpit for a while, and Hallie loves it. Bree and I continue to use some of the buckets and spades to build little sandcastles, only for Hallie to knock them over with the most hilarious laugh. Girl's good at destruction, I'll give her that.

"Why don't I take her on the swings for a bit, and you head over to the coffee cart and get us some drinks?" Bree asks, pointing to the coffee cart in the corner of the park. I also see her eying the muffins up lovingly. Despite Bree having a figure to die for, she's put herself on a diet in preparation for her wedding. We've all told her it's crazy, and that she looks unbelievably good without losing any weight, but she won't be told. I think she's sending me to the cart because her willpower only stretches so far, and apparently her breaking point is a raspberry and white chocolate muffin.

"Okay, I will grab us some drinks and go to that picnic table over there. Bring her over in a bit," I say as I stand, brushing sand off my ass in the process.

Bree picks up Hallie, who begins flailing her arms and screaming because she doesn't want to leave the sandpit. Sand she had in her hands when Bree picked her up flies all over Bree, including in her hair and mouth. I give her an apologetic smile before walking away, leaving her with a screaming baby. I can hear exactly when Bree gets Hallie on the swings because the screaming stops and giggles ring loud instead. She loves being pushed on the swings.

Joining the back of the queue, with around five people in front of me, I notice a blonde woman comes to stand behind me. It feels as though she's just a little too close. I can't even explain it, I just get a strange vibe from her. So, when she starts talking to me, my stomach starts to sink.

"Mia, please don't yell or act alarmed. I promise, I'm not here to hurt you or to cause problems," she says, which admittedly doesn't settle my nerves. I turn to face her, and as our eyes meet, a strange feeling comes over me, like I've met her before.

"Who are you?" I ask.

"I'm Shayla, and Hallie is my daughter." Her eyes glance towards the swings, and I'm grateful that Bree seems to have Hallie distracted. A rage I probably have no right to feel descends over me. Hearing her call Hallie her daughter, it angers and hurts me because she has no fucking right to that title.

"You can't be here. Not without Kellan." I start to walk away, but she grabs hold of my arm and pulls me back into the queue. Her grip isn't bruising, but it's tight, and her expression looks serious.

"I'm not here to see her," she nods towards Hallie, pain etched across her face. "I'm here to see you. I need to know what role you play in my daughter's life. I know you're her nanny, and you look after her nearly every day, but I need to know if it's more than that."

Rage I've never felt before descends, and I spin to face her, yanking my arm from her grip so forcefully that her nails drag along my skin. I don't bother looking to see if the action has drawn blood, it was my fault.

"How is that any of your fucking business? Are you coming back to claim Kellan or Hallie? You can fuck off if you think I won't fight for them," I shout, gaining looks from others in the queue. I'm just lucky Bree hasn't looked over to see me arguing with her. I don't know if Bree has met Shayla before, but I don't want to risk it.

Shayla gives me a small, sad smile. "I'm not here to get them back. I couldn't get Hallie back even if I wanted to. And Kellan…as much as I loved him, and despite what I'm sure he's told you, I really did fucking love him, but we weren't ever supposed to be together. He deserves to be with someone who makes him the happiest he can be, who can help him to realise what love really is. What I'm asking is whether that's you or not."

My heart skips a beat and I release the breath I didn't know I was holding. Hearing her say she isn't here to claim back my family, it's exactly what I needed to hear. I only just got them, I'm not ready to let them go.

"We aren't anything official yet, but I'm hoping so." As soon as the words leave my mouth, Shayla's face falls. Her eyes that were filled with pain before now look almost vacant, and she's staring at me like I just said the last thing in the world she wanted to hear. Why does she look so fucking annoyed when she literally just told me she's not here for him? Did she lie to me?

"Excuse me, Miss. What can I get you?" shouts the young lad behind the coffee cart. I'm so caught up in our discussion, I didn't realise I'd reached the front of the line. I place my order and step aside, joining an equally long queue to collect my coffees when ready. Shayla joins behind me and pulls my arm to gain my attention.

A sinking feeling I can't explain begins in my stomach, nausea twisting my insides as I wait for what she has to say, knowing nothing good will come from this. "Did you know his mother filed for sole custody, claiming he's an unfit parent?"

Hearing her say those words causes me to fly into a fit of rage, anger rippling away beneath the surface, as this woman brings out my bad side. Terrified she could turn my whole world upside down, I step forward until I'm right in her face, grabbing hold of her T-shirt at the same time, trying not to make too much of a scene.

"Don't ever fucking say that. Kellan's the best parent that little girl could ever ask for. His mother is a spiteful bitch who wants what she can't have. The worst thing for Hallie would be for anyone to take her away from the only family she's ever known." I let go of her T-shirt, taking a slight step back now I've regained some composure. She looks at me like I'm telling her what she wants to hear, so I decide to be honest, and hope it works. "Did Kellan struggle as a single parent for a while? Yeah, he did. Hallie was going through a phase where she didn't sleep any longer than an hour at a time. When she was getting her first tooth and was in pain, she would only sleep in Kellan's arms. He felt like he was drowning, and so he asked his family for help. His mother babysat on three occasions, and each time she brought a nanny to do the work. Kellan didn't want Hallie being looked after by a stranger, so he turned to the only person in his life that's never let him down..."

Just as I'm about to say the final word, Shayla beats me to it. "Liam."

Hearing us both say the same word results in matching small smiles. My heart aches as there's no denying this girl knows Kellan. I can't deny that it makes me crazy jealous.

"Liam and his fiancée, Bree, who's over there with Hallie, took them in and helped Kellan become the amazing father he is today. I'm Bree's best friend and I needed somewhere to stay. Kellan needed someone to watch Hallie when he was at work. I'm doing my early years educational qualification through an online university. This job's part of my university placement, and without it I can't graduate," I explain.

"I'm sorry to hear that, but it's not going to change what I have to say." Shay tries to hold herself taller, taking deep breaths before continuing. Clearly terrified to utter the words, but she wants to sound strong. I knew I wasn't going to like anything she has to say.

"Which is what?" I snap. I know I sound like an asshole, but this is my family, I have to protect them.

"My lawyer contacted me when Marianna put in the custody request. I'm not sure if Kel ever read the papers I signed giving away my parental rights, but they clearly state that if ever Kellan can't be a parent, for whatever reason, or his ability to parent is ever brought into question, I will be contacted to have a say on who cares for her. This isn't to get her back, I just didn't want something to happen to Kellan, and for Hallie to end up with strangers. They've asked me if I think Kellan or Marianna is the better parent, so I started doing my research. I figured there had to be a reason why Marianna would do this, there's no smoke without fire, as they say."

"There's so much wrong with what you just said. Firstly, if you're not part of Hallie's life, what the hell makes you think you know enough to have a say over who raises her. As for Marianna, she's nutty as a fruit cake. She abandoned Kellan at six years old, so what will make her a better parent this time around? I've only seen Marianna with Hallie once, despite living with them a couple of months, and she never even held her. I promise you, there's no better parent for Hallie than Kellan. That shouldn't ever be in question." My voice is stern, but if ever there's a time to fight, it's now for the people I care about.

Shayla gives me a small smile. "I already know that. I just wanted to see how much you love him. I want to know if you love him enough to do the right thing."

Her eyes flick across to Bree and Hallie, obviously looking to see if they're coming over here soon. I don't need to look, I can recognise Hallie's shrieks of joy from across the park. Hearing her talk about my feelings for Kellan, causes my anger to bubble again.

"Why is that any of your fucking business?" I snarl, as the lady making the coffees calls my name.

I head forward, ignoring whatever Shayla was about to say, grabbing the takeaway bag holding our muffins and the cups carrier with our coffee in it. Thankfully, the picnic table I pointed out to Bree is still available. If Shayla has any sense, she'll leave now. I don't want her anywhere near Hallie, and if Bree learns who she is, she may just kick her ass, and I might let her.

Sadly, she doesn't take the hint, and I hear her footsteps running after me. She places a hand on my shoulder and I spin around. Meeting her gaze, I let her know how serious I am, and she has the good sense to look embarrassed, her eyes shifting around to make sure nobody's watching our exchange. I need to make it clear we're done here. I tried the nice approach, now I need to be more forceful.

"Bree will be here any minute. Either you leave now, or I'll tell her who you are. I'm sure if you know Kellan, and have done your research, you'll know who Bree is." Shayla takes a step back, appearing almost startled by the growl in my tone.

"I know who she is. It's you I'm worried about. I know who your father is, Mia. I know what type of man he is, and I don't want you or him anywhere near Hallie. So, you have a choice. You can stay on as Hallie's nanny until you finish your course, and then you have to leave. Leave the house and never speak to Hallie or Kellan ever again. Let me be very clear, I'm only saying you can stay on as her nanny, as long as that's all it is. You end your relationship with Kellan, and stop playing mum to her. You are not her mother and I don't want someone like you pretending to be." Her words aren't said nastily, yet

I feel as though she's just slapped me around the face. I can't help but take a step back, and my breath catches in my throat.

"No," I mutter, shaking my head as I bite down on my lip, trying to stop the tears from welling up in my eyes. I hate the fact that this woman is judging me on my past, using it as an excuse to stop me from being happy. My brain feels fuzzy, and I can't find the words to reply to her.

"If you don't agree to my terms, I'll tell the judge Kellan's an unfit father and ask for custody to be given to Marianna. I have evidence of Kellan's criminal activities. The Reapers keep track of people they work with, as they never know when they'll need dirt to use on others. I hate to do this, but—"

She hasn't even had the chance to finish when I interrupt her lies. "No you fucking don't. Don't lie. You are using my past, of which you really know nothing about, to blackmail me into staying away from Kellan and Hallie. How fucking pathetic are you? Is this about keeping Hallie safe, like you claim, or is it more to do with making sure Kellan doesn't find happiness? Is it a case of you can't have him so nobody else can either?" I shout, my hands physically shaking now. I feel like I'm fighting for my life, and I really don't know what to do.

"Think whatever you like. You're right, I don't know you, but I do know your father and I don't want him in my daughter's life. So, if you love Kellan the way I think you do, and you want Kellan to keep custody, you will do the right thing. I have an appointment with my lawyer in half an hour, so I need an answer. And don't even think about telling me you've dumped him and still crawl into his bed every night. I have my ways of finding things out. If you break our arrangement, I'll have Hallie taken away instantly. If you know anything about me, you'll know I have no problems hurting Kellan if I'm trying to keep Hallie safe," she states, her eyes seeming almost sad at the end. Like she feels bad about hurting him, but that doesn't make any sense.

My head's swimming, my breathing ragged. Why now? I've literally just become happy, for the first time in my entire life, and I feel it all being ripped away in the blink of an eye.

"You can't take Hallie from him. He wouldn't survive without her."

Every word I say is the truth. He adores Hallie, and I don't think he'd survive without her. The question is, can I live without them?

Shayla's face morphs into a scowl, and this is the first time she actually looks like the evil bitch Kellan claims she is. Before, I saw the broken girl, lost and confused, and I could relate to her. I always thought Kellan's views about Shayla were tainted by how she treated him, that she couldn't really be that malicious. But, right now, that's exactly how she looks.

"So, you're done with them?" she questions, and out of the corner of my eye, I see Bree looking our way. Thankfully, Hallie's still on the swing, but it won't be long before they come over.

"You can't stop me from caring about him. Keeping my distance isn't going to change how we feel about each other. You're hurting him all over again. Do you not give a shit who you hurt?" I snap as she tries to avoid eye contact, I place my hand on her arm to get her full attention. "You're a heartless bitch, and I hope you live a long, lonely life. You can chase me away all you want, but Kellan will fall in love again. He will date, and you can't chase everyone away. What you are doing here is wrong and judgemental. I cut my father off years ago and have nothing to do with him. Not only do I truly care about Kellan and Hallie, I would never hurt them. You should want them to be with someone who loves and cares for them, and that's me."

"Look…"

I cut Shayla off, needing her to hear everything I have to say. "When you first came over here, I recognised something in you. You have the same haunted look in your eyes that I've had for years. I thought you, of all people, would understand that when you find someone you care about, who cares about you, you should hold on to that. But, apparently you're a sick, twisted bitch who's so incapable of love you couldn't even hold your new baby, and cared so little it was easy for you to abandon her."

"It was never easy," she mumbles, her eyes glazing over with unshed tears.

"Then don't make me do the same," I beg.

"She's on her way over, so you better decide now." Shayla nods her head to indicate Bree's currently trying to prise Hallie away from the swing, while she holds on for dear life, her screams echoing around the park.

"You haven't really given me a choice. Give me one day to end it with him. Tomorrow we'll go back to him just being my boss, but give me one last night. Please!" Hopefully my plea will resonate with some part of her...that is if the callous bitch even has a heart.

"You can have tonight, but that's it. The day after you graduate, you move out and cut all contact, or I promise I'll go through with my plans. I will provide the judge with so much evidence, Kellan will never be able to see Hallie again. Do we have a deal?" she asks, holding her hand out for me to shake.

I look down at her hand, and back up to her face. I'm sure there's a look of repulsion on my face because she quickly lowers her hand. "We have a deal, but let me make this perfectly clear. You will regret this. Whatever your reasons are for doing this, they're all kinds of messed up, and you're so fucking wrong."

She shakes her head in disagreement before giving me a small smile. "It may not look like it to you, but everything I do is in Hallie's best interests. One day, I hope Kellan learns the truth, but right now, I'll settle for being the bitch in his story. As long as it keeps Hallie safe."

She doesn't wait for me to reply, which is good because I'm not entirely sure what to say. Instead, she walks off without looking back. But as she turned, I could have sworn I saw a rogue tear falling down her cheek. I don't care if she thinks she's acting in Hallie's best interests, or that there's more to her story. It doesn't make up for what she's doing to us now.

I can't believe when I set off this morning, I had it all. The only thing I had left was to take things all the way with Kellan. I thought we'd have time to build up to our perfect future. If I'm being totally honest, I thought we'd have forever. I should've known life doesn't work that way. I should've known I have no right to be happy.

"Who was that?" Bree asks when she reaches the table. Hallie's screams have died down to a normal decibel, but it isn't until she's sat on my knee with the stuffed penguin Liam bought, her tucked under one arm, that she finally begins to calm down.

If I thought it'd be difficult saying goodbye to Kellan, I never even considered how hard it would be to stop loving this little girl. I've always known that with time it'll be easy to fall in love with Kellan. Hell, I think I'm almost there. But with Hallie it was instantaneous. I challenge anyone to spend a couple of hours with Hallie and not fall in love with her. Every day she achieves something new, or she gives me a big, beautiful gummy smile, and I'm sunk. The thought of leaving her, after everything she's already lost, kills me. I know that when I leave, I'll be leaving a piece of my heart with each of them. I just hope I'm left with enough that it will still carry on beating.

"Nobody. We just made small talk in the queue. She's a nanny too, in between jobs, and was asking if I knew of anyone hiring, that's all." The lie falls off my tongue easily, but it feels like acid. I hate lying to Bree. As she stares at me, suspicion heavy in her eyes, I don't think my lie's as convincing as I hoped. I need to make my lies a lot more convincing because I'm spending the afternoon with Kellan, and when I break his heart tonight, I need it to be convincing.

Pacing up and down the living room, my brain feels like it's about to explode. Why the fuck am I so nervous about a bloody date? It's not like it's with a stranger either, it's Mia. She knows me, and I know her. It's not going to be one of those weird first dates where you have to try and hide all your annoying habits while attempting to function like a normal adult who can hold a proper conversation for a couple of hours. All while hoping the awkwardness will go away quickly.

"Will you stop pacing, you are wearing out the carpet," Liam snaps from where he's lounging on the sofa. His feet are up, and he's reading something on his tablet. No doubt doing research for a new job that he will tell me about tomorrow. He knows there's no point asking me anything while my anxiety is like this.

Mia and I agreed to not tell Bree and Liam about us dating, and I didn't exactly tell him, he guessed. "Are you going to tell me where you are going on this date? It better be good if it's got you this nervous," Liam asks, as he places the tablet down and picks up the can of Coke next to it, taking a gulp while he waits for my response.

"You aren't even supposed to know we're going on a date," I reply stubbornly, as I throw myself into the chair opposite Liam.

Looking down at my dark jeans, black Converse, and the tight white T-shirt that will pair nicely with my leather jacket, I wonder if I'm not dressed up enough. I mean, for what I have planned, it'll be fine, but I'm not sure if Mia will expect me to be more dressed up. I should have asked her. When she asked me what to wear, I told her casual, so hopefully this is fine. I try to quiet my brain, demanding it stop bringing up such trivial things that aren't even an issue until my brain makes them one. I hate when my anxiety does that, it's crippling.

"It's not exactly hard to miss the way you are together. It's obvious you like each other. I know I said I was against it originally, but you deserve to be happy. I like Mia, and after learning what she's been through, I'm sure I don't need to tell you how important it is she doesn't get hurt." Liam gives me that glare that you would imagine a father giving his son. Whenever Liam becomes a dad, he will have the role down, it comes naturally to him. This is why I feel absolutely no hesitation over leaving Hallie with him.

I know I told Mia that Hallie was coming with us, and that it wasn't a date, but after a lot of panicking, I realised this was the perfect time to do the date we talked about. Bree and Liam were both off to take care of Hallie all night, and the weather was lovely. Why wait for the perfect time when it's right here and right now.

"Aren't you supposed to be the one threatening her about not hurting me? Why do I have to get it twice? When Bree finds out, I'm sure she'll threaten to remove my bollocks, and she'll be pissed about being the last to know." Liam's face falls and he bolts upright instantly.

"Oh fuck. What am I going to do? Never mind what she'll do to your bollocks, what about mine?" Liam shrieks, his eyes darting around like he expects Bree to walk in any second. She really doesn't like to be left out of the loop on things, and as her boyfriend, Liam is responsible for keeping her updated. But, technically, neither of them should know about this.

When Bree and Mia brought Hallie back in from the park earlier, for just a moment I considered not asking Mia if she wanted to make this our first date. I can't really put my finger on it, but she looked different. When she realised I was looking at her, she schooled her face like she always does, but not before I saw the look of sadness in her eyes. I just couldn't explain it. Bree said they had a lovely time at the park, and Hallie was fast asleep, so it can't have gone too badly. Yet, Mia isn't quite behaving like herself.

"Bree quite likes your balls, so I think you'll be fine. Me, on the other hand, I'm fair game," I answer Liam, who instantly relaxes.

With a small smile, he replies in his usual cocky manner. "Yeah, she will rip your bollocks off and feed them to you if you hurt Mia."

Now it's my turn to laugh. "Oh, I already know that. Actually, speaking of dying…"

"What?" Liam interrupts, as I think of a way to continue this conversation. It's one I've been meaning to have with him for a while now, but the timing has just never seemed right. Only, now we're on a deadline, and I have to get the paperwork completed and sent to my lawyer, so there's no time like the present. I think I already know the answer, but that doesn't mean I'm not still nervous as hell asking.

"Since my mother started this custody bullshit, the judge needs to know the ins and outs of not only my life, but Hallie's too. I've already identified you, Bree, and Mia as my support system, to help me with raising Hallie. So the judge knows I'm not doing this alone. Ryleigh, Freya, Evan, and Finn are also included as my family, and even though I'm not sure I would want Hallie spending any long periods with them —well, maybe Freya would be fine—but, they are still my support system. Besides, they were fucking adamant I put them down," I add with a chuckle. One that is replicated by Liam.

"That sounds like them," he adds, giving me the biggest smile. When I joined the Doughty family as a kid, I never thought I'd be seen as one of their siblings. I always thought they'd taken me in because I was Liam's best friend, and nobody else would have me. But the longer I spent with them, the more I got to know the whole family. I became friends with each of them in different ways. Even Desmond and Von treated me like part of the family, even though the Doughtys aren't exactly an ordinary family. I still got Christmas presents, and they celebrated my birthday. They became my family, and now they're Hallie's.

"There's one thing the judge is very adamant about knowing. He wants to know, given that I'm a single parent, who will get custody of Hallie if anything were to ever happen to me. They can't just hand her over to Shayla. That bitch signed away all her rights, and she can't ever get them back." My voice becomes sharp, like it always does when I talk about her. Hallie doesn't need people in her life that are going to let her down, and I just need to prove to the judge that sometimes it isn't the family you are born into that care about you the most, it's the family you choose for yourself.

"Doesn't fucking deserve them back," Liam chunters, not necessarily to me, just in general. I don't know who hates Shayla more, me or Liam.

"Anyway, I need to tell the judge what my plans are if anything were to happen to me. Obviously, Hallie doesn't have any blood relatives I would want her to stay with. If it's okay with you and Bree, I would like to put you down as her guardians. Both you and Bree will be named, if you are together, but if something goes crazy wrong and you are no longer together, then it will just be you." I know I haven't really asked him a question, that I'm more just telling him what my plans are, but I still wait for him to answer.

A big, cocky grin spreads across his face and for the slightest of seconds, I could have sworn I saw the glisten of a tear in one of his eyes. "Thank you, bro. You know I would do anything for the both of you, and I'm kinda blown away that you would trust me with her."

With a small chuckle, I make my reply cocky to try and cut through all the emotion that seems to be clogging up the air. "Well, I don't exactly have many options." Liam knows I'm joking. There are a lot of other people I could leave Hallie with, but nobody I would trust more than Liam. Besides, I think Hallie would be pissed as hell if she went to anyone except her uncle Liam. She loves him more than she does me.

"Fuck you," Liam retorts with a laugh. "Wait…who gets her if I'm dead. If we die together?" he asks, and I shrug my shoulders. This is a hard one, and it's one I've been going over and over in my head recently.

"The honest answer is that I don't know. I was thinking of Mia, but this is our first date, and I don't want to scare her away by asking her to take custody of Hallie if anything happens to us. Bree is also in the running, obviously. The only hesitation I have is that if she doesn't have you, I see her throwing herself into her job, and she could end up getting herself killed too. I don't want Hallie to lose more people. At this stage she has already lost plenty. I think out of all our siblings, Freya would probably give Hal the best life, away from all our drama. I just need to make sure she's kept away from my mother and Shayla," I explain, and Liam nods his head.

"I think Mia would be more than happy. I think you're right, if I'm not around, Bree will be very unstable for a while, but I think having Hallie would keep her grounded and give her an excuse to keep surviving. So, don't count her out just yet. Freya is definitely a good choice. I know she's young, but she's so much older than her age. Freya's the most likely to leave this life behind to live a normal life. She would give Hallie a lot of stability, but her age could be an issue if we're dying soon."

"Well, I have to give the plans to the judge this week, but I'm really hoping we don't die anytime soon. I only have to give two names, so I'll have to think about it. Maybe talk to Mia, and if she doesn't want to do it, I will talk to Bree and Frey. Please don't talk to them before I get a chance to. That includes Bree." I give him a pointed stare, and he rolls his eyes at me.

"If you keep making me hide things from my wife-to-be, it will be me who dies first!" Liam states, and before I have a chance to reply, footsteps hitting the stairs in the hallway next to us pull our attention back to the room. Fuck, I almost forgot that I'm supposed to be freaking out about my date.

Bree and Hallie walk through the door first. Bree's knowing smile, and the little wink she gives me, lets me know she's no longer in the dark. She clearly knows we're going on a date, and I can hear Liam release the breath he's holding, as he realises his bollocks will live to see another day. Hallie gives me a small chuckle from in Bree's arms, and I lean down to kiss her on the forehead, but of course she smacks me around the head, indicating for me to get out of the way so she can reach Liam. She wastes no time, squawking until Bree hands her over to him. Yeah, I've definitely made the right decision picking Liam.

I'm too busy looking at Hallie, I miss Mia's entrance. But, as soon as I see her, I feel like I've been hit around the head with a frying pan. This girl is out of this world beautiful. I've heard people talk about their heart skipping a beat, and I always thought it's just what people wrote about in love songs, to make them sound more chaotic. But, as I take in her beauty, for the shortest of seconds, my heart really does miss a beat.

When I first met Mia, she had bright blonde hair, and I liked the blonde, but her natural brunette colour makes her look so much more like Mia. Like she's slowly becoming more comfortable in her own skin, which is something I love to see. Her darker hair, that hangs just below her shoulder blades, has a slight wave to it, and does an excellent job of helping to accentuate her beautiful brown eyes. She's wearing a white flowy sundress that stops just above her knees, and there are beautiful blue flowers dotted all across the fabric. I've never seen her looking so feminine, and fuck does it suit her.

"Mia...you look..." I mumble, hoping my new-found confidence will start to kick in soon. Hell, at this rate, I would just settle for the anxiety being gone.

Mia gives me the biggest, most beautiful smile, and I realise it's not the make-up she has on, it's the sunshine that radiates from her the more she smiles. She looks like she's about to answer, but Bree beats her to it. "You better be about to finish that sentence in a positive way."

Everyone laughs, but I'm too busy losing myself in this woman's beauty. I've woken up next to Mia on more than one occasion, and I've also seen her naked. I've seen her while she was recounting the worst moments of her life, and I would like to think that I feature in at least some of her greatest achievements. Throughout each of these, I've noticed how stunning she is. Yet, as she stands here in front of me now, I feel as though I'm seeing her for the first time all over again, and all I can do is stand here, open-mouthed, gasping, as she takes my breath away.

Ignoring Bree's comment as though she never even spoke, I keep my eyes fixed on Mia, so she knows how serious I am. "You are beyond beautiful, Mia. You look so amazing."

I take a step towards her, almost on instinct, and I notice her breath hitch before she starts breathing again, faster than she was a second ago. I don't exactly know what I'm doing, it's as though my body has a mind of its own. I think I want to touch her, to feel if she is real, maybe? But, I'm put off by Liam and Bree staring like we're their favourite soap opera. I certainly can't kiss her the way I would like to with them watching.

"Thank you. You look great too," Mia replies, as a bright red blush floods from her cheeks to across her collarbones. I love that she's more embarrassed admitting that she was checking me out, than she ever got while I was practically eye-fucking her in front of our friends. "Should we get going?" she asks, and all I can do is nod.

Liam stands from where he's sitting on the sofa, picking Hallie up with him. She gives a loud shriek before her hand clasps onto some of Liam's hair tightly. He tries to pry his hair out of her fingers, but to no avail. She holds on to it like a starved woman who just discovered a bar of chocolate. She isn't letting go of that anytime soon, and each time he tries to get her to let go, she yanks just that little more.

Walking over to where he stands with her, I gently pry her hand off Liam's hair, much to her annoyance. I give her seconds before she does it again, so I decide to capitalise on it while she's still in a happy mood. Leaning forward, I plant a kiss on one of her big, chubby cheeks, and that's enough to pull her attention away from Liam, even just for a few seconds. "Okay, Hallie Bear. Daddy and Auntie Mia are going out for a bit, and you are staying here with Auntie Bree and Uncle Liam. Please, try to be a good girl. I hope to take Auntie Mia on lots more dates, and I can only do that if you don't scare away the babysitters. How does that sound?"

Hallie stares at me with those big, beautiful blue eyes that look so much like my own, and I can't help but smile at her. She gives me a small squeal which I take as confirmation that she has heard and agrees with what I just said. Obviously, the chances of that being true are next to none, but I want to at least feel as though I tried.

I reach over to stroke the hair out of Hallie's face, and she reaches out to grab onto me with her hand. Her little hand grabs two of my fingers and she holds on to them with a grip that's impressive for a girl of her age. That's when the babbling begins, and we all try desperately to hear whether she's learnt to form any actual words, but no.

Mia takes a step forward and grabs hold of Hallie's hand. "Hey, beautiful girlie. I'm only stealing your daddy away for a couple of hours, and I promise I will bring him back to you. Have a good time here with Auntie Bree and Uncle Liam, okay? I would say try to be a good girl, but we both know you are going to run rings around them. Try to be good all the same, please. See you in the morning, beautiful. Love you."

Fuck. Hearing this gorgeous, perfect girl talk to my daughter in that way is doing ridiculous things, not only to my cock, but my heart too. I felt like it started to beat again. My heart skipped a beat, and with each new beat that follows, I feel them all. It's like my heart is beating just for these two girls.

Liam must have seen the change in my expression, that bastard is in tune with everyone, and his voice seems to bring us all out of the mini trance we're in. "You two better get going, before we change our minds about babysitting this little terror," Liam jokes as he nuzzles his head into Hallie's neck, much to her delight.

I lean over and give her a kiss again, but she doesn't give a shit right now. She has Liam, and that makes me smile. I know without a shadow of a doubt that I've made the right choice when it comes to caring for Hallie if I'm not here. The lawyers were right, I don't want just anybody to raise my daughter. If I don't have an advanced directive, the courts can decide who she lives with. That could be my mother, or even worse, it could be Shayla. I don't want that. My mother couldn't raise a plant, let alone a child. She will just pay a nanny to do it for her, and I don't want that for Hallie. But even that is preferable to the thought of her going to live with Shayla and

Whiskey in the Reapers' compound. No way in hell is that happening.

Taking hold of Mia's hand, we say our goodbyes, and I lead her to the garage. "Are you okay putting on leathers with that sexy dress on? If not, I can ask Liam to lend me the car," I ask, pointing towards my bike and the bike leathers I already have laid out.

This will be the first time Mia has been on the bike with me, so I took the time to buy her some leather trousers and a leather jacket that she should be able to put on over what she is wearing now. I also bought her a black and purple helmet, which will do a perfect job of keeping her safe. I had to buy them all new as I've never had anyone on my bike with me before.

"I've always wanted to go on a motorbike," Mia says, as she picks up the helmet I bought for her, turning it around to inspect it.

"Well then, it's your lucky day. Do you need a hand getting into your leathers? They might be a bit tight to start with." I hold the trousers out for her, and with a nod of her head I drop to my knees in front of her.

I've always thought taking a woman's clothes off is one of the sexiest things ever, but as I slowly pull Mia's leathers up, over her creamy, silken skin, I have to hold back a groan. Thankfully, I haven't put my leathers on yet, because my jeans are starting to feel impossibly tight, and I'm sure it would be damn painful if I had them on already. Pitching a tent in leathers is fucking torture.

As the leathers reach the top of Mia's thighs, she slowly pulls her dress up, until it is bunched up above her belly button, revealing a sexy pair of black lace shorts. The intricate lace design barely covers her pussy, and I'm trying really hard not to rip them off her body right now. Instead, I turn her around under the guise that I'm trying to get the leather up over her ass, but really I just want to see what she looks like in the panties from behind. The curve of each cheek is beautifully exposed, as the material sits high on her ass. It looks like a perfect juicy peach, and it's taking every ounce of strength to not take a bite out of her right now.

Reluctantly, I pull the leathers the final part of the way up, and I can't hold back the groan that rips from my throat when Mia has to shimmy her hips to get the trousers over the last hurdle. As her hips sway from side to side, my cock pulsates as it strains to seek freedom from its denim constraints. I try to think of anything to distract myself. I start to list all the Liverpool Football Club's current players, then as many facts as I can think of, anything that could distract me from the beauty in front of me long enough for my dick to go down. If it doesn't, my leathers most definitely will not fit.

Finally, I feel my plan starting to work, so I close my eyes tightly to avoid catching sight of her and starting the process all over again. I pull the leathers up quicker than I ever have in my life. So quickly, in fact, that I have to hop from one foot to the other, and I almost crash into my bike as I reach out looking for stability. I feel her hand touch mine, and I pull it away quickly, so I can get the leathers fastened. Once they're safely on, I finally open my eyes. It's a good fucking job I kept them closed. As soon as I open them, I'm greeted with a view of Mia, dressed head to toe in leather, looking like a badass. Instantly, my cock becomes rock hard again. It hasn't been this sensitive since I first learned to wank as a teenager.

Biting her lip, when she finally speaks, her voice is low and gravelly, sounding exactly like sex. "I like you in leather."

That sexy, coy smile she has etched on her face lets me know she's thinking some very naughty things, and that makes it even worse. I reach down to try and adjust myself, but there's no point. There's no more room in the leather, nowhere to move it to. The only option is to get my cock out, and as much as I would fucking love to do that, it's not really the best start to a first date. So, I settle for throbbing pain instead.

"You don't look so bad yourself, Flower." I give her a little wink, since I know how much she hates her nickname. She rolls her eyes, and the urge to bend her over the bike is fierce. Obviously, she deserves better than that for our first time.

I instruct her on what to expect while she's riding on the back of the bike, since she's never been on a bike before. I know she'll love it and I'm glad I get to be her first for this.

Once we're all set to go, I climb on, and she follows me. Her arms wrap around my waist, just like I showed her, and I try not to think about the fact that I can feel her pussy grinding against my ass. Her hands swipe slowly over my abs, like she is trying to take as much time as possible, trying to feel as much as she can before her fists grip hold of my leathers. Reaching behind me, I scoop my hands under her petite ass and pull her so that her front is plastered against my back. Now, there's not even enough room to slide a piece of paper between our bodies.

As I bring my hands back, I make sure to drag my fingers along her thighs, scraping along her new leather trousers, and she squeezes her legs tighter around my hips. I hear the most amazing moan escape her lips and shivers ripple down my spine. It's taking all my energy not to pull her around so she's sitting in front of me and I can smash my lips against hers.

"Put this on. If you don't, I will kiss you and we may never leave this garage. And that wouldn't be a great first date, now would it?" As I hand over the helmet, she chuckles.

I feel her breath against my ear before I hear her speak. "I don't know, it sounds like a pretty good first date to me." Her voice has that gravelly, raspy tone that seems to have an instant connection with my dick. Hearing her say that, combined with her breath tickling my ear, I can't help but groan.

"You'll be the death of me, Flower. Now, put your helmet on," I growl, as I push the helmet over my own head. As soon as I know she's safe, I bring the bike to life.

Her legs grip tightly around my thighs, and her arms pull me impossibly closer. I can feel her tits pressed against my back, her helmet resting on my shoulder. The deep rumble of the engine rips through us, and the power I feel between my legs is intoxicating—I can only imagine how Mia feels. I've often wondered if these vibrations are enough to turn women on, which is something I'll have to check with Mia when we arrive.

Reaching the main road, I open up the throttle, shouting back to Mia as I do. "Hold on tight." Although, it seems a stupid thing to say as I don't think her grip could get any tighter.

Once we are off the main roads, and away from all the traffic or stop lights, I show her what the bike is really capable of. Though, I don't go as fast as normal, as I have precious cargo on board. I know how fast I can go and still be in control of the bike. As it reaches around a hundred miles an hour, I hear Mia's squeals of delight followed by infectious laughter as the wind sails through us.

We travel for just under an hour, and just before we arrive, I think Mia's worked out where we are going because she starts to do a happy dance with her hands against my abdomen. The closer we get, the more I can feel her buzzing with excitement.

Seeing the turn off I'm looking for, I slow down and pull into the dirt road. It leads all the way down to a very small beach. Most people will travel farther along the coast, to the more popular part of the beach that is used by tourists. This section is small and secluded, with caves on both sides. When the tide comes in, it's like this little patch of beach doesn't even exist. Luckily the tide is starting to go back out for the evening, and so it's the perfect place to sit and watch the sunset. I park the bike at the end of the road, just before the few steps that lead down to the beach. I turn to try and help Mia off the bike, but she springs off easily, bouncing from one foot to the other in excitement.

As she pulls the helmet off and places it onto the seat of the bike, her hair sticks up at all angles, looking like sexy bed hair, but it's her wide eyes that really grab me. She takes in the beach, and as her astonished gaze flicks to me, they begin to glaze over. As she speaks, her voice seems almost clogged with emotion. "Thank you."

Two little words is all she's able to say, but it melts me. This is such an everyday thing for most people. I think a vast portion of people in England have been to the beach at some point. Yet, Mia hasn't. While we've been talking, I've found out that there's a lot she's missed out on. She's never been to an amusement park, a theme park, or even a fair. She's never been on a roller coaster, or played hook-a-duck. Luckily, hearing all about her troubled past has given me lots of date ideas. I've been talking to Liam about planning a family trip to a theme park. I know if I invite one Doughty, I have to invite them all. Hallie might be a bit young at the moment to enjoy it, but there are some rides she will love. Hell, my daughter's a beautiful weirdo, so she will probably want to go on all the death-defying rides, which is a good thing. I want her to be fear-free. I also don't ever want her to have a childhood like Mia's, where she misses out on such simple things.

"I can't believe you brought me to the beach," Mia exclaims, looking at me in awe, like I've given her the best gift ever. She looks torn between coming to me and running onto the beach. So I make the decision for her.

"Let's get these leathers off, and your shoes, then we can go and feel the sand beneath our feet. I've got some blankets because when the sun starts to go down it will get cold here," I tell her, as I reach for the bag I threw over the back of my bike before leaving.

Mia wastes no time stripping the leathers off, and she practically throws them onto the floor, along with her slip-on shoes. I haven't even started to get mine off yet, I'm too enthralled just watching her, as she bounces on her feet in excitement.

"You go ahead, I'll be down with our stuff in a second." She doesn't wait for me to finish before heading in the direction of the beach. She's only made it a couple of steps when she stops and turns abruptly. She runs over to me and before I have a chance to figure out what she's doing, her lips crash against mine. I drop everything I'm holding, and I lower my hands to cup her ass. It's the only hint she needs and as she hitches one of her legs up, I lift her. Mia's legs clamp around my ass, as her arms fly around my neck. Her lips continue their mission as her tongue demands entry into my mouth. At this point, I would give her anything.

Mia's beautiful sundress is hitched around her waist, and I can feel the lace of her panties under my touch. Just my strained jeans, and her thin, lace panties separate us. She can feel my hard dick grinding against her clit and she arches her back as she moans into my mouth. Thank fuck there's nobody else around as what we're doing shouldn't be done in public.

Slowly, and with incredible difficulty, I lower her to the floor. Pulling away when she tastes this good is fucking painful. I lean in to whisper in her ear. "If we don't stop now, the only view you will get of the sunset is while I'm fucking you over this bike." My voice is a growl, and she shivers with pleasure, biting her lip to try and hold back a moan I know she's trying to stop.

Straightening her sundress, I point towards the steps leading to the beach, and spank her on her ass cheek when she doesn't move straight away. Her responding yelp is music to my ears, and her giggles ring out as she skips towards the beach while I gather up all our stuff and follow behind her.

As soon as I make it onto the beach I freeze, just watching Mia enjoy the sand for the first time. I watch as she crinkles her toes, watching as the sand squishes out around her feet. With each step she takes, she marvels at the footprint left behind. She does this all the way to the edge of the water, where she tests the different texture of the wet sand. Small waves begin to crash around her toes, covering up to her ankles and her shrieks of delight and surprise—no doubt at how fucking freezing the water is—echoes all around us. November isn't usually the best time for a trip to the beach, but the weather's surprisingly nice, so I capitalised on that. The sea is far too cold to go in, but Mia doesn't seem to mind, she wants to feel the waves.

"It's freezing," she calls back to me, and I can't help but laugh.

"Well, get out then."

She shakes her head to indicate she doesn't want to. "The waves feel so funny crashing against my legs." I marvel at the bright smile on her face as she runs around in the shallow water, a bit like you would see a kid doing. Her voice is loud and free, and her laughter fills the air. But it's the bright smile on her face that makes this whole trip worth it. She looks like I've just given her the best gift ever. I want to see her like this all the time. Happy, free, and mine.

Despite hating the idea of freezing cold water crashing around my feet, I know I would do anything for this girl, so when she calls me over, I dump all our stuff on the beach and run to her. Picking her up, I twirl her around, loving the sound of her laughter as she shrieks at me to let her down.

We play around in the sea for what feels like ages, before the cold starts to get to us, and I can see Mia's teeth starting to chatter. She doesn't want to admit it, but I can see she's cold, so I pick her up and carry her over to the towels I've laid out next to our things. Sitting us down on the big blanket I brought, I waste no time in wiping each of her feet until they are both clean and dry before wrapping her up in the towels and blankets. I can feel her watching me, her lip clamps between her teeth. It's like she's waiting to say something, but can't quite find the words. I look up, meeting her gaze with a big smile, but I don't say anything. I want her to trust me enough to tell me things in her own time. Even though the wait is killing me, I bite my tongue. Thankfully, I don't have to wait too long. When she speaks, I'm stunned by her words.

"Tonight, after we've watched the sunset together, I want you to take me home and make love to me. I want to know what it's like with someone I care about. Eventually I want to learn to fuck, and to enjoy a rougher type of sex that I think I would enjoy, without feeling like a whore. But to start with, I just want to feel something I've never felt before." She tries to avert her eyes, like she's too shy to wait for my answer. Reaching out, I take hold of her chin, holding her gaze so she can't look away and she'll see how fucking serious I am.

"Fuck, Mia. You have no idea how much I want to show you what sex should really be like. What it feels like when it's all about you. And when the time is right, you can bet your fucking ass I'll be right there for you. But we don't need to rush. I'm not going anywhere, Flower. I'm in this now, and I have no plans on it ending. We have all the time in the world."

Mia's eyes fill with tears, and I have no idea if they're happy or sad tears. I don't think anything I just said warrants tears, but you just never know with women.

I watch her gulp, like she is trying to swallow the tears she's desperately trying not to shed, and when she speaks it's clogged with emotion. "You don't want me now?"

Fuck!

Hearing that literally breaks my heart. That's not what I'm trying to say to her. I'm trying to be the good guy, the one who doesn't take advantage of someone on the first date. I had no idea this could backfire on me.

"Mia, that's not at all what I meant. If you're one hundred percent sure that tonight is the night, then you know I'm in. How can I not be? You're so fucking gorgeous, it actually hurts my dick every second we aren't together. I was just trying to think of you." As soon as the words leave my mouth, a bright smile crosses her face and it warms my heart.

"I'm scared," she mutters, so quietly it's almost hard to hear with the waves crashing around us.

"What? Of sex? Because you know I would never hurt you. Even when we get to the stage where you want me to really fuck you, to experiment with you, it will all be on your terms. We will have a safe word and you can always stop, no questions asked. You can trust me, Flower. I won't ever hurt you," I exclaim, as I pull her into my arms. She lays her head against my chest, listening to the beat of my heart, and I can tell she's grateful we don't have to make eye contact any more.

"I'm not scared of sex. I trust you completely, and I know you would never hurt me. What scares me is how much I like you. How easy it is to like you. Every time you make me smile, or laugh, or you kiss me, my heart expands a little more. It feels like I was made for you, like my heart was made to beat in time with yours. I'm scared that I'm falling in love with you."

My heart stutters, and I freeze when I hear those words coming from her lips. I know what she means because I feel it too. Like we are destined to love each other, no matter what life throws our way.

Only one other person has ever said those words to me, and at the time I thought I felt the same. I soon realised I couldn't be more fucking wrong. Shayla never loved me, and I never loved her. Mia's different. I can feel it building, growing. She's right, it's like our hearts were made for each other, and that scares the shit out of me.

"You don't have to be afraid, Flower. If you give me your heart, I promise to cherish it and protect it, for as long as you let me keep it." I'm not ready to say those three words yet. I know I will get there soon, but I'm not just going to say them because she does. She deserves better.

I feel a tear trickle down my chest, and I pull her up to look at me. I wait, giving her the time to talk, knowing she needs a minute to find the right words. "I'm not worried about me. I'm worried about you. What if I can't keep your heart safe? What if I break it?" she asks, tears streaming down her face, and I can't stop my brow from furrowing in confusion. Why is she so worried about hurting me? She's the kindest girl in the world, I don't think she is capable of hurting anyone.

I must've said that part aloud because Mia responds. "Broken people are only capable of causing pain. I will hurt you, Kellan." Her voice sounds so lost and hopeless. Such a difference from the bright, bubbly person who was laughing and joking just a second ago. Mia telling me she loves me shouldn't be a sad event. We should be singing about it from the fucking rooftops because I'm the luckiest man alive.

"Mia, I trust you with my heart. You don't have to worry. If you do end up breaking it, that's okay, as long as I get to love you for just a little bit." I capture her lips with mine, silencing whatever negative thing she was going to say next. "No more negative talk. I want to sit on the beach, cuddling the woman who makes me the happiest man in the world, as we watch the sunset together. Then, when we go home, we will take things a step at a time."

Mia nods her head, a small smile crossing her face, and I pull her farther between my legs. My arms surround her, and she lays back, her head against my chest. We lay there together, just talking, waiting for the sun to set. We talk about anything and everything. All our fears are long forgotten, we just live in the moment. As the sun sets, we sit there in silence, and I spend more time watching Mia than anything else. The look of marvel on her face as the sun disappears beneath the ocean is a sight to behold. She is more stunning than the sunset itself.

As the moonlight shines over our bodies, the creamy silk of her skin that has started to develop goose pimples from the cold, makes her look even more gorgeous. I know she wants to stay here longer, but even covered with all the blankets and coats that we brought, I can still feel her shaking. So, I lead her over to the bike.

"One step at a time, Flower. If you say llama, I will stop at any point." She looks at me with pure confusion etched across her furrowed brow.

"Why llama?"

"A safe word has to be something that wouldn't normally come up in conversation, and definitely not something one of us would say during sex," I explain, and Mia smiles when she realises what I'm implying.

"How do you know I don't scream llama every time I come?" she whispers in my ear. Fuck, it physically hurts when I hear this beauty whisper the word come in my ear. I can feel the shiver ripple down my spine and into my balls.

"You better hope that you don't. The last thing you want, as you are just about to come, is me hearing the word llama and stopping whatever I'm doing. Leaving you desperate, gasping for more. That would be a shame, wouldn't it?" I tease, and given the way she trembles, it obviously works.

"I want to try it all with you. I want to be able to fuck like a whore, and know that's okay, because I'm only a slut for you. One of the things I'm most scared about is doing things with you that will make me feel like I'm just going through the motions, doing what I was taught."

I shake my head, trying to keep the anger off my face. "I know that scares you, but you don't ever have to worry about that. You follow how you feel. If the idea of doing something excites you or turns you on, then try it. If the idea makes you feel sleazy, then avoid it. If you follow your body, and trust me to make you feel good, then you will be okay. There's nothing wrong with being a little slutty for your man. Women should never be afraid of showing their sexy side, and being proud of their sexuality. Anyone who ever made you feel like a slut was wrong. You own your body, nobody else. I'm just here to help you to feel it all," I explain, and Mia gently places her lips against mine, before whispering into my mouth.

"Let's get home, now. I can't wait to get slutty for you."

Fuck! Now not only do I have to drive home with the biggest erection straining against leathers, I also have to drive with that in my brain the whole way home. It'll be a miracle if I keep to the speed limit.

Mia

The ride back to the house seems to take forever and with each minute that passes, I can feel the tension between us growing. The feel of his hard muscles beneath my touch as I hold on to him for the drive home, it makes my fingers tingle. They're so desperate to move and explore, but the back of his bike is not the place to do that. I don't know if it's because I know our time together comes with a deadline, but I don't want to waste another minute. I want to be with Kellan, I want to give him all of me, and tonight is the perfect night to do that.

Would I be in such a rush to do this if Shayla hadn't given me this ultimatum? Probably not, but I can't say for sure. I care very deeply for Kellan, and the chances are we would've easily got to this stage anyway. I'm just moving things along a little quicker. But, no matter what, I know I won't regret tonight. I don't think I could ever regret anything involving Kellan.

When we arrive back at the house, all the lights are out, and we move through the house as quietly as possible. We've enjoyed it in our own little bubble these last few hours, and I don't know about Kellan, but I'm not ready for that to end just yet. If Bree and Liam see us, or if Hallie wakes up, the bubble will burst and we'll be forced back into our lives again. Kellan must have the same idea because he doesn't even bother to turn the lights on, and instead takes hold of my hand, guiding me through the house. We have both lived here for so long, we can navigate this place in the dark.

The closer we get to the bedroom, the more my heart pounds and my body tingles. I can feel the anticipation coursing through my body like I've just taken a hit of the best drug available. The high I'm feeling right now is all Kellan, and I'm nowhere near ready for it to end.

The second we are in Kellan's bedroom, I close the door behind me and Kellan wastes no time. Pushing me firmly against the back of the now closed door, his body presses flush against mine and our lips meet. At first they are soft and gentle, like he wants to give me a moment just to feel him, and I'm not surprised by his action. He's touching and holding me like I'm a china doll, one that could break at any moment, and I don't want that. I want him to show me what it's like to really feel. I want all of Kellan, not a censored version.

"Don't hold back with me, Kel. Give me everything. I can take it, I promise," I whisper against his ear, and can't deny how much I love the way his body ripples from the feel of my breath against his skin.

"Are you sure this isn't too soon? I don't want you to regret it," Kellan replies, as he kisses along my jaw.

Fuck, could this man get any more perfect?

I shake my head. "I could never regret anything with you. You're the first person I've ever given this to willingly, and despite how terrifying it might be, I trust you. I know you won't ever hurt me." Each word gets louder, said with more conviction. I absolutely mean every single word. There is no way I could ever regret anything concerning Kellan. Well...until tomorrow. I will regret having to leave him tomorrow. No matter how necessary it is.

Once Kellan's heard all he needs to hear, his hands reach towards the bottom of my dress, and in one quick swoop, he lifts the dress over my head and throws it to one side. He takes a moment to admire my very exposed body, as I stand before him in just a black lace bra and matching panties. I didn't even own any sexy underwear before I met him, but when I bought this, I pictured this moment in my head a thousand times. I knew he would love it, but I could never have predicted the hunger in his gaze. His normally bright blue eyes appear almost glazed over, like he's entranced by what he sees before him.

I reach out to remove some of his clothing, so that we're equal, but before I can, his hands cup underneath my ass and he lifts me until I have no choice but to wrap my legs around his tight ass and throw my arms around his neck. With my back pressed firmly against the back of the door, and Kellan's body plastered against my front, I'm sandwiched in the best way possible. Kellan manoeuvres me to get comfortable, and I feel his denim-covered cock, rock hard and straining to get free, it presses hard against my panty-covered clit. A deep, grumbling moan rips out of my body, and I tilt my pelvis even further, desperately seeking more.

Kellan chuckles against my lips as he taunts me in between kisses. "Someone is eager, Flower."

I don't bother giving him a reply, instead I crush my lips against his, our movements becoming more frantic. Our hands claw at each other, and I realise Kellan's no longer needing to hold me up, I'm so tightly sandwiched between him and the door that I couldn't move even if I wanted to. As soon as I realise this, I move my hands from around his neck, and drop them to the hem of his T-shirt. Clawing at him, I try to pull the T-shirt up and over his head in a desperate attempt to expose his silky tattooed skin. I want to see, and feel, all of him.

After a few frantic attempts, Kellan takes pity on me and breaks our hold. Gently, he guides me until my feet are firmly on the ground. He takes a step back, and my legs wobble from the intensity of the situation. I notice the heat in Kellan's eyes, they almost appear black as lust takes over his beautiful face. He's wearing the cocky grin I love, and he winks at me before pulling the top over his head. As he does, he begins walking backwards, towards the bed, but I can't move. It's like I'm in a trance, and all I can see is his gorgeous ink-covered torso.

Almost his entire chest, arms, and back are covered in the most elaborate, beautiful, black ink designs. I'm sure there's a story to most of them, but every time I've asked, Kellan doesn't answer. I do know that Liam has the same tattoo on his back. A Celtic tree of life, with the most beautiful branches above the surface with little leaves on them, and small birds that I think are meant to show the beauty in the world. Below the tree's surface is a mess of roots that are all interconnected and weave together into the shape of a heart. Some then branch out, looking like they almost reach outside the circle of the tattoo, and they mingle with the branches from above the surface to create a Celtic cross. It looks like it has two hearts, interwoven together with a larger one on the outside. All they will tell me about the design is that it's personal to them and that it has a different meaning to traditional mythology. If I were to hazard a guess, I think it's a symbol to show that the family you choose can be more important than the family you are born with.

"Are you going to keep staring at me, or can I taste you now?"

Holy fuck, what a way to be pulled out of my own head. I'm not entirely sure how to answer that, so instead I try to embrace my inner sexy as I slowly walk towards him. Swaying my hips as much as I can without stumbling over my jelly legs, I reach behind and unclasp my bra. Crossing my arms to grab the straps, I pull the garment away from my breasts, and as it falls to the floor, I keep my gaze firmly on Kellan. His eyes widen as he takes in my naked breasts, and when he licks his lips like a starved man looking at the most decadent buffet, I walk towards him faster.

"Fuck, you really are the most gorgeous girl I've ever laid eyes on," Kellan growls, and before I know it, he reaches for me, picks me up, and throws me onto the bed. I squeal, more out of surprise than anything else, and I can't help but laugh because he's so invigorating. I'm feeling multiple different emotions, and I don't know how to deal with them all at once, which is how the laughter bursts free.

As Kellan begins to crawl over my body, the look of pure desire in his eyes is anything but funny. I bite my lip, unsure of what his next move could be. I don't even know what I want him to do, but I want to feel all of him, to have all of him devour me, and given the way he's staring at me, he clearly wants the same thing.

I'm lying in the middle of the bed, propping my top half up on my elbows, so I can see exactly what Kellan is doing. At first he just stands at the bottom of the bed, his gaze raking over my almost naked form, and I can feel the path his eyes take as my skin burns under his gaze. As he lowers himself into a kneeling position, my breath hitches and I feel as though my heart stops beating just for a second as I await his next move.

Reaching up with his hands, he takes my left leg in his hands and he slowly brings my ankle towards his lips. Gently, he presses his lips against my ankle bone, before peppering kisses along the top of my foot and inside my calf. As he kisses higher and higher up my leg, my body becomes tense with anticipation. Each kiss is teasing and drives me that little bit more crazy, and I'm desperate for more.

When he reaches the top of my leg, he kisses around my hip before moving around to my inner thigh. His fingertips scrape across the bikini line of my panties, and I whimper when he doesn't touch me where I desperately need him to. Instead, he uses his hand to spread my legs wider, so he can kiss my inner thigh. He works his way higher, the brush of his stubble against my sensitive skin is driving me wild, and I can feel the heat from his body right next to my waiting pussy. I can feel myself becoming wetter the more he teases me, and I'm sure he will be able to tell from his current position. His mouth is right next to my panty-covered pussy, and I'm sure he will be able to see the wet patch.

He places a light, tender kiss right over my clit, and despite it being covered by lace, the heat and feel of his touch is too much and a guttural moan rips from my body as my back arches. "More," I plead, but it falls on deaf ears. Kellan is enjoying torturing me too much, and instead of giving me what I ask for, with a little chuckle that vibrates through my pussy, Kellan shuffles back down to the bottom of the bed and begins his path again, only this time he travels up my other leg.

Each kiss is like pure torture, and I can't help but grab hold of his hair and try to pull him higher. I don't pull hard because I don't want to hurt him, but if he doesn't give me the attention I need soon, I won't be worried about hurting him.

He reaches the top of my inner thigh again and spreads my other leg wide, so my pussy is almost completely exposed, except for a small stretch of fabric. I wait for more agonising kisses, but instead Kellan uses his finger to swipe down my slit, pressing the fabric in between my lips. As soon as I feel it hard against my clit, I groan, barely able to hold it together.

"More, please, Kellan," I beg, as I desperately arch my back and tilt my pelvis, trying to get any kind of friction to help with the ache between my legs.

Kellan lifts himself off me, and with those fiery eyes trained right on me, he crawls up the rest of my body, his cocky smirk trained on me the entire time. "What's the matter, Flower? Tell me what you need." As soon as the words are out he presses his lips against mine, preventing me from answering him, as his body hovers over mine, pressing into me in all the right places.

"You can start by evening the playing field and removing your trousers," I whisper against his ear before returning my lips to his. Our lips crush together and we devour each other, hands everywhere, as I scrape at his back, desperately trying to bring him impossibly closer.

I'm so distracted by everything that is Kellan, I don't notice as his hand snakes down between our bodies and under the hem of my panties. It's not until he swipes his finger through my dripping slit that he finally gains all my attention. I groan as I arch my hips, trying to get more of that delicious friction. This time, instead of teasing me like he has been doing, he continues to move his finger up and down my slit, swirling his finger around my waiting entrance before pressing hard against my throbbing clit. Each time he repeats this pattern, my body begins to coil, muscles tightening as I desperately try to reach that edge I'm so close to. I've never felt this way, other than with Kellan, and even though the idea of me losing myself, and just allowing my body to feel, scares the crap out of me, I trust him to catch me when I fall.

The more I moan, the harder he presses against my clit, and then each time he reaches my entrance, I think he's going to press his finger into my waiting hole, but instead he starts the whole process again. It's maddening, but so infuriatingly sexy, and I love it. I can feel the muscles in my stomach begin to coil, like I'm building up to the best orgasm of my life, but it all stops when Kellan pulls his fingers away. I start to protest, looking at him with such venom in my eyes, until he pulls his fingers in front of us. The light glistens off his dripping wet fingers, and for a moment I'm embarrassed I did that, but as soon as he places one of his fingers inside his mouth, sucking on his digit like it's the best tasting lollipop he's ever had, my embarrassment is replaced by heat. That has to be one of the sexiest things I've ever seen, and when he pulls his finger out with a pop, I'm almost hypnotised watching him. I can still see my juices on the finger he didn't suck on, and I watch with bated breath, waiting for him to take the remaining digit into his mouth, but he doesn't. Instead, he reaches out and brings the finger closer to my mouth.

"Taste yourself, Flower. Do it and I will give you exactly what you asked for." His words are like a low growl now, as passion and lust have begun to consume him.

I don't even hesitate to do as I'm told, and I open my mouth, eagerly awaiting his finger. I've never tasted myself before, and if you had asked me before this, I would've said it's not something I'm interested in, but as soon as his finger touches my tongue and I taste the salty, sweet taste, it's surprisingly okay. What I enjoy more than anything is the way Kellan's eyes grow wide, and his nostrils flare, not to mention the way he has to bite his lip but still can't hold back the insanely hot moan that bursts free.

As soon as I've licked his finger clean, I smile up at him, waiting patiently for him to give me exactly what I want, just like he said he would. But instead, he rips my panties from my body, the tattered pieces of fabric thrown into the corner of the room. I'm about to complain, I don't exactly have a whole heap of nice stuff, but those thoughts fly out the window when I feel his tongue press against my clit.

Holy fuck! As his tongue sweeps through my slit, dipping into my waiting entrance before circling around my swollen clit, I feel like I'm about to lose my damn mind. Even though Kellan has done this once before, other than that I've never had any experience of being licked and touched in this way. Abusers tend not to be concerned with my pleasure, which is good because this is so fucking intimate. Even without having anything to compare it to, I can say without a shadow of a doubt that Kellan is a fucking sex god when it comes to this. The warm, moist touch of his tongue against my sensitive areas drives me crazy.

My back arches off the bed, and my hands fist the bedsheets as I groan and writhe around, desperate for more. In fact, my body doesn't exactly know what it wants, but I know I want more. I want to feel more. Something I am only too happy to tell Kellan. Well...it comes out more as begging and pleading, but I'm not ashamed of that. For the first time in my life, I'm embracing the way my body feels, and fuck do I want it all. Kellan is only too happy to oblige.

As he swirls his tongue around my clit, and I feel my body starting to climb towards that edge I'm desperately seeking, Kellan very gently presses one of his fingers into my pussy.

"Ohhh fuck. That feels so good," I cry out in pleasure, tilting my hips to meet his hand.

He presses his finger in so fucking slowly, and as my pussy gets used to the feeling of having something in there, I quickly start to get a pleasurable sensation each time he moves. It's like all my nerve endings are electric, and my heart races as I desperately chase the orgasm I'm so close to.

Clearly knowing exactly what I'm searching for, Kellan is only too happy to oblige, and as he pulls his finger out, when he pushes it back into my pussy slowly, this time he adds a second finger. The sensation of having two fingers stretching me out has me feeling deliciously filled, and I'm grateful that Kellan gives me a few seconds to become accustomed to the feeling. He doesn't stop the assault with his tongue, and it's not long before I'm begging him to move.

"Kellan, move your fingers. Please, I need to feel more," I beg, thrusting my hips upwards in an attempt to force his fingers farther inside of me. I never knew it could feel this amazing to be touched in this way, and I'm not even thinking, I'm just acting and following my body.

"You are so tight and wet, Flower. I'm really struggling not to fuck you with my cock right now." Hearing his dirty, delicious words, a groan rips from my body and my hands fly to Kellan's hair. I clasp hold of his dark, black locks, and without thinking I pull his face impossibly closer to my pussy. It's like I'm acting on instinct, not even thinking about what I'm doing.

Kellan's groan ripples and vibrates through my pussy, pulling me out of my instinctual behaviour, and I let go of Kellan's hair. "Sorry," I mumble, trying to hide the blush that is spreading across my cheeks.

Pulling his head up to look at me, I bite my lip to hide the frustrated groan that threatens to burst out of me when his talented tongue leaves my aching pussy. His hands that had been hooked over my hips, holding me in place to prevent me from moving too far away from his tongue while I'm writhing around, releases my legs and clasps hold of my arms.

With the sexiest smile I've ever seen, and a gravelly, lust-filled voice, Kellan melts me. "Don't ever apologise, Mia. Follow what your body is telling you. Use me however you want because it's incredibly fucking sexy, Flower." He places my hands back onto his head, threading my fingers through his hair.

Before giving me a chance to respond, his hot mouth covers my aching clit, and his tongue begins swiping around my engorged bundle of nerves. At the same time, his fingers begin to thrust in and out of my wet pussy. The combination of both occurring at the same time causes me to lose my mind. Screaming out in pleasure, my hips thrust upwards to meet his fingers, while my fingers grip Kellan's hair tightly and I hold him firmly in place. He continues the onslaught of his fingers and tongue, and my nerves feel like they're about to explode. My muscles coil, and my skin begins to prickle. I can feel my body building towards the orgasm I'm desperately chasing. At first it's hard for me to let my body lose control, and I start to overthink it. Until I feel Kellan's tongue exploring my most intimate of places, and I just allow myself to feel. That's when it occurs to me that I don't just trust him, and know he's going to catch me when I fall, I want him to do that. I want him to be there for me because I fucking love him. The realisation hits me at the same time as the orgasm, and it literally feels like my brain is exploding.

My back arches, and I use my hands to grip hold of Kellan's hair as tightly as I can, making sure he doesn't move, even the slightest. My muscles spasm, my heart races, and Kellan has to cover my lips with his to muffle the cries of pleasure. My clit that had until a second ago been covered by Kellan's mouth, is now exposed to the cool air, and the sensation against my swollen, wet clit is amazing. Spasms and jolts of pleasure shoot through my pussy, adding to the already amazing experience, and it takes me a moment before I'm able to catch my breath.

When I finally come down from my bliss, Kellan slowly removes his fingers, and once they are out completely, I feel like I'm missing a piece of me. I've never felt like this, and I want more. As I look down at Kellan, knowing how I feel and that I can never tell him, I realise that I have to find a way to show him. We have tonight, and only tonight, and I don't want him to ever question what we have together. I may not be able to tell him how I feel, but I can show him.

Finding a confidence I didn't know I had, I place my hands on Kellan's shoulders and give him a slight push. Realising what I'm trying to do, Kellan allows me to push him until he's lying on his back. Let's be honest, there's no way in hell I could manhandle this guy without a little help from him.

Once he's lying on his back, I waste no time climbing onto his thighs so that I'm straddling his hips. Sitting on top of him, completely naked and exposed, I expected to feel a little embarrassed, or at the very least, use my arms to cover my exposed breasts. But, I don't. The way he looks at me, eyes hooded and darkened with lust, I've never felt as sexy in my life. His gaze rakes over my body, and his hands grip at my hips, holding me in place. The only thing separating my pussy from his rock-hard dick is a flimsy piece of cotton, and I know I need to get his boxers off straight away.

Even though Kellan and I have messed about together before, I've never seen or touched his cock. I've seen the outline in his boxers, so there's no denying that he's incredibly well endowed. I've already had the discussion in my mind over whether or not he can fit inside me, but the more I've got to know Kellan, the more I believe we were made for each other. If you had asked me this morning, I would've said we were meant to be together, but Shayla's made it very clear that isn't our future. But, we were meant to impact each other in a big way, of that I'm certain. He is helping me to heal, and to feel normal for the first time in my life. He has taught me how to put my trust in someone, and how to open up enough to love someone. This is my opportunity to show him how I feel.

With the best seductive smile I can manage, I slowly slide down his body, kissing along his rock-hard abs as I go. I kiss along the path of those delicious black swirls that I love looking at so much, and I follow their journey down Kellan's body.

Fuck! This man is quite literally built like a god.

My heart races and I try to push all thoughts out of my mind because if I start to think about what I'm about to do, I may just check out. Instead, I focus on exactly what I'm doing right now, and I slide off Kellan's body until I'm kneeling in between his legs at the bottom of the bed. Without halting, and keeping my eyes trained on Kellan, I reach up his thighs and waste no time pulling his boxers off.

Kellan's breath hitches, and I release the breath I didn't know I had been holding. I want to try and be slow and seductive, but I just can't. Once I've fully removed Kellan's boxers, I finally allow myself the time to look over his naked form. His cock is so much bigger than I was expecting, and that's a massive fucking understatement. His hard dick stands tall and falls all the way up onto his lower abdomen. I'm drawn towards the swollen tip that looks angry and purple, with beads of pre-cum seeping out.

Reaching out to grab hold of his dick, I take a moment to appreciate how beautiful it is. I may not have any fucking experience with this kind of thing, but there's no denying that his cock is quite a vision. Before I'm able to grasp the big erection, Kellan reaches out to stop me. "Beautiful, you don't have to do this if you don't want to. I would never force you to do this, and I can hear how much you're hyperventilating. Don't do anything you don't want to do, Flower."

Shaking my head and my hands, I shrug off his grasp on me. "I'm not hyperventilating. I'm trying to get control of my breathing because I'm so fucking turned on. I know I don't have to do this, Kel. I actually want to. I want to taste you the way you just did for me. I want to make you fall apart on my tongue."

A shiver ripples down Kellan's body as I take hold of him. I'm quite surprised by how silky, velvety smooth his hard cock is, and I love the feel of it in my hand. Tightening my grip around the base of his shaft, my fingers struggle to meet, given how much girth he has. My hand looks so small compared to his long, thick dick. I don't hesitate, and begin to pull down gently, before letting my hand travel upwards towards the swollen head and then back down again.

After a couple of thrusts, more beads of pre-cum pool on the tip of his cock, and Kellan's responding groan is like music to my ears. I have never felt more powerful, beautiful, and in control than I do at this moment. It's almost like I'm hypnotised by the glistening cum on the tip, and so I lean forward until I'm bent over. My tits are hanging low next to Kellan's thighs and my ass and pussy are up in the air. I'm sure it's quite a sight from behind, but I don't care. I have one focus, and I firmly hold his shaft to direct him into my mouth.

As I wrap my lips around his swollen head, I flick my tongue across the head, tasting the salty fluid leaking from the tip. Kellan's resulting groan echoes around us, and it's the sexiest noise ever. It spurs me on further, and after swirling my tongue over the tip, I close my mouth over the top of his cock, and suck as though it's my favourite lollipop.

After sucking the tip, tasting the saltiness of his pre-cum, I then slowly begin moving my mouth farther down his cock, taking in as much of it as I can. As Kellan's breath hitches, I look up at his through hooded eyes in time to see Kellan closing his eyes, his mouth falling open as his moans fill the air.

Seconds later, I slide my mouth up and down Kellan's cock a few times, revelling in the taste and feel of his erection as it slides across my tongue. I thought I knew how I would feel doing this again for the first time in years. I thought it would be a triggering act, and something I would hate doing, and so I'm surprised to find that it's quite the opposite of how I'm feeling. Not only am I enjoying bestowing pleasure on this beautiful man, but it's actually making me feel confident and powerful. With each moan, each shiver that ripples through his body, and the way he quivers under my touch, it's invigorating. It pushes me further.

I push my mouth farther down Kellan's cock, forcing him deeper into my throat, and I watch as Kellan's eyes fly open. Our eyes meet and he looks at me with awe as I push his cock farther and farther until he's fully embedded in my throat. As I swallow, the bobbing sensation in my throat must feel amazing as Kellan doesn't hold back in his moans. I watch his hands flutter, and I realise his instinct is to place his hands on my head, to guide or maybe even to control me, but he's resisting doing this. He pushes his hands down by his sides and he grabs hold of the duvet cover to gain control over his hands. But I don't want him to be in control, I want him to act on instinct.

Pulling his cock out of my throat, I make sure to look him in the eyes as I explain, ignoring the saliva dripping from my mouth after having his cock so deep. "Don't hold back, Kellan. I want all of you. I want the full Kellan experience…"

Before I have a chance to explain, he cuts me off. "But, Mia, I don't want to trigger…"

Now it's my turn to interrupt him. Looking him straight in the eye, I give him my cockiest smirk, as I scoop the saliva off my chin before spreading it across his cock using my hand. "Unless, of course, you want me to stop playing with your big, hard cock?"

Kellan growls. "Fuck. You better remember your safe word, Mia."

"I remember, and I have no intention of using it. Now, are you going to put your hands on my head?" I ask, goading him with my eyes and the cocky smile I learnt from him.

Kellan doesn't hesitate and he grabs hold of my head, threading his fingers through my hair until I can feel my roots stinging as they are pulled from my scalp. It's not painful, and although Kellan is taking charge in a forceful way, it at no point feels like he is manhandling me in a bad way, I just think I'm finally getting him to let go enough to show me how it really feels to be with him.

He pushes my head onto his cock, and I let him guide it deep into my mouth, sticking my tongue out farther to allow him deeper access.

I'm balls deep, and my tongue actually touches his ball sack as his cock sits deep in my throat. Kellan holds my head in position, and my eyes start to water and my lungs begin to burn as they are prevented from getting air. My hands grip tightly against Kellan's thighs, and it's like he knows exactly what my limits are because as soon as I start to panic over the loss of air, Kellan pulls me off his cock. I cough and splutter, gasping for breath as water from my eyes mixes with the spittle that drips from his mouth all the way to his wet cock.

"Fuck, Mia. That feels amazing," Kellan growls before gently guiding my head back down onto his cock.

We repeat this process a few times, Kellan loving the way I'm able to take all his cock deep into my throat, and in between while I'm gasping to collect as much air as I can, I use my hand to pump up and down his shaft.

After a while his groans become more guttural and his movements more frantic. I can feel his cock beginning to swell impossibly further in my mouth. I can tell he's reaching his peak, so when he pulls me off his cock, I can't help but groan in frustration.

"If you keep doing that, Flower, I am going to come for sure," Kellan explains, and I can't help the cocky, proud grin that spreads across my face.

"That's kinda the point, babe," I retort, letting the nickname just fall off my tongue without even thinking about it. I know he calls me Flower, but I've never really had a nickname for him. Babe may be corny as fuck, but it just felt natural to say it.

"You don't have to swallow my cum, Mia. Besides, I would much rather come while I'm buried deep in your pussy." Fuck, his words do delicious things to my insides. I want that too, but I'm torn because I also want to taste him the way he did me.

Suddenly, an idea pops into my very dirty mind. "Why can't you do both?" I ask, not meaning for it to come out as a challenge, which Kellan took it to be. I think he thought I was questioning his virility, and his ability to come twice in one session. As he stares at me with one eyebrow cocked, like he is more than happy to accept that challenge, my stomach begins to flip at the thought.

"Oh I can most definitely go twice, maybe more. Whenever you're around, you literally drive me fucking crazy. I have a permanent boner, thanks to you. Now it's time you make it right. Don't you think?" he asks, that cocky smirk spread across his face.

He doesn't wait for me to answer before he pushes my head back down onto his cock. Using my hand, mouth, and tongue, it doesn't take me long to get him back to the edge again, as he was before. His hand is fisted into the hair on the back of my head, and even though there's a delicious sting when he pulls, he never causes me pain. I feel his muscles start to coil beneath my hands on his stomach and thigh, and his breathing becomes erratic. The vein running the length of his cock begins to pulsate, and I hear Kellan's voice grinding out through his gritted teeth. "I need to come, Mia. Now. You can pull away if you want."

I don't move, I simply continue my sucking action and it's not long before I feel his cock begin to pulsate. Before I know it, ropes of cum are shooting into the back of my throat, and I have to pull my head back slightly so as to not choke.

I let the salty fluid build at the back of my mouth, sitting on my tongue, and I use my hand around the shaft to continue to pump him through the remainder of his orgasm. I waste no time swallowing it all, and I'm actually quite surprised by the taste. I expected it to be horrible and make me sick—thanks to previous experiences—but this was nothing like that. He tasted salty, but with a slightly sweet element. In fact, I quite enjoyed the whole thing.

I think it was the actual act of having power over Kellan, and being able to give him as much pleasure as he gives me. I even enjoyed the way he took control, guiding my head and being responsible for my breathing. If you'd asked me this morning, I would've told you there's no way in hell I'd give that power to someone else, but this is Kellan. I didn't even consider it, I just acted.

Kellan continues gasping, trying to catch his breath, and I sit there on my knees in between his legs, just looking at this beautiful man. I stare in amazement at his cock that's still semi-erect, and I wonder how the hell he can do that after he just came so fucking much.

Kellan's chuckle lets me know I must have said that last part aloud. "I told you before, Mia. It's you. You drive me fucking crazy, and my cock will always be ready for more with you. But we don't have to," he explains, looking almost sheepish at the end. It's so sweet to see him blushing over me. I don't know why it's so hard for me to believe that I'm capable of eliciting that kind of a response from a guy like him. He only has to look at me with that cocky grin and I'm physically dripping, so why can't he feel the same?

Kellan pulls me up into his arms, until I'm laying on his chest with my legs on either side, straddling his hips. I can feel his cock just below my pussy, and all it would take is a few shuffling motions, and a tilt of my pelvis, and I'd be able to slip him inside me. Something I didn't realise I wanted so much until the opportunity presented itself. I can't deny that thoughts of tomorrow do flash through my mind. How much worse will things be when I have to end this if we do take things all the way? I try to push the thoughts to one side, but the truth is, it's going to hurt like a motherfucker, whether I've fucked him or not. I love him, and that isn't going to change in the next couple of hours.

"We don't have to do anything more tonight, Mia," Kellan says, as he strokes my hair in a soothing way. I think he mistook my silence, my deep thought, for regret, or something else.

I shake my head and decide to cover myself with humour. "Why? Don't you think you can go again, old man?" I ask with a chuckle, and before I even have a chance to finish the laughter that bursts out of me, Kellan picks me up and rolls me until he is hovering over me, his body pressing against mine. He's so close I can feel his breath against my lips, and I can feel his hard cock sitting against my pussy lips. It wouldn't take much for his cock to slide in.

I try to wriggle to get my legs open a little more, as that will make it easier for his cock to find my entrance, but Kellan holds me tightly in place. His eyes are hooded, and his cocky grin is hitched up on one side before he leans forward, closing the impossibly small gap, and places his lips against mine. It's a sweet, chaste kiss, and I try to deepen it, loving the taste of him as always, but this time he pulls away. I can't help the childish groan of frustration that escapes.

"I would be more than happy to show you exactly how many times I can go, but I wouldn't want to destroy your pussy on the first night.

That doesn't mean I'm not going to fuck you so hard that you feel me long after I've gone." His words sound almost like a growl and his dirty words speak directly to my waiting pussy. I feel myself starting to get wet and I try desperately to tilt my hips, desperate to relieve the ache that's growing between my legs.

"Please, Kellan." I don't exactly know what I'm begging him for, but I do know that I want whatever he is willing to give me. Unfortunately, that's not enough for Kellan.

"Tell me exactly what you want, Flower. Or you won't get it." To emphasise his point, he grinds his cock hard against my pussy lips, creating the most delicious friction against my clit. I want to be able to open my legs, to feel him touching me everywhere. I've never been asked what I want, and I'm not entirely sure what to say.

"I want everything. All of you, Kellan," I whisper, averting my gaze from his as a blush spreads across my cheeks. He reaches up until his hands are on both of my cheeks, making it impossible for me to turn away from looking straight at him.

"Don't ever be embarrassed with me, beautiful. Listen to your body and use your words. I want to hear every dirty detail of what you want me to do to you. I want to know exactly what you need."

Fuck! My heart literally aches as he says the perfect words to me.

I take a deep breath to settle my nerves, and I follow his advice. I listen to exactly what my body wants from him and I push aside all of the embarrassment I feel and just talk to Kellan. I realise I have nothing to be embarrassed by. I trust him, and I know he's only getting me to do this to help me become more in tune with my body and my desires. And I can't deny that the whole dirty talking part is sexy as fuck.

Leaning in so that I can whisper in his ear, I tell him exactly what I know he wants to hear. "I want you to let me open my legs for starters. Then I want to feel the tip of your cock swiping through my slit, making sure my pussy is dripping wet, which we both know it will be. It's constantly dripping when you are around. Then I want you to slowly push your big, hard cock deep into my pussy. But don't forget to pause for a bit when you are deep inside my tight, hot cunt. I will need some time to adjust as your dick stretches me more than ever before. Then I know you will start by moving slowly, and that's okay at first. Until you get into a beautiful rhythm, but once we are both starting to go a bit insane, then I want you to fuck me exactly how you like to do it. Pull my hair, spank my ass, call me a dirty whore. Whatever turns you on. I want to experience all of you, Kellan. I want you to listen to your body the whole time, and don't ever hold fucking back. We were made to fit each other, so I know I can handle all of you."

Kellan looks at my eyes wide with awe, his mouth flopping open and then closed as he struggles to find the right words. I can feel his cock becoming harder between my legs, and I know it's taking every ounce of strength that Kellan has not to move right now. He seems to take a few minutes to fully take in everything I just said, and once he has it's like someone flips a switch and he springs into action.

Pushing my legs apart, he follows my instructions to the letter by swiping the swollen head of his cock through my slit, making sure to press hard against my throbbing clit. I couldn't be more desperate and ready for him if I tried. I feel him spreading my moisture around my pussy lips, before pulling away with a groan.

"Fuck, I wasn't even thinking just now. Your dirty words have me all confused. I forgot about a condom," Kellan whispers, looking a little sheepish like he's expecting me to get mad at him. I'm not surprised he's so keen on condoms given Hallie wasn't exactly planned.

"We can wear a condom if you like, but I have the implant in my arm. I got tested recently and I was all clean. But it's entirely up to you, Kel. I understand if you would prefer to use one," I explain, giving him the choice. I want to tell him that I've never had sex without a condom before.

My dad couldn't put me onto any kind of birth control until I started having periods at around age thirteen, but he always insisted on everyone using condoms when they were with me. Even he wore one. At the time I didn't really even think about it too much because I barely understood the risks. As I got older, not only was I grateful that I couldn't get pregnant by these monsters, but I was also protected from whatever diseases they were carrying. It also means I'm able to have sex without a condom for the first time with someone I choose. I don't want to put that kind of pressure onto Kellan, particularly given his history with Shayla. So, I keep all this hidden and let him make his own choice.

"Mia, if I have a choice, I want to feel all of you. I want to bury my bare cock deep into your pussy, feeling your heat and how wet you are just for me. But, it's up to you? I will wear a condom if you tell me to."

Shanking my head, I tell him that I want to feel him, and that's all Kellan needs to hear. He gathers his cock into his hand, grasping it just enough to guide it in the right direction, and he uses his other hand to spread my legs open wider, opening my pussy up to him. With a deep groan Kellan slowly pushes the head of his cock into my waiting hole.

"Fuck!" I shout in pleasure, my back arching off the bed as my fingers grip tightly into the skin of his back. My nails scrape down his skin as I try to pull Kellan closer while he moves his hips.

He presses his cock into my tight wet pussy, moving just as impossibly slow as I predicted. As much as I hate to admit it, I need him to go slow because he feels so fucking big. If I thought he felt huge in my mouth, it's nothing compared to this. The sensation of feeling wonderfully full and stretched is amazing, but with each inch he pushes inside of me, I worry I'm not going to be able to take any more.

"So big," I moan as Kellan grunts and pushes a little more.

"Fuck, Flower. You are so fucking tight. Your cunt fits so tightly around my cock, hugging me like a glove that was made just for me." His voice is low and gravelly, and as his breath hits my ear, I can't help the spasm that ripples down my spine. Like little electric shocks are travelling through my body, with a direct link to my pussy. I wonder if Kellan can feel my pussy pulsating around his cock.

With a final push, followed by the most delicious grunt, he finally pushes himself fully inside me. He pauses for just a second, and I gasp, trying to gain control of my breathing as Kellan does the same. He waits for me to become adjusted to having him so deep. At first it stings and the feeling of fullness is a little overwhelming at first, which is why I try to get control of my breathing. My heart is racing, and I can feel beads of sweat forming across my body.

It doesn't take long for the sore, full feeling to turn into a pleasurable sensation, as my pussy starts to pulse with need. I tilt my pelvis slightly, moving my pussy off his cock just slightly before rocking the other way. Kellan takes the hint and starts to move. His cock pulls out agonisingly slowly, the head just sitting at my pussy entrance. Kellan's hands grip my hips, preventing me from moving as I desperately try to seek more of him.

When I least expect it Kellan pushes back in all the way to the hilt, and I scream loudly before remembering where we are. I don't exactly want Liam and Bree to hear us, or worse would be Hallie. Taking my hand, I cover my mouth as Kellan chuckles. "Don't worry, Flower. They are on the other side of the house, you won't wake them. Besides, I happen to know that all these rooms are soundproof. So you can scream as much as you want. In fact, I encourage it." As soon as the words are out of his mouth, he pulls my hand away from my mouth, pinning it above my head. He then begins to really fuck me. Thrusting his cock in and out of my pussy with wild abandon.

At first his thrusts are deep, fast, but coordinated, and so it's not hard to miss when he begins to lose control. His thrusts become more frantic, and I can feel why. My pussy is beginning to tighten, pulsating with need as I get ever closer to that orgasm we are both chasing. I'm so close, and given the way Kellan his fucking me, I would say he is too.

I'm concentrating so much on how fucking amazing it feels to have him deep inside my pussy, and how he is making me feel things I didn't think I could physically feel, I miss the moment where he lets go of my hand and uses his hand to snake between our bodies. Before I even realise what he's doing, he presses the pad of his fingers against my swollen, aching clit.

"Fuck," I scream as he presses hard, his fingers rubbing against the tight bundle of nerves.

"I want you to come, Flower. Fall apart on my cock. Put your trust in me, I will catch you. Now come!" His dirty demand and reassurance is the only instruction I need. It's like his words hold the key and I fall apart in his arms. My muscles that were clenched tightly now begin to spasm, my moans turn into cries of pleasure, and my pussy grips hold of his cock tightly.

"I'm coming," I shout, although it's not really necessary to tell him this, because I'm sure he can feel it.

Kellan takes his fingers off my overly sensitive clit, and he stops moving, giving me the time I need to ride out my orgasm. With panting breaths, I desperately try to lower my heart rate. Just as I'm finally starting to come down from the most amazing experience of my life, Kellan starts to move again. He moves with slow, deep thrusts to start with, before he soon starts to increase his speed. It's not long until he is on the edge just like I was, and I'm shocked to find my body is beginning to show signs of another orgasm. This time I want to fall with him.

"Come for me, Kellan. I want to feel you coming deep inside my tight, wet cunt." I use the dirty language I know he loves so much, and I turn the words he used for me onto him.

It works. As Kellan thrusts deep inside of me, his loud groan of pleasure fills the room and I can feel his cock begin to pulse as he empties himself deep inside. The feel of him spasming deep in my pussy is all it takes to trigger my own orgasm, and although it was considerably smaller compared to the other one just a second ago, my muscles still coil and spasm, and my pussy grips Kellan's cock.

In the midst of our orgasms, Kellan presses his lips against mine and we cling to each other as we ride them out. Knowing we came at the same time, it feels so incredibly amazing, and I'm reluctant to pull away from him. Sadly, my need to catch my breath overtakes the need I feel to keep connected to Kellan, and we both part, gasping and panting as we desperately try to catch our breaths.

Kellan flops down onto his side, and as his cock slides out of my pussy, I hate how empty I feel. I never knew it was possible to physically crave a cock, but that is exactly what I feel right now. Bringing his hand up to my face, he gently sweeps my sweaty hair out of my eyes, tucking the stray strands behind my ears as he looks at me with an expression I can only describe as awe. He's looking at me like he can't quite believe what just happened, and I can appreciate that feeling. I don't even know how to explain it, but I feel so much closer to Kellan now. There's no doubt in my mind that I'm crazy in love with him, and I think given the way Kellan is looking at me, he might feel the same. Thankfully he doesn't say anything, we just sit there in companionable silence, staring at each other with love in our eyes.

As our eyes begin to droop, Kellan pulls me farther into his arms so I'm encased by him, my cheek resting on his chest. I can hear his heart beating against my cheek, and I have no doubt in my mind that it's beating for me, the way my heart beats for him. As we both begin to fall asleep, I imprint this entire moment, this whole night, into my memories. I know I will need to hold on to this, to feel this love, because I won't ever get the chance again. Tonight is my first and last night in Kellan's arms. No matter how much he might hate me come tomorrow, I hope he will always know that my heart beats only for him.

Waking up without having Hallie next to me is still one of the most bizarre experiences, and I don't think it's one I will ever get used to. Maybe that's why I'm so reluctant to let Hallie sleep in her own room. Just for a fraction of a second, when I wake up without her, panic starts to set in. My heart races and I sit up so quickly, eyes darting around the room while I look for her. Every possible worst-case scenario flicks through my brain, but they all involve me losing the best thing to have ever happened to me. That overwhelming fear that one day I may no longer be Hallie's dad, and that thought scares the shit out of me.

This morning, even though I have that moment of panic yet again while I try to look around the room for my daughter, my mind is calmed almost instantly when I feel the beautiful girl curled up beside me. Her head is resting on my chest, brunette locks fanned out covering my tattoos, and her leg is tossed over my leg as she grips my side.

Just the feel of having her silky soft skin against me, is more than enough to have my cock standing to attention. Apparently I just can't get enough of her. We had what can only be described as the best sex I've ever had last night. I honestly didn't know what to expect when Mia said she was ready. I'd have been more than happy to wait as long as she wanted, but when she said she was ready, I was more than on board. I still kept checking in with her throughout the night, waiting for her to change her mind. Yet at each and every stage, she wowed me. I knew this girl was strong, but each time she pushed her fear to one side and simply just followed her own feelings, I was amazed by her.

I thought when we fell asleep that would be it for the night. So, when she woke me up a couple of hours after that first time, I was expecting her to freak out. She didn't, quite the opposite in fact. It was like talking to a different Mia. Her confidence was sky-high and she had absolutely no regrets. She just said she was surprised, and plans to capitalise while she feels sexy.

Instantly, she threw her legs over my hips and slowly sank down onto my cock. Her breasts swung as she arched her back in the sexiest way. Seeing this hot as fuck woman, completely naked, riding my cock with vigour, I'm surprised I didn't blow my load there and then. But Mia just wanted to follow her body, and experience many different positions to see what feels best. Obviously it wasn't exactly a hardship for me to fuck this woman, and each time we tried a new position was better than the last.

When we finally fell asleep just a couple of hours ago, we were both exhausted, but I knew I wouldn't get away with sleeping too late. Even though Liam and Bree are used to having Hallie, and they know her daytime routine, that doesn't mean they are used to managing it. Hallie can be quite a handful depending on if she's in a mood or not. Besides, I can't bear to be separated from her for too long.

Gently, without trying to jostle Mia, I pull away, lowering her head back onto my pillow so she can continue to sleep for a little longer. On my way to the bathroom, I grab some sweatpants, and I jump in for a quick shower. When I come back out, water droplets dripping from my hair, running down my exposed abdomen, I notice Mia sitting up on the end of the bed. She's pulled one of my T-shirts over her body, and it dwarfs her petite frame.

It's not her attire that grabs my attention, it's the look on her face. Her eyes are downcast at the floor, and she's fiddling with her fingers that are resting on her knees.

"Morning, beautiful," I say when I walk into the room. I hit her with my best cocky smile, but she doesn't reciprocate. In fact, her eyes barely meet mine before they are back to focusing on her fiddling hands again.

Walking over to her, I sit down beside her, before reaching over to take hold of her hands. I want to stop her from picking at the skin on her hands, something I've learnt is a nervous habit Mia engages in when she's highly anxious. I try to stroke at the fresh red, sore skin that she's just ripped from around her nails.

Before I've even had a chance to stroke all of the raw skin, Mia snatches her hand out of mine and stands up in a hurry. I'm so fucking confused. All night we've been surrounded by nothing but bliss, yet couldn't be further from that now. Mia's pacing like a caged, wild animal, preparing to strike at any moment. I'm just worried that when she does, it will rip me up.

My heart starts to race as a sinking feeling overwhelms me. I run all the possible scenarios through my head, and I try to find the right words. I want to simply ask if she's okay, but I can already tell I won't like the answer. So I wait, and give Mia a chance to talk when she's ready, which thankfully isn't too long.

"I'm sorry, Kellan," she mumbles as she stops pacing. I expect her to look at me, but she is trying to look everywhere except at me.

"You don't have anything to apologise to me for, Flower."

"Yes, I do," she shouts, and she finally meets my gaze. Her eyes are full of unshed tears and there's an emptiness in her gaze that makes the sinking feeling even worse. "Last night was amazing, but it should never have happened. We have so many reasons why us being together is a bad idea, and last night we went too far. I'm not saying I regret it, I'm just saying we shouldn't have gone as far as we did."

What the fuck? "That's the same thing, Mia. What are you trying to say?" I shout, desperate for her to stop beating around the bush and just tell me what she is getting at.

"I'm not ready for a relationship. I'm sorry. I thought I was, but I'm not. I love being Hallie's nanny, and I don't want to lose the friendship I have with you, Kellan. But I don't want more. Last night shouldn't have happened."

My heart sinks. I physically feel my body deflate, and I just don't know what to say. Even though her face is covered with the tears that have now broken free, Mia is standing tall, determination clear in her voice. With each word she says with conviction, it feels like she's slicing me open with a knife.

"You can't say you won't regret it, but that it shouldn't have happened, Mia. Make your fucking mind up. Tell me what the hell has made you change your mind. When we fell asleep just a couple of hours ago, you were happy. We were fucking happy. You said you thought you could be falling in love with me, how the fuck has that changed?" I want to shout, to make her hear exactly what I'm trying to say, but it just comes out empty. I know Mia, and once her mind is made up, she won't change it. Well…that's what I would have said about her up until a couple of hours ago, but this has just come out of the blue. Or maybe I simply missed the signs? Did I push her too far last night? Did I trigger her in such a way that she simply can't trust being in a relationship with me?

"I don't want to talk about it, Kellan. But I'm not going to change my mind. We should never have happened, and we can't happen again. I need to stay on as Hallie's nanny until I graduate. I know you probably hate me right now, and I promise that after I graduate I will disappear and you will never hear from me again. All I ask is that you let me finish my course here as promised. Please," she begs, wiping the tears away from her cheeks.

My brain feels mangled. How have we gone from being blissed out in the perfect relationship just a couple of hours ago, to her now talking about leaving and never seeing us again? That thought hurts me more than anything else.

"Mia, I don't ever want you to leave and never see you again. Of course you can stay on as Hallie's nanny, she loves you. But I really would like to talk about this, please. I want to understand what has brought on this change. If we talk about it, we may be able to sort it out."

Mia shakes her head and groans, running her fingers through her hair. "There's nothing to discuss, Kel. I have made my mind up, and my reasons are irrelevant. If you want to be friends, we can do that. If not, I can simply be your employee. But that is all I have to offer right now, and I ask you to respect my decision and not try to change my mind. I need you to respect me and keep your distance."

I place my head in my hands as I blink away the tears that are threatening to break free. I feel like I'm losing her, and I don't know what to do. Maybe if I give her the distance she thinks she wants, then eventually she will trust me enough to talk to me about what the hell is going on. Something has obviously triggered her enough that she's too scared to jump into this relationship with me.

Reluctantly, I look up to meet her gaze and give her a small smile. "If that's what you want, we can be friends. But just for the record, I'll always want more. I genuinely believe we're meant to be together, and you know that too. I think you are scared, and that something has caused you to feel this way. I'm going to hold out hope that one day you feel comfortable enough to discuss this with me, and once we've talked it out, we can be together."

"I wish I could talk to you, Kellan, but this is just one of those things that you wouldn't understand. Please believe that I'm acting with your best interests in mind. I don't want you to wait for me, I want you to move on," she mutters, and hearing her say that causes my blood to boil.

I try to take some deep breaths, so I don't lose it too badly, but I can hear my pulse pounding in my head from the anger. "You do not get to tell me to move on, and you sure as fuck don't get to say this is all in my best interests. It's selfish, and if you had the balls you would talk to me about how you're feeling. What you're doing is running away," I shout, and watch as Mia flinches at the harshness of my words.

With a small smile on her face, she moves to stand in front of me.

Raising her hand, she places it against my cheek, and I resist the urge to flinch. Her hands are cold but it's the tingles that shoot all throughout my body that shock me. How can someone who makes me feel so alive with just the slightest innocent touch not feel the same?

"I'm going to my room now, Kel. I'll give you space today because I know you aren't working and can have Hallie. In the morning, we'll start as just employees, and I'll respect the boundaries like we always should have. I'm hopeful that one day we can get back to being friends, but that's all on you. I don't regret what happened, Kellan, but it can't happen again."

Before I have a chance to reply, Mia turns on her heel and flees from my room. I flop back down onto my bed, head in my hands, and for the first time in a very long time, I let the tears fall. I cry because for the first time in my life, other than when I first met Hallie, I felt sure that I'd love this woman forever, only to have it taken from me. It's like I was given a small insight into what my perfect life could be like. I was able to touch it, to feel it, for just one evening. Only to have it ripped from me. I imagine some cheesy game show host shouting, "Here's what you could have won!"

My heart breaks, and I give myself just a few minutes to wallow in the feelings before I get up and go to my little girl. I may not be able to live my perfect life, but I can still be happy with Hallie.

The next couple of weeks pass by painfully slowly. Each day seems to get more awkward between Mia and myself. The first week I just went about my business, hoping she'd regret her decision, and eventually we could get back together. But it didn't happen. In fact, Mia seems to go out of her way to avoid being in the same room as me alone. I don't blame her either. The sexual chemistry between us hasn't got any easier. Every time she is close, I want to hold her, touch her, kiss her, and the silence just crackles. I have a perpetual hard-on whenever I'm near her, yet she just moves away and pretends she doesn't feel it, but I know she does. I can see the way her cheeks blush, and she bites her lip. Or the way she squirms on the sofa when I sit just that little bit too close.

I know I shouldn't wind her up, or try to make things awkward between us, but I can't just admit it's over. I have to fight, and if that means flirting with her continuously, that's exactly what I'm going to do.

To say that Bree and Liam are pissed about the scenario is a massive understatement, and the following morning, I got one hell of a lecture from Liam. This is the exact reason he gave for us not being together in the first place. But, after he got through chewing me up and spitting me back out, he finally let me tell him exactly what happened. Both Liam and Bree were as stunned as I was by Mia's change. I never asked them to take sides, but it was impossible for them not to be pulled into the middle of our mess.

It's not like we argue, in fact, our voices have never been raised. Instead, it's mostly Mia trying to ignore me, or getting snappy at me when I hit on her. I allow my cocky, sarcastic tone to dictate most of our conversations, which obviously pisses Mia off. Then Bree and Liam end up in the middle, acting as go-betweens for us. It's really fucking childish, but I feel like I have to do something. I can't just pretend that my feelings for her have just gone away. She might be able to turn hers off, but I can't.

This mess has been going on for around two weeks when Bree and Mia fall out. Bree won't tell us exactly what happened, they were at an appointment for the upcoming wedding, but when they came home, they weren't talking to each other. All I know is that Bree got pissed over Mia not confiding in her, and it spiralled from there.

Liam and I gave them some time to cool down because both girls can be hot-headed and stubborn, but after a week we decided to step in. The wedding is just a week away, and we can't have the bride and the maid of honour fighting.

Liam sits both girls down on the sofa, and I sit on the chair with Hallie, keen to watch his intervention. "Okay, this crap has gone on long enough. You're both going to go out for a meal tonight, and when you come back, you are going to be best friends again. Bree, if Mia doesn't want to open up to you about something, you have to honour her wishes and just trust in your friendship. And, Mia, you need to seriously think about who you can trust in this world. If you keep alienating the people who love you the most, you will end up alone. I'm not telling you to confide in Bree about whatever has caused this argument, but what I'm saying is that you have to put your pride aside and realise that part of being in a friendship or in a relationship means trusting the other person. Knowing that they have your best interests at heart, nothing else. We are getting married next week, and the girls will be here soon to plan the hen party. By the time they get here, I want all the animosity that's suffocating this house to be gone. Understood?"

Both girls look at each other before returning their gaze to Liam, and neither looks like they want to be the first to reply. Liam pierces Bree with his gaze and I watch her roll her eyes before responding. "You better be paying," Bree grumbles at Liam, which gets a laugh from Mia.

Her laugh is faint and short, but it's the most animated we've seen her in the last couple of weeks. She could only be described as acting like a robot recently, so that laugh is like music to my ears. I may not be able to fix what's happening between Mia and myself, but I don't want her to fall out with Bree over this. They've been friends for too long to let that come between them.

Thankfully, when they both come back from dinner that night, they're laughing and joking like their falling out never happened. Seeing how Mia's face is lit up, her cheeks flushed, my heart begins to race. Seeing her happy and carefree, like she used to be before that night, it's a bittersweet moment for me. I don't want her to ever think I have changed my mind, I think I will always believe we are supposed to be together, but I don't want her to be miserable. It's like a lightbulb moment for me when I realise that my persistence is making her feel like crap. New plan. If I remind her of our friendship and dial back the flirting, maybe it'll give her the time she needs.

"I'm so excited," shouts Ryleigh as she comes running down the stairs, wearing a skirt that is far too short for an eighteen-year-old girl.

Ryleigh, Freya, and Shane all arrived a couple of days ago. The decision was made to combine the hen and stag nights and to just have one big night out for all of us. Initially there were a few grumbles, particularly from Ryleigh, who I think had planned a crazy blowout for Bree, but eventually she came around.

Evan is the only one that's unable to attend, apparently Desmond sent him on a mission, but he'll be here for the wedding. The decision to combine the party only happened when I found a babysitter. Thankfully, Annette offered to come over and look after Hallie for me.

Annette and I stayed in touch, talking almost every week after I left Ireland. She regularly talks to Hallie over video chat, and she's been over to stay with us on a couple of occasions. It sounds so strange that an older woman is one of my best friends, but she's like the mother I don't have. She cares for me, and she absolutely adores Hallie. So, when she offers to fly over from Ireland to look after Hallie, I pay for her to get on a flight straight away.

The house feels like a fucking hotel right now. It's a big house, and when it's just us, it feels just right. But now that Freya, Ryleigh, Shane, Finn, and Annette are staying with us, it feels very crowded. There are still a couple of spare bedrooms, and I know there's talk that Kian will move in with us, but at this moment, I'm so fucking glad the stubborn bastard is refusing. Bree wants him to move in because he keeps getting threats sent to his flat, and she takes all of our safety very fucking seriously. But Kian's very determined, saying this isn't related to his work with Bree. He thinks he's pissed off someone in the underground fight scene, and that he can deal with it himself. If I know Bree, he will be moved in before the wedding is over. She tends to get exactly what she wants.

"Keep your voice down, Ryleigh. You will wake up Hallie," snaps Liam, and I can't help but laugh. I think it's my job to say that, but Liam is on edge with Ryleigh at the moment. They've been arguing on and off since she got here. Ry is at that age where rebellion is her middle name, and everything she does seems to wind up Liam. I caught him yesterday putting the fear of God into Shane as he gave him the big brother warning. Shane swore blind that he isn't dating Ryleigh, and Liam made it very clear that this lecture applies for any time in the future too.

"I saw Annette take her up into Kellan's room. Stop being a party pooper, this is a celebration," she shouts, before turning in the direction of the staircase. "Bree, get your cute butt down here."

I shake my head, but I can't deny that Ryleigh's excitement is contagious. She has been helping the girls to get ready. Freya looks different to how she normally does, dressed in a tight, short purple dress. Ry has managed to highlight her natural beauty and make it stand out even more, and I don't miss the way Kian practically drools on the floor when Freya walks into the room.

The men are all gathered, dressed similarly in smart jeans and shirts or T-shirts. Ry did try to tell us how we needed to dress, but we shot that down very quickly. The girls, on the other hand, didn't escape her.

"Frey, don't forget your sash," Ry shouts, as she runs over to Freya and places a sash over her shoulder that reads 'Bride Squad'. Freya has a look of terror on her face, but doesn't resist. Or at least she doesn't until Ryleigh pulls out a headband with two bobbles on it that are in the shape of cocks.

"No! Not a chance, Ry. You can fuck right off," Freya shouts, as she backs away from Ryleigh until her back is pressed against the wall.

Ryleigh starts to moan, but it's Kian who is standing beside Freya that speaks. "Come on, Freya. You would look cute with two cocks on your head."

Freya turns to face him, and despite his cocky smile that seems to win everyone over, it clearly doesn't work on Freya. She glares, and I don't envy him right now. Freya is one of the sweetest people you'll ever meet, but if you cross her, she will cut you down. She's a

Doughty, after all. "I think you should wear the headband. You are the biggest dickhead in the room, so it will suit you."

Laughter rings out as Freya hands the headband over to Kian. He takes it from her and places it on his head. "I can make anything look good, babe," he retorts with a very obvious wink. Liam's groan echoes around the room and I can't help but laugh.

Kian and Freya continue to banter, while Liam threatens Kian every time it's obvious that he's flirting with Frey. While that's happening, my attention is pulled towards the stairs. There's no noise or indication that someone is making their way down the stairs, but somehow I just know. It's like there's a magnetic force field that pulls me towards her whenever she is near.

As Mia begins descending the stairs, she is looking around almost timidly, like she is anxious about walking into this crowd of people. As soon as her full silhouette comes into view, I can tell why Mia's nervous. She looks like a fucking supermodel. Her shoulder-length brunette hair is curled and pinned back away from her face, which helps to emphasise her beautiful face. She is wearing dark, smoky eye make-up that makes her eyes pop. But it's the luscious red on her lips that is really driving me crazy. All I can think about is the way those red lips would look perfect around my cock.

Fuck, I really need to get her out of my head. She has made it abundantly clear over the last few weeks that friendship is all she has to offer, and I really am trying to get on board with that. But then she comes in here wearing this short, light blue silky dress that falls to just below her knee. The silky material clings to her curves, showing off what a fucking amazing figure she has, and as she puts her left foot down onto the next step, it's hard not to miss the slit she has up that side, stopping around mid-thigh.

She isn't exactly showing off a lot of skin, even the straps and the scoop neck at the top doesn't show off a load of cleavage, yet she still looks stunning. My heart races, and I take a moment just to appreciate her beauty while nobody else is even aware she's entered the room. Sadly, the pull we seem to have for each other goes both ways, and her eyes instantly connect with mine. I don't avert my gaze and neither does she. I watch as she takes a few seconds to take in my appearance, dragging her gaze over my body. I try to hide my smile when I see her bite her lip, Mia's classic sign that she likes what she sees.

I obviously didn't do a very good job of hiding my cocky smile, and as soon as she realises I've caught her checking me out, she tries to look away. It doesn't take long for Ryleigh to notice Mia's in the room, and everyone turns their attention to her, telling her how stunning she looks, which is a fucking understatement. She's the most beautiful girl I've ever seen, and I suspect wherever we go tonight, she'll be the most beautiful girl in the room.

"Here's your sash, Mia. What kind of headband do you want to wear?" Ryleigh asks, as she holds the sash in one hand, and a selection of novelty headbands in the other.

"Erm…is that a pair of boobs on one, and a cock?" she replies, trying to take in all the designs as she takes the sash that says 'Maid of Honour' and places it over her head, wearing it across her body like a beauty queen.

"Yeah, do you wanna take them and have a look?" Ry holds out the selection, attempting to spread them out as best she can so Mia can take her pick.

Mia looks like a rabbit caught in headlights and is staring at the penis-shaped headband like it is a lethal weapon. I know I shouldn't interfere and it's not my job anymore to stick up for Mia, but I can't help it. "Ry, leave the poor girl alone. She doesn't have to wear a headband if she doesn't want to. She is wearing the sash so be happy with that."

Mia's eyes dart towards me, and I brace myself for the retort I'm sure is going to come. Telling me she can fight her own battles and that I shouldn't get involved, but instead she just smiles at me. It's the smile I love seeing, one that's been absent from her face the last couple of weeks. I sound like a teenage girl when I say that the sight of her smile quite literally makes my heart soar, but it's true.

The interaction is over before it's even begun, as Bree makes her big entrance. She is dressed in a beautiful white dress that stops mid-thigh. The stark white colour makes her bright red hair stand out even more, and if the way my best friend is staring at her is any indication, she looks hot.

"I am one lucky guy," Liam says, as he pulls Bree into his arms and presses his lips against hers. I can't help but look away. Their love shines so bright and it feels almost intrusive to witness them together.

"No, enough of that nonsense. I agreed to a joint party, but she is still ours for the night, Liam. You don't get to steal her," Ryleigh moans, as she pulls Bree out of Liam's arms and pulls the sash over her shoulder. Its gold lettering reads 'Bride To Be'. Ryleigh then pulls out a headband that has a veil on it, and places it on Bree's head, so the white netting falls down to her lower back. She then produces a big L plate—that learner drivers usually have on their cars—and she pins it onto Bree's sash.

"Perfect. Now for some pictures," she shouts, as she throws her phone at Shane, giving him instructions on what kind of shots she wants.

Ever since Shane moved to be at the same school as Ry, they have become best friends. Well...they are more than that. It's painfully obvious that they both have feelings for each other, but I think the only people who don't know that are Shane and Ry.

After posing for what feels like a million different pictures, Ryleigh then has a lightbulb moment and informs us she has forgotten something important and to stay where we are. Groans fill the room as she runs upstairs.

"Now. If we sneak out now we can lose her," Kian jokes, or at least I hope he is joking. Everyone laughs except for Shane.

"Come on, guys. I know she sometimes can go a little over the top with things like this, but she has a good heart. You have no idea how much the first wedding affected her. I was with her when she came back to school. She is doing this because she wants to eradicate any memory of the last wedding. She wants your wedding to be a memorable occasion, not one overshadowed by pain. So, give her a break. I will get her to dial it down, but I would be very grateful if you would all make an effort, just for a little bit. Please." Everyone looks at the kid in awe. He has always been pretty high in my estimation after the way he went out on a limb to save Bree, but now he's just gone up even further. It takes balls to stand up in front of a room full of people and say what he just did. Kid's got more balls than he thinks he does.

I'm glad we have managed to get him out of the game, though. He deserves to have a life, to be a teenager.

"Sorry, Shane. We really do appreciate everything Ry has done for us," Bree says, as she pulls Shane in for a hug. Ever since he helped her get free, they have become friends. He refused to leave the hospital until he knew she was okay, and from that moment on he became family. Bree in particular bonded with him, and I know they talk a couple of times a week on the phone. I think she sees him as her unofficial little brother.

Before anyone has a chance to say anything more, Ryleigh comes bursting into the room. As soon as I see what she is carrying, I can't help but burst out laughing. It's like a Mexican wave of laughter. As soon as people see what she is holding, they have no choice but to laugh. Well…all except Bree, who is currently looking at the four-foot inflatable penis like it is a weapon of mass destruction.

Her eyes flit between Ryleigh, Liam, and Shane. She is looking at Liam with pleading eyes, which coming from the leader of the biggest UK based crime family is actually quite funny.

"Come on, boss lady. Take your cock so we can get going. I think we are all in need of some drinks," Kian says, as he points at the inflatable cock while trying to keep a straight face. Something he is incapable of doing when he starts laughing as Bree takes hold of the cock. Ry manages to take a few more photos before we all bundle into some taxis and make our way to the local club.

We were originally supposed to be going to one of Kian's fights, but with all the death threats, he made the very sensible decision that the girls most definitely should not be in that environment. Kian worked with Ry to plan the new location.

We pull up to a new club that I've never been to before. Not that I was a big partier, and when I did go out it was mostly in Ireland. I've had a few nights out in London with Liam, but we've never been here before. There's a queue around the block, people waiting patiently for access. The sign above the door says 'Belle's Rose', and there's a picture of a rose in a glass jar lit up alongside it.

Once we are all out of the taxi, I hear chuntering from Shane and Finn about how much they don't want to stand in the queue for what they are sure will be a crazy long wait. I'm about to agree with them, when Kian steps towards the door and is greeted by a couple who have just come out of the club.

The man is tall with dark hair and the beginnings of a beard covering his cheeks and chin. He's wearing a suit but without the tie and the top two buttons of his shirt are open. He's wearing a very brooding expression that lifts just slightly into the shadow of a smile when he pulls Kian in for a man hug. The girl by his side is beautiful. She is shorter than him, but taller than the other girls. Her long black hair falls down below her shoulders, and she's wearing a small amount of make-up. Just enough to show off her classic beauty. When she sees Kian, a big smile spreads across her face and she pulls him in for a hug, kissing him on the cheek at the same time.

Once Kian has said hello to his friends, he turns around to introduce them. As they get closer, I can't help but think I've seen this guy somewhere before. I can't quite remember where, but his face looks so familiar.

"Guys, I want to introduce to you my best friend, Declan. And this is his beautiful fiancée, Belle," Kian says, as he points at each of them in turn.

Everyone begins saying hello all at the same time, and I can tell by Belle's shrinking posture that she is quite shy, and all these loud people are beginning to overwhelm her.

"Welcome to Belle's Rose. We are so happy to have you all here for this special occasion," Declan says, as he points at the club like he owns it. Which given the name matches the name of the girl hanging off his arm, it doesn't take a genius to guess that he does.

"Dec is basically my brother. He has agreed to let us use the VIP section of his club for the party." Kian has a tone of pride as he talks about Declan, and it's clear this guy means a lot to him, which means our family just got that little bit bigger.

Bree looks like she is about to thank them, but Ryleigh butts in. "This is so cool. When Kian told me we could use the VIP room here, I thought he was taking the piss. Even though you haven't been open for very long, Belle's has quickly become one of the most sought-after, in-demand clubs in London. You have no idea how exciting this is. I am going to Instagram the shit out of this," Ryleigh shouts as she begins taking photos of the club.

"Well, I would have let Kian use it anyway. But, I could hardly say no to Desmond," Declan explains, and with the mention of Liam's father's name the ears of all the Doughty children prick up. That's when my memory finally kicks in.

"That's where I know you from. I knew I recognised your face, but I didn't know where from. You work for Desmond," I explain, and everyone turns to face me. Liam looks pissed, like I expected him to. He hates it when his father interferes in his life in any way.

"Actually, I used to work for him. He does own a small share in the club, but he's a silent partner. He gave me the investment money I needed to get this place started, but that's all. This place is one hundred percent legit, before you ask." He directs that last part to Liam, who does appear to be giving him an evil glare.

"Well, thank you for having us, and you are more than welcome to join our little party. It will be great to get to know you further. Do you want to lead the way?" asks Bree, as she attempts to diffuse the tense situation.

We all walk towards the entrance, but Liam falls back until he is standing beside me. "Is he legit?" he whispers for only me to hear.

Nodding, I tell Liam what I know. "From what I remember, he used to run Shades, your dad's sex club in Ireland. There was some trouble surrounding one of the monthly auctions that are held there, but I don't know the specifics. Shortly after, Declan handed in his letter of resignation because he wanted to move to England to be with Belle. She goes to medical school at Oxford Uni. From the research I did, and it wouldn't have been a full deep dive, but he came up clean. Des invested as a silent partner only, and he agreed there would be no illegal activity. Declan wanted to build a life here for him and Belle. That's all I know." As soon as I finish, Liam begins to nod, like what I've just told him is enough...for now. I already know that I will have to run a deep dive on this guy tomorrow. Liam likes to know everyone his father is in business with. It's the only way we can stay on top of what he's planning.

As we reach the door, Kian comes over to us. "Look, I know you have issues with your father, and from what I've heard, I don't blame you. But Declan is practically my brother, and I trust him. And he trusts Desmond. He has always looked out for Dec, and that means something to us both. So please, keep the hatred you have for your father to one side, and just give Dec a chance. I think you might actually like him if you get to know him."

Liam claps Kian on the back and we both give him the nods he needs. "We promise to give him a try. Thank you for organising this. You have made Ryleigh very happy," Liam jokes as we make our way into the club.

The minute the doors open, it's like we are hit with a blast of noise, the loud beat of the bass echoing through our bodies. Belle is leading the way, and Ryleigh appears to be using the giant cock to move people out of the way so we can make our way to the VIP section.

As usual, my gaze instantly finds Mia, and as I suspected, she looks to be a bit uncomfortable. Her head is shooting from left to right as she takes in the mass of people, and I watch as her shoulders stiffen and she tries to make herself smaller. She hates crowds or any sort of attention, and we aren't even halfway into the club yet and I've seen a couple of guys leering at her.

I know I shouldn't do anything, and that I should keep my distance like I promised. But, fuck it!

I move closer to her, using my body as a shield so nobody is able to get too close to her. I then place my hand against her lower back, not only for her to use as a guide, but also to give her the comfort of knowing I'm there for her.

As soon as she feels my hand, her head whips around. She has no idea who is touching her, and I'm guessing she is about to tell me off. I think for a moment, even after she sees that it's me, she still considers shouting at me. Then she seems to sigh, almost like she is relieved, and she continues to walk.

Just a few steps later I feel her hand reach around to where mine is, and she takes my fingers in hers and pulls my hand around so that my arm is wrapped around her, and her hand is intertwined with mine. She doesn't look at me, or even acknowledge that it's happened, she simply continues to walk. But I don't miss the way she walks just that little taller, with a bit more confidence. It's like the dark shadows of the club can hide the secrets we aren't meant to have.

Belle leads us into the VIP area, and as we all take our seats a waitress comes over holding a tray of shot glasses. "First round's on me," Declan states, as he picks up a shot glass and holds it in the air. Everyone reaches for a glass, and as we all sit there looking around at each other, the silence starts to become a bit awkward. I'm waiting for either Bree or Liam to make the toast, but they appear to be looking at me or Mia, who I'm trying to pretend isn't practically sitting on my knee. We're all crushed into the booth that wasn't made for this many people. Kian is next to me, and obviously I don't want to sit on his knee, so I'm naturally leaning closer to Mia. She's the better choice, after all.

"I think it's the best man who is supposed to do the toast," Kian whispers in my ear, and I realise everyone is looking at me expectantly.

"Shit. I didn't know that. My bad...okay. Everyone, please raise your glass and slam it back to celebrate Bree and Liam. May they live a long and happy life together," I say before leaning forward, clinking my glass with Liam's before downing the shot. The burn of the vodka as it slides down my throat is delicious, and everyone else follows suit as they congratulate Bree and Liam before slamming back their shots.

"A round of Jagerbombs next, please," Ryleigh shouts, and groans echo around the table. The loudest of which is coming from Shane.

"No. You promised no Jager tonight. You know how you get when you drink Jager. Last time you ended up in the middle of the dance floor, dancing around your handbag while you threatened to take off your bra." Shane's voice has taken on an extremely high pitch, and I don't miss the red mist that descends over Liam's face at the mention of his baby sister taking off her bra.

"Oh, shut up. It was one time. And we don't know if it was the Jager or the tequila that was to blame." Ryleigh waves him off and instructs the waitress to bring the drinks. Shane shakes his head disapprovingly, but doesn't bother to say anything. He clearly knows Ryleigh well enough to pick his battles.

Liam, on the other hand, is not happy. "Let me make it very clear right now, Ryleigh, before you drink any more. The first sign that you have had too much to drink and you are in a taxi home. And so help me God, if you even think about taking any of your clothes off, you will be straight home. Understood?"

Ryleigh's face twists into her typical pissed-off teenage expression, and I have seen this look many times before. If somebody doesn't diffuse the situation right now, it will descend into chaos. The problem is, Liam sees Ry as the baby of the family, and his dad mode kicks in. But she isn't a little girl anymore, and I think Liam is struggling with that. Even though he isn't the eldest, he has always been the one to look after the girls, and Freya has never caused him any trouble. But the same can't be said for adventurous, rebellious Ryleigh.

Bree, thankfully, has also read the situation and steps in. "Okay, enough of the lectures. We are here to have fun, and that is what we are going to do. I'm not carrying a giant inflatable cock around for no reason. Ryleigh promises not to overdo it, and Liam promises to try and lighten up, even if it's only for a bit. Now, shall we get this party started!" Bree shouts, as the waitress puts the tray down and everyone reaches to grab their glasses.

We all place the tumbler that is filled with Red Bull in front of us, and take hold of the shot glass full of Jager. Holding them up, everyone looks around for who will be the one to make the next toast. They can fuck off if they think I'm doing another. I expect Liam to take the hit, so I'm surprised when Mia begins to talk. "Here's to a great night. Thank you to Ryleigh and Kian for helping to organise this. You deserve the best, Bree, and I think you have found it with Liam. Congratulations!"

As soon as she finishes her speech, we each drop the shot glass into the tumbler of Red Bull, before swallowing the whole thing. Fuck, that shit is strong. I can already feel the alcohol beginning to flow into my bloodstream. It's like I can feel it travelling through my body, relaxing each of my nerves in turn. Making me a whole lot more chilled than I was before.

It also seems to have electrified my nerve endings because the ones that are currently touching Mia's soft, silky skin, it feels like I'm being electrocuted. I'm on edge each time her arm brushes against mine, and every time she laughs she seems to lean in towards me, and I have to resist the urge to put my arm around her.

We manage to talk Ryleigh down from another round of shots, and we all just order whatever we want. I ordered a bottle of beer, and Mia got her usual Jack Daniels and Coke. I don't really pay much attention to what else is going on around me, my attention is always on her.

Everyone seems to break off into mini conversations, and Kian starts telling me all about his recent threats, and asking me if I will look into it for him. I agree, but tell him he will have to come to me with all the details another time. I blame it on the drinks I've had, saying I won't be able to remember, but in reality it's because I'm only half listening. The other half of my attention is with Mia, who is talking to Freya about her college course.

Freya has just finished sixth form, and was going to go to university, but has decided to take a gap year, much to Liam's annoyance. Freya has always been the good girl of the family, determined to get as far away from this life as she can. Growing up surrounded by death and mayhem, she doesn't exactly know how to live a normal life. She has no idea what she wants to do with her life. She could've just chosen a random subject she enjoys and gone to university with no clear plan, like a lot of people her age do. But Frey wants a plan. She wants to find what makes her happy. At the moment she is staying with a friend in Ireland, but has been talking to Bree about coming to stay in London for a bit. She wants to explore and find herself.

"So you just left your family and went on your own? How did you do it? Weren't you scared?" Freya asks, and Mia shakes her head in reply as she circles her finger around the rim of her glass.

"Honestly, no. But that's because for me it was scarier to stay and be part of my family. I'm not saying it's easy. If I'd taken my father's money, I could have done a full-time course and graduated two years ago. Instead, I did a part-time, online-based course so I could work during the day to pay off the money for the course. I'm in my final semester now, and this is the only module I have to do in a placement.

So the university basically sends out assessors and has Kellan fill out paperwork about how I care for Hallie. He will be the person who decides if I pass my course or not," Mia explains, and I'm shocked for a moment because she never told me that. I knew I would have to assess her. I received all the paperwork and did a video call with her assessor, but I didn't know it was my decision.

"You are so lucky that you have been able to use this as a placement. Not that I think Kellan would be biased. In fact, he is probably the harshest judge when it comes to Hallie." Mia just laughs at Freya's comment. It's more of a sarcastic chuckle that lets Frey know she knows exactly what she's talking about.

"He is, but I don't blame him." Mia discreetly turns my way, I can just see her out of the corner of my eye, but thankfully I had already turned to face Kian. I may not be looking directly at her, but my ears prick up as she starts to talk about me. "He really does love Hallie, and is a genuinely great dad. She is a lucky little girl to be surrounded by so much love. I know Kellan sometimes tries to compensate for what Hallie lost so early on in life, but he really doesn't need to. She may not have a mum in her life, but she has everything that matters. She is loved, and if I can be part of that, even just a little bit, then I will take it."

"I guess for you it's different, but I would be worried about having to leave the family when the assignment is over. Nannies build a bond with the child, and then when they aren't needed anymore they just move on. I don't know how you do that. I guess it's good that you will always be in Hallie's life."

Mia picks up her glass, and takes a drink as she tries to find the words to respond. "I think leaving someone you have grown to love, no matter the reason, is one of the hardest things anyone has to do. But, like you said, people leave because they have to, not necessarily because they want to." Mia's voice takes on a sad tone, almost like she is talking about when she has to leave. But like Freya said, even when Mia is no longer needed as Hallie's nanny, probably when she starts nursery school, she'll still be around to see her every day. So, I don't know why she'd get sad talking about that.

I don't have time to dwell on her comments for too long because as soon as the song changes to "Dirrty" by Christina Aguilera, Ryleigh insists all the girls and the giant penis head to the dance floor. Even the new girl, Belle, ends up getting dragged along too.

The conversation between the guys stops as we all turn to watch the girls dance. I'm sure we tell ourselves that it's a security thing. That we have to make sure they're all safe. But in reality, I think we are all watching our own girl.

My gaze locks on Mia instantly, and at first she looks a little out of place, like she isn't entirely sure what to do. Her head swivels around and she begins to get overwhelmed with the amount of people around her. Almost on instinct, she turns to face me and with a smile and a nod, I let her know that she can let her hair down and I'll watch over her. Mia constantly has her guard up, waiting for her father or Kyle to strike at any moment, but there's no way in hell that's happening while I'm around. Even though we aren't together, I still fucking care about her.

The girls dance through a couple of different songs, their moves becoming more raunchy as they swirl their hips to the music. It doesn't take long for the guys to say fuck it, and they join their girls on the dance floor. Liam, surprisingly, caves first, and he joins Bree and the giant cock, which is definitely the funniest sight I've seen in a long time.

Declan caves next, joining Belle, and it's not long before Ryleigh pulls Shane onto the dance floor. I hear Kian make a comment about going to dance so he can see more clearly if there's a threat. Guy must think we're stupid. His lovesick ass goes straight for Freya, and it takes less than two minutes for her to shoot him down. Kian is everything she's not looking for in a guy. He fights, and he's in the world she's desperately fighting to be free from. Still, Kian doesn't seem like the type of guy to give up easily, and he continues to persevere, just dancing near her until she caves.

I'm left here with Finn, who seems more interested in his phone than being here. He appears to be texting furiously, his fingers banging on the touch screen of his phone. His eyebrows are furrowed and in deep concentration, concerned with whatever he's reading. I'm about to ask him if he's okay, when he turns to me first. "Tell Liam and Bree that I'm sorry, but I need to leave. Evan has got himself into a fucking mess with the mission Dad sent him on. I've gotta go and help him. Tell them I'm sorry." He stands to leave, but I grab hold of his arm to get his attention.

"Wait, do you need any help? Is Evan okay?" I may have a serious liking for the asshole, and think he needs to get over his hero worship of Desmond, but I would still throw down for him, the way I would with any of the Doughty siblings.

"No, it will be fine when I get there. Don't tell them anything that will ruin tonight. I will text and keep you updated. I promise, you all should stay and enjoy your evening." With a nod, I let go of his arm and we say our goodbyes before Finn heads towards the door.

Looking over at the group, nobody has noticed Finn has left yet, which is good. I don't want Liam chasing after him and ruining this evening. Everyone is dancing, even Freya has allowed Kian to dance with her now. My eyes naturally go to Mia, who has started to relax and is letting the music take over her body. I watch as she sways her hips to the beat, and I'm hypnotised.

Then I notice the tall guy standing beside her, who is trying to dance his way towards her. Every so often he puts his hand on her hip, but she moves it out the way and turns her back on him. It couldn't be more obvious that she doesn't want to dance with him, yet he is persisting. I let it happen twice before I stand and charge my way onto the dance floor. By the time I reach them, I've calmed down enough to know I'm not going to punch the guy in the face. Instead, I walk straight up to Mia and pull her into my arms. At first she's shocked, and the guy behind her starts to protest. So, I make it very fucking clear she is unavailable by pressing my lips against hers.

It was supposed to be a sweet kiss, just enough to show him that she isn't on the market. But the moment our lips touch, it's like these last few weeks never happen and all the lust we feel between us explodes. I pull her body against mine, and she wraps her arms around my neck, threading her fingers through my hair so she can pull me impossibly closer. Her tongue slides across my lower lip before giving it a slight nibble, and I'm putty in her hands. Our tongues mingle, battling for dominance, and I savour her taste. It's just as perfect as I remember, and there may as well be fucking fireworks going off in the background. That's how explosive and perfect kissing Mia is to me.

After a while we pull apart, panting as we try to catch our breaths. She keeps her arms wrapped around my neck, and mine stays pressed into her hips. She begins to sway to the music, and it's as though the whole world falls away around us, and it's just the two of us dancing to the music. I couldn't even tell you what happened to the other guy, I'm assuming he left. I don't even give a shit if any of our friends saw us kiss. I've never hidden how I feel for Mia, so it's not news to them.

As the song changes, Mia turns in my arms, so her back is plastered against my front, and she begins to grind her ass into my cock. Pulling my hands around to the front, she keeps hold of them while she sways and grinds against me. With a confidence I've only ever seen her have in the bedroom, she takes full ownership of her body and she moves it with purpose. She knows that each and every twist, turn, and grind is turning me on. She can no doubt feel the painful erection I have that is straining against my now incredibly tight jeans. For the first time since I was a teenager, I worry I might actually come in my pants, just from dry humping alone. She doesn't even seem to mind that we are in the middle of a nightclub, surrounded by people. And I know why. It's because when we are together it's like nobody else even exists.

We continue to dance for a long time, until finally I feel Liam pulling on my arm, and Bree appears to be doing the same with Mia. "Sorry to break up whatever the hell this is," Liam says, looking pointedly between Mia and myself, before continuing. "We're going to get a taxi home. Ryleigh's had too much to drink and Shane wants to take her home, so I said we would go too. Freya and Kian are coming too, I think. You guys are welcome to stay if you like?"

Mia looks over at me as Bree finishes her sentence, no doubt giving her the same option Liam just gave me. I give her a slight nod, knowing that she won't want to stay here without Bree. I hate that our bubble has to burst, but maybe I can keep it going just a little longer.

As we start to head to the door, Shane is in front of us carrying Ryleigh like a bride as she cuddles up to the giant, inflatable knob.

Even Freya looks a little wobbly on her feet as Kian lets her lean on him for support. I think we all drank more than we realised while we were dancing.

While we are outside waiting for our taxis to arrive, Mia shivers from the cold weather, and without thinking I throw my arm around her and pull her against me. I don't have a jacket to give her, the best I can do is give her some of my warmth. We seem to have drifted away from the group slightly, which, as I look over, I realise is a good thing. Ryleigh begins to puke her guts up, with Shane holding back her hair, while Liam lectures her about drinking too much.

Ignoring the drama, I turn Mia towards me and wrap my arms around her. "I've enjoyed tonight," I say with a smile, and my heart races when she smiles back, wrapping her arms around me too.

"Me too. It's been a lot of fun. I don't think I've ever danced like that before." The blush that spreads across Mia's cheeks as she mentions our dirty dancing does absolutely nothing to help my strained cock.

"I'm glad I got to be another of your firsts," I say, as I gently push a rogue strand of hair off her face and tuck it behind her ear. Using that hand, I cup her cheek and guide her lips against mine. It's short and sweet, but fuck is it hot. I want more. No, I need more.

"Come back home with me," I say, and Mia chuckles.

"We live together, silly."

Shaking my head, I fix my intense gaze on her and pull her body closer so she can feel my cock against her body, and she will know exactly what I mean. "No, Flower. I mean, come back to my room with me. Just for tonight if you want. I just need one more night with you." I can hear the desperation in my voice, and for a moment I think she wants it too. Then it's like something clicks and she takes a step back. She's still in my arms, but the distance speaks volumes.

"Kel, we both know one night will never be enough. I'm sorry. Tonight should never have happened, it isn't fair on you. We can't be together, and doing this is only going to make it harder. Before you say anything, yes, I do want you. Fuck, my body craves yours. But that doesn't mean we can be together."

I want to argue, I want to scream and shout, but it's pointless. She has a reason why we can't be together, and she doesn't trust me enough to share it with me. Until the love we feel for each other overpowers whatever is going on in her brain, we don't stand a chance. So, I keep hold of her in my arms, and I don't try to close the distance between us. I don't try to kiss her at the end of the evening. Instead, I'm just grateful that for a little bit of time, I was able to experience what it's like to be with Mia. I know our hearts and souls were made for each other, I'm just waiting for her brain to catch up.

Kellan

The next few days in the lead up to the wedding pass by relatively quickly. The house feels like a fucking bus station with all the people coming and going. Even though Bree and Liam didn't want a big event, there's still a lot of fucking effort that goes into putting on such a high-profile wedding. The security alone is a nightmare, and I don't think I've ever seen Kian as stressed. Normally the cocky asshole always has a smile on his face and an overly sarcastic comment to share, but this last week I've noticed he seems very stressed. I guess after what happened at the last wedding, it's important they get this one right.

After the joint party, Mia and I never spoke about what happened, but the tension between us seems to be worsening. Obviously we have to interact regularly every time she takes care of Hallie, but we haven't exactly gone back to the being friends stage yet, and thankfully she isn't trying to force me. I just can't ignore the electricity that hums through my body every time our hands touch slightly, or the swooping feeling I get in my stomach every time she walks into the room. My heart literally races whenever I catch her looking at me. Those feelings don't just go away because she says they have to.

Luckily, the mass of people in our house has given me a constant distraction. I did some work for Liam looking into Declan, who thankfully is clean. I say thankfully because the girls really took to Belle, and she's become a regular fixture around here since then. Bree and Mia particularly really hit it off with her, and Declan seemed pleased because apparently since moving here Belle has struggled to make friends. Also, Declan doesn't seem too bad either. How he has been friends with Kian all these years, I will never know. They are complete opposites, yet whenever they are together they bring out the best in each other, and are definitely more like brothers than anything else. Actually reminds me of Liam and me; we aren't exactly compatible on paper, but we work.

Thankfully, Desmond and his wife, Siobhan, and Paddy, and his wife, Clodagh, all agreed to stay in a nearby hotel. They could have fit, at a push, but I think this whole event is stressful enough, without asking Desmond to move in for a bit. He's too unstable, I have no idea what he is going to do from one minute to the next.

We've all been building bridges lately. The girls have started talking to their mother again, Liam has started at least acknowledging Desmond, and we finally feel like we have Finn back. We are even making progress with Evan, and it's all thanks to Bree. She has an amazing ability to bring people together, and they trust her which means they have no problem standing beside her in a fight. Even Desmond appears to have that approach—or at least he does for now.

"Kellan, for fuck's sake, we need to leave in half an hour and you aren't ready," Liam shouts as he comes barging into my bedroom. I turn to face him with a scowl on my face.

"That's because your evil goddaughter decided last night that she didn't need sleep. I was up and down with her almost all night. Then this morning whenever I tried to feed her, she just either refused or threw it all up. I'm starting to worry she might be getting sick. She feels hot to me. Does she feel hot to you?" My words come out in a rush as I hold the gripy baby in my arms out for Liam to feel. He isn't yet dressed in his suit, otherwise I would try to keep her as far away from it as possible.

Liam places his hand on Hallie's forehead and his eyebrows furrow with the same concern I know is etched on my face. "She doesn't feel crazy warm. I'm gonna ask Mia to come have a look at her and do her temperature. She's better at all that stuff than we are. She can bring some medicine if that's what she needs."

Before I even start to object, Liam has pulled the phone out of his sweatpants pocket and is dialling. I hear him relay everything I just told him and then he hangs up. "You shouldn't have called her. She is trying to get ready, and to help Bree get ready. Besides, we are supposed to be splitting the house. Is she even allowed to see us?"

Liam rolls his eyes. "She isn't the bride, dumbass, and this is an extenuating circumstance. Besides, if she can help get Hallie settled, we may stand just the slightest chance of getting to the wedding on time."

I start what I'm sure will be a very sarcastic retort, but I'm halted when my bedroom door bursts open and a very concerned-looking Mia flies in. She is wearing a silky pink robe that stops mid-thigh, and the back reads 'Maid of Honour' and below it says Mia. She has her hair in big rollers, and it looks like she was halfway through having her make-up applied when she left to come here. One eye looks more spectacular than the other. But I do my best not to comment, she is doing me a favour, after all. But the truth is, even looking completely unready, she still looks absolutely fucking beautiful. That swooping feeling, that I refuse to refer to as butterflies—I'm a grown-ass man, for fuck's sake, we don't get butterflies—continues in my stomach, and my heart races. Even like this, my cock is beginning to harden.

"Is she okay?" Mia asks, as she rushes over and sits next to me on the bed, placing her hand on Hallie's forehead.

"Oh yeah, she does feel a bit hot. Let me grab my thermometer from next door. Liam, we've got this. Please, for the love of God, go and get dressed. Also, can you check on your brothers? Ryleigh said she saw them a few minutes ago in the kitchen having some breakfast, they weren't dressed yet either. Kian says that because our security is run with military precision, being late is not an option if we all want to stay safe," Mia explains, and as she heads towards the door, Liam charges in front of her, spitting out a bunch of expletives about how unreliable everyone is. He also may have mentioned something about having a heart attack, and that seriously may happen before the end of the day. Liam is quite possibly the most stressed I've ever seen him, and I know my job is to help take the burden off, or even just make him feel excited for today, but I can't do any of that while I'm worried about Hallie.

While it's just me and Hallie, I carry on rocking her in my arms, whispering and singing to her. It helps to keep her calm when I sing. Ever since she was born I've always sang "Mockingbird" to her by Eminem, and while most would argue it's not the most appropriate song for a baby, she loves it. My beautiful little weirdo laughed for the first time when I was singing about breaking the birdie's neck. Thankfully, it seems to be doing the trick right now, as her eyes begin to droop from the song and the swaying motion. She is fighting it, desperate not to fall asleep, but I know she must be exhausted.

Mia comes rushing in with her children's ear thermometer. She looks at me for permission, which I instantly give. She should know by now that when it comes to Hallie, she doesn't need my permission for things, but she still gets it anyway. Mia has more than proved how much Hallie means to her, and despite a rocky start, I know she will always put Hallie's wellbeing before anything else.

The thermometer beeps and the display screen turns an orange colour. Meaning she has a fever, but it's not too high. "That's good, it's not too high. But I think it's something we should keep an eye on during the day. If we give her some medicine now, that should help it go down, and she also might sleep through the ceremony then."

Nodding in confirmation, Mia strolls over to the chest of drawers where I keep all of Hallie's things, and pulls the medicine and syringe out of the top drawer. After reading the instructions once more, despite us both knowing them off by heart, she draws up the correct amount and holds the syringe out for me to take. "It's okay, you give her it and I will keep holding her."

I appreciate her offering to let me administer the medicine. When she first started working as my nanny, I was crazy overprotective of Hallie, and when it came to things like this, I didn't want her to use her own initiative. I wanted to know if my child was ill. But, the more we've worked together, she knows now that I trust her judgement, possibly more than I do my own sometimes. And, even though Hallie doesn't get ill often, I know Mia only has her best interests at heart.

Stroking my daughter's cheek, Mia gently presses her finger against Hallie's lower lip, encouraging her to open her mouth. Gently she places the syringe into her mouth and Hallie responds by lapping up the medicine like a little cat would. Mia strokes Hallie's beautiful curls and pushes them off her forehead. She leans down and presses her lips to her head and my heart stops.

How the fuck am I supposed to not fall in love with a woman who cares for my daughter in this way? If I was a woman, my ovaries would have just exploded. When I became a single dad, I always worried about dating. It was hard enough for me to date before, but finding someone who could not only deal with my shit, but take on my daughter too, I pretty much ruled myself off the eligible bachelor list. Then I met Mia. She cares for me and my daughter, so why can't I have her?

Acting almost on instinct, given how close we are to each other while she is kissing Hallie, she reaches up and strokes my hair in the same way she did my daughter. Cupping my cheek she gives me a small smile, and she is so close now I can feel her breath on my lips. It wouldn't take much to lean in, to close the gap between us and press my lips against hers. But I don't. There have been too many times in her life when men have taken what they want from her without listening to what she wants, I won't be like them. She has to be the one to move first every time.

"I need to finish getting my make-up done, but Ryleigh is having hers done now. So I have a little time. Why don't you go shower and get dressed while I look after Hallie?" Mia asks, and the feel of her words against my skin sends shivers down my spine.

Please close the fucking gap and kiss me, I think to myself, being very careful that this isn't one of those times where I'm supposed to be thinking the words, but in reality they are tumbling out like word vomit. But not this time, thank fuck.

"Are you sure, Flower? Aren't you supposed to be helping Bree get ready?" I ask, as I reach up and push a stray lock of hair behind her ear. I don't miss the way her breath hitches when my hand touches her skin. I wonder if she feels the electricity pulsing through her body the way I do?

Her eyes glance down at my mouth, and I know she is watching as my tongue travels around my lips. I'm not trying to be sexual when I lick my lips, but the way she is looking at me is driving me fucking crazy. I don't miss the way she bites her own lip, no doubt to hold in a groan.

"She's fine. She only needs to put her dress on, and we won't be doing that until after all the men have left the house. It's more important that you all get ready and leave on time. You need to be waiting at the venue to greet people," Mia explains, and with each word she drives me more crazy.

If I didn't have a baby in my other arm, I would've taken hold of her neck and her hip and pulled her into me, taking the kiss we both know she's trying not to give. Whatever is holding Mia back, it's big. I just wish she would talk to me about it. Maybe then we can stop all this bullshit and just be together.

I move slower than I normally would, giving her plenty of time to move away or not consent, whilst still making my intentions perfectly clear. She doesn't retreat, if anything I think she moves in farther, and it doesn't take long for our lips to meet. Her soft, supple lips press against mine, and I want to deepen the kiss, to taste her fully, but she has to be the one to change the kiss. She doesn't, but she doesn't pull away either, and I savour this moment.

Slowly she pulls back, resting her head on my forehead, and for just a moment she looks really sad. When she speaks it's barely above a whisper, and I struggle to hear her. "I miss you." It's like she's frightened to say the words aloud. Like admitting she misses me brings her pain. When, it's me that feels like she's stabbing me in the heart.

If she misses me, why can't we be together?

She pulls back, staring at me, and I realise I just said what I was thinking. Fucking hell, I really need to learn not to do that.

"Kellan...please don't ask me that. Being apart from you physically hurts, but one day you will trust that I've done the right thing. No matter how much we both want to be together, we can't be. So, please, I'm asking you to be strong during the times when I'm not. I'm asking that you be strong and remind me of this moment, when I'm being weak and wanting you," Mia begs, as she places her hand on my cheek.

Shaking my head in confusion, I try to hold back the annoyance I feel at that statement. "Please don't ask me to do that. The times you are weak, they are the only times I get to be happy. Just for a short space of time, I get to live the life I want, with the woman I am falling for. Don't ask me to take that away. If you have to do it, then that is all on you. But don't ask me to walk away from you, because I can't."

Tears well in Mia's eyes, and I reach up with my free hand to wipe them away. One eye smudges, the one that already has make-up on. Oops, looks like they might need to start again. "You think you're falling for me?" she whispers, averting her eyes. I feel like I shouldn't have told her that, like it will just cause us both more pain and suffering. But she needs to know what she's walking away from.

"Yes, how can I not. You are the perfect girl for me, Mia. You love my kid, even when she's a pain in the ass, and I know you care about me. Even with all my flaws. The more time I spend with you, the more I fall, and I wish I could stop it. I know the more this feeling grows, the more we're going to get hurt, but I can't stop it. I'm not even sure I want to." I take a slow, deep breath and confess something I've never told her before. "When I was with Shayla, I thought I loved her. Hell...when I found out about Hallie, I wanted to love her. I wanted to have the feelings everyone else talks about. Don't get me wrong, I hate her with a passion now, but at the time I had pretty strong feelings for her, but there was always doubt there. Liam kept telling me that if it was love I would know. It might not be the insta-love I felt when I held Hallie for the first time, but the feelings would grow and grow, before eventually taking root in my heart. He said they would grow and make their presence known, even if I didn't want them to. That's how I feel about you. You've taken up residence in my heart, Mia, and I can't lose you without you taking a big piece of my heart with you."

Without even a second thought, Mia presses her lips against mine. It's not sweet and chaste like it was a minute ago. This is raw, passionate, and says everything we've been struggling to admit to each other. Her tongue sweeps into my mouth and I can't help but groan with pleasure as I taste her. We try to pull each other closer, forgetting about the baby in the middle of us. It's not until Hallie screams to let us know she's still here do we finally spring apart.

Mia's cheeks are flushed and her eyes are bright. Fuck, her lips are swollen and bruised, and fuck does she look hot. "Pass her to me while you get in the shower. I think we both need a minute to cool down," she says, as I stand up and hand over Hallie. I don't miss the way her gaze settles on my hard cock that is pitching a tent in my grey sweatpants.

Looks like I'm going to have to have a quick wank in the shower. I can't go to a wedding with a hard-on. Liam would fucking kill me.

"I didn't realise I would feel this nervous," Liam states as we stand at the top of the aisle, the music has just begun to play, indicating we are about to get this show on the road.

Luckily, I finally managed to get both myself and Hallie dressed, with a lot of help from Mia, and we made it to the venue on time. Hallie is obviously not feeling great as she has been clinging to me like a little spider monkey. Thankfully, she went across to Mia without too much of a grumble, but I'm not sure how much of a flower girl she is going to be. Although, a few minutes before Mia took her, she was laughing with Liam. She kept smacking me around the head because I wouldn't let Liam hold her. I would rather get beat up by a baby than face the girl's wrath if I let Hallie dirty Liam's suit in any way before the wedding. Once the pictures are over, she can do whatever she wants. But until then, we all need to stay as clean as possible.

"No regrets?" I ask, with a cocky wink. I already know the answer. No matter how nervous Liam is, the idea of marrying Bree doesn't even come into question. He's been a nervous wreck since we got here, counting down the minutes until Bree was due to arrive. I know he is trying not to think about the last time, but the fear will always be there. I feel it too, and when Freya texts to say they're here, I feel like I can finally breathe again. I don't think my best friend could survive without Bree.

"Not in a million years." Liam gives me and his two brothers a big smile, before turning to face the barn door that has just swung open.

Ryleigh is the first to enter, and she's followed closely behind by Freya. They are both wearing long, silky gowns that are a deep purple colour. They look stunning. The dress almost appears black at times, until the light hits it when it glistens a brighter purple. They are both holding bouquets of white and purple flowers. Everyone is looking at them, the murmurs of how beautiful they look fill the barn. Ry loves all the attention, and she walks at a super slow pace to soak it all up. Freya, on the other hand, practically sprints down the aisle, her eyes looking straight forward, but not really seeing anything. Frey hates attention, so it's not surprising that she would try to block out everyone looking at her. I also don't miss the way Ryleigh chastises her for walking too quickly when she reaches her side.

Before they have a chance to start to argue, Mia enters the room. Holy fuck, I feel like my heart is about to explode. If I thought the dresses looked magical on my sisters, it looks fucking gorgeous on Mia. The way the silk clings to her, emphasising the delicate curves of her body, she looks like a model. My eyes rake over her body, and my heart literally skips a beat when I take in the full sight.

Sitting on one of her hips is my gorgeous daughter. She appears to have temporarily perked up a bit, and she is reaching into the basket Mia is holding to grab the rose petals before she throws them on the floor. Her chubby fists scrunch up the flowers, and she literally throws them at the guests as she passes, giggling her little head off. I also catch the moment she tries to put the petals in her mouth, only to be told off by Mia. In retaliation my beautiful Hallie Bear decides to throw the petals at Mia's face, much to everybody's amusement.

Hallie does go back to throwing the flowers properly, and together they look perfect. It physically hurts me to see them together. Knowing this could be my future. One day this girl could have—no, should have—been walking down the aisle towards me. I know how I feel about her, and I know one day we could have had this happiness. Hallie could have had a real mum, but that has all been snatched away, and seeing this, being able to see what our future could be, it breaks my heart.

Pushing my own dark thoughts out of my mind, I smile and simply embrace the here and now. When Mia reaches the end of the aisle, she looks unsure of what to do. We never really planned how this would go, so we are all winging it, minus a few last-minute instructions Ryleigh threw our way. Seeming to make a decision, Mia walks over to me and I take a couple of steps forward to meet her. Leaning down I place a kiss on my daughter's head, and she giggles before grasping hold of my tie. I manage to prise her little hands off it, but it's almost like Hallie isn't there at all. I'm so close to Mia, I can feel her breath on my face. It feels so natural to lean forward to kiss her, and I feel my head move of its own accord.

Before I have a chance to do something I can't take back, particularly at our best friend's wedding, and in front of all our family and friends, I pull away. She lets out a small moan that only I can hear, and I realised she wanted me to kiss her. Fuck, this girl is giving me whiplash!

"Can you keep hold of her during the ceremony, please? Or give her to Freya if Bree needs you. Is that okay?" I whisper against her ear. I lean in to whisper, not because it's a private conversation that shouldn't be overheard, but because I want an excuse, just for a second, to be close to her.

She nods and we both take a step back, that's when I hear the gasps from the people sitting behind us. They had obviously witnessed the whole thing and thought we were going to kiss too. It's like a fucking pantomime and I can't help rolling my eyes at them. Nobody really knows what is going on with Mia and me. They know at some point we were seeing each other, and now we aren't. I haven't even told Liam that I know her secret, about the abuse. Mia has spent a long time hiding that, and she trusted me with it, and her trust is something I would never break.

I watch as Mia hands Hallie over to Freya, who looks over and gives me a reassuring smile. Mia then comes to stand at the front of the venue, next to the registrar's table, opposite where me and Liam are standing. I'm so distracted looking at Mia, I miss the music starting, and it's not until I hear gasps from everyone in the room that I realise Bree has started walking down the aisle.

Looking like the most beautiful, gothic princess, Bree begins walking, arm in arm with her Gramps, Paddy. She's wearing a black, flowy dress that seems to sparkle in the light. She looks every bit the princess that Liam tells her she is. I turn to my friend, and I almost feel overwhelmed by the love and adoration that's etched across Liam's face. I can see the slight hint of tears in his eyes as he watches his entire future walk towards him. I have no doubt that they will have a long and happy life together. Well…they will do it if everyone stops plotting to kill us all.

The wedding goes off without a hitch, and we all gather in the large marquee that is set up behind the barn. Everyone has done an amazing job of putting together such a gorgeous, intimate event. As we all feast on the meal that's served to us, my heart begins to race. It suddenly dawns on me that as soon as the food's been eaten, it'll be time for my speech. This was the one reason why I didn't want to be Liam's best man. I know I'm his best friend, and practically his brother, so I'm the obvious choice, but I'm no public speaker. In fact, I hate people. Give me a computer screen and a dark room any day. But, a room full of people, no matter how much I might know and love them, it's still terrifying.

You have no idea how many times I've re-wrote this fucking speech. I've rehearsed it so many times, I know it off by heart, but I still have it on my phone, just in case. When the person who works for the venue announces it's time for my speech, my stomach starts to flip. Luckily I haven't eaten too much, or it could be making a reappearance sometime soon. The order was decided by Bree, and so Paddy did his first, then Liam got up and did his. Soppy fucker nearly had us all in tears. Then it's my turn.

I give a nod to the man who works for the venue, giving him the instructions we had previously discussed. I had met with him a few days ago to tell him what my plan was, but I still hadn't managed to get his name. Luckily, he has remembered all my instructions as I see his team standing in the wings, awaiting my cue.

Liam hands me the microphone, and I give him a nervous smile. His responding nod of encouragement is all I need. I take a big, deep breath to settle my nerves, then I start my speech. "Thank you everyone for being here. Firstly, I want to let you all know that I absolutely hate giving speeches, or doing any kind of public speaking, for that matter. So, please bear with me, and only laugh at the appropriate places."

I turn to face Bree and Liam, and with a smile on my face, I recite the words I have practised non-stop for the last couple of weeks. "As most of you are well aware, Bree and Liam didn't have the most conventional start to their relationship. Bree was tied to his bed before they even knew each other's names. And I don't know of many relationships that start with one person shooting the other but still work out okay. I knew Bree was a keeper when she put Liam in his place." Laughter fills the room as we all fondly remember how these two love birds got started. I can still remember Liam's astonishment that this girl was able to catch him unawares enough to pull a gun and shoot him. If it hadn't been for the vest, things would have gone very differently.

I continue my speech, telling a few funny, embarrassing stories from when Liam and I were kids, and thankfully the speech goes down really well. Now it's time for the bits I was told to include by Bree. "Before I close off this speech, there's a few people I want to thank on behalf of everyone here. Firstly, to Paddy and Clodagh. Thank you for helping to make this Bree's dream wedding. I know the love and support you have shown her, more specifically over the last couple of months, it has meant the world to her, and to Liam. Next I have to thank Kian, even though I would rather not. His head is big enough as it is. But, seriously, mate, you have done a cracking job at organising all of this. Special thanks also goes out to Ryleigh, who helped with lots. Thank you to all the Doughty family for your support, I know Liam is so grateful to have you here. Let's hope this new-found bond, brought back together again with the help of Bree, will last for a long time." I stare pointedly at Desmond, hoping he listens to my words. The family has only just got their shit together, I don't want his thirst for power to pull them all apart again.

My heart rate begins to return to normal, because I only have a couple of people left to mention, then I can get another drink and forget all about this moment. Maybe then I can start to enjoy this party. The next part comes easily, and then I turn to look at Mia, who would have been sitting next to me, if it weren't for the high chair separating us. Mia is holding Hallie's hand and has a beautiful smile on her face as her eyes meet mine. "Now, I may be a little biased when I say this, but can we get a massive round of applause for the most beautiful, talented flower girl, my daughter, Hallie." The room erupts into loud clapping, and Hallie wastes no time, giggling and clapping her chubby little hands together. She literally is the most adorable girl I've ever seen. Even with what looks to be mashed potato and gravy covering her pretty, pink party dress, and I think it's mashed carrots in her hair.

Looking over at Mia, I'm impressed she isn't covered in Hallie's food too. Whenever Hallie smacks her hands together, whatever mashed food she had in there, it flies around like an exploded bomb. But she doesn't care. Mia's eyes meet mine, and I can feel the electricity crackling between us. "In addition to having the best flower girl, I also want to point out how beautiful Bree's bridesmaids look. I know you have all helped Bree out so much today, and I thank you for that. Especially you, Mia. You look absolutely stunning, and I think you are doing an amazing job at being Bree's maid of honour. As Liam's best man, I would like to formally ask you to do me the incredible honour of joining me on the dance floor with Bree and Liam, later on, to help them celebrate their first dance as husband and wife. I don't think I could ask for a better, more stunning dance partner."

I watch as the blush travels across Mia's cheeks, embarrassed at being called out like this. But, I don't want her to deny me, and this way she can't. Unable to find the words to reply, she nods and the room applauds. I release the breath I didn't even realise I'm holding. Everything with Mia, at the moment, seems to make me nervous.

Turning to Bree and Liam, I raise my glass to finish the speech. "Obviously, I'm supposed to thank Liam for asking me to be his best man, but let's be honest, he didn't really have anyone better. But, seriously, Liam is my brother in all the ways that matter. He taught me that family isn't always the one you are born into, but the one you choose for yourself. I was only six years old when we chose each other, and it's been us against the world since then. Now our family is extending even further, and I am so pleased to welcome Bree. You are one hell of a woman, Brianna O'Keenan, or should I say, Doughty. To the outside world you are hard, ruthless, and pretty fucking scary, but to your family, you are everything. You are one of the sweetest, most caring people I've ever met, and I am so honoured to stand by your side. Believe me when I say, it was hard for me to admit Liam had found a partner. Someone who he will turn to first, before me or his family. I'm not even ashamed to say I was a little jealous at first. That was until I got to know you. I know that nobody will fight stronger for Liam, nobody will stand by him and support him more, and nobody will love him harder. You are both lucky to have each other."

Looking between them both, I smile and try to hold back the emotion I can feel is clogging my throat. "I'm not ashamed to admit for the longest time, I didn't know what love really looked like. I had never experienced or felt it, until Hallie was born. Since then, my family has closed the gap and started to get along again, and we have widened to accept new people into the mix. I'm surrounded by love more now than I ever have been and that's all because of you two. Your love shines bright, and I, for one, feel blessed to be a part of it. I don't need to wish you luck for the future, or wish you a long and happy life together, because I already know that is guaranteed for you. You are soulmates, and you are not only lucky that you have found each other, but that you are strong enough to fight and hold on to each other." I can't help but look at Mia as I added that last part. That was not part of the rehearsed version, but it's another example of where my mouth speaks before my brain can think through the consequences. But it's all true. I do believe I've finally found love, but Mia isn't strong enough to fight, or maybe our love isn't strong enough. Either way, I'm sitting here with a broken heart, talking about love. It's a fucking miracle I kept it this light-hearted.

Holding my glass in the air, I address the room. "I would like you all to raise your glasses, to help me toast the new Mr. and Mrs. O'Keenan-Doughty."

Rounds of applause and cheers fill the room, and as they die down, Bree reaches over the table to take the microphone from me. This was most definitely not part of the plan, and I can see Liam looking concerned too. With a smile, Bree addresses the room. "Sorry, everyone. This isn't another speech, although I would like to thank you all for coming to make this day so special. Please make sure you sign the guestbook over on the back table. Shortly, we are going to move this outside onto the deck for cocktail hour. This is so they can spend the hour changing the room around and getting things ready for the party to come. I hope you can all stay, and there will be quite a few people coming just for the evening event. Everyone is under strict instructions that this is a party, no business will be discussed. If we see it, you will be asked to leave. Eat, drink, and most importantly, please join us on the dance floor to let your hair down.

"Anyway, now I've got all that over with, there's just one thing I wanted to point out, and I know it's something I had been very undecided on up until about five minutes ago. I would like to announce that legally I will be changing my name to Brianna Doughty. For work purposes, I will remain O'Keenan-Doughty, but nothing would make me happier than to join the Doughty family. I didn't grow up with any siblings, and I never really wanted any. Then I met Kellan, Finn, Evan, Freya, and Ryleigh. You may fight and fall out constantly, but when it comes down to it, you always have each other's backs. Desmond, you may be a crazy bastard, but you are incredibly lucky to have such a great family, and I thank you for making me feel welcome." She turns to face Liam, and the smile she gives him lets me know that the whole room is fading away, and it's only them. "I know I said it's archaic and sexist, but a girl reserves the right to change her mind. So, what do you say Mr. Doughty, can I share your name?"

Liam stands up, and places his hands on her hips, pulling her a bit closer to him. "You can share anything you want of mine, Princess," he growls before pressing his lips roughly against hers. Hollers and catcalls, shouting about them getting a room and that children are present fall on deaf ears. They are happy and that is all that matters.

The rest of the evening passes by without a hitch, we even manage to fit a small detour into the schedule. Bree went to see Jimmy, even though Liam and I both told her it could wait, but once she gets an idea in her head, that's it. She had made the decision that Jimmy needed to die. He was being kept alive for this supposed information that he has, but he's never shared it, only snippets. We were all starting to think there isn't any info, and that he's simply just trying to get us to keep him alive. But that all ends tonight. Bree basically gave him an ultimatum. She said that she will be back tomorrow afternoon, when she is finished with her wedding night, and then she will kill him. He dies tomorrow, no matter what. The only difference is whether he dies with a clear conscience or not.

As she is leaving, he calls her back, and I can see Bree is physically shaking. It'd taken all her effort to give that speech; she doesn't look like she can take much more. Without thinking, I take hold of one hand and Liam the other, so she knows she isn't alone.

Jimmy's voice sounds hoarse and croaky, which given the length of time he's been a prisoner with minimal water and company to talk to, it's not surprising. "Brianna, I'm not going to beg for my life. I know you will do what you need to do. When you come back tomorrow, I will tell you what I can. You should go and enjoy your wedding. You look absolutely stunning, by the way." He gives Bree a small smile, but she just turns her head away from him. It looks like she's indifferent to his comments, but I can see the pain in her eyes. She's fighting the emotion that is battling to get free. This guy was more of a father to her than Vernon ever was, that's why his betrayal stung the most.

"Bree, you need to know that while Vernon is alive, he will always be a threat to you. He is power mad, and he has somebody backing him with very deep pockets. I overheard one of the guards mentioning that you have sent him into exile, and have cut him off under strict instruction to never return. That won't ever be enough, Bree. As long as this backer has money, Vernon will have a plan. He isn't gone, he's just hibernating. Lulling you into a false sense of security, waiting for the day he can strike when you least expect it. He will tear you all down. He doesn't give a shit who he hurts."

Liam's growl echoes around the room as he turns and bellows at Jimmy. "And yet you were willing to fucking help him. You didn't care who got hurt either. You were prepared to let Bree die so that—"

Jimmy cuts off Liam's rant and begins shouting over him. "No! I absolutely didn't want Bree to get hurt. Yes, I helped him for reasons I can't explain. But I was assured Bree wouldn't be harmed."

Upon hearing this, Bree spins around and steps closer to Jimmy, her voice low and deadly. "Well, I was hurt. I was beaten, tortured, abused, and sexually molested. But you know what, I could have coped with all of that. What I will never be able to get over is the fact that you murdered my baby."

Jimmy looks like he has been slapped across the face, his eyes filling with unshed tears. When he finally speaks, his voice is low and barely audible. "You were pregnant?"

"Yes. I didn't even know. But you and my father took that baby from us. You stole the life of what I'm sure would have been the most loved child. I can't ever forgive you, or Vernon, for that. If it were up to me, he would be facing death tomorrow with you, but Gramps asked for mercy. He couldn't kill his only son, and I can't hold that against him. As a parent who has lost a child, I can only imagine how difficult that decision was for him. So, yes, Vernon has been given another chance, but if he remains a threat like you say, he will be joining you before you know it."

Jimmy shakes his head, and I've never seen him look so small and defeated. Hearing what Bree and Liam lost at his hands, I think it may have broken him. Liam takes hold of Bree's hands and leads her towards the door, but I turn around asking the question that has been on my mind since he mentioned it. I know Bree wants to get all the info tomorrow, but I have an awful nagging feeling in my gut. It is screaming at me to find out the answer. But, if I'm right and have already managed to guess what he's about to say, we could all be in a lot of fucking trouble.

"Jimmy, before we go, you can give Bree all the details tomorrow, but I have to know…what's the name of the person financially backing Vernon?" I ask, and Jimmy looks across at Bree, like he needs her permission to answer me. She gives him a nod, and with a big sigh, he says the words I was dreading to hear.

"Whitlock. Mortimer Whitlock."

I groan as Bree, Liam, and I all look at each other with trepidation. It appears Bree's father is a lot further involved in all of this bullshit than we planned. I'm not even the slightest bit concerned when Bree informs me that one day soon, we are going to have to take Whitlock out of the equation. Maybe then Mia won't have anything holding her back from being with me.

Mia

It's been a couple of weeks since the wedding, and I think for a while we all seem to go into a bit of a slump after such a beautiful day. The day itself was gorgeous, and to watch my best friend be so happy, it was amazing. I was only like five percent a jealous, hateful bitch. I honestly didn't mean to be, but as I walked down the aisle towards Kellan, carrying his daughter in my arms, all I could think about was the future I'm missing out on. I pictured myself in a beautiful white dress, walking down to meet Kellan and Hallie, asking them both if they will accept me into their family. I know they would have done it in a heartbeat. I hate that we can never have that.

I didn't miss Kellan's sarcastic comment in his speech that was aimed directly at me. Telling me I need to be braver and fight for love. What he doesn't realise is that I am fighting. I am fighting every fucking day to stay away from him, to not fall into his arms, because I want him to keep custody of his daughter. The love they have for each other will always come before mine.

All of that meant absolutely nothing when Kellan held me in his arms for the first dance. Bree and Liam started the dance to Ed Sheeran's song, *"Perfect"*. As soon as the chorus started, Kellan took my hand and pulled me onto the dance floor. Other couples quickly followed suit, and it meant that all eyes weren't on us. I was able to rest my head on his chest, with my arms around his neck, and our bodies crushed together while we swayed to the music. I have fallen asleep every night since picturing that moment, imagining how his hand felt against my lower back as he pushed our bodies closer together, and how his breath felt against my neck. Whenever the main part of the chorus rang out, he would sing the words softly into my ear, just for me to hear, with his lips almost touching my lobe.

"Darling, you look perfect tonight."

"I see my future in your eyes."

"Now I know I have met an angel in person...I don't deserve this."

Each lyric seemed to have more meaning to us and our situation, and we just held each other. Shivers rippled down my spine and I held back the tears that threatened to fall. I know Kellan, this was his way of telling me, without having to say the words, that he loves me. For a guy like Kel, who when I first met him would have been the first to confess he didn't even know what love was, for him to feel comfortable enough to show me how he feels, I know this is a big thing for him. That's why I let myself stay in the moment. We danced all night, to a whole host of different songs. We slow danced, we dirty danced, hell...we even did the Cha Cha Slide. It was the perfect night that ended with the perfect kiss.

To say I wanted to go back to his room with him was a massive fucking understatement, and it took every ounce of energy that I had to keep out of his room. I wanted to fall into his bed, to let him love me, and to show him that I love him, but it's not that simple. I've spent every day since then wallowing.

Being apart from Kellan is literally driving me crazy. I can hear Hallie waking him up constantly throughout the night, and it takes every ounce of strength not to go and help him. Stubborn asshole that he is says he doesn't need help. That nannies don't come into the guy's bedroom in the middle of the night, join him in bed to help with the childcare. He does have a point, but I'm more than just an employee. I'm supposed to be his friend too.

There's also a very selfish reason for wanting to help him overnight, my nightmares have started to return and the fear is crippling me. I wake up screaming a couple of times a night, and combined with Hallie screaming, Kellan and I get no sleep. I know he hears me, there's no way he can't. Every time I expect him to waltz in and scoop me into his arms, to rescue me from the monsters in my mind, but he never does. Sometimes I'm mad at him for it, but I know that's not logical. I told him to stay away, so I can't be mad at him for doing as he's told. Still doesn't stop me from being any less lonely.

With the exception of the nightmares and Hallie's very disturbed sleep pattern, things go back to normal around here pretty quickly. But I don't think they will stay like that for long. It's Christmas in a few weeks, which means the Doughty's will be descending for another round of chaos, and this time, I have been invited. Given that it is being hosted in my home, I'm grateful for the invite. I'm still not quite used to the big, loud family gatherings. I never had that growing up. In fact, with the exception of the times I was being abused, people rarely even acknowledged I existed, and after a while, I was pleased with that.

The Doughty's are due in a couple of days, but everyone is under strict instructions to stay away from the house today. Even Kian, who is in the process of moving in with us, is instructing security to be on guard but not visible. Today is the day the social worker appointed by the court is coming to do her visit. She has done two unannounced spot checks, but this is the formal interview process. The court has instructed that Bree, Liam, and I are also there. I'm guessing they just want to make sure the people living with Hallie are not a danger to her.

Kellan is probably the most nervous I've ever seen him, and he is pacing so much he is close to wearing a hole in the carpet. He made sure we were all dressed smartly, and we rehearsed possible questions multiple times. I think we have literally prepared for every eventuality, but still Kellan isn't calm. Liam has tried, but has got nowhere. He pleads at me with his eyes, and as I hand Hallie over to Liam, I stand and walk towards Kellan.

Stopping in front of him, I take his hands in mine and wait for his eyes to meet mine. Once they do, I'm blown away by the emotion I see. He is genuinely terrified that this woman will take his daughter from him. Over my dead fucking body!

"Kel…babe, you have to calm down. We are prepared, but even if we weren't, it doesn't matter. The minute this woman steps into this house, she will see exactly what she has seen the last two times she has visited. She will see that Hallie couldn't be more loved. She is well looked after, cared for, and is surrounded by her family. We may not be her blood, but we are her family. I genuinely mean it when I say this, you don't need us. There isn't a person on this planet who can deny what a fucking amazing father you are. You love Hallie and you put her first, always. All you have to do is let this woman catch just a glimpse of what we see every day, and you will win her over. Like you did me." I hadn't meant to add that last part at the end, but it's true. Kellan is one of those guys that you can't help but love. Even when he's being sarcastic or cracking inappropriate jokes, even when he's so anxious he can barely function, even then they will still love him.

My words seem to be enough to settle Kellan, and he squeezes my hands in his own form of thanks. I don't let go like I should, instead I thread my fingers through his and clasp his hands tighter, pulling him that little bit closer. It's like this every time we are together. Our bodies just take over, and they don't want to be apart.

BUZZ!

The loud shriek of the doorbell has us jumping apart like teenagers who had just been caught doing something we shouldn't. Kellan walks to the door, and I join Liam and Bree on the sofa. Hallie stays on Liam's knee and she is quite happy just bouncing up and down on his knee. In fact, she is always perfectly content when Liam has hold of her.

Kellan brings the social worker through and introduces her as Sarah, which is good because I don't think I've ever caught her name during the previous visits. She takes a seat in the armchair opposite as she takes off her coat to greet us. I shuffle over so that Kellan can sit in between Liam and me. I know he will want to hold Hallie's hand, and I'm not surprised when he grabs it. I am surprised when he discreetly, shielded by our legs, takes hold of my hand before giving it a squeeze. If he needs to pull a bit of courage from me, I don't blame him.

The interview seems to go on for ages. She asked us all a lot of questions. The hardest for me was when she asked me about my plans for the future. About if I planned to nanny for a new family when I'm qualified and Hallie no longer needs me. I could tell everyone was looking at me, desperate to hear my answer. I know I made promises to Shayla, but I also made promises to Kellan, and right now, he is my priority.

"Obviously there will be a time in the future, when Hallie no longer needs a nanny, and then I will of course take a job with another family. But, my relationship with Hallie is more than just being her nanny. I live with her, I'm friends with her father, and so there won't ever come a time when she isn't part of my life and vice versa. No matter what job I'm working, even if one day Hallie and Kellan move out to get their own place, that will never change the bond we share. I love Hallie, and I plan on always being part of her life."

I meant every word I said, and it was impossible to miss the smile on Kellan's face. It's the first time I've seen him really smile in a few days, other than when he's laughing with Hallie. Once the interview is over she informs us that she will be notifying the court of her findings. They will then get in touch to discuss if a court case is needed.

The date to attend court came around scarily quickly and just two weeks later we were descending on the local court. When I say we, I mean not just Kellan, Liam, me, and Bree, but also Ryleigh, Shane, Finn, Freya, Kina, and even Evan came too. They all wanted to sit in the stands and show their support. So that is exactly what we did. Even Hallie sat on Liam's knee and behaved through the whole proceedings, which was surprisingly short. The judge entered and once she was settled, her steely eyes fixed firmly on Kellan, before looking over at his mother, and she then began to address the room.

"I have proceeded over a lot of custody cases, but I have to say this one did surprise me. After reading the case put forward by your lawyers, Mrs. Mattherson, I expected a very different person to be standing before me. You presented your son as a criminal delinquent, someone who can barely take care of himself, let alone his child. You stated he was struggling as a single parent and didn't have either a secure home, or a reliable support network. So, imagine my surprise when the facts of this case turn out to be very different. Mr. Burke's lawyers have stated that you are in fact the one who abandoned him at just six years old. He was lucky enough to have been adopted into a family that cared for him. If the amount of people here today wasn't a good enough indicator, the abundance of character references I received certainly were. Mr. Burke very much has a strong and stable support system. As for talk of him being involved in criminal activity, I had instructed the court to do a thorough search, and I can tell you that nobody in Halle's life is or has ever been involved in criminal activity. I want to make that very clear." The judge's voice is harsh and all her anger is aimed at Kellan's mother. I don't miss the cheeky grin that passes, just for the slightest second, when she mentioned the deep dive the police did. Kellan made sure that none of our pasts, or our present indiscretions, for that matter, were ever found. Of that, I never had any doubt.

The judge takes a few seconds as she fiddles around with the papers in front of her, then she continues, "I have received a full report from children's social care, and not only have they not identified any areas of concern on any visit, they even went as far as to highlight how happy and healthy Hallie is. Her medical records and the visits she has with the health visitor all show she is in good health, and she is progressing on target with the expected milestones, if not a little advanced in some areas. As for the support system, they noted that she was surrounded by love and support, which I can see in front of my eyes. I did ask them to clarify regarding Mr. Burke's home life, and they stated that Mr. Burke moved in with his friends to get the help and support he needed to help raise Hallie."

She pauses for a moment, and I know we're all waiting for the ball to drop. She has been saying nice thing after nice thing, and I can't help but worry she is about to add in that ever dreaded 'but'. She turns her steely gaze to Kellan and speaks directly to him. "Mr. Burke, I want to commend you. It takes a lot to admit when you need help. I have read the statement provided by Hallie's birth mother, and she goes into a lot of detail about how she left and how alone you were. She never doubted that you would be the perfect parent to raise Hallie. You identified that while you were back in Ireland you were isolated from your support system, so you gave up everything to come to London and to give Hallie a better life. You not only found a great support system, but you managed to build a life here. It may not be the most conventional housing arrangement, but I don't think that matters. As long as everyone in the house has Hallie's best interests at heart, I think that is all that matters, and from the statements I've seen before me, I more than agree that is the case."

I can hear Kellan's loud sigh of relief from where I'm sitting in the row behind him. The judge then turns to face Kellan's mother. "Let me be very clear about this, Mrs. Mattherson, I personally feel that you have wasted the court's time with these accusations. It is more than clear that your son is a fit parent, and therefore I have no choice but to grant him sole full custody. As Hallie's legal guardian, he has the right to make decisions on her behalf, and that includes who is part of her life. My best advice to you would be to work with your son, build a relationship again and discuss visiting access. This mediation will be supplied by the courts, as will supervised visits, if needed. However, you could walk away from here today and sort this out as a family without the need for legal intervention. Obviously you have the right to appeal my decision. In which case it will go to a full tribunal, and both sides will be presented in court in front of a panel of judges. But, a bit of personal advice from me, don't go down that route. If you do, you risk not being able to see your granddaughter at all. Work together as a family and try to fix this, for Hallie's sake.

There's already one too many people absent in her life, don't make it more."

With that, she adjourns the court, and that is it. The decision has been finally made and my heart feels like it's souring for them. Kellan has tears running down his cheeks as he grabs Hallie out of Liam's arms and pulls her in for a hug. At first she grumbles, smacking him around the face as she tries to reach for Liam again. Then Kel starts spinning her around and gently throwing her up in the air in celebration, her giggles fill the room.

There's so much laughter I didn't see Kellan's mother walk over to us. Kel hands Hallie back to Liam and tells him we will meet him by the car. Everyone starts to leave, so I turn too, but Kellan grabs hold of my hand. I stay because I know he needs me.

"Maybe the judge was right," Marianna says, as she tries to avoid meeting Kellan's gaze. "I would like to be part of Hallie's life. Maybe we can meet sometime to discuss it?"

Kellan squeezes my hand and I can feel him trying to rein in his anger. After everything this woman has put him through, she has a fucking nerve. "Mother, you have just put us through hell for the last couple of months. Our privacy has been trashed, our entire lives are in upheaval, all because you wanted something you couldn't have. I'm not saying that you can't see Hallie, I'm just saying not yet. I need time. Don't make contact or pressure me. When I feel like I can, I will contact you. Don't force this, or you will regret it." It's not hard to hear the threat in his tone, and she clearly sees it too as she backs away, leaving just Kellan and me, standing there.

"I'm really proud of you, Kel. I knew this would be the outcome, but it was still nice to hear it."

Kellan places his hand on my cheek and leans in until our foreheads are touching. My heart races and I can feel shivers rippling down my back. "I hope you meant it when you said you would stay with us forever." As soon as he finished speaking, he places the softest, sweetest of kisses onto my lips. I want to pull him into me, I want to take more, but I know I can't. This moment is just for him.

As we pull away and are making our way to the car, my phone vibrates. When I pull it out, I recognise the number instantly. She has only made contact a couple of times, but it's enough that I won't ever forget her.

SHAYLA

I'm glad Kellan got the outcome he was looking for, but you need to remember our deal. Stay the fuck away, or you will regret it. Don't test me!

Fuck! Did she have a spy here at the hearing? Did they just see Kellan and I kiss? Fuck, I need to be more careful. If not, this celebration will mean nothing and he could lose Hallie for good. I'm not worth that. His daughter will always come first.

Kellan

The few days leading up to Christmas pass by in a blur. It's always like that when the Doughty's are in town, and this time it's all the siblings that are staying with us. Plus, that annoying prick Kian has also moved in. Even though he is living a floor above me and Mia, it's still a shift in the balance that we were used to. And even though we only got a couple of days with him living here before the siblings descended, we barely noticed he had moved in. I expected him to be a pain to live with, but he works out in the gym a lot, but otherwise he's working most of the time. I think the longer he lives with us, he may eventually get closer to us, but at the moment his dumb ass is sulking because Bree forced him to move in.

Hallie, although I'm pretty sure she has no fucking clue what is going on, you can definitely tell she's getting more interested. Everyone is excited for her, and they keep talking to her about Father Christmas, asking what she wants for Christmas. Like all of a sudden she is going to stand up, walk over to us, and hand her shopping list for Father Christmas. Instead, she gurgles what I am convinced sounds like "Dada," and she giggles a lot. She's attracted to the lights on the tree, and if you take your eyes off her for a few minutes, she will crawl over to the tree and begin pulling the baubles off. Typically, she then either throws them at us, or tries to eat them. I am dreading the day when she can walk. I think we are all going to need eyes in the back of our heads to stop her from destroying everything.

Christmas Eve night, we all sit around the living room, and engage in what has been a long-running Doughty tradition for as long as I can remember. Siobhan usually does all of the cooking on Christmas morning, and starts to prepare it the night before. So, because the kitchen is usually deep in the prepping phase, we order pizza to be delivered. This is a tradition that all the Doughty's appear to have continued. When Bree announced that she wanted to cook Christmas dinner this year, with the help of Mia, the only stipulation Liam and I had was that our pizza Christmas Eve dinner must be honoured.

As we all pass the pizza around, laughing and joking amongst each other, I take a moment to appreciate what I have in my life. When I realised I was going to have to raise Hallie by myself, I thought it would be such a lonely experience, but my beautiful baby girl has me anything but lonely. She has brought my family back to me, and I can't thank her enough for that.

With a pizza slice in one hand, while I'm rocking Hallie to sleep in the crook of my other arm, I realise I'm fighting a losing battle. My girl's big blue eyes are wide open as she giggles along with everyone else. She's a nosey baby and I know she doesn't want to miss anything. I know I'm going to have to take her up to my room soon because there's no way I will get her to sleep in this room. The only problem is, I'm still not comfortable with Hallie sleeping in a different room to me. I have just about got used to her being with Bree and Liam, or Mia. And, even though her room is completely set up, I can't move her into it just yet. I promised Liam and Mia that I would try it in the new year, and I fully intend to do this, it just scares the shit out of me. I could leave her in my room, with the baby monitor on as it is all set up, and that way she will get some sleep and

I don't have to leave the gathering. But, I still can't bring myself to do it.

As I'm pacing up and down, rocking Hallie in the futile hope of getting her just a little sleepy, the doorbell rings. Looking around, we all have the same confused look on our faces over who the hell it could be. Everyone we know that would call on Christmas Eve night, they're all already sat in this room. Since I'm standing already and nearest the door, I say I will get it. I quickly hand Hallie to the person nearest me, who happens to be Kian, and he holds her like I've just handed him a live explosive. He's never had much experience with children before, and surprisingly, despite Kian struggling with how to be around Hallie, she has taken to him. She loves to play with him, and in the morning he is her favourite target for when she's throwing her breakfast around. This is how we discovered Kian is not bright and friendly all the time. The guy is essentially a monster until he's had his morning coffee, and Hallie has got a fantastic ability of hounding him while he is trying to make that first cup. I loved my girl even more after that.

Rushing to the door as the doorbell rings again, I mumble about the person on the other side being an impatient asshole, as I rush to answer. Throwing the door open, I'm shocked to see Desmond Doughty standing on the doorstep. I stand there, just staring at him, like I can't quite believe that he's here, which would be accurate.

"Merry Christmas, son. Are you going to invite me in, or wait until my balls freeze and drop off?" Desmond asks, as he basically pushes his way into the house. He doesn't wait for me to say anything before he starts to make his way into the living room.

The once lively room descends into silence when they see Desmond enter the room. As I follow in behind him, I see that all of the Doughty children are looking at each other, shock written across their faces. They all seem to be looking at each other, wondering which sibling will be the first to speak. Thankfully, Bree steps in, as we may have been sitting in silence for a while waiting for one of the siblings to speak.

"Merry Christmas, Desmond. We weren't expecting you, what are you doing here?" she asks, trying to make the question sound more inquisitive as opposed to confused and accusatory, which I think it really is. We all want to know what the hell he's doing here.

"Well…as soon as I found out all my children would be here for Christmas, Von and I decided to come over and spend the day with our children, if you don't mind having us. It's been far too long since we all sat down as a family, and after the lovely time we all had at the wedding, I want to make a conscious effort to be part of this family a bit more." Desmond sounds like he genuinely means what he says, and I don't miss the way we all look at each other, unsure whether we should believe him or not.

Liam doesn't look happy, and instead scowls at Des. "You can't just invite yourself over the night before Christmas. You have to wait for an invite," Liam grinds out through gritted teeth, and I can tell he is only just managing to keep his shit together.

While Des appears to be making progress with his other children, and even with Bree too, Liam is going to be a much harder nut to crack. Liam has been fighting against his father for as long as I can remember, and it's hard for him to believe he is no longer a threat. I've done a lot of research, and he is still very much under my watchful eye, but I can't deny that since meeting Bree, he has only ever shown loyalty towards this family. I'm not saying I believe he is no longer a threat, but for the moment, he appears to be on our side.

"Well, son, if I waited around for an invite from you, that beautiful little girl will be a teenager," he says, pointing towards Hallie who is now cradled in Mia's arm. My heart skips a beat, the same way it always does when I see Mia with my girl.

"Maybe that is the point," Liam mumbles, but Bree smacks him on the arm, chastising his behaviour.

"We didn't know you were in London. But since you are, of course you will be welcome to join us for dinner. We will be eating around two, but you are welcome to come around any time after twelve midday." Bree gives Des a small smile and it's met by a groan from Liam. I can see both Ryleigh and Freya don't exactly look thrilled he will be in attendance either, so I decide to set out some ground rules.

"Listen, Desmond. You can come for dinner but I want to make it very fucking clear that this is my daughter's first Christmas, and nobody will be ruining that. There will be no drama, no arguing, and if you even think about bringing a weapon into this house, I will kick your ass out myself. Do you understand me?"

Desmond nods his head while I'm stating my expectations. "Son, believe it or not, I have no interest in ruining that little girl's first Christmas. When we adopted you years ago, in my eyes you became a Doughty, which means that little girl is my only grandchild. I know I've never been the greatest parent, and I'm not going to apologise because you can't change the past. I can, however, make an effort for the future." Desmond's voice sounds the most sincere I've ever heard, and I'm sure I look like a stunned goldfish, my mouth flopping open and closed as I struggle to find the words.

Desmond has never talked about adopting me, ever. Nor has he ever specifically stated that he sees me as his son. He calls me it, but I saw it as more of a nickname than a factual account. Desmond isn't exactly a role model parent, and I'm sure there aren't many people who would be thrilled to have Des call them his son, and honestly, I'm not sure how I feel. I've never had a family, so hearing him say this makes me feel strange. I've always felt like a Doughty, and the siblings have always made me feel part of it, but this just cements it.

Everyone is waiting for me to respond, but I honestly don't know what to say. I'm speechless, and having all eyes on me, expecting a reply, while I attempt to make sense of what he just said, I feel like a zoo exhibit. They're all watching to see how I react. Thankfully, Mia realises that I'm starting to panic at the thought of everyone watching for my reaction, and she speaks, dragging the attention to her.

"Well, this little one is starting to get sleepy, so I think it might be a good idea if we get her put to bed. If not, she will be Little Miss Cranky Pants tomorrow, and we don't want that," Mia jokes as she walks towards me, Hallie very much awake in her arms. I literally could kiss her right now, and when Bree jumps onto her comment, I feel so incredibly cared for in that moment. Two people, who haven't known me for very long, they both now know me well enough to know when I need help, and they know just how to give me it too.

"I think that's a good idea. We can all part ways and spend the rest of the evening doing whatever you had planned. Then we can meet back here in the morning. I think it's going to be a quiet morning, so, Desmond, you are welcome to come back any time after twelve. That's when Gramps is coming too," Bree adds, as she stands up gesturing towards the door. It couldn't be any clearer that she is kicking him out, but she manages to do it in such a polite way.

I see the moment of panic in the Doughty kids' eyes, as they all waited for Desmond to kick off. We have all seen it happen so many times before. If he thinks he is being offended, or he just doesn't like their tone, he can flip out at the drop of a hat. So everyone is in complete amazement when Desmond simply smiles and walks towards Bree. He stops in front of Mia, and leans down to place a kiss on Hallie's forehead. She giggles, which surprises us all. She doesn't always get along with new people. As she tries to get hold of Desmond's hair, he takes hold of her hand, kisses it and chuckles. "I will see you in the morning, pretty girl. Grandpa has lots of presents for you," he coos, and I see Liam's eyes widen in shock.

What the fuck? Have we entered some kind of fucking parallel universe? I don't think I've ever seen him this happy, and I sure as fuck have never heard him using baby talk and cooing before. We all look equally as stunned as Bree leads him out the door. Once the door is closed, and we are sure he has gone, Ryleigh is the first to break the silence. "Does everyone else feel like they just entered a parallel universe where Dad is a normal human being who likes everyone?" Her voice becomes high-pitched, and almost like we all have one voice, we all agree that what we just witnessed was batshit fucking crazy.

"Well, I am definitely going to take my girl to bed and probably have nightmares over how jolly he was," I say, but I make no effort to take Hallie out of Mia's arms. Mia is already heading towards the stairs, and I'm more than happy to follow.

We shout good night to everyone as they continue discussing the possibility Desmond has been possessed by pod people. Once we get up the stairs, their laughter starts to become less noisy. When Paddy bought this house, before he gave it to Bree and Liam, he made sure all the rooms were soundproofed. He also got planning permission and designed the house so it could be expanded on. It can have another two floors added onto it, and if more Doughty siblings keep moving in, we may well need to start building. Liam and Bree always make it clear that the second floor, on the right side, is all just for me and Mia. There's a room for each of us, and a room for Hallie—if I ever can pluck up the courage to put her in it—then we also have a lounging area that we rarely use, and I have my office. It's like our own little flat, and Liam has offered on a couple of occasions to build a wall, essentially making our space into its own area, but I don't want them to do that. This is our home for now, but it won't be forever. Eventually, Liam and Bree will have a family of their own, and when that happens they won't want people living with them. Hallie and I will have to find a place of our own when that happens. Thankfully, that's not anytime soon.

As we reach my bedroom door, Mia pushes it open and walks in, not even hesitating. I know things have been awkward between us lately, but when it comes to Hallie's routine, this is one area we are doing well in.

Mia lays Hallie on the bed and begins undressing her, to get her ready for bed, while I gather the cute little Christmas onesie we bought her to sleep in. I offer to take over to change her nappy, but Mia shoos me away, and instead I make sure Hallie's crib is all set up. Most importantly, I make sure her stuffed penguin is in there, the one Liam got her. She won't sleep without the damn thing. Hence, why I have a drawer with three exact replicas in it. As soon as I realised this was the key to helping her get to sleep, Mia told me to buy spares, but I was adamant she wouldn't lose it, and that if we gave her a replacement, she would know. I learnt the hard way. Of course Hallie lost it, and we got absolutely no sleep that night, until Mia went out first thing and bought a replacement. Hallie had no idea it wasn't her original teddy, and I learnt my lesson. I went out that afternoon and bought five. We have since lost another, but I panic a whole lot less about it now.

Once Hallie is in her cute baby onesie, and we have taken a few photos, including a gorgeous selfie with us all in, I begin the night-time routine of getting Hallie to sleep. I start rocking her, walking up and down the room while singing to her gently. This is normally when Mia leaves, but tonight she doesn't. Instead she sits on the end of the bed, a cute as hell smile on her face as she watches us.

It's not long before Hallie falls asleep and I lay her in her crib. Thankfully she stays asleep, and I know we should get a couple of hours before she wakes up again. She has started to settle a little more with her sleep recently. Turning to Mia, I give her a small smile, but I don't really know what to say to her. I'm curious as to why she is still here, normally she avoids any alone time with me. But, I don't want to say anything in case I scare her away.

Averting her eyes to look at the floor, when she speaks, her voice is barely above a whisper. "I know I have no right to ask you this, and the last thing I want to do is mess with your feelings. So, when I ask you this, please take it as a friend asking. Please can I stay with you tonight? I would love it if I could be here when Hallie wakes up for her first Christmas. But I also don't want to be alone."

My heart breaks for her, and I know what she means about it being confusing. There's no way in hell we can spend the night together and it doesn't mean anything. I know I should say no, but I can't. The truth is, I want her here. Fuck, I always want her here. I want her to be part of Hallie's first Christmas. But more than that, I want her in my bed, in my arms. Maybe it will be okay if we pretend for just one night?

"Of course you can stay. Would you like to watch a movie together?" I ask, and the smile that crosses her face is blinding. Fuck, there goes my dick getting excited. It isn't possible for me to be around her and to not get turned on.

"I would love that. I'm just going to go and get changed, if that's okay?" Mia jumps up and heads towards the door. Just as she is about to leave, I whisper-shout enough to get her attention, but quiet enough that I don't wake Hallie.

"Shall we watch it in the lounge next door? I know she often sleeps through our movie nights, but she's been a lot more unsettled on a night recently and I really want her to get a good night's sleep tonight." She agrees with me and we arrange to meet in the lounge.

I waste no time changing into my grey sweatpants, and I throw a baggy white T-shirt on too. I pull the duvet cover off the bed and drag it through into the lounge. While I'm waiting for Mia, I go to the fridge in the corner of the lounge and pull out a cider for me, and I make Mia her usual Jack Daniels with Coke. I also grab a bag of popcorn from the cupboard above. It's our movie night cupboard, and it's full of popcorn, crisps, and sweets. As I'm about to close the cupboard, I decide to grab a bag of M&M's too, as I know she loves them.

When Mia walks back into the room, I'm literally floored by how fucking gorgeous she looks. I can tell she hasn't gone out of her way to make herself look good; she doesn't have to try, it's completely natural. Her glossy brunette locks fall down around her face, and she isn't wearing any make-up at all, yet her eyes glisten and stand out. Same goes for her plump lips that do nothing to stop my cock from standing even more to attention. She is wearing a short, baggy T-shirt that is cut off just above her belly button, showing the most gorgeous patch of skin. The T-shirt is falling off one of her shoulders, and I don't miss the fact that she isn't wearing a bra. The T-shirt is red with Christmas decorations on it, and she's wearing a matching pair of booty shorts. They stop mid-thigh, exposing her luscious legs.

Mia sees me sitting on the sofa with the duvet, with all the treats for our movie night, and she practically skips into the room. I haven't seen her this carefree and happy around me in a long time. Normally she tries to keep a healthy distance from me, but tonight she wastes no time throwing herself down right next to me on the sofa before pulling the duvet over us both.

Snuggling further against my side, I can feel the warmth from her skin against mine and I can't help the shiver that cascades through my body. This is why she doesn't get too close any more. Our bodies can't be this close without us feeling each other. Feeling the want and desire we both can't deny still exists.

"What movie do you want to watch?" I ask, trying to ignore the sensations, while I discreetly adjust my cock under the covers to make things a little more comfortable. As soon as my hand makes contact, to move him to a more comfortable location, it twitches and springs even further, thinking this is the start of the action. Sadly, he has become used to my right hand.

Mia turns to answer me, and I quickly move my hand away. Last thing I want is her thinking I'm playing with myself next to her. Fuck, that really wouldn't be good. "Erm…could we watch…*Love Actually*? I know you secretly love rom-coms, and this is a Christmas movie. So, it definitely counts," Mia states with a cheeky smile on her face as she uses the remote to start playing the film. I did say she could pick, so I can hardly change my mind now.

We sit together, cuddled up on the sofa like none of the past couple of months has happened. She lets me put my arm around her, and is more than happy to curl up into a ball by my side, with her head on my chest. I know she can hear my heart racing, but I don't care. I may not be able to tell her how I feel, but she will know. She can hear the way my heart beats just for her.

The movie ends and she looks up at me through hooded eyes, neither one of us wanting this evening to end. "Shall we pick another movie?" I ask, not even wanting to look at the time. Hallie is sleeping peacefully next door, and I've probably spent just as much time watching the monitor as I did watching Mia. I barely saw the movie at all.

I know it's getting late, and we should call it a night, but neither of us do. She bites her lip, like she is contemplating exactly what to say. A blush spreads across her cheeks, and I can't hide the cocky grin because I know there's only one reason she would blush like this, she just thought of something very dirty, and I'm so here for that.

Before I even realise what's happening, Mia throws herself up onto her knees and climbs over my thighs, until she is straddling my hips. Just as my hands clasps hold of her hips to steady her, she lowers her lips and crushes them against mine. It's not sweet or innocent, this is pure passion and my heart races. Instantly, I match her kiss, letting her tongue sweep into my mouth, loving the taste of her, just like I always have.

She pulls back suddenly, her hands cup my cheeks and she tilts my head so that I meet her gaze. Her lips are swollen, her cheeks flushed, and she's panting to catch her breath. I'm sure I look the same. "This can only be a one-time thing, Kel. Think of it as a Christmas present, but tomorrow we have to go back to normal. I know you don't understand it, but you have to. Please agree to this, it's the only way I can carry on," she mumbles, pleading with me.

Fuck, I would have sacrificed a fucking kidney if it means we get to finish what she has just started. My body craves her, and even if I can't have her permanently, I will take whatever she is willing to give. "You have my word, Mia. I will always want you, but I can respect your decision."

She barely waits for me to finish my sentence before she acts. As soon as I agree, she pulls her T-shirt over her head, revealing her fucking amazing tits, before she throws it onto the floor and crushes her lips back against mine.

This is so different from any other time we have been together. This is frantic and desperate, where we both literally can't stop grasping at each other, desperate to take things further, quicker. I think for me, I want to get straight into it, as I am worried she is going to change her mind at any moment, so I want to enjoy as much as I can for as long as I can. She appears to have the same thoughts, as we both fumble around desperately trying to rid each other of our clothes, but not wanting to stop touching or kissing each other.

I don't know how it happens, but we eventually both end up naked, with me hovering over her, as I use my body to cage her in. I then waste no time sliding down Mia's fucking gorgeous body, and once I reach her stomach, I quickly part her legs, hooking them widely over my shoulders. My head is straight in front of her glistening pussy, and I have to bite my lip to stop myself from diving straight in. Looking up at her through what I'm sure will be hooded eyes, I'm like a starved man and Mia is my last meal. I take a second, just staring at the beauty lying in front of me, and I realise that even though we are rushing and are desperate for more, I still want to make sure Mia is completely on board with this and most importantly that she gives me her full consent.

With a small nod of her head, it's all the encouragement and permission I need, and I use my fingers to spread open her glistening slit. With a sweep of my finger, I feel just how ready she is. I can't hold back the resulting groan and it vibrates against her pussy, and given the way she shivers every time my breath hits her sensitive clit, she clearly is enjoying what I'm doing.

"Fuck, Flower. You are so wet. Is this all for me?" My voice sounds almost like a growl, and I hear her chuckle slightly, which is most definitely not what I want to hear. I look up at her, wondering what she could possibly find funny about the way my tongue feels against her pussy.

"It's always just been you."

Fuck! Does she really mean that? I feel like I've waited forever to hear that, but at the same time, she has made it very clear that I can't read into things too much. This is a one-off. I will hold what she just said close, but this is by no way over between us. I will find out what is keeping her from me, and I will prove to her what a load of bullshit it obviously is.

Upon hearing those words, I waste no time at all running my tongue through her slit, circling her pussy entrance, before travelling back up to flick it over her already sensitive clit. I repeat the same process enough times that she starts to moan, arching her back, desperately seeking more.

That's when I push my fingers into her wet pussy. Combining my tongue flicking over her clit, and the way I use my spare hand to tweak her nipple between my thumb and forefinger, making sure to roll it around and squeeze it just enough, the way I know she likes it. This works exactly as I planned, and my touch becomes too much for her. It doesn't take long before her muscles are coiling, her hands fist in the cushions of the sofa, as she mumbles almost incoherently.

"Please, Kellan. Oh fuck. How are you able to do this to me every fucking time? I need more. I need all of you. Please." I love that even though it's been a while since we were together, the confidence she gained while we were together, and the lessons I taught her, have stuck with her. I can't tell you how much fucking harder my cock becomes when I hear her words.

I give her exactly what she is asking for, and continue my efforts with both my tongue and my fingers. I keep the rhythm, making sure that when my fingers pull back, that's when my tongue flicks over her clit. It means she doesn't get any respite, and her breathing becomes more erratic. I can feel her becoming wetter, and the walls of her pussy are grasping on to my fingers. She begins chanting my name as her orgasm rips through her body.

"Kel...fuck, babe...oh fuck, Kellan. I'm...I'm coming. Kel," she screams, and I don't even bother to quieten her. My tongue is too busy lapping up her fucking exotic taste. I can't get enough of her.

Her fingers have been threading through my hair, gripping my head and holding me in place between her legs, and I couldn't move my head even if I had wanted to—which I very much fucking did not! But, as she begins to come down from her orgasm, she pulls my head away from what I'm sure is her overly sensitive clit. This time, I let her.

Pulling gently on my hair, she guides me up her body, and without even a hint of hesitation, she pushes her lips against mine. The moan that vibrates through my mouth is intoxicating, and I know she must be able to taste herself on my tongue.

"Do you like how you taste, Flower?"

"Mmm," is all she is able to respond with. When she finally pulls her lips from mine, she has the cheekiest grin on her face and through hooded eyes, she keeps eye contact with me as she pushes me backwards until I'm laying down and she slides down my body. "There's something else I would like a taste of too."

Fuck, could this girl get any more fucking perfect?

The answer to that becomes a very quick yes as she grasps hold of my cock, her small fingers barely able to circle completely around the shaft, before guiding it into her mouth. Her plump, red lips encase my swollen tip, and I feel her tongue swipe across my slit, tasting what I'm sure is beads of pre-cum.

As she begins to push my hard dick farther into her mouth, my cock twitches and my eyes roll backwards. Fuck, her hot, wet mouth feels fucking amazing, as she pushes my cock deep into her throat. When she finally bottoms out, she begins to swallow and the sensation of her throat closing, squeezing my cock, drives me crazy.

Mia pulls back, coughing and spluttering as she begins to gasp for air. At first I'm concerned she stayed on my cock for too long, but she is the one that was calling the shots, my hands are firmly gripping the sofa cushions rather than taking control the way I usually like. The cheeky grin she has on her face when she finally catches her breath lets me know she is enjoying this just as much as I am, and before I have a chance to tell her she doesn't have to push it so far, she begins to swallow my cock again and all rational thought falls away.

Her hand that is circling the shaft begins to pump up and down, while her mouth sucks on the tip and her tongue flicks over my slit. The combination of it all together is too much, and it's not long before I feel like I'm going to blow my load. Usually I can last longer than this, but I have been dreaming about this moment since Mia called it quits on our relationship, and even though I have whacked one off at the thought of this, nothing compares to the real thing.

"Fuck, Mia. I am so fucking close to coming. You have to stop," I mumble, letting her know that if she carries on, I won't be able to stop myself from coming in her throat. I'm not worried about him being ready to go again very soon afterwards, because he is always ready and raring to go where Mia is concerned, but she will always have the right to choose with me.

She pulls her lips off my cock just long enough to say the words every man fucking loves to hear. "I want you to come in my mouth. I want to taste you on my lips."

With that, her lips begin to swallow my cock inch by inch until it's fully seated in the back of her throat. She then begins bobbing up and down, her tongue licking along the shaft as she pulls in her cheeks, creating a sucking motion that nearly kills me.

I can feel my balls tighten and the muscles in my lower abdomen begin to coil. I can feel myself getting ready to fall over that ledge, and the more she continues to fuck me deep into her throat, the closer to my release I get.

After a few more pumps of my shaft while she sucks the head into the back of her throat, I feel that sweet release and give her the warning she needs. "Fuck, Mia...baby. I'm going to come. Pull back if you want to, but do it fucking quickly."

She doesn't move, and instead looks up at me through hooded eyes as she continues to suck. With a roar that fills the room, I begin to spurt ropes of cum into the back of her throat. Mia tries to swallow, but the ropes of cum are coming quicker than she can keep up with, so instead she pulls back slightly so the spray is hitting the back of her tongue. She waits, collecting every last drop, and once she is sure I have finished, she pulls my cock out of her lips and licks the last few drops off the tip. Then, opening her mouth wide, she shows me the pool of cum that has collected in the back of her throat, and without dropping eye contact she gives a very cheeky wink at me before swallowing my cum.

Fuck, I think that is legitimately the hottest fucking thing I've ever seen. I'm just in awe of this beautiful; girl and the strength she has to push her past behind her enough to fully enjoy this with me.

If there was any doubt over whether my cock could get hard again quick enough to fuck Mia, that went straight out of the window upon seeing that. My dick had barely gone down before it is springing straight back up again, straining towards Mia. She looks down at my cock that is glistening with her spit, and when she looks up to meet my gaze, she has that mischievous smile that I love to see. It's Mia exposing her most playful side.

"Looks like you are ready for more. That didn't take long," she says playfully with a cheeky wink.

"Flower, that was the sexiest thing I've ever seen. But you know my cock is always hard and ready whenever he's around you. That's never changed." I don't mean to make a reference to our time apart, or to cast a damper on our moment. Thankfully she just focuses on the cock comment.

"I know you like to be in control, but do you think you could let me take control this time? I want to pin you down, and ride your cock." Fuck, what do I say to that?

"Flower, you are always the one in control, even when I'm dominating you. But I guess, just this once, I can let you take control. But I can't promise how long it will last."

Before I've even had a chance to finish the sentence, she climbs up my body until she's hovering over my cock. Holding the shaft, she gently guides my dick into her wet, waiting pussy. She just gets the tip in, and freezes with a gasp. "Fuck, I forgot how big you feel."

I can't help but chuckle in response and she playfully hits my arm as she lowers herself onto my cock. The more she descends, the faster our playfulness disappears. It's always been like that with her, no matter the situation, we always feel at ease with each other.

All thoughts of anything else quickly disappears as she descends fully onto my cock. Mia holds herself there for a few seconds, placing her hands on my chest as she takes some slow, deep breaths. No doubt giving herself some time to stretch to accommodate my cock. I forget that we have only done this a few times, but when I'm with her it feels so natural. Like we were made for each other.

Moving my arms to grab hold of her hips, she quickly clasps my wrists in her hands and pulls them away. Pushing them above my head, she leans over until her tits are right in front of my face. This change of position results in my cock being deeper in her pussy, and her moan mixes with mine. She leans down to whisper, and as her breath touches the sensitive spot beneath my ear, I can't help the shiver that I know she feels rippling over my body.

"I told you, I'm in charge," she whispers against my ear, and before I have a chance to respond, she begins moving on my cock. Swirling her hips up and down, she moves off my cock until just the tip remains in, and then she pushes herself back down again. At first she starts off slow, while her lips kiss and suck along my jawline, but it doesn't take long for her movements to become more frantic. After pressing her lips firmly against mine, she kisses me with a passion that I can feel deep in my core. She then pulls away panting, desperately trying to catch her breath.

Letting go of my arms, she straightens her back and rests her hands on my chest so that she is fully upright, impaled on my cock. She changes the position of her legs so that she is essentially squatting on my cock, and with her feet on either side of me, she is able to use those to bounce up and down more aggressively on my cock.

I let her take charge and do whatever the hell she needs to chase her orgasm, because anything she does, any position she's in, feels fucking amazing. Once she has the position she's aiming for, she wastes no time bouncing up and down on my cock, and is finally able to get into a rhythm. As her pussy squeezes my cock while she rides me, her tits bouncing up and down while Mia moans and gasps for breath, it's clear she is getting close to her peak. Her pussy is tightening, and my cock is getting there too. I'm amazed I didn't blow my load earlier after feeling her tight, wet pussy milking my cock.

"Oh fuck. Kellan, I'm going to come. Fuck, this feels so fucking good," she moans, as she continues to ride me as quickly as her legs will allow. Her dirty words, and the urge to reach out and take control, are literally driving me crazy.

"Come on my cock, Flower. I want to feel you milk my cock dry."

That is all it takes for Mia to fall apart, her pussy gripping my cock as her body spasms on top of me. Her hot wet cunt tightening around my dick pushes me over the edge, and with a roar, I begin shooting my load.

I can't help myself, I reach up to put my hands on her hips, to steady her, as her legs start to tremble. Upon feeling that I have hold of her, Mia collapses into my arms, resting her head on my chest, her hair fanning out around her, as we both try to catch our breaths.

"Why does it always feel so fucking good with you?" she mutters, barely above a whisper. I'm not sure if she is asking me, or if it's just a statement she didn't mean for me to hear. I don't bother to answer her, there's no point. She knows why it's so good, it's because we were made for each other. Even if she fucks hundreds of other men—which I really fucking hope she doesn't, the idea makes me want to kill them all—it will never feel as good as it does with me. Our bodies were made for each other. Her pussy fits my cock perfectly, and that's why it's so good. Yet, despite knowing this already, she still has her reasons for us not being together. I don't want to ruin this moment, or remind ourselves that we are living on borrowed time right now, so I simply savour the moments. I run my fingers through her hair, kissing her neck gently, and I grab hold of her ass, keeping my cock in her pussy. I'm not ready to let her go just yet.

We must have fallen asleep in that position as we wake up a couple of hours later to the sound of Hallie crying through the baby monitor. Looking at the clock I see it's only two in the morning. She probably just needs a nappy change and a bottle before she goes back to sleep again. Without even talking about it, we both spring into action, engaging in a routine we have perfected. Mia pulls my T-shirt over her head, and as she climbs off my body, my cock slides out of her cum-soaked pussy, and I can't help but smile. There's something so fucking primal about seeing my girl coated in my cum that turns me on.

Pushing all those thoughts out of my mind, I pull my sweats on and run next door to soothe Hallie. I change her while Mia cleans herself up and prepares the bottle. We then all climb into bed together and cuddle up. Hallie lays in one arm, while Mia lays beside me on the other side, her head on my chest while she holds the bottle for Hallie to drink from. I can't help but think this has been the perfect start to Hallie's first Christmas. I also vow to do everything in my power to make sure Mia is there for every fucking Christmas, from here on out. I don't have a plan just yet, but I need one. I have to fight for my girl.

Christmas morning passes by so quickly, and I try to treasure every moment. Hallie wakes us up again around half past six in the morning, and even though she has no real idea of what is going on, we make a big deal of telling her that Father Christmas has been. We show her the plate that we left out the night before, and she is in awe of the half-eaten carrot that we tell her Rudolf must have eaten. But she is even more taken with the stocking Father Christmas left on the end of her crib.

All her main presents are downstairs under the tree, but I wanted her to have some things that she opened with just Mia and me. With each present she opens, her laughter becomes more infectious. Wrapping paper was thrown everywhere, and on more than one occasion we have to stop her from putting it in her mouth. I think I would even go as far as to say she enjoyed playing with the wrapping paper more than actually opening the presents. But as long as she is laughing, I don't care how or what brought it on.

Mia heads next door to get ready, and comes back wearing the cutest Mrs. Claus dress. It stops just above her knees, and there's no doubt that she's the sexiest Mrs. Claus ever. I dress in my dark jeans and a Christmas T-shirt with Peppa Pig and her dad both wearing Christmas hats. It says 'Merry Christmas, Daddy Pig, love from your little monster'. Mia bought it for me from Hallie, and despite the fact that I'd rather shoot myself in the head than watch another episode of *Peppa* fucking *Pig*, Hallie loves it, and so of course I wear it for her.

As Mia goes to grab Hallie so we can go downstairs for breakfast, I hold my arm out to stop her. Grabbing hold of her wrist gently, I pull her until she is just inches away from me, her breath hitching as she waits in anticipation for what I'm going to say. "I know we said no presents, but I couldn't get you nothing. I don't want you to open this in front of everyone. I bought it a few months ago, and I didn't want to return it. It's yours, so I'm giving it to you anyway. If you want to open it later by yourself, then you can. It's up to you," I mumble, word vomit dripping out of my mouth as I struggle to find the words to explain my gift. I bought this when I realised I loved her, and this was supposed to be my way of telling her.

Handing over the small rectangular box that's wrapped in Christmas paper, with Father Christmases all over it, Mia's eyes widen as she takes in the shape of the gift. Fuck, does she think this is an engagement ring? I fucking hope not. Even I wouldn't be stupid enough to propose like this. When I propose to her, it'll be romantic, and there won't be any question over her answer. I will already know she'll say yes. Can you tell I've put a lot of fucking thought into the idea of proposing?

Mia takes the box from me and slowly starts to open it, revealing a velvet black box. I hear a release of breath as she sees the shape of the box definitely isn't a ring. She snaps it open to reveal a delicate white gold necklace, with a pendant in the middle. There are two hearts intertwined and in the middle, where the hearts crossover is a beautiful diamond.

She doesn't say anything for the longest time, she just stares at the necklace, her finger lightly tracing along the shapes of the hearts. She seems lost in the moment, and it's not until she finally looks up at me do I see the unshed tears that are glistening in her eyes.

Fuck, I don't want to make her cry. That was never my intention.

I'm about to apologise, to tell her I will take it back, when she finally speaks, but it's barely above a whisper. "It's beautiful. Thank you. Can you put it on for me?"

She holds the box out for me, and with fumbling hands, I do my best to secure the chain around her neck. It sits perfectly just below her neck, and almost without thinking she reaches up to touch the pendant.

"It suits you," I say with a smile, pleased she's agreed to wear it.

"I can't even find the right words to say how much I love it. Thank you, Kellan," she says, as she stands on her tiptoes and presses her lips against mine. It's a soft, gentle yet passionate kiss, and I think it tells me everything she isn't capable of saying. I take this moment and commit it to memory. This is the moment I realised we do stand a chance. We both love each other, that much is obvious. When I start the new year, I'm going to make it my business to find out exactly why Mia has decided we can't be a couple. I know she's hiding something from me, and I've given her plenty of opportunity to talk to me about it. I've sat back, waiting and hoping for the time to come where she realises she can trust me and we can sort this shit out. Now I'm done waiting. I'm going to fight for my girl, even if it means invading the privacy she is so desperate to maintain. I have to know I've done everything, that I've fought for her in the best way I can.

Christmas dinner is the loud, rowdy affair that we expected it to be and everyone had a lot of fun. Even Desmond was surprisingly jovial, and engaged in lots of fun, jokes, and laughter as we all enjoyed each other's company. Hallie was passed around the group and showered with gifts. I think after a while it became a lot for her to handle and she started to get a bit grumpy. I managed to get her to have a short nap while we all had our Christmas dinner. Bree and Mia did an absolutely fantastic job of cooking, and I have to confess I was a little surprised. They cook at home, but nothing to this magnitude, with this many people. Yet they coped with it brilliantly, and the food was amazing.

We all sit around the table, too stuffed to move, just chatting in our little groups about anything and everything, when my little monster wakes from her nap. I go to grab her from the crib while Mia goes into the kitchen to grab the small plate of food she prepared for her earlier. We left it in the oven to keep it warm. It's only some mashed potato, mushed-up carrots, and some gravy, but Hallie will love it. I sit with Hallie on my knee, and of course because I'm sat next to Liam, her instinct is to reach out, demanding he hold her. I tell her no, that she has to have her dinner first, and she grumbles for a bit, but doesn't say anything.

Mia returns to the dinner table, but she doesn't hand over the dish yet, saying it needs to cool down a bit first. She instead hands Hallie a bottle of juice, which she grabs with both hands and starts to drink from. Every time I look at her, she seems to have grown that little bit more and it's fucking terrifying.

I hear Bree and Liam beside me start mumbling to each other, obviously trying to have a conversation they don't want everyone to hear, so naturally I'm intrigued. Thankfully, I don't have to pester Liam into telling me, as a big smile spreads across Bree's face and Liam clears his voice loud enough to get everyone's attention. Liam hates speeches almost as much as I do. The cocky bastard must have something good to say, given his cocky grin, and the room descends into silence, with the exception of Hallie who is cooing away to herself about nothing in particular.

Liam holds his hand out and Bree takes hold of it, giving it a squeeze before Liam begins to speak. "So, we have something exciting that we would like to share with you all. It's still early days, but you are our family and we don't want to keep this a secret from you. We want you to share the happiness we are feeling right now. We are going to have a baby."

As soon as the words leave his lips, the room erupts into applause and cheers. Everyone gets up from their seats and rushes towards the couple, desperate to hug them and congratulate them. I can't move given the baby on my lap, but that doesn't stop me reaching for my best friend's hand. We do this weird man-style hand shake that soon begins to look like we are holding hands, so we drop that pretty quickly, but I reach to pat him on the back instead, trying to make this less fucking awkward.

"I'm so fucking happy for you, bro. You are going to make a great dad. After all, you are the one who taught me how to do it." Both our eyes drift to Hallie, who giggles as she does whenever Liam pays her any kind of attention.

He kneels down so he is level with Hallie and he takes hold of one of her hands in his. "What do you say, Hallie Bear? Are you looking forward to having a little cousin to play with?" Liam asks, and she giggles like she understands exactly what he's saying, which earns a round of laughter from everyone watching the interaction. Liam then has no choice but to take hold of her, as she has already latched on tightly to his T-shirt, making it very clear she wants to cuddle him. Something he is only too happy to oblige with.

Once Liam takes Hallie, I get up and move towards Bree. She and Mia are hugging and whispering to each other. I see tears in both their eyes as they pull away, so I stay back to give them their moment. Until Bree notices me nearby and gestures for me to come closer.

Holding her arms wide for me, I pull her into a big hug. "Congratulations, Bree. I'm so happy for you both. You'll make excellent parents." I try to ignore the very obvious lump in my throat as Bree holds on to me tightly.

Whispering in my ear, her words shock me, but I understand them. "I'm so fucking terrified. I have no idea what I'm doing. Will you help us?" I can't help but smile. I went through the exact same thing when I found out I was going to be a dad. I had no idea what the hell to do with a baby, and even after she was born, I felt like I was winging it the vast majority of the time. But Liam and Bree were here to help me, so I'll be here for them and their beautiful baby. This house is about to get a whole lot crazier.

The days after Christmas are thankfully a lot quieter. I get to spend a lot of time by myself, everyone wants to spend some time babysitting Hallie, which means I get lots of opportunities to catch up on my sleep, and to spend some time with Mia.

Ever since Christmas Eve night, our relationship changed again. Things haven't turned sexual since, but we're back to being friends. We spend a lot of time hanging out together, watching movies, or just chatting, like we used to before we acted on our feelings. Mia made it clear this is all we can be, but she hasn't gone back to being distant. She sleeps in my bed, we fall asleep in each other's arms, and we hug each other a lot. That's as far as things have gone, but if that's all she can give, for now, then I will take it.

The day before New Year's Eve, Bree and Liam have taken Hallie to the park, and everyone else has plans. I decide to catch up on some much-needed sleep, since Mia's treating herself to a shopping trip. I see her off before going to bed. She only plans on being gone an hour or two to buy a new dress for the party we are having at the house tomorrow.

"I'll probably be back home before you've even woken up," she says, as she gathers her bag to head out of the house.

"Well, if that's the case, then you really should come and join me in bed when you get home." I know she can hear the flirty suggestion in my voice, and she rolls her eyes at me. She's gotten used to me flirting with her again, but she never reciprocates. If her smile is anything to go by, she likes the attention.

"Go to sleep and stop being a cocky asshole," she jokes, and we both say our goodbyes. It doesn't take long for sleep to draw me under when I'm comfortably tucked up in bed, not having to worry about a baby waking me.

I wake up naturally, which feels weird to me, and when I realise that nobody has woken me up, I actually start to panic a little, sitting up in bed quicker than I should. Looking around, I catch sight of the clock telling me I've slept for close to three hours, which is very unusual. Mia must have decided I needed the sleep instead of waking me. I would much rather have woken up with her in my arms, but I think that will always be the case.

Pulling on my sweatpants, I adjust my half-mast cock that has sprung up at the mere thought of Mia. I don't want to be pitching a tent when I go downstairs. I also pull a black T-shirt over my head. Normally I wouldn't bother, much preferring to walk around without my shirt on, but our visitors complain, and then Liam whacks me round the head. So, I'm saving myself from a traumatic brain injury today.

Walking into the living room where everyone is gathered, my first instinct is to look for Hallie, and she's playing in the ball pool I bought her for Christmas. Ryleigh and Shane are sitting on the floor playing with her, which basically involves my little monster throwing balls at them, while they run around picking the balls up and filling the pool back up. Once I know she's okay, I look around for Mia. I'm shocked she isn't with everyone else. Sitting next to Liam on the sofa, I pull the phone from my pocket. I check to see there's no messages or calls when Liam begins talking.

"Nice to see you, Sleeping Beauty. Did you catch up on your sleep?" Liam jokes.

With a deep chuckle and a sarcastic grin, I reply. "Just you wait until you are in this position. Babies hate sleep. When you get the chance to sleep, you will grab it with open fucking arms, trust me. I was actually freaked out when I woke up by myself. I can't remember the last time I woke up naturally. How fucking terrifying is that? And pretty soon, that will be you too, bro." Liam doesn't look quite so cocky anymore.

"I'm choosing to pretend my baby is going to be a little angel, and will be sleeping through the night from day one." I can tell he doesn't quite believe what he's saying.

"You are fucking delusional. Where's Mia, by the way?" I ask, trying to drop her into conversation, making it sound like my enquiry is casual. Liam's eyes narrow; he sees straight through my bullshit. I think he's secretly amazed I lasted this long without asking about her whereabouts.

"Is she not with you? We got back about an hour after she left to go shopping, but we haven't seen her since. Honestly, we assumed she was with you. I don't think Bree's heard from her, but I can ask." He turns his attention to his wife, who is sitting on the seat opposite, talking to Kian, no doubt about work. "Princess, have you heard from Mia?"

Bree's eyes narrow as she quickly takes out her phone, her brow furrows as she looks. "No. I thought she was with Kel." She can obviously tell by the look on my face that isn't the case. She begins dialling and holds the phone up to her ear. Shaking her head, she tells me that it's gone to voicemail. I don't know why, but I have a sinking feeling in my stomach. Something doesn't feel right and my heart is racing as panic begins to set it. I know Bree has just tried, but I have to try myself. I pull the phone out of my pocket and start to dial Mia's number. It goes to voicemail without even ringing. Could her phone be turned off?

"I've just put a call into the main gate, they are checking security footage to find out if she came home at any time," Kian states, and by this time the room has descended into silence as they all listen to what is happening.

"Fuck, she's missing, isn't she?" I snap, standing up and beginning to pace around the room.

"Kellan, bro. Calm the fuck down. We don't know that she's missing. She could still be out shopping, for all you know. Just keep trying her while we check she hasn't come home," Liam says, trying to calm me down.

Shane jumps up from his position on the floor. "I will go and check the house, just to make sure she isn't here somewhere," he says, as he starts sprinting towards the staircase. I'm grateful for him wanting to help, and it's not a bad suggestion, but I already know she isn't here. I can feel it.

Pulling up the software I need on my phone, I start entering the computer code that I need, and the program works perfectly, just like I designed it to. I'm basically running a trace to find her phone. I created an app that'll let me do it from my phone. The only way I won't be able to locate someone is if their phone is turned off or damaged. Then all I can see is the last location they were at before their phone lost connection, for whatever reason.

It only takes a few seconds for the data to flash up on my screen, and it doesn't help the impending fear of doom I feel in my chest. "Her phone is off. It was last connected two hours ago down by the high street," I explain to nobody in particular.

"So her phone could just be dead?" asks Freya, and fuck do I want to believe that is true. Yet everyone is wearing the same sombre expression that tells me they don't believe that either.

My heart feels like it's going to beat out of my chest, and my palms are sweating as that impending fear of doom spreads through my stomach, making me feel sick. A very out of breath Shane quickly returns, letting us know that she isn't in the house, and Kian confirms that security hasn't seen her since she left the property. Bree continues to call her, despite me telling her that her phone is off. We are all starting to panic. I can feel the tension in the room, but nobody says anything.

I can't take the silence any longer. I have to voice how I feel, and we have to deal with this. "Fuck, she's missing, isn't she? What are we going to do?" I don't mean for the last question to come out sounding like a plea, but I look to Liam because I desperately need him to step up now and tell me exactly what to do. We need a plan, otherwise I'm going to lose my shit.

"We don't know that she is missing for sure, so that's the first thing we need to look into. We can go to her last known location, ask around and see if anyone has seen her? Meanwhile, you can check her phone's history to see if there's any information in there, anything she may have been hiding that could give us answers," Liam instructs, and Bree nods in agreement, before adding more demands.

"Kian and I will get in touch with Whitlock. If she is missing, there's a good chance he will know something about it." Fuck, I hadn't even thought of her dad. Now that I think about it, that's probably the most obvious reason for her being missing, but there's also a part of me that thinks she has left me. Women always leave me; I just thought Mia would have been the one to break that cycle.

"Honestly, there's a lot of routes we could go down. Why don't

Kellan and I go and do the deep dive now? That will give us all some areas to focus on. Keep trying her phone. We will come back down as soon as we can and we will have an action plan," instructs Liam, and I don't blame him for wanting to come up with a plan before we all spring to action. The truth is, there's a million different reasons for why Mia might be missing, and so we need information so we can focus our efforts more.

"Can you look after Hallie, please?" I ask Bree, but everyone in the room replies. Kneeling down in front of my daughter, who is still happily playing in the ball pool, oblivious to the scare going on around her. I lean down to give her a kiss, and I tell her I will bring Mia back to her very soon. The only reply I get is a ball thrown in my face, but I will take it. At the moment she is unaware Mia is even missing, I don't want her to have to suffer the loss of another female in her life. It's hard enough for me to live through the heartbreak, I don't want her to have to suffer too.

Liam and I waste no time, running up the stairs towards my office. Shuffling the mouse, all my computer screens spring to life. I make myself comfy in my chair and try to focus my thoughts. I need to keep a clear head. I will find her, if it's the last thing I do.

Using software I created, I manage to hack into her phone, grabbing coordinates for her last known address. I then go deeper, trying to grab as much information as I can. Mia doesn't use her phone much. Other than texts to the people here in the house, there's only a couple of other numbers that I don't recognise. As soon as I open the latest one that was sent just a few days ago, my blood begins to run cold. I recognise the number, and now everything is starting to make an awful lot of sense.

Turning to Liam, all the colour drained from my face, I show him what I've found. "This is the reason Mia ended our relationship. Fucking Shayla. She made contact with Mia and threatened to give the judge enough evidence to have her take Hallie from me. The only way to stop me from losing custody of Hallie was if Mia agreed to stop seeing me. So she did. But Shayla tells her she is always watching, and if she attempts to start a relationship again, at any time, or she doesn't leave once she has finished her university degree, then she would regret it. Shayla fucking threatened Mia. I'm going to kill her," I scream, pushing myself up from my office chair so quickly that it flies into the wall.

Liam grabs hold of my arm. "Whoa, calm down, Kel. This does look damning, and we do definitely need to sort it, but Shayla is in Limerick with the Reapers. There's no way she is over here stalking Mia. I have no idea why she felt the need to interfere with your relationship, but we also can't ignore the other texts on her phone. Her father there makes it very clear she belongs to him, and that she has to marry Kyle when she graduates. All of this is a lot for one person to deal with. We will explore every option, but I think we do need to keep in mind the possibility that this all became too much for Mia, and she just left." I start to protest, because I know for fucking certain that she wouldn't just leave, not without saying goodbye to Hallie.

"She wouldn't," is all I manage to croak out, and I feel my body beginning to deflate. Liam throws my arm around his shoulders and takes my weight for me. I think he is the only reason I haven't collapsed into a heap on the floor.

"I know. Let me call Evan to find out what he knows, since he's in Ireland. I promise we will look into this. But if Shayla is in England, or she has taken Mia back to Ireland, there will be a trail. So you have something to look for. If it comes to it, I will storm the Reaper compound with you. But before we start a war, we need proof. Can you keep working? You can't just focus on the Reapers, you have to investigate Whitlock too." I nod in agreement, and he pulls his phone out. He calls Evan who went back to Ireland a couple of days ago. I think he had planned to come back here tomorrow to celebrate the new year with us, but he had some business he needed to attend to these last couple of days. Which works out in my favour because everyone else is here in London.

I'm surprised when Liam next calls his father, but if anyone can find out what Whitlock is up to, to find out if he's involved, it's Desmond. It's a fucking massive thing for Liam to contact his father. I'm not sure if times have really become that desperate, or if they really have started mending some of the broken fences between them.

Desmond is only too happy to help. He hates Whitlock almost as much as I do.

Being active and feeling like we are doing something is helping to settle my friend's nerves, but I can't deny the feeling that's still in the pit of my stomach. I don't know how I know, but I know Mia has been taken. I know she is in danger and scared. It's almost like I can hear her body calling out for me to help her. I make her a promise that I will find her, or I will die trying. And so help me God, whoever has taken her, they will regret the day they ever thought this was a good idea. Then, if it isn't Shayla, I will deal with her. She can take back her fucking threats, and stay out of my life. I decide who I want to be with, and that is Mia. When I bring her home, she is never leaving my side again.

That night is the longest night I've ever endured in my life, and that's coming from a sleep-deprived single father. I've never known fear until I realised Mia was missing. I've also never felt so fucking helpless. I feel like I've explored every single piece of CCTV that I can find, and the few glimpses of Mia that I caught on the high street caused my blood to boil. She made it to the shop, and had bought the dress she'd been telling me about for weeks. I watched her choose it, walk into the dressing room, before exiting and purchasing the dress. I followed her movements, watched as she bought a takeaway coffee, and then she disappeared.

I've explored several surrounding cameras, but she went missing in a dead spot. That does give us an area to explore, which Finn and Shane were more than happy to do. Everyone has been keen to help in any way they can, and it makes my heart soar to see the love that my family has for my girl. They want to see her returned home safe and sound, just as much as I do.

Ryleigh and Freya take turns looking after Hallie, as I don't have the emotional capacity to care for her right now. She has experienced so much loss in her little life, and I sure as fuck am going to do everything in my power to make sure she doesn't lose Mia too.

Bree, Liam, and Kian have all been exploring our criminal aspects to find out if Mia has been caught up in some of our bullshit that has gone wrong. Personally, I think they are barking up the wrong tree. The evidence suggests Shayla is our number one suspect, but we also can't rule out Whitlock. If it is Shayla, then Mia is as good as dead. The Reapers would only keep her alive if they could gain something from her, but Mia has nothing they want. If it was about me, I would've had a ransom demand by now. But it's been radio silent, which fills me with dread. It means we have no idea if they plan on returning her, if she isn't already dead.

Fuck…this is all my brain has been able to focus on last night. All I can think of are the worst-case scenarios, and all the ways that I might already have lost her. We have wasted so much time being apart, and Shayla will fucking pay for that. Mostly, I just want to hold Mia in my arms, and tell her how I feel. It feels so stupid now, waiting for the perfect time to tell her that I love her, and now that opportunity might be gone. She's either in a shit situation, probably one where she fears for her life, or she's already dead. I need her to know I love her. I want to be the reason she fights, the thing she has to live for. I need her to come back to me and Hallie.

"Kellan, come downstairs and get some food, bro. My father is on his way over with an update," Liam says, as he taps me on the shoulder to get my attention. I've been looking at the same computer monitor for the last few hours, and it makes my blood boil that I don't have any more information than when Liam checked on me a few hours earlier. He was going to try and get Bree to have a few hours of sleep, given her pregnancy. I didn't bother to tell him that he is fighting a losing battle. Bree loves Mia almost as much as I do, and she won't stop until we've explored every avenue, no matter how much her body is telling her to sleep.

I guess Bree's the one person who knows how Mia feels right now. Bree was kidnapped, and the memories still terrify her. I sure as fuck hope Mia isn't going through what Bree did. Mia's already suffered so much in her life, but she survives it all, and I have to hope she will survive this.

I let Liam push me out of my office and down into the living room. Despite it being early, all the Doughty's are awake. Hallie's in her high chair, and it looks like Freya and Ryleigh are trying to get her to eat her porridge, but instead my cute little monster is throwing it everywhere. Shane and Ryleigh appear to have got the worst of it, and Freya is cleverly standing behind her.

The sudden urge to hold my little girl, to be near her, propels me towards her. When she sees me she starts to clap and giggle, and I honestly have never felt so loved in all my life. Tears glisten my eyes as I watch Hallie look around, and I realise she's looking for Mia. It's usually Mia who gets her to eat her breakfast without painting the walls with it.

"Hallie, my beautiful little monster. You either eat the porridge or I take it off you. You don't throw your food. Understand?"

She looks up at me with the big blue doe eyes that are the exact same shade as mine, and she even sucks in her bottom lip, like she's trying not to pout. My girl is becoming an expert at wrapping everyone around her cute little finger. She is nowhere near crying, but she looks at me like she's about to be in floods of tears.

Thankfully, before we can get into this any further—as I'm more than sure she will eventually—we're distracted by the doorbell ringing. Bree enters the living room with Desmond in tow. Everyone finds a chair, surface, or the floor to sit on. I sit on the sofa with Bree and Liam, and Desmond sits in an armchair opposite.

"You didn't have to come all the way over here, Desmond," I say, not wanting to sound too ungrateful for his help, but I'm not entirely sure why he is being so helpful.

A smile, that I know is supposed to be friendly, but actually comes across as a little sadistic, spreads across Desmond's face. "Your girl is missing, of course I'm here to help. But if you can all stop getting your girls kidnapped, that would make our lives a lot easier," he jokes, with a head nod towards Bree. Stupid fuck, why the hell does he think now is the time to mention such a traumatic experience.

"Nobody asked you to be here," Liam snaps, but I see Bree lay her hand over Liam's arm, no doubt to try and calm him.

"I've gotta admit, I'm questioning your motives with this one too," Ryleigh shouts from in the kitchen with Hallie, and I hear Shane and Freya both tell her to be quiet and stay out of things. But Ryleigh's never been one to shut up, not unless she wants to. "What? I can't be the only one questioning his motives?"

"Ryleigh…" Desmond starts, but I cut him off, stopping the argument before it starts.

"Answer Ryleigh's question."

"I don't think now's the right time for us to talk about this. We can do it, just the two of us, at a later date. For now, shall we focus on the information I have?" Desmond somehow manages to look even more shifty than usual. Everyone looks to see if I'm going to let that slide, or if I'm going to demand he talks. I've never lied or kept things from Liam, and I'm sure as fuck not going to start now.

"I think now is the perfect time. I hate people who keep secrets and lie to me. So you better start fucking talking, right now," I snap, and Desmond just rolls his eyes.

"Fine, but remember, I advised you that this is a conversation that should be had in private, when we have a lot longer to talk about it." He pauses for a moment, looking to me for permission to continue, and I nod my head for him to carry on. "Do you remember when you came to live with us when you were a kid?"

"Of course I remember. What does that have to do with anything?" I snap, looking at Liam to see if he knows what his father is talking about, but he looks just as confused as I do.

"When your mother decided she couldn't look after you anymore, she asked if we'd look after you. You had no other family, so I didn't hesitate to take you in."

I cut him off, adding in the part I remember, "No. Liam asked you to take me in, not my mother."

I look to Liam who confirms my version of events. Desmond shakes his head, making it clear our recollection isn't correct. "No, you and Liam had grown up together and were friends, and yes, Liam did ask us to let you live with us, but the decision had already been made at that point. What do you remember about your father?" Des asks, and my brow furrows in confusion.

"Why is that relevant? My father worked with you and one of your shady deals got him killed before I was even born," I snap, confused as to why he would bring all this up. Besides, that's about the extent of my knowledge on the subject. I know Mum was married to a man called Kaden Burke, for a couple of years before I was born. They never planned on having children, and he didn't even know he was going to be a father. He died on a job gone wrong, getting shot in the head while working for Desmond. That's all I know. I don't know anything else about him, not even stupid things like what he was like, or what kind of person he was.

"Look, before I tell you the rest of this, I want to make it very fucking clear that I have never wanted to keep this from you. I wanted to tell you a long time ago, but your mother was very set against it. Even now, she will be very fucking pissed that I've told you, but I don't care. It's time you knew." Desmond's voice raises and becomes more animated as he talks about arguing with my mother.

Snapping at him, I can't keep the anger out of my voice. "Tell me what you know. Now!"

"There's no easy way to say this, but I'm your father." Before he has even got the last word out, the room erupts around me.

"WHAT?"

"What the fuck are you talking about?"

"Liar!"

"For fuck's sake."

I can't tell which comment comes from whom, but I can relate to them all. I sit there stunned into silence, wondering what the hell he's talking about. My eyes feel like they're bugging out of my skull, while my mouth flops open like a goldfish. I'm literally stunned into silence.

"Please, everyone, shut up. Let Desmond finish what he has to say, then we can talk," Bree shouts, silencing the room.

Desmond shoots her a smile, but as I look over at Bree, I can see it isn't reciprocated. Her steel gaze is fixed on Des, but her hand is stroking Liam's leg, trying to calm him down.

"Thank you, Bree. I'm not proud of this, but I had an affair with Kellan's mother. It was short, a couple of weeks at the most. Von and I were going through a rough patch, she had just found out she was pregnant with Liam and was struggling a lot with morning sickness and we were arguing more than normal. I knew Marianna, having met her through Kaden, and she pursued me. I know her and Kaden's marriage was on the rocks, and I'm not proud of it, but I did engage in a brief fling. It was never serious, and it was over long before I found out about you." He takes a deep breath and reaches for the glass of water Freya had put next to him before we started, taking a gulp.

"Are you sure?" I don't need to elaborate. He knows I'm asking if there's any doubt about my paternity.

"I'm sure. When you were born, we did a DNA test, confirming that I'm your father. I just want to make it very fucking clear that from the moment I found out I was your father, I wanted to be part of your life. I told Von straight away, and even though she was incredibly pissed, she supported my decision to be part of your life, Kellan. It was your mother who said she didn't want that. She refused to put my name on the birth certificate, and I didn't want to cause you any upheaval. I made it very fucking clear that a time would come when I would tell you the truth, but honestly, the longer I left it, the harder it became."

"So, why now?" Liam snaps, and I nod my head in agreement.

"Because you were all questioning my motives over why I'm here. I'm here because Kellan is my son, and I love him just as much as I love each and every one of you. His girl is missing, so I am moving heaven and earth to get her back, the same way I did for Liam when Bree was taken. I may have been a shitty father for the majority of your lives, thanks to a few piss-poor decisions on my part, but I won't ever have you say that I don't love each and every one of you."

We all look at each other, matching expressions of shock on each Doughty's face. Fuck, this makes them my real siblings!

"Bullshit. You tried to pimp Ryleigh and me out to sexual predators. How the hell can you say that you care about us? After all, you made it very fucking clear that we aren't your real daughters," shouts Freya, and everyone freezes. I don't think I have ever heard Freya lose her temper like that. She's the most chilled out of us all, but her cheeks flush with rage.

"Frey...you know that isn't true. There's so much going on that I can't tell you all about. But please don't ever think that I don't love you," Desmond says, looking Freya in the eyes, and I have to admit, he looks very fucking serious.

"Wait...fuck. You talked to Declan about this. About putting under-aged girls in your auctions at Shades. I remember him saying you had someone manipulating you, and you had to protect your girls," Kian states, and all eyes quickly flick towards the blond sitting beside Freya. I don't miss the way he's gently stroking Freya's back, trying to comfort her.

"Kian. We're not discussing that now," Desmond snaps.

"I want to hear what he has to say," Ryleigh shouts, while Freya and Liam mumble agreements.

"Look, I know you don't trust me, but I need you to. I need you to trust that if I'm keeping something from you, there's a pretty fucking important reason. I'll tell you when I can, but for now, you have to believe I'm doing the best for our family."

Nobody is willing to put their trust in Des, and the room erupts into noise, everyone demanding he stop lying and tell the truth. I agree with my siblings—fuck, it feels weird saying that now I know it's real. As much as I want to know exactly what he's hiding from us, my patience is wearing thin.

I shout, making sure everyone hears me. "Look, I know there's a lot we need to cover, and you can fuck right off, Desmond, if you think this is over. A time will come, very soon, where you will have to give us the answers we need. But right now, I have to find Mia and I don't have time to deal with your bullshit." I pause, looking around at each of the Doughty children. "I'm sorry, but I have to find Mia before I can deal with any of this shit. Can we, just for now, focus on her?" I plead, watching their anger melt away.

"I'm sorry, Kellan. We shouldn't have hijacked this moment. Mia is the priority," Freya apologises, a small smile on her face, but it doesn't quite reach her eyes. We definitely need to have a long fucking talk with Des, but it'll have to wait for now.

Bree somehow manages to sum up exactly what we're all feeling. "Look, Desmond. Let me make this very fucking clear. Mia's our focus, for now. But, once we have her back safe and sound, I expect you to sit down with everyone in this room—Finn and Evan too—and you will answer all their questions. I personally do not work with people who keep secrets, but more than that, we're supposed to be a fucking family. If you want to be part of this family, you will trust us, and you will tell us everything. Do I make myself very fucking clear?"

Desmond chuckles and smiles that sadistic smile he thinks is friendly. It's downright fucking scary. "You are one hell of a leader, Bree. I'm very lucky to have you in our family. I promise, we'll have a long discussion and I will answer all your questions."

Nods come from all around the room, and I see Bree smile, happy to have mediated this shitstorm. I need to forget all about the whole 'he's my father' rubbish. I'm putting that into a box and sealing the lid, for now.

"Right, now that's sorted, what do you know about Mia?" I ask, grabbing Desmond's attention.

Des finishes taking a gulp of his water, and places his glass back onto the coffee table, as he takes a deep breath. "Firstly, I want to tell you about when Finn and Evan visited the Reaper compound. Evan almost got shot, as apparently Doughty's aren't welcome on the compound. It wasn't until Shayla recognised Finn that they were finally allowed inside. Whiskey, who I believe is Shayla's husband, took Evan on a tour of the compound, to make it clear that Mia wasn't there. Finn stayed behind to talk to Shayla, as I believe they met before."

I nod, remembering the experience well. Shay and Finn got along well, and when he learnt of Shay's true colours, he was more shocked than me. We grew up learning to identify liars. Hell, we're fucking experts at lying and deception. But neither of us saw her coming. Desmond pauses just for a second, like he's trying to gather his thoughts about what to say next.

"Shayla did admit to making contact with Mia. She thought she was doing the right thing by keeping Mia away from you and Hallie. She knew who Mia's father was, and his reputation. She didn't want him to be around Hallie. She knows she isn't entitled to a say in Hallie's life, but when she was contacted about the custody debate, that's when she started looking into things. But, she hasn't made contact with Mia since that last text after the court case. According to Shayla, her text came out as more of a threat than she intended. She just wanted Mia to adhere to her promise and stay away from you and Mia. But Finn says she was shocked to learn Mia had been taken. She knows nothing about it, and did say she regrets her interference."

I can't help but interrupt with mumblings I hadn't meant to say aloud. "Too fucking right, she shouldn't have interfered."

"So if Shayla and the Reapers aren't involved, does that just leave Whitlock?" Kian asks, voicing the question on everyone's lips.

"Well...that was my thinking. But, last night I sat down with Whitlock, and I told him about Mia's disappearance. He was genuinely surprised, and pissed too. Whether you like it or not, he still sees Mia as his daughter, as an asset. So, he took her disappearance as a personal insult. Honestly, I have to say, I completely believe him. I know he's a master manipulator, but not about this. Don't make the mistake of thinking he was upset that his daughter's missing, it wasn't about that. This was more about someone taking something that belongs to him. He's still a cold, hard, calculating bastard, but he didn't know about Mia."

"Fuck!" I can't hold back my rage as I stand up and begin to pace, running my hands through my hair in despair. "So we have nothing? We're exactly where we started yesterday. We have no fucking leads at all."

"Kel, calm down, bro. The more leads we cross off the list, the more we narrow down our search. I know it seems like we have nothing, but that isn't true. We will find Mia," Liam states, as he stands up and walks towards me. He pulls me into a hug, and my body just sags against him.

"Liam...I can't lose her." My voice is thick with emotion, and I try to hold back the tears that are threatening to fall.

"Bro…I promise you, we will find her," Liam mumbles into my ear. "Come on, sit down and we will all brainstorm together."

Liam leads me to the sofa and I flop onto it. Almost like she knows exactly what I need, Freya walks over to me and places Hallie into my lap. My beautiful little girl is oblivious to all the drama going on around her. She reaches up and grabs hold of my cheeks, squeezing them in her chubby little hands. Her resulting giggle echoes around the room and it's more than enough to bring a genuine smile to my face. My bright star in a world full of darkness.

Pulling my daughter close, squeezing her tightly, I take comfort in the hug, making a silent promise to her. I vow to bring back the woman I know we both love. I vow that I will make her mine, and we will get our happily ever after.

Mia

I wake up drenched in a cold sweat, my voice hoarse after no doubt screaming through my nightmares. As I open my eyes and look around the unfamiliar bedroom, the fear and despair I felt in my dream doesn't disappear. I'm living my nightmare.

The room itself isn't exactly a prison. It's a medium-sized room, decorated with beige walls, and a large king-sized bed taking up most of the room. There's a bedside table on each side of the bed, and a table with two comfortable fabric chairs under the window, but that's the only furniture in the room. The bed is covered in a floral duvet that matches the curtains—that are currently drawn—covering the large window. There are three doors leading off the room; one leads to an en suite, one into a walk-in closet, and the other is the door to get into the room, which is currently locked.

Everything about this room screams normal, maybe even homey. The bathroom is lovely, with a large Jacuzzi bath and a walk-in shower big enough for two with beautiful marble tiling. Don't even get me started on how big the walk-in wardrobe is, and it's filled with rails of women's clothing, shoes, bags, accessories, and lingerie. If it wasn't for the fact that this room is being used to hold me prisoner, I might have some serious envy.

I've been here for three days, and today is the start of a new year. I fell asleep last night dreaming of where I should have been. I should've been at a party at my house, surrounded by all the people I now class as my family. I should've held my beautiful little Hallie, and rocked her to sleep, while she fought against me as much as possible, desperate not to miss out on the party. I should've counted down to midnight, and said goodbye to last year and hello to the new year in the arms of the man I love. I should've kissed him hard, vowing I would start and end the new year kissing him. The way I want to start and end all my years, for the rest of my life. Kellan's my soulmate, and when I get out of this fucked-up situation, I plan on telling him. No matter what the consequences might be. If Shayla comes for us, we will fight her together, like I should've done all along.

The lock for the door begins to turn and I scramble into a sitting position, pulling my legs up to my chest as I drag the duvet cover around me. I know who's about to walk through that door, but when he first walked in last night, I have to confess I was shocked. I didn't think Kyle Fratacello had the balls to kidnap me.

"Happy New Year again, my Little Bunny. Did you sleep well?" Kyle asks as he lets himself into the room, making sure to lock the door again behind him. I watch as he places the key into the inner breast pocket of the suit jacket he's wearing. I store that piece of information away for if I ever need it to get out of here.

I don't bother to answer him. What's the point?

"Oh, come on, Little Bunny. We had such a lovely night last night, seeing in the new year. Why are you in a mood now?" he snaps, and as I lower my head I can't help but clench all the already sore muscles in my body, waiting for the blows I expect he's going to deliver. I'm shocked when they don't come. I'm not sure if he's luring me into a false sense of security. I'm still covered in cuts, bruises, and welts from his 'lovely night'.

The first two days locked in here, I was mostly left to myself. The odd lackey would come in and bring me food, or pass along instructions to me, but none of them physically hurt me. They were a bit rough at times, throwing me around when I refused to cooperate, but I think they had instructions not to harm me. At that point, I still had no idea who my kidnapper was.

Last night, when he came into the room, I was shocked to see Kyle. He said he was here to celebrate the new year with me, but he was practically vibrating with rage. Ranting about how I didn't honour my promise to marry him, furious that I whored myself out—as he called it—to Kellan. To say he was jealous about Kellan was a massive fucking understatement. This built until I ended up spending New Year's Eve being beaten, tortured, and sexually assaulted, all in the hopes it keeps Kellan alive. Hallie will not lose another parent if I can help it.

"Mia, I thought we made a deal last night, or do you need a refresher?" His voice is thick with the threat. Memories of last night taunt me, as I try to forget them.

"*Y*ou?" *I ask incredulously when the door opens and I find out for definite who's responsible for kidnapping me. Kyle Fratacello, the person who stole most of my childhood, and who I was supposed to marry prior to meeting Kellan.*

By kidnapping me, he's put a target on his back. Kellan, Bree, and Liam will be coming for him, but more than that, he will have pissed off my father. I may not like the fact that my father views me as his property, but in this case, Kyle's not only gone against my father's instructions, but he's taken something that doesn't belong to him yet. That means my father will be hell-bent on destroying not only Kyle, but Kyle's entire family. My father is a powerful man, and he isn't concerned about me, but he will not stand someone challenging him.

"Are you happy to see me, my Little Bunny?" he sings, with a sadistic smile on his face.

"Why am I here, Kyle?"

He moves towards the bed where I'm sitting, and with each step he takes towards me, I shuffle farther back towards the headboard. It doesn't take long until my back hits the board, and I have nowhere else to go. I pull my legs up and tuck my arms around them. It's a technique I learnt years ago, making myself seem as small and fragile as possible.

"You are here because you are my fiancée, Mia. I gave you some time to live your life, and I feel like I've been more than amenable, giving you your freedom. But, I will not let you humiliate me any longer. As soon as I found out that you have been acting like a slut behind my back, I knew I had to act."

I freeze, stunned by his words. I think this lunatic genuinely believes that I've cheated on him with Kellan. I don't really know what to say. It's obvious he isn't living in the real world, so anything I say will no doubt just piss him off more.

"What do you have to say for yourself, slut? Are you even going to try defending yourself?" he snaps, acid dripping from every word, as his face contorts into an evil sneer. This is Kyle showing his true colours.

"There's nothing for me to say. I didn't know we were engaged. I left my family five years ago, and I thought that meant I was leaving any obligation that had been made prior to that. I wasn't whoring myself out, and it wasn't just a fling. I love Kellan, and I want to be with him. I'm sorry if that hurts you." I don't know why I'm telling him all this, it's certainly not what he wants to hear. I know I should have lied, but the truth is, I'm so fucking sick of lying. I've spent the last few weeks lying to Kellan, telling him I don't have feelings for him, that I don't want to be with him. Kellan deserves better than that.

Kyle lets out a low, sadistic chuckle. "Do you think any of that matters to me, Little Bunny? I couldn't give a shit if you think he's your soulmate. As far as I'm concerned, you're a whore. You cheated on me, and humiliated me, and it stops now."

His face begins to tinge with red as he flexes his hands in and out of fists. He appears to be getting more angry, and my heart starts to race. He's always been volatile, and is capable of anything when he loses his temper.

"So, I've decided that tomorrow will be the start of our new lives together. Tomorrow we will start our lives as a married couple. I'm sick of waiting. So, this will be your last night of freedom. I have everything set up. We will get married tomorrow."

What the fuck? Is he serious right now? I think he's very fucking serious, if his steely gaze is anything to go by. That sadistic smirk lets me know he means what he says. This isn't open for discussion as far as he's concerned. But he can fuck right off if he thinks I'll let him do this without a fight.

"You can't force me to marry you, Kyle. There isn't a legal officiant in the country who will marry us once they see you're doing it by force," I retort, hoping like hell that's actually true. His responding cackle lets me know he already thought of that.

"Oh, you would be very mistaken. I've already found someone. He will be here tomorrow, and he's more than happy to make sure the marriage will be legally binding, no matter how reluctant you may seem during the wedding. I think now would be a good time to tell you exactly what I expect from you, not only during the wedding, but through our entire marriage," Kyle replies, his tone far too happy.

I freeze, unsure of what to say. It seems like he has an answer for anything I'm going to say. Before I even have a chance to think about this, an overwhelming painful sensation spreads over my scalp, as Kyle grabs hold of my hair into his fist, dragging me across the bed. As he pulls me, I reach to grab hold of his hand, trying to pry it from my hair, and I thrash around, desperate to get away from him. My scalp burns, and the fear that's pooling in my stomach is now very much alive.

His voice takes on an even more menacing tone. "The first thing you need to learn, my Little Bunny, is that you will NEVER ignore me! Whenever I speak to you, it's imperative you respond to me. You will refer to me as 'Sir'. Is that understood?"

I try to nod my head, but I'm limited by what I can do. He continues to grip hold of my hair tightly, ensuring I remain laying on my back, my head closest to where he's standing.

SLAP!

Pain spreads across my cheek as his other hand makes contact, hard. I actually hear the slap of his palm against my cheek before I feel the pain. My head's thrown to the side with the force of the blow, and I reach up to cup my cheek.

"You are not learning, whore. What did I literally just say to you?" he snarls, his face just inches from mine. His tobacco-infused breath is right in front of me, offending my nose and causing my stomach to roll. Normally, I take deep breaths to try to stabilise when I feel nauseous, but I can't do that here.

I try to focus, thinking back to what he said, so I can do as I'm told. Anything to avoid getting hit again. But I must've taken too long to answer, as Kyle throws his fist into my stomach. Pain explodes in my gut and I instinctively draw my knees up to my chest, trying to tuck my arm around where he hit me. Fuck, spasms of pain continue long after the blow and I can't think straight. Tears roll down my face as I try to catch my breath.

There's a ringing in my ears, no doubt from the overwhelming pain, and it means I can't quite hear what Kyle is saying, but I'm guessing it has something to do with me doing as I'm told. With emotion clogging my throat, in between gasps, I tell him what he's waiting to hear. "I understand...Sir." I tag the last part on quickly, and the sadistic smile that widens across his face makes me feel even sicker.

"Good girl. That wasn't so hard, was it?"

Sadistic fuck. Once again, he doesn't even give me a chance to answer before he rains three more punches down on my ribs and abdomen. The pain becomes too much and I cry out, tears rolling down my face as I beg and plead for him to stop. I try to curl up into a ball, desperate to protect all my major organs.

"Please, Sir...please stop. It hurts." My pleas are loud and desperate. The pain in my ribs makes it excruciating to take in a full breath. Whenever I do, there's a sharp, stabbing sensation that prevents me from inhaling fully. Fuck, I could have a rib fracture.

"Are you ready to learn the rest of the rules now?" he asks, pulling me by my hair until I'm sitting up on the edge of the bed. I don't like this position, it leaves me far too exposed.

"Yes, Sir," I mumble, making sure I gave him the title he's desperate for me to use.

"Good. Now I finally have your attention. I'm going to tell you what I expect of my wife. Firstly, you will call me Sir at all times, and respond whenever I address you. You will never embarrass or contradict me. You will keep your appearance up to the highest standards. To facilitate this, I will book and pay for regular appointments for your hair, and waxing. You will make sure your cunt is bald at all times. If and when required, you will undertake any plastic surgery needed to keep you looking as young as *possible. The most important part is that whilst you will appear to be the perfect housewife to the outside world, when it comes to the bedroom, you are my whore. You will do whatever I tell you. You will take whatever I give, in any hole I choose. You will not complain, you will simply beg for more. Do I make myself clear?" he snarls.*

I try to formulate words, but the blow I sustained has obviously caused some damage because all I can concentrate on is trying to breathe. The pain is unbearable. Clearly it takes me too long to reply to Kyle, as he lets go of my hair, causing me to slump down while I try to sit up on the bed, and he rains down more blows than I can count.

Slaps ricochet across my face, causing my ears to ring and my head to ache. But he doesn't stop there. In between slaps, he punches my abdomen, ribs, and sides. Pain echoes around my body and I don't know what to do. I only have two fucking hands to use to block the blows, and whenever I manage to block one body part, he simply finds another free area.

I can't hold myself up any further, the pain vibrates all over my body, and I slide from the bed into a crumpled sobbing heap on the floor. "Please... Kyle...Sir... N-no mo-more... S-stop. Please," I sob hysterically, begging for Kyle to stop.

His hands stop pummelling my poor, broken body, and instead he begins tearing at my clothes. The T-shirt I'm wearing is ripped clean off my body, and while my hands are protecting my abdomen, Kyle begins ripping off my jeans. That's when I really start to panic. I know exactly where this is going. Fuck, I've been here far too many fucking times before. It's obvious what Kyle's intention is, and I can't allow that to happen.

Since I found my freedom, and Kellan taught me to take back control of my body, I hoped that I'd never find myself in this position again. I gave my body to Kellan, and I don't intend on giving myself to anyone else. Kyle's trying to take something that belongs to Kellan, and it breaks my heart. Kyle seems to realise that he's finally broken me.

Grabbing hold of my hair, he pulls me up until I'm sitting on my knees at his feet. The scream that rips from my body is music to Kyle's ears, and that sadistic grin spreads across his face. When I first met Kyle, all those years ago, I actually thought he was quite cute. His face is all angles, and it's something he's grown into. With the exception of a bit of a beer belly that he appears to be developing, he looks the same. The older he's got, the more sick and sadistic he's become.

"Look at you. Those titties have gotten bigger. Normally I would prefer a younger-looking body, but I can definitely get on board with bigger tits. Take your bra off," Kyle instructs, and I don't even hesitate. What would be the point? If I were to object, Kyle would just beat me further.

Pulling the black lace bra away from my body, I place it on the floor, and avert my eyes. Humiliation and shame floods my body, a blush spreading across my cheeks as I keep my eyes firmly downcast. All I have left covering my throbbing, painful body is a small pair of black lace short panties, and given the predatory look in Kyle's eyes, they won't be on for very much longer. I need to push beyond the crippling pain I feel so that I can start thinking logically.

"Sir, I am very sorry for any offence I have caused you. That was never my intention. Please accept my humblest of apologies, and allow me to make it up to you," I mumble, the words tasting like bile on my tongue. But, if I don't play Kyle's game, there's a very real possibility he could kill me.

"Look at you, Little Bunny. You're learning. I like hearing that you will do anything for me, but I already knew that you would. You've always been a natural submissive little slut." His words burn me, humiliating me further, and the damage he's doing to my confidence is far worse than any damage he's done to my body. "I forgot how fucking good you look on your knees. Now, tell me what you're going to do to make it up to me."

I take a deep breath, as much as the pain in my ribs will allow, and I try to focus my mind. This is going to be my main chance at getting this right. I need to embrace all the training I've spent years trying to put behind me, to manipulate Kyle without him realising that's what I'm doing. "Well, Sir, firstly I want to thank you for giving me another chance. I know I've let you down and have humiliated you with my actions. I can only apologise greatly for that, and promise it won't happen again. I'm thrilled that you still want to marry me, and I can't wait to become your wife." I flutter my eyelashes and smile up at him through hooded eyes, trying to give off the sweet, submissive impression he gets off on.

"Obviously, I'm going to have to punish you for the humiliation, but your apology goes a long way, Little Bunny. I'm so excited to marry you

tomorrow. Once you are my wife, there will be nothing holding us back." Kyle smiles, and I try to amp up my manipulation.

"I completely agree, Sir. Which is why I want to ask your permission to hold off on anything more between us tonight. This is the night before our wedding, and if we want our marriage to last, we shouldn't mess with fate. We should sleep separately, only so that when we consummate the marriage, it will be so much more special." I keep my eyes up, holding his gaze as I try to look as timid and non-threatening as possible.

"Hmmm. I hadn't thought about that. It's true, this is the night before our wedding, and superstition does say that we should spend the night apart. Obviously I want our marriage to be long and successful. So...I think I will agree to this," he mutters, almost to himself rather than to me. I want to smile, to celebrate the small win, but I know better than to let him see how I feel. Unfortunately, he continues talking. "I can't deny my body craves you, and I do need to punish you. I can't start our marriage with that hanging over us. I will class the beating you've taken as part of your punishment, as I think you have learnt from this, but it's still not enough."

Fuck! I thought I'd got him.

He continues to mumble to himself, until he finally reaches a decision. "Right, I have decided how we can rectify this. I will spank you to make sure you understand your punishment, and then you will suck my cock. I have waited far too long for you, Little Bunny. I will wait for the full experience once you are my wife, but I think a little cheat tonight won't hurt anyone."

My body shakes as I realise I'm not going to be able to make him change his mind. I cast my eyes down to the floor, and mumble my agreement to his terms. If I don't agree to this, fuck knows how much worse this can be.

The terror in my eyes must be clearly visible to Kyle as the sick, sadistic smile spreads across his face. "I will give you the choice. Which do you want to do first? Shall I spank your ass until you accept the pain you have caused me, or shall I fuck your face first? Fair warning, if you choose the blow job first, and I get turned on while I'm spanking you, I will have no choice but to have you take care of that. Can't go into my wedding with blue balls now, can I?"

He waits for my answer, and I want to ignore him. He's making it sound like he's giving me a fucking choice, but he isn't. I don't want another beating, so I reply instantly, "Please can you spank me first, Sir. Hopefully *that will get you very hot and horny after punishing me, and then I can help make you feel good, if you allow me to do that, Sir."*

"Would you like to suck my cock, Little Bunny?" he taunts, reaching down to stroke my face, holding my chin to make sure I maintain eye contact with him.

"Yes, Sir," I reply, my voice remains monotone as I try to say what he wants to hear.

"Come on, Little Bunny. You can do better than that." He grabs hold of my hair and roughly pulls my head back, making it clear he's becoming frustrated. He wants me to play the role I adopted years ago, the one he taught me to play. Humiliation floods my cheeks as I realise I have no choice but to play along.

"I'm nothing but a dirty whore, Sir. My holes all belong to you, and I live simply to make you happy. Of course I want to taste your cock, and to make you happy, Sir. Please, spank me and show me what a bad little girl I've been. I promise to be good from now on. I promise to make you feel good. Please let me swallow your cock, Sir." The words sound like I'm reading from a script. As Kyle lifts me to my feet by my hair, he throws me over his knee, and fear trembles through my body.

No! I don't want this. Please. I don't want this. I allow myself just a moment to go to my happy place. I think of lying in bed with Kellan's arm around me, while Hallie lays on top of us, giggling while we play together in the morning. I think about all the good in my life, blocking out the pain and humiliation Kyle's forcing upon me.

T try to force the memories out of my mind, but the physical pain I feel whenever I try to move my body, the throbbing ache in my head, the sharp stabbing pain in my lungs whenever I try to take a breath, they all act as reminders. No matter how many times I brushed my teeth last night, I can still taste his salty vile cum on my tongue.

I stayed in the large tub for over an hour after Kyle finally left last night, hoping the delicious hot water would burn away the itching disgust I feel spreading across my skin. No matter how much agony my broken body is in, it's nothing compared to the break in my soul. I thought I'd escaped this cycle of abuse, I thought I was free, but now I'm right back to where I started. I want to fight back. I want to fight for the life I've built with Kellan and Hallie, but I can't. Years of training, learning that I'll be punished more severely if I don't do as I'm told, it brought my submissive side back to the surface.

I'm not the same person as I was the last time I was here. I'm not truly submissive. He can intimidate me, cause me pain, or try to break me, but I have so much more to fucking live for this time. I don't know exactly how I'll get out of here, but you can bet I'm not going to just sit here and allow Kyle to win. I will get free and I will get back to my family. Yet, for now, I need to make him think that I'm on board, that he has control over me. So when I do fight back, he won't ever see me coming.

"I'm sorry, Sir. I'm just very tired this morning. It was a long night last night," I speak quickly, trying to ensure he doesn't punish me further. Last night I couldn't even sit on my ass. When Kyle got bored with spanking my ass using his hand, he rained the last few blows down on my ass and upper thighs using his belt, drawing blood in a few places. So it's not surprising that sitting down is so fucking painful today.

"Good, Little Bunny. I'm glad you learnt your lesson last night. Now, I know we aren't supposed to see each other on our wedding day, but I don't believe in that sort of bullshit. I know our marriage will be a success, why would it not? Anyway, in the next couple of hours I will be sending in a girl who I've worked with before. She'll come in and do your hair and make-up and will get you ready for the wedding. But, before she gets here, I want you to shower, and remove all the hair from your body. In just a couple of hours, you will be my wife, and I want to make sure you look your best. Do you have any questions?" he asks, like I have a choice in this shitshow. But, I decide to try, just in case.

I take a deep breath, embracing the sharp stabbing pain in my ribs that I'm used to now. "Can I ask about the wedding, Sir? How big is it going to be? Will any of my friends be invited?" I maintain the eye contact Kyle insists on, and give him a small smile, trying to show him I'm embracing the wedding.

"It'll be held here, and all of my family and friends will be here. I think there will be around sixty people coming, if not more. It's a bit last minute, so not everyone can get here. I would have invited some of your friends, if I trusted them not to ruin the wedding. I'm sorry, Little Bunny. I will be inviting your father. He'll believe he's coming to discuss our situation, but once he's here, I'll update him. I figured you'd want your father to walk you down the aisle. Are you happy I thought to give you this gift?" That sick, sadistic smile on his face appears genuine, and I have to school my features so he can't see what I'm really thinking. This asshole genuinely believes this is my dream wedding. I hate my father and there's no fucking way, if I was really getting married—I try not to think about Kellan when I think about what my real wedding would be like—but, I can tell you this for sure, my father would be the last fucking person on the invite list.

I quickly respond in the fake, cheerful voice I know he expects. "That is so thoughtful of you. I will be sad that Bree won't be here, though. Is there any way we could make this happen?"

"No!" he snaps, and I flinch, waiting for the blow that thankfully doesn't come. "Sorry, Little Bunny, but it won't be possible. I just don't trust her not to try and ruin our wedding. Once we're married and settled into our lives together, I will revisit this, but for now I believe she's a bad influence on you."

I don't bother to reply, I simply smile and nod my head, letting him know I support his decision. He's right, if Bree was here, she would burn the world down to make sure she got me out of here. So, as much as it pains me, Kyle's actually being incredibly smart. I'm going to have to think of another way to escape. I'm holding out hope that Kellan will find me. He'll leave no stone unturned until he finds me and brings me home. Once I get home, you can bet your fucking life I won't ever leave again.

Kyle holds out his arms, indicating that I'm to go to him, and I waste no time because I know exactly what will happen if I don't follow his commands. I crawl across the bed, ignoring the pain that ricochets all over my body, trying to keep my face neutral. This sadistic asshole takes pleasure in seeing my pain, so I'll do everything I fucking can to avoid him getting that power.

Once I'm at the edge of the bed, he pulls me into his arms, and presses his lips against mine. I freeze, closing my eyes to try and block everything out, but he places his hand on the back of my neck and pulls me even closer. His kiss is bruising and his tongue pushes through my closed, unmoving lips. When Kyle realises I'm not reciprocating his affection, he pauses. I hear the slap of his hand against my ass cheek before I feel the pain. It's so much worse than a spank would normally be because his hand lands directly on the bruises and welts that already sting from last night. I know what he wants and so I open my mouth and kiss him back. I try to close myself off, to think of other things, but thinking of my happy place, of Kellan and Hallie, while this man is kissing me, just feels wrong. So I imagine fighting him. I think about all the ways I could fight against him, and all the ways I will kill him when I get the chance. I also make a mental note to get Kellan, Liam, and Bree to train me when I get back home. I never want to be this helpless fucking damsel in distress ever again. I want to know how to fight, how to kill, because if I ever get taken again, I need to know how to hold my own. I'm done being the submissive little walk over these men clearly think I am.

After Kyle finishes kissing me for a few minutes, making sure he gets a good grope of my ass in the meantime, he pulls away, looking at me with the same dark eyes. "I'm going to go and get everything ready for our perfect day. Make sure you get yourself ready. I will not marry you if you're anything less than perfect, do you understand?" he asks, and I reply with the usual acknowledgement that pleases him. He walks towards the door, freezes, and turns towards me. "The girl will be here in about an hour. See you soon, Little Bunny."

He turns and leaves, and I waste no time doing as I'm told. I go to the bathroom and brush my teeth as many times as I can, until my gums start to bleed. No matter what I do, I can't rid my mouth of his taste. Hopefully, a scalding hot shower will burn away my shame.

After showering and shaving to Kyle's standard, I towel myself dry and wrap my hair in a smaller towel. I walk back into the bedroom, and once I'm dry, I assess the damages in front of the mirror. I gasp at the reflection I see before me. There's black, purple, and blue bruising covering my right side and across my abdomen.

Along the tops of my thighs on the front and back there are red welts, no doubt from the belt, along with what looks to be scabs from where the belt buckle sliced open the skin. You can see handprints across my ass. There's also crescent-shaped piercings across my hips and arms, accompanied by small bruises that are consistent with a hand gripping me tight enough that his nails punctured my skin.

Quickly I run to the wardrobe, pulling out the longest T-shirt I can find, pulling it over my body. I can't bear to look at the damage he's caused. It just reminds me of how fucking weak I am. I curl up into a ball on the bed, trying to comfort myself as best I can, when the door swings open. I don't bother lifting my head, I know who it will be. It's the start of the worst day of my life.

A deep, rumbly voice I recognise as belonging to Kyle's bodyguard, Lionel, speaks. "Mia, this is your assistant for the day. She is not our usual girl, so I want to make it very fucking clear, I will not tolerate any nonsense. You have two hours to get Mia ready, and I would appreciate it if she's ready early. I will not tolerate tardiness. It's my job to get her to the altar on time, and you will not fuck that up. Do I make myself very clear?"

Both myself and the girl mumble agreements, but I don't bother looking up. I hear Lionel moving towards the door, but the girl stops him. "Sir, I don't mean to cause any problems, but in order to get her ready for this wedding, please do I have permission to give her some medication. She's clearly in pain, and if I can help take the pain away, then that will help me get her ready quicker." Fuck, I hope Lionel says yes, because I'm in so much fucking pain.

"Fine, but I don't want her high as a kite. None of the hard stuff." As soon as Lionel has finished speaking, he slams the door closed, and I hear the lock clicking. Now we are both locked in here.

I feel the bed dip beside me, and a gentle hand touches my shoulder. I think it's supposed to be reassuring, but I can't help but flinch away. I can't bear to have anyone touch me. I look up, and as soon as my gaze locks on the woman sitting beside me, my eyes widen in shock.

"You?" It's all I manage to squeak out, not entirely sure what else to say. I thought this woman had ruined my life enough, but now she's here to dig the knife in. Fucking Shayla!

Scurrying away from Shayla, I climb off the bed, desperate to put some distance between us. Her face crumbles to sadness, and I'm so fucking confused. "Mia, I know you don't trust me, but I promise you, I'm not working with Kyle. I'm here to get you out safely. Kellan knows I'm here, and it won't be long until he arrives, along with his small army, to help get you out of here."

"Why the fuck would you help me? You ruined my life," I spit, anger bubbling under the surface, and I can't even feel sorry for her when Shayla's face drops with shame.

"I'm so sorry. I should have listened to you. Fuck, I know I shouldn't have interfered in your life. Please believe me when I say I was acting in Hallie's best interests. I was raised by abusers, and my childhood was a shitstorm. Everything I've ever done, all the pain I've put people through, it has always been for Hallie. I didn't leave her because I wanted to, I did it to keep her safe. Everything I've ever done is to keep Hallie safe. I have experience of working with Whitlock. I know exactly what he's capable of, and I don't want someone like him in her life. When you said you weren't in his life, I should've believed you. I'm so sorry. I know there's no way I can give you back the time I took from you and Kellan, but I sure as fuck will do my best to get you out of here, so you can live your lives together," Shayla explains, sadness and shame lacing every word.

I have no idea if I should believe her, but right now, she's my only hope of getting out of here. There's a whole fucking lot that we need to discuss, and she's going to have to prove herself before I start to trust her, but I'm willing to try. I don't have a whole host of options right now.

"Okay...well, if we can start with the pain relief, then I'll hear this plan of yours to get me the fuck out of here. I can't trust you right away, but I sure as fuck am going to give you the chance to prove yourself. Get me the fuck out of here, then we can talk. Agreed?" I ask, stepping towards Shayla as a smile spreads across her face. She reaches over to her bag that's sitting on top of a suitcase, it looks like the type a mobile beautician would carry, and she pulls out a pill bottle. She shakes a couple loose and hands me them along with a bottle of water. My gaze flits between looking at the pills and looking at Shayla, unsure whether I should take them or not.

Seeing the distrust on my face, she holds out the bottle for me to read. As soon as I see the word 'codeine', I'm reassured she is only giving me strong pain killers, and I swallow two instantly. Once I've done that, I look at her, raising my eyebrow in question, silently asking where we go from here.

"Right, now we get ready for the wedding. I know it doesn't seem like a plan, but it is. I need Kyle to think that everything is going exactly as he planned. In reality, Kellan and his team will be getting ready, waiting for the exact moment to strike. I've sent them all the information they need from the inside. It won't be long, Mia, until your rescue party arrives. But until then, it's business as usual. Okay?"

I nod my head and allow myself to hope for just a moment. I imagine Kellan getting everything organised, and all my friends banding together to come and rescue me. I've always believed they would come for me, I just hope they get here and do it before I have to marry this asshole. I would much prefer to kill him.

Kellan

We're all gathered in the living room, everyone is shouting out plans or suggestions, while the others bat them down as stupid or not feasible ideas. I simply pace around the living room, listening to what everyone has to say, but at the same time my brain is working continuously, evaluating and analysing everything I've done so far. Trying to think of what I've missed. Any little clue I may have overlooked that could help me find her. But there's nothing.

A buzz vibrates in my pocket, and I pull it out instantly, praying that it's Mia. That she's been able to find a phone to ask for help. The number is unknown, and I open it as quickly as I can.

Obviously I have no reason in this world to trust her, but I don't hesitate even for a second before I click on the link. My phone would alert me if she was attempting to do anything dodgy. All it does is take me to a secure server with a couple of links. I open the one that says 'open me first' and it looks like a letter.

Kellan,

First of all, I want to apologise for interfering in your life. I should never have done that. I have my reasons, and I will share them when the time is right, but for now, please know that I'm trying to make amends.

I've found Mia, and I've gone undercover to get you the information you'll need to come and get Mia. As soon as it's safe, I'll email you everything you need. Please promise me you won't make a move on the location before I tell you. You could be putting a lot of lives, mine and Mia's included, in danger. Please, I know you have no reason to, but trust me on this one. I want to get Mia home to you and Hallie. Please let me do this. I'm sorry for all the hurt I've caused you. This is my meagre attempt at putting things right.

The next couple of links contain details of where I am and who has taken Mia. It will give you all the information you need to prepare. The files are password protected, and I will share the password with you when you need to access them. Until then, I need you to stay calm. I want to get Mia out safely, and I promise I can do that. Just give me the chance.

Shayla xx

"Motherfucker!" I shout, as I try to access the other files. They're all password protected and after I try typing in a few obvious choices, I know I'm going to have to run a password detection scanner, which could take ages depending on the size of the password. I can hack in, but it will take forever. I may be left with no other choice than to trust Shayla, to wait for her.

My cursing catches the attention of the people around me, and Liam jumps up from the sofa along with Bree, asking what's happened. I decide to tell everyone at the same time, rather than having to explain myself over and over.

Once I've finished, the room erupts into shouts, as everyone has a thought on whether I should trust Shayla or not. I look to Liam for his advice, as he's the person I trust most, but he looks perplexed. "Honestly, bro, I have no idea why she would want to help you. If she means what she says, that this is her way of helping, then we have no choice but to go with it. We have no reason not to trust her."

"You mean, if we don't include the fact that she lied and abandoned Hallie and you back in Ireland," Ryleigh adds with a sneer. She's never met Shayla, but she hates her nonetheless.

Finn, who is normally one of the quietest of the Doughty kids, stands up and he looks almost shy as he starts to speak. "Look, Kel, before I say this I want you to know that I don't approve of what Shayla did to you, and if it ever comes down to it, I will always side with you. I saw you as my brother before the revelation, but now you really are my brother, and I'm with you. But I haven't been totally honest with you. You know I bonded with Shayla when I came to help her get ready for the job in Ireland. We became close, and we texted a bit afterwards. I never interfered, I was just there for her to talk to me if she needed. I'm sorry if it upsets you knowing I stayed in touch with her, but I always got the impression she could use a friend. We never talked about what happened, not really, but she did tell me she believes she acted in Hallie's best interests. I don't agree with her decisions, but having gotten to know her a little over the last year, I don't think she is a malicious person. I think she is broken, and maybe this is her way of trying to fix the things she had a hand in breaking."

"You kept in touch with her after what she did?" I choke out, and Finn just drops his head, looking almost embarrassed.

"I'm sorry. I genuinely believe she needed a friend," Finn explains, but my anger is already bubbling over. Hearing this is the tipping point.

"That didn't have to fucking be you, did it? How the fuck could you do this to me?" I shout, pacing towards Finn, who seems to almost cower. Fuck, does he think I'm going to attack him?

I look down to see my hands are curled into fists, my rage causing my face to distort, and I hate the guy I'm turning into. I would never hit any of my family, no matter how much they piss me off.

Kian, who is the closest to us, stands to act as a barrier preventing me from getting closer to Finn, and that just pisses me off even more. There's no way I would hurt Finn. "Okay, Kellan, why don't you go and sit on the sofa until you've cooled down a bit? Clearly we have no choice but to follow Shayla's demands. It's the only lead we have. We don't have to trust her, but we do have to listen to her." Kian guides me to the sofa as he speaks, and I flop down, resigning myself to the fact that he is right. Stupid, smug asshole. Who would have thought he'd be the voice of reason.

I agree to wait it out, to follow Shayla's plan, but that doesn't mean I can't start running the hacking software to crack the password, just in case. The longer I have to sit here and wait, wondering what kind of hell Mia is having to endure, my patience begins to wear thin.

After about an hour of waiting and wondering, there's a loud pounding on the door. It sounds like someone is about to break the door down. Bree goes to answer it, but both Kian and Liam push her aside, chuntering about how a pregnant woman should be trying to stay away from danger, not being the first to run towards it.

We all try to listen, to find out what's happening, but initially all we can hear is muffled voices, until the door to the living room bursts open and things become a blur. The next thing I realise, the large man who burst into the room strides straight over to where I'm standing, grabs my T-shirt in a large fist, and pushes me against the wall.

"Where the fuck is Shayla?" Whiskey shouts, his leather Celtic Reapers MC cut prominent over his muscular body.

Finn, Shane, Liam, and Kian rush to where I'm pressed against the wall, everyone shouting at Whiskey to let me go. The way he presses his fist against my larynx is preventing me from fully breathing. I try to focus on what he's saying, but all I can see is the fury etched across his face.

When the boys finally manage to pull him away from me, I gasp, trying to catch my breath, while Whiskey seems to collapse to the floor in a heap. Kneeling down, I lay a hand on his shoulder, and the pain I see in his eyes is something I recognise. The girl he loves is missing, potentially in danger, and I sure as fuck can relate to that. I appreciate he's scared and acting out of fear, the same way I am.

"Whiskey, I think, for once, we're both in similar situations. So, how about you put the macho bullshit aside, and we can try to work together to get our girls back?" I try to calm him down. He's obviously here for a reason, and all I can think is that Shayla led him here, which means I need to know whatever he knows.

"Fuck! I just don't understand how she's ended up in this mess. No offence, Kellan, but I thought you were long gone from our lives. I've only recently managed to get Shay back on the right track. She's starting to enjoy life, after spending months in a black hole. I'm starting to get her free from the Reapers who have terrorised her, and then she gets caught up in this bullshit. Ever since your fucking mother and her custody case, it brought it all back. She barely survived leaving the first time, and I think she'll risk her life to make things right for you." Whiskey's voice sounds desperate, like all the fight is leaving his body.

"No offence to you, Whiskey. I thought you were gone from my life, too. I'm finally happy, and I have no idea if Shayla is at all responsible for what's happening with Mia. All I know is that Shay has a plan to get her back for me. I received an email from her about an hour ago. I'll share what I know with you, but in return, I need your help. Our girls are together, and we need to work together to get them back." I take my phone from my pocket, load the link that Shayla sent me, and I hand it over to Whiskey. He takes a moment to read what she sent me, and his eyes widen.

"Well…this message makes sense now. I received it from Shay a couple of hours ago, and it gave me your name and this address. It basically says you need my help and we need to work together to put her plan into action. This email came through just a few minutes ago, and before you ask, I haven't spoken to Shayla. It appears these messages are on a timer, to be sent at specific times." Whiskey hands over his phone as he explains.

Whiskey,

I know you don't agree with me interfering, but after everything I've put Kellan through, I need to help him. He was finally starting to be happy, and I took that away from him. I know I thought I was acting in Hallie's best interests, but that wasn't the right decision. I shouldn't have got involved. I took the woman he loves from him, and that wasn't fair.

By now you will have received the message asking you to visit Kellan. I need your help with this. Mia has been kidnapped by a sick, twisted prick who abused her for most of her teen years. I found out he plans on forcing Mia into marrying him, and I've gone undercover to get as much info as possible.

The plan is that you, Kellan, and Kellan's friends will breach, but only when I tell you to. There are a lot of innocent people here for the wedding, and all our lives will be put in danger if you enter the property before I tell you to.

I've sent over to Kellan the floor plans to the estate and my plan. There are three links in total and you need to give Kellan these passwords:

1 - Halliebear
2 - Tothemoonandback
3 - KellanandMia

Please work together. You've done it before, and I know you will keep him safe. Don't mistake this as love for Kellan. He will always hold a special place in my heart, but he's nothing compared to you.

I love you with all my heart, Jamieson. I know you will come and help me save Mia because it's the right thing to do. I walked away and left Hallie without a mother once, this is my chance to give her back the mum she deserves.

All my love,
Shay xxx

Fuck! I'm literally lost for words as I read the message on Whiskey's phone. I've spent the last nine months hating Shayla for what she put me and Hallie through, and I didn't even think about her reasons for acting that way. As far as I'm concerned, there's no reason for her to abandon her daughter and I won't forgive her for it. But actually, present madness excluded, things have worked out for the best for us all. She found her happiness and I found mine.

Without wasting any time, I pull the links up on my phone and using the passwords Whiskey gave me, I open up the files Shay sent. "Motherfucker!" I yell, when it suddenly hits me who has Mia, and I'm pissed that we didn't even consider him.

"It's fucking Kyle Fratacello that has her. Why did we not even suspect that cuntwaffle?" I ask, speaking to the entire room. Everyone's gaze seems to be flitting towards someone else, and I know that we are all to blame. Particularly Bree, Liam, Kian, and me. We had a meeting with Kyle. We knew how much he wanted Mia, yet we thought our threats had worked. We never even considered he was a danger.

"I'm sorry, Kel. We haven't heard anything from him since our meeting, not a word, and so I thought our threats had worked. I don't know why the fuck we didn't consider him," Bree says, her voice thick with emotion as she reaches out to grab my hand to help me up off the floor. I take her hand, but I pull myself up. I can't have a pregnant girl pulling me up.

"I didn't rule him out. He was part of the research I did yesterday. I spoke to his father who reassured me that Kyle had no intention of going against Bree. So, either Kyle's dad doesn't know about it, or he lied to us. Either way, the Fratacello family are living their last day," Kian explains, as he runs his hands through his hair and begins to pace. Much to my surprise, Freya stands up and holds her hand out to stop him from pacing. She gently strokes her arm down his side, and I almost feel as though I'm interrupting a private moment.

"Kian, you're not to blame," she says, before turning to address the whole room. "None of you are to blame for this. This is all Kyle. I think what you all need to do is communicate and come up with a plan. It sounds like Kellan and…I'm sorry, I don't know your name." Freya looks at Whiskey with a wince, and I forgot that most people in the room won't have a fucking clue who the big biker is.

"Sorry, everyone, this is Jamieson, but he goes by Whiskey. He's a member of the Celtic Reapers MC, and the husband of Hallie's birth mother, Shayla." As I explain, gasps fill the room, everyone looking at Whiskey like they aren't sure if a Reaper can be trusted or not. Paddy has been tracking the Reapers, keeping us updated on whether they are a threat or not. I personally have tried to keep away from hearing anything Reaper-related, but I've heard talk of a mutiny. The new generation, led by Whiskey, are getting ready to make their move against the sick fucks who currently run the MC. Can't say I won't be glad to see the back of them.

Freya smiles, and continues with what she had been trying to say. "Sorry, Whiskey. As I was saying, I think you and Kellan have a lot of information, and if you share it, and we all work together, we can bring everyone home safely. So why don't we put all the information on the table and come up with a plan?"

Almost an hour later we have gone through all the information that everyone has, and we've formulated a plan of attack. Apparently, the sick, twisted fuck thinks today is his and Mia's wedding day, and the ceremony starts in roughly two hours. Shayla's going to let us know the exact time to breach and where, so she can try and make it as safe as possible. It looks like Kyle has planned the wedding down to every detail, and his security is tighter than ever before. Luckily, the stupid fuck has invited people to the wedding, which means there will be a short time window when most of the security guards will be distracted screening the guests. They're only being admitted ten minutes before the wedding starts, which means Mia will be in position. The plan is a good one, the only problem is that the wedding is in Liverpool, and we are in London. Even if we broke every speed limit, there's no way in hell we can get there in two hours.

We all sit there, head in hands while we try to think of a solution. Bree, who's been typing furiously on her phone, suddenly yells in excitement. "I've just spoken to Gramps. Thankfully, he's here in London, which means so is his helicopter. If we can get to his downtown building, which is about ten minutes away, he'll make sure the pilot is there to fly us to Liverpool. We'll be there in plenty of time. The problem is, the helicopter only holds six people."

Everyone looks around, counting who should come and who should stay behind. Liam is the first to speak. "Obviously Kellan and Whiskey are going to take the first two spots. Then me and Kian will take three and four. We don't need to take anyone else if nobody wants to come."

Bree looks like she is about to say something, but Whiskey cuts her off. "My friend Joker is here. I would prefer for him to have a seat. For all of you, Mia is your priority, and that's fine. But I need someone there with me, who will be there for Shayla. Please, it's only fair."

Bree nods. "I agree. I think that's more than fair. So, I will take the last seat." The look on Bree's face is fierce and unwavering. She's determined to be on that helicopter, and there's a million reasons why she shouldn't, but I don't bother saying anything. I see the looks of concern on Liam's and Kian's faces, and I wait for one of them to take the risk.

Liam steps in front of his wife and places his hand on her very tiny bump. If I didn't know she was pregnant, I would think she was just a little bloated, but knowing he's holding his hand over their future kid, it's almost painful to watch. Bree's face softens slightly as Liam places his other hand against her cheek. "I know I shouldn't ask you to sit this one out, but I am asking. I can't go into battle worrying about you, Bree. If you're there with me, that's exactly what I'd be doing. I'd be worried about you and our little peanut. So please, for me, don't go."

Kian steps forward and speaks before Bree gets a chance to answer Liam. "I'm with Liam on this, boss lady. My job is to keep you safe. When I go into this, I can't be worrying about protecting you."

Bree gently places her lips against Liam's, before pulling away with a small smile on her face. "I'm pissed as hell at you two right now, but I get what you're saying. So, let's compromise. I want the last seat on the chopper. I promise not to take part in the job, I will stay as far away as possible from any danger, staying in the helicopter the whole time. But, when you find Mia, I need to be there for her." Her voice breaks at the end and the emotion fills the room.

"I think that's more than fair. Can Paddy arrange transport home for an extra two, since we will have Shayla and Mia when we are done?" I ask, and Bree nods her head.

"He is working on it as we speak. By the time we land in Liverpool, he will have a plan."

"Right. Let's get going then," I say, and everyone stands in a blur of movement and activity. They all disperse into different directions, gathering what they need for the job. I make my way over to Hallie to say goodbye.

The helicopter touches down literally around the corner from the Fratacello house, which is good because we have just thirty minutes before the ceremony is due to start. The flight took just over an hour, and even though I feel like we're actually doing something, sitting down is hard. I have no option but to think about what kind of situation we'll be walking into. What kind of pain Mia has suffered while I've been unable to help her. The idea that this asshole thinks he's going to marry my girl, sends me into a rage. I need to make sure he never gets a chance to hurt Mia again.

Exactly thirty minutes before the ceremony is due to start, just as we are landing, my phone buzzes to indicate a new notification. Opening up my phone, I find a new link has appeared from Shayla. It's password protected again, and I look over at Whiskey, to see he's also received a message.

Once the helicopter has landed, we swap information and I don't hesitate to log in. She's managed to get me backdoor access to the Fratacello security system, and it's also a blueprint of the house. The note only says that no matter what we see, no matter how much my instinct tells me to breach early, Shayla begs me not to act before she sends me a sign.

"How the fuck will we know what the sign is?" I ask Whiskey, reading through all the information again to make sure I haven't missed anything.

Whiskey simply smiles as he takes his phone off me. "I know my wife, Kel. I will know what the sign is."

Well, that's pretty fucking vague. But, I guess I have no choice but to trust him.

Opening my laptop, I get the security feed set up and curse myself for only bringing one laptop. The house is fucking huge, and there are numerous security cameras with important things going on. But, because I only have one screen, I'm limited by which I can show first. I must have voiced this concern aloud as Liam replies, "I know this is hard, bro, but you have to take Mia out of the equation. This is just any other job for us, and we have done fuckloads of them. Let's scout the footage the way we would any other job. Methodically, do the external grounds, move through the front door, and sweep each floor in a clockwise motion, the way we would if we're going in for real. We will find Mia when you do the sweep, but we also need to assess any danger before we even think of stepping foot through the door. There are civilians in there who have no idea what they're in the middle of. Nobody can lose their life today. Understand?"

I nod and thank him for helping my brain to stay focused. When I'm anxious like this, my brain isn't always able to focus.

Everyone huddles around the screen as I do the walk through. I try not to go too fast, and with each new camera I bring up, we all discuss the security of the house and things we need to be aware of. We're planning how we can move through the house, who will take out which security guards, and how we then go about getting the girls out. Thankfully, the wedding appears to be set up in the sunroom at the back of the house. The guests appear to be entering through the side gate, keeping the house relatively free from civilians, with the exception of the staff who were catering the event.

It isn't until we get up to the top floor that I finally find Mia. She's in a plain-looking bedroom and Shayla's with her. I watch on the computer screen as Mia stands in front of the mirror, and all I can see is my beautiful girl dressed in a stupidly large, poofy wedding dress. I'm not going to deny that she doesn't look fucking stunning in the gown, but even if I didn't know that this wedding was a massive fucking sham, I would have known she didn't pick the dress. Mia is so petite, and she's always said she would prefer a smaller, more form-fitted dress. I know this because Bree and Mia made us sit through far too many fucking episodes of *Say Yes to the Dress* while they were prepping for Bree's wedding. It never occurred to me how fucking much I want to see Mia in a wedding dress, but not like this. I want her to be in the dress of her choosing, walking down the aisle towards me and Hallie. Not like this.

I try to zoom the camera in as much as I can, but they're fucking shoddy cameras, and I'm unable to properly assess whether Mia is unhurt or not. Regrettably, once I've assessed that she and Shayla are both alive and well, we continue the rest of the scan. Once we've finished, there's only around fifteen minutes before the ceremony is due to start, and Shayla made it clear that we would be breaching in approximately five minutes' time.

Bree takes control, directing each of us and assigning roles for how we'll enter, and what all our jobs will be. "Kellan, do you want to breach or provide guidance from here? Nobody's better at manning multiple security cameras and providing instructions than you are. I personally think you will be most useful here, but I won't ask you to stay behind if you don't want to."

My heart races, I knew eventually I'd have to make this decision, but now the time is here, I'm so fucking lost. Bree is right. Strategically, I would be better suited to running the command centre, keeping an eye on the CCTV, and guiding people from here. But, my heart couldn't fucking disagree more. I need to be in there. I need to get to Mia, and I need to make sure Kyle never torments her ever again.

"Kel, Bree won't tell you what to do, but I will. For the safety of each of us, I need you to stay here. I know why you want to be in there, and I can promise you, not just as your best friend, but as your brother, I will make sure Kyle has breathed his last breath. As soon as Mia is safe, we will get her straight out here and get her to you. Please, monitor the CCTV and keep us safe, and in return we will get Mia out safely," Liam says, his hand on my shoulder as he matches my gaze.

I know he can see the fear and the anger in my eyes. My breath hitches when he addresses the fact that we are legitimate brothers. It's something we haven't had a chance to talk about yet, and we will probably need a fuck-tonne of therapy to deal with that shit in the near future, but to hear him address it makes my heart swell. It feels like I finally have the family I've always hoped for. Now I need to trust Liam to bring home the girl I love and complete our family.

"I swear to God, Liam, you better get her out safely. Promise me." My breath hitches and I hate how much the emotion clogs my voice. Bree places her hand on mine, giving me a small smile to let me know she feels exactly the same way. Her instinct is to run in there, guns blazing, and destroy anyone and everyone who stands in her way. This is what she does, and she is fucking better at it than me.

Liam promises me that he'll do his best, like always. With that, we all sit and repeat the plan, making sure everyone knows their role. I watch as people file into the sunroom and begin taking their seats. It appears that the last of the guests have entered, and security is moving into position around the sunroom. There are now very few security guards manning the grounds. Stupid fucker, he's moved all his team to one room, which is where Kyle appears to be heading, leaving the vast proportion of the house unprotected.

As I watch Kyle moving through the house, another link appears on my phone. Opening it, I find Shayla has sent me the information I need to take control of the security alarms. I actually didn't need it, as I'd already run one of my programs to make sure I have control over it.

"There. Look, Shayla's giving us the signal," Whiskey shouts, pointing at the small window I have open at the bottom of the screen, keeping an eye on the girls. I make the window bigger and see a security guard opening the door to the girls' room. Whilst he's unlocking the door, Shayla stands squarely in front of the camera, and holds a shot glass up. She appears to be saying something, so I activate the sound, and Shayla's voice echoes loudly out of the laptop speakers.

"We should toast your wedding. I personally love a shot of Whiskey. In fact, I love a whole load of Whiskey, and I can't wait to get more. I need it now!" Shayla shouts, holding the glass up to the camera.

Whiskey chuckles. "I told you I would know the sign."

"Right, gear up, we need to go now," Kian shouts, as everyone rushes around gathering up the weapons and security vests they need. Bree keeps her eye on the security feed, while I get everyone's communication devices up and running. Once I've made sure they're all working, the guys leave the helicopter and run around the corner to the house.

I take the laptop into my hands and begin altering the security footage, cutting down the alarm, so we can freely access the house.

From then it's a blur of movement as Liam, Kian, Whiskey, and Joker breach the house. They move with expert precision, like they're a well-oiled machine, instead of a hastily put together group of people who barely know each other. But, they all have a common goal, to get the girls out of there without anyone getting hurt.

I keep my eye on the monitor, giving them directions and warnings whenever I see someone approaching. They all have silencers on their guns, since the aim is to get into the wedding unnoticed, and loud gunshots would definitely cause people to panic. Out of the corner of my eye, I see the security guard walking Mia and Shayla through the house. For a short period of time, he goes off camera, using a back staircase that doesn't appear to have a working camera covering it.

Cursing, I let Liam know, and the decision is made that we can't extract them from a blind spot. We have to have visuals so we can assess the risk. For all we know, the blind spot is deliberate and he's trying to draw us into a trap. I mean, I highly doubt that given the vast majority of Kyle's men are manning the main wedding ceremony room, but we have to consider everything.

It's not long before the girls reappear on camera and they're in the room just next to the sunroom. There's only two ways into the sunroom; the external door that all the guests have used, and that leads out to the garden, or the internal door that leads into a type of dining room. That is where Mia and Shayla now are. The security seems to be split between those doors, with the occasional person manning the perimeter. Everyone else has been taken out by the team.

Joker appears to have taken control of the staff, moving them all into the kitchen and locking them in there. He is treating them as hostile civilians, as he doesn't want any of them to raise the alarm. We will get them all out safely afterwards.

I watch as the guys move closer, until finally they're around the corner from Mia's room. Once they round this corner they will be faced with several security guards, and I doubt they'll be able to extract the girls without anyone noticing. Liam gives everyone some last-minute instructions via the communication devices they're wearing in their ears, and they get ready to go. They're just waiting for my signal. I want the security guard to turn his back, and given the way he's pacing, it won't be long until he does that. It's the only way they will get the element of surprise.

Just as I'm about to give the warning, the door to the sunroom opens, music begins to play and the security guard indicates it's time for Mia to walk down the aisle. All eyes are on the room Mia is in, meaning there's no way we're going to have the element of surprise now. Shayla has obviously come to the same conclusion as she looks straight at the camera and mouths the word, "Now!"

"We have lost the element of surprise. You're going to have to go in, all guns blazing. Go now!" I shout, and the guys waste no time at all.

Liam goes around the corner first and ducks so he's kneeling down, and Kian is behind him in a flash. At the same time they both shoot their weapons and the first two security guards drop to the floor. Their bodies create a loud bang, and all eyes travel to the open door. Joker and Whiskey run around the boys and begin brawling with four security guards that have rushed to the door. There are people everywhere, moving at such speed as they battle it out. I watch as the bodies fall, making sure none of them belong to our team. At the same time, I keep my eye on the girls.

Kyle, along with three of his men, is fighting to get through the mass of people that are all panicking and trying to flee from the battle. Thankfully, their panic stops Kyle from getting to Mia. He's obviously instructed a few of the guards nearest to her to make sure she's kept safe.

I watch as Shayla catches the security man closest off guard. She kicks him in the bollocks, and as he bends over in what I'm sure is blinding agony, she lands a couple of blows to his head, knocking him down for good. Once he is down she picks up his weapon, and using the technique I taught her, she checks if the gun is loaded and gets it ready to be fired. She then pushes a terrified-looking Mia into the corner of the room, and puts her body between Mia and the action.

I have had a lot of bad things to say about Shayla after what she did to me, and I didn't think I would ever be capable of forgiving her, but that action right there just put her a lot fucking closer. She is using her body to protect the woman I love, and I couldn't be more fucking grateful.

I try to keep my eye on the carnage, but there's so much going on. You would think we have a whole army on our side, rather than four ruthless guys, but as each member of the opposition falls, there's no doubt that our team has the upper hand. Each guy methodically takes out all of the security that charges them. They don't even have to move forward, Kyle has been instructing his men to charge them, which is working out in our favour as the guys are able to hold their positions, supporting each other as they take the men out.

"Liam, all of the security are now in your vicinity. There's a few manning the external sunroom door, a few with Kyle in the sunroom, the rest are in Mia's room or guarding the internal door to the sunroom. But there's only around ten left." I aim the update at Liam, but I know everyone can hear me.

"I'm going into the dining room. Kellan, where are the girls so I know where to avoid?" asks Whiskey, who is closest to the door into the dining room.

"When you go in through the door, they are in the north-east corner. Shayla is armed and is attempting to keep two security guards away from them. She appears to have the situation under control."

Whiskey chuckles. "That's my girl."

He then charges into the room, pushing his way past the two guards blocking the door, and while they are distracted by Whiskey, Joker takes them out, clearing the doorway for the rest of the boys to follow. Whiskey starts shooting, and again as everyone converges into the dining room from both sides it's a blur of bodies, and as much as I try, I'm struggling to keep up with the action.

Kyle's voice rings out loud as he shouts to get everyone's attention. "Stop right now, or you will regret it!"

Everyone freezes instantly, and I watch as the guys scan the room, trying to identify where the noise is coming from. I follow the sound until I see my worst fears being played out before me. Kyle is standing in the corner of the room with Mia tucked in one arm, while he holds a gun to her head with the other. Shayla is next to him, blood running down her face, the gun that was once in her hand is now long gone, and Kyle's bodyguard has her secured against him, a knife to her throat.

"Kyle, think very carefully before you do this," Liam says, his voice steady and even while he tries to negotiate. I look over at Bree and see the matching fear in her eyes. She turns away from me and begins rummaging through the boxes we brought with us in the helicopter. I can't watch what she is doing as I'm too busy staring at the hostage situation on the screen.

"Oh, I'm thinking very carefully. I want to marry Mia, and nothing you do will stop that. My father's next door along with the registrar.

You may have scared off all the guests, but it doesn't matter to me. I will marry Mia today, no matter what," spits Kyle, and I check the cameras for the adjoining room to confirm what he's saying. His father, along with two bodyguards I'm assuming are allocated to Mr. Fratacello, are in the corner of the sunroom, alongside the registrar.

I'm so focused on Mia, looking at all the cuts and bruises that are littered across her exposed skin, and the way she is barely holding herself upright, and it breaks my heart. My broken girl looks defeated and I'm so consumed by her, I miss the second wave of security that arrived from the dead zone that I couldn't see on the cameras earlier. Around ten men all charge into the room and one by one they pull Liam, Kian, Joker, and Whiskey away from the dining room. They're trying to drag them out long enough to get the registrar in to perform this shitshow of a wedding, and it seems to be working.

Once Kyle is sure that the guys have been pulled in from the sunroom, he shouts for his father to bring in the registrar. The guys are fighting hand-to-hand now, having run out of ammunition. Fear is etched on my face as I look over at Bree. She has pulled the last remaining gun from the gun storage and is starting to put on a safety vest.

"No way!" I shout at her, as I snatch the vest from her hand. "There are already two girls in danger in there, Liam won't forgive me if I let you risk yours and your baby's life. Mia would never want that either. The majority of the work here is done. I know where all the remaining security is. I'm going," I explain as I pull the safety jacket over my head and grab the gun from her.

Bree looks torn, like she wants to argue with me but she knows she can't. "I'm very pissed right now that I'm pregnant and can't help. But I'm not risking this baby's life. You've got this, Kellan. There's only six bullets left in this gun, and no extra ammunition. Use them wisely." Bree pulls me in for a quick hug before practically pushing me out of the helicopter.

"I will bring them all back safely," I shout as I run off in the direction of the house.

I'm met instantly by two guards, who I take out without even a moment's hesitation. My heart races as I bring up a blueprint of the house in my head, and mentally instruct myself the safest way to get to the action. I don't know exactly where the guys have been dragged off to, but I can hear sounds of scuffles in the rooms next to the dining room. As I approach down the corridor, I'm met by two more security guards. They are manning the door, and in a move that I saw Liam and Kian do not ten minutes earlier, I turn the corner, crouch down and shoot, catching both guards by surprise. They drop like flies, but I'm very aware I now only have two bullets left.

I approach the door slowly, keeping my back to the wall so that nobody can catch me unawares. Keeping low the way Liam did, I slowly move into the dining room. I manage to get all the way into the room before one of Kyle's father's bodyguards spots me and raises his gun to aim at me. I don't even hesitate, I shoot before he's able to shoot me. He drops to the floor, blood spilling from the wound in his chest.

I quickly assess the situation. Kyle's father, the registrar, and a bodyguard are in the north-west corner of the room, and I can hear his bodyguard talking on his communication device asking for a team to get Mr. Fratacello out of the house. His job now is to make sure Kyle's father walks out of this alive, and so I don't think he will be much of a threat. Over in the north-east corner of the room, Kyle has a gun pointed at Mia's head, and his bodyguard has a knife at Shayla's throat.

"Fuck! I only have one bullet!" I thought I had said that in my head, but clearly I said it aloud as Kyle begins to chuckle.

"That's too bad. It looks like you're going to have to give up now. No matter who you choose to shoot with your last bullet, it will not end well for you. If you aim for me, as I suspect you will, Lionel here will slice this pretty girl's throat, while Malcolm—my father's bodyguard—will shoot Mia here. Then once you have watched her bleed out slowly, my father will exact his revenge by killing you slowly. So, I would think very carefully about your next move." He sounds like a psychopathic lunatic, something I'd definitely not thought after our last meeting. His voice almost sounds like a hiss as he threatens us all.

I look over the camera, silently asking Bree about my back up. "I'm sorry, Kel. They're all still busy. It doesn't look like it'll be long, but for now you're on your own. There's a car that's just pulled up, and from what I can tell, they're getting ready to extract Mr. Fratacello. I think it would be in your best interests to let him leave, then you only have two hostiles to deal with," Bree explains, and I nod slightly to let her know I hear her.

Bree called the situation right because Mr. Fratacello holds his hands out in a sign of surrender and drops his gun to the floor. "Look, Kellan, is it?" he asks and I nod in confirmation, my eyes continuously flitting between him and his son, making sure this isn't a trick to split my attention. "I never wanted a war with Mrs. Doughty, and I don't agree with what my son is doing right now. If Mrs. Doughty is the leader I know she is, then I'm sure she is here somewhere and can hear me."

I nod in confirmation. "She can hear you."

"Good. I would like to ask permission to leave this room. I will leave the country and I promise not to return. I understand what my son has done here will be seen as an act of war, but I want you to know I had no part in it. I didn't even know this wedding was happening until a couple of hours ago, and believe me, I've tried to talk him out of it. I know you need to end his life as punishment, and as much as I would like to beg for his life, I understand your situation. All I ask is safe passage for myself and my wife. We will go to a European country for a while. Maybe one day when the dust has settled we can start to build bridges again, but for now I appreciate the damage is done. So, Mrs. Doughty, I beg for your mercy and ask for forgiveness." Mr. Fratacello keeps his arms raised, and he speaks as though he has the utmost respect for Bree.

"What the fuck are you doing, Father?" Kyle spits, and his father turns to him, a look of pure anger spreading across his face.

"I'm trying to get your mother out of this fucking mess with our lives. You have fucked up, Kyle, and you will have to accept the consequences."

Kyle laughs manically and his hold on Mia must tighten because she yelps. I look at her, something I've been trying not to do since I entered the room. I know if I look at her and see her pain, I'll get distracted. But, the more she sobs in pain, I can't help it. Tears stroll down her face, and I do a quick scan of her body to find out why she's in pain. I see that in the hand gripping her hip, holding her against his body, Kyle has a small dagger. He clearly doesn't even realise he has it in his hand, but every time he pulls Mia against him, the knife is slicing into Mia's abdomen. Her bright white wedding dress is stained with bright red blood as the wound seems to get bigger.

Fuck! I can feel my pulse pounding in my head as I try to evaluate this shitshow of a situation. Then I hear Bree's voice over the pounding and she instructs me to repeat what she is saying aloud. "Mr. Fratacello, I'm repeating what Bree tells me word-for-word, so please take in exactly what I say." He nods and I listen for Bree to take over.

"Mr. Fratacello, I can't even begin to say how disappointed I am in this situation. The people fighting your men are my family and friends. Your son has put us in a terrible position, and you are correct in saying he will need to pay with his life. However, I'm not sure I can just let you walk away like this, with no punishment at all."

Mr. Fratacello shakes his head, the look of defeat is apparent on his face. "Apologies, Mrs. Doughty, I don't mean to offend, but let me be clear, if you allow me and my wife to leave this mess, I will not be leaving unpunished. I'm being forced to flee from the very good life I've built here. I know you will freeze most, if not all, of my assets, so I'm not even in a position to live comfortably. I'll also have to explain to all of my business partners that I'm no longer in business, which could place a very big target on my back, if you're not able to replace me quickly. But the biggest wound of all will be knowing my only son —my only child, in fact—is dead. That is a pain no parent should have to suffer."

Bree replies and I speak her words aloud. "That's something I can agree with you on. I lost a child and there's no pain like it. Unfortunately, mine was never given the chance to take its first breath. Yours, on the other hand, has put the lives of all the people I care about in danger. I cannot save him. But, I do grant you permission to leave. Go now and don't look back. But, let me make this very fucking clear, Mr. Fratacello. If you even think about double-crossing me, or about stabbing me in the back, I'll end you personally. Do you understand?"

Mr. Fratacello agrees, and along with his bodyguard and the registrar, he starts to leave. I quickly back up so my back is against the wall and I can still cover his exit and Kyle. Kyle's face drops and his eyes bug out like you see in a child's cartoon. As his father leaves the room, at first he is stunned into silence, then the rage starts. "Fuck you, Father. How dare you fucking abandon me. We were winning. We have him outnumbered. He only has one fucking bullet left. What the fuck are you thinking?" he shouts manically, his face turning feral as he spits through the snarls.

Mia's cries of agony get louder, and I see her cut is getting worse. Fuck, if I don't end him soon the wound is going to be too deep and he could cause some real fucking damage. My eyes glance between Mia and Shayla, and my heart races as I try to work out what to do. Kyle's right, whoever I shoot, there will be casualties. But now that his father and his bodyguard are no longer a factor, there's only one gun —Kyle's. If I take him out, his bodyguard can come at me with a knife, but that will give me a chance to fight him off. Either way, I need to take out the only remaining gun. The problem there is I don't know what Kyle's bodyguard will do next, and that puts Shay in a whole heap of danger. He could lay down his weapon if his boss is beat, or he could slit her throat in retaliation and charge at me. Both are very real possibilities, but I have to act.

Shay must be able to see the indecision and pain in my eyes, as she meets my gaze with a sad smile on her face. "Kellan," she starts, and the bodyguard slams his elbow into her stomach to silence her, causing a scream of pain. But, she doesn't let that stop her. When she speaks to me, I can see the pained expression on her face as her eyes fill with tears. "I understand what you have to do. Save Mia. Live a long and happy life together. But, please promise me you'll look after Hallie. Mia, I gave you my blessing to be her mum. Maybe one day you can tell her about me, that I fought for her, even when it didn't look like it. I will always love our little Hallie Bear. Please, Kellan, save your family."

Shayla manages to get the whole thing out before Lionel slams his elbow into her again. The tears that started to flow while she was talking, now they stream down her face as sobs rack her body. I know exactly what she's telling me. She's saying that I can only save one of the girls, and she gives me permission to save Mia. Shayla knows she's going to die, and she's okay with that, but I'm not.

"How fucking touching. Why don't I take the decision away from you and shoot you first?" Kyle asks, but he keeps the gun trained on Mia. If he even starts to move it in my direction, I will have no choice but to shoot him.

"Bree, is there any backup coming?" I mutter into my communication device, hoping the boys have got rid of the security guards by now and are on their way to help me.

"I'm sorry, Kellan, more arrived and I can't free one of them. Do you want me to come?" she asks, and I don't even hesitate.

"No. I've got this." Bree would be coming in blind with no weapon and no safety vest, as I took the last. We didn't bring more stuff than we needed, as the helicopter can't carry everything. I'm on my own, and unless I want Mia to bleed to death in front of me, I need to act now.

"Do it, Kellan," Shayla shouts.

Mia must see the moment I make my decision, as her scream rips through the room. "No!"

I turn briefly to Shayla and give her a small smile. "I'm sorry." As soon as the words leave my mouth I lift my gun, aim with the precision I was taught by Desmond as a kid, and I gently pull the trigger. Everything seems to happen in slow motion. The bullet travels from the barrel of the gun, aiming straight towards Kyle's head. Seeing the bullet coming, he tries to move his gun to aim at me, which is exactly what I hoped he'd do. Obviously he didn't get far before the bullet connected with his skull, smack-bang in the middle of his eyes.

Mia's scream echoes loudly as she drops into a heap on the floor, Kyle's body crumpling behind her. At first I thought it was just the terror of what she just witnessed that scared her, until I look down and see Kyle's dagger sticking out of my beautiful girl's body. Her hands are next to the knife, not really sure if she should touch it or not. I rush to her, but I don't get far before I hear another scream from beside Mia.

In all the drama, I'd almost forgotten it wasn't just Mia in the room. I look over just in time to see Shayla trying to fight back, but Lionel is jabbing at her repeatedly with his knife. Blood is squirting everywhere, and it's obvious given the amount of blood and Shay's screams that he's hitting his target. Fear freezes me. I know I need to help her, but I don't know how. That's when my brain suddenly kicks into gear.

Sliding across the floor to where Mia is crumpled on the floor, my instinct is to comfort her, but I need to make it safe first. Grabbing hold of Kyle's gun, I quickly check it's loaded, take the safety off, and aim.

Fuck, Shay's in the way. I can't get a clear shot.

"Shay. Drop, now!" I scream, and Shay reacts on instinct, dropping to the floor, her high-pitched scream echoing through the room as a loud bang overtakes it. Kyle's gun doesn't have a silencer the way all ours do, so the shot is loud, causing my ears to ring. My shot hits the target and Lionel drops to the floor behind Shayla. Once I'm sure he's dead, lying beside where Shayla is kneeling with her back to me, I finally turn to my girl.

I scoop her in my arms as gently as I can and I wipe the sweat-coated strands of hair from her face. "Fuck, Flower. I always knew seeing you in a wedding dress would be the death of me, but this is ridiculous," I joke, and thankfully Mia laughs in between her sobs.

"Oh, fuck. Kellan, don't make me laugh. It hurts. Should I take the knife out? It hurts so much," she sobs, and I quickly shake my head, putting my hands over hers to prevent her from pulling the knife out.

"No, baby. You need to keep it in until the paramedics arrive. Just stay strong please, Flower. I need you to be okay. I don't think I can live without you." All the emotion I've been holding back since I found out she went missing, come rushing forward and sobs rack my body as I hold my beautiful girl in my arms. "I thought I was going to lose you, Mia. Please, don't ever leave me."

"Shush, Kellan. I'm here and I promise I won't ever leave you again. I'm sorry I lied to you before. Of course I want to be with you. I want forever with you and Hallie, and I shouldn't have said any different. I don't want to live another day without you," Mia sobs as she gently presses her lips against mine. It's short and sweet, but fuck is it everything I've longed for.

Gasps of breath and sobs from beside me pull my attention and I turn towards Shayla. She no longer has her back towards me, and now I can see her fully, panic sets in. Blood is seeping out of three large wounds over her chest and abdomen, she has a cut that's dripping blood across the side of her neck, and she has a knife protruding from her left rib cage. It's no wonder she's gasping for breath. There's no way on this earth that knife hasn't punctured her lung.

Gently, I lay Mia down and apologise for leaving her, but she gives me a small smile and tells me to go. As I close the short distance to Shay, I shout out to Bree. "How long until the ambulance gets here. Shay is in a bad way, and I'm sure Mia isn't far behind. Fuck, Bree, we need help now."

I scoop Shayla into my arms as best I can while Bree replies. "They're only a few minutes out, Kel. I've told them to step on it."

Seeing the blood pouring out of Shay's wounds, I know I need to stop the bleeding somehow. As gently as I can without moving her too much, I take off my security vest and then my shirt. I rip it in half and press it against the two knife wounds that appear to be causing the most problems.

"Wow, I didn't think I would ever see you strip for me again. Don't tell my husband, but you aren't bad to look at," Shayla jokes, coughing up blood. I pull her close, my eyes continually looking over at Mia to make sure she's okay. She's still conscious, but she's getting pale, though not as quickly as Shay is.

"I have to tell Whiskey that, you know how much I love messing with that guy," I joke and Shay's smile breaks my heart. For a split second, all I can see is the poor, broken girl, abused by her family, who turned to me for help. The beautiful girl who helped make the most important person in my world, Hallie.

"I'm sorry for everything, Kellan," Shay starts, and I cut her off.

"Don't. You don't have to apologise." If you had told me a couple of days ago that I would say that to Shayla, and that I would mean it, I'd have told you to fuck off. But, it's true, or at least, it is while I'm fuelled by emotion and adrenaline. She's the reason I get to take my girl home, and I will forever owe her for that.

"Please, Kellan, let me get this out. We both know I'm dying and I can't go without getting this off my chest," she pleads and my eyes fill with tears.

"You aren't dying," I sob, not entirely sure I believe my own words.

"I am, and of course I wish I wasn't. I was just starting to get my shit together, to really be the Old Lady that Whiskey deserves. Please tell him how much I love him…to the moon and back." Whenever she tries to talk too much, her breathing becomes more laboured and shallow. With every cough, she splutters more blood, and my heart breaks for the girl I once thought I loved. Even if it wasn't the type of love I feel for Mia, I cared for her more than I ever had anyone else, and the love we shared made Hallie.

"You need to hold on, to tell him yourself," I cry, and she nods her head.

"Kellan, I need you to know, you were never a target. I left Hallie and you because I thought it was the only choice I had. The Reapers made it clear I'd only earned one freedom, and if I took it then Hallie had to stay with them. They said I could stay with her if I chose, but only one could leave. I couldn't have her growing up like I did. Abused, tortured, beaten daily by the people who call themselves family. She deserves a better life, and I knew you could give her that. Taking your money was payment for Hallie's freedom. I'm so sorry I didn't tell you this before, but you would have tried to fix it, and I didn't want that. I just wanted Hallie safe. You're a great dad, Kellan, and Mia will make a great mum to Hallie. You have my permission to be happy, not that you need it." It takes her a long time to get the words out, in between gasps of breath and coughing up blood. The words penetrate my soul and I feel so lost.

For the last several months, almost a year, I've spent all that time vilifying Shayla. Making her the enemy of my story, but all along she was the victim too. She's a victim of the Reapers, and everything she's ever done has been for Hallie.

My heart breaks as I think of all the awful things I thought. How many times did I wish her dead? And now she's laying in my arms, and I have to watch as the light fades from her once sparking green eyes.

"I had no idea. Shay, I'm so sorry. You have to live, you have to fight. Our little girl needs to know her mum is a fighter. I promise, when that little angel gives you a hug, you will know why you need to stay strong." I wipe the tears from her eyes and move the stray hair from her forehead.

"You would really let me see her?" she asks, hope ringing in her words.

"Yeah, I don't see why not." At first I wonder if I'm just saying this to get Shayla to fight, to give her something to live for. I've never wanted her to be part of Hallie's life before, and I know I will never give her custody or any kind of permanent access, but the odd visit I can definitely get on board with. I don't ever want Hallie growing up and thinking I kept her mother from her.

I hear a commotion coming from the doorway, and I hold Kyle's gun out, just in case the people trying to get in are a threat to us. As soon as I see it's Liam, I drop the gun and sag to the floor. If Liam's here, the threat has been neutralised and the paramedics can come in as soon as they get here, if they aren't already.

Whiskey's sob shatters through the room and I hear him before I see him running towards us. He looks at a very battered and broken Shayla in my arms and the big, strong biker disappears. In his place is a scared, young guy who's about to lose the love of his life. Without saying a word, I gently pass Shayla over to Whiskey, who takes her in his arms, and the smile that lights up her face is beautiful. There's no denying the love they share, it's almost painful to witness.

"Babe, you promised me you were going to stop putting your life in danger. I know you want to make amends, but killing yourself is not the way to do that," Jamieson cries, as he places little kisses along her forehead. Shay almost hums in appreciation, but it's getting harder for her to breathe and to keep her eyes open. I can feel her body getting colder in mine.

"Kellan has agreed I can have a cuddle from Hallie when I'm better.

So, obviously it did work," she says, sticking her tongue out at the end, which causes Jamieson to laugh, even as the tears continue to fall.

I see Liam go to Mia out of the corner of my eye, and she's looking at him and talking to him, which reassures me. I want to go to her, but right now, Shayla needs me more, and I know Mia gets that.

"Thank you," Jamieson says, and I realise he's speaking to me. "Giving Hallie up broke Shay, and she's only just starting to get her shit back together. I have plans to take down the old Reapers, and replace it with the next generation. I want to make Shay's life safer for her. But, no matter how much I rid her of her demons, you're the one that will make her day by letting her see Hallie."

"Hey," Shay says, grabbing both our attention. "Yes, Kellan saying I can see Hallie is exactly what I want to hear. But you're the one that's making my life safe. Once they are gone, we can have babies of our own, that don't have to live in fear. You are my whole world, Jamieson, and don't you ever forget that." Shayla reaches out and pulls Jamieson down to kiss her, but it's short-lived as Shay begins coughing and gasping, as she struggles to catch her breath.

Her eyes flutter into the back of her head and her body goes limp. Whiskey's cry sounds like a wounded animal, and it breaks my heart. Thankfully, the paramedics arrive and swoop in to look at both girls. They begin doing CPR on Shayla, whose heart has just stopped beating. Joker has to pull Whiskey away because he doesn't want to let go of her hand. They need to shock her, and so I take his hand from hers and grip it in my own. He looks at me, pain and anguish in his eyes, and I squeeze his hand in reassurance.

"We've got a pulse, but we need to move. Now," shouts the paramedic, and I think my heart has finally started to beat again too.

I watch as they carry Shayla away, Joker and Whiskey tailing after them, and I turn to find Mia being loaded onto a stretcher. She's paler than she was before, and she looks like she's struggling to breathe. She looks exhausted, and I rush to her, taking her hands in mine.

"I'm sorry. I didn't choose Shayla over you. I wanted to help you, but I didn't know what to do," I mutter, not entirely sure why I'm feeling the need to explain my actions, but I do feel guilty for not staying with Mia. I don't want her to think I chose Shayla because I have feelings for her, or anything like that.

"Kel, I told you to go and help her. You did a good thing. She needed your forgiveness. If anything happens to her, she'll be happier knowing you forgive her," Mia says, her voice faint and weak.

"You will always be far too good for me, Mia, but I hope you'll always have me anyway," I joke.

Mia smiles, but before she gets a chance to reply, we are interrupted by a loud beeping on the monitor. I look around to see what's going on with Shay, but she's already been taken to the ambulance. That's when my world starts to collapse in slow motion. The noise on the heart monitor is coming from Mia, and the paramedics try to move me out the way, shouting about how her heart has stopped beating and they need to restart it.

Liam pulls me out of the way, and wraps his arms around me. All I can think is 'not Mia too'. I thought Shayla was worse off, I should've been with Mia. I should have told her all the things I never got a chance to tell her. I swore once I found her I would tell her I love her, so why the fuck didn't I do it? I told myself I was waiting for the right moment, that I didn't want her to think I'm saying it just out of fear of losing her. As usual, I fucking overthought it, and now I may never get the chance to tell her. She can't die not knowing how I feel.

Sobs rack my body and each time the paramedic slams his hand down into her chest, doing CPR in an attempt to revive her, I feel like he's stabbing me in the heart. Each shock that doesn't revive her, it kills me just that little bit more.

L oud beeping wakes me up, and as I try to open my eyes, pain overwhelms me. I've never known physically moving my eyelids to be painful, but my entire body aches. There's a pounding in my head and a ringing in my ears. My mouth feels drier than the Sahara Desert, and I feel like I've slept for longer than I normally would.

As I try to force my eyelids open, to the bright lights burning my vision, I try to think back to what I last remember. My brain feels like it's shrouded in fog, and I can't physically wade through it all.

My eyelids flutter and after a few blinks I'm able to focus my vision. I try to mentally scan my body, but the pain is literally everywhere. Though there's a stabbing pain in my abdomen that feels worse than the other aches.

I scan the room and it's not difficult to work out that I'm in a hospital bed. The loud beeping is coming from the heart monitor, and

I have numerous fluid drips travelling into my arms. The pain tells me something really fucking bad happened, and I guess part of me always knew my life would wind up here.

Looking down to see if I can see any physical injuries, but instead I'm greeted by a mass of black hair laying next to my side. Kellan is sitting in one of the hospital chairs at the side of my bed, but at some point he's leaned over to rest his head on the bed, and he's fallen asleep. His hand is gripping mine, our fingers interlaced, and the warmth from his hand heats my body.

Memories start to flood back to me, like flashes of pictures in my mind that are used just to terrorise me. I see Kyle. He kidnapped me, beat me, tortured me, and sexually assaulted me. Then, he had the audacity to think I'd marry him. I thought of Kellan and Hallie. They were the people that kept me going when I didn't think I possibly could go on. All I dreamt of was getting back to them, putting things right with Kellan, and starting our lives together. For a while, I never thought we'd get that chance. I was sure Kyle was going to kill me before I got to see Kellan again.

I remember having to be separated from him, of how much I hurt him. That's when images of Shayla flash into my brain. For a while I hated her. She took everything from me for no fucking reason. Until she showed up in Kyle's bedroom, declaring she wanted to help me.

Fuck! Flashes of her with the paramedics, covered in blood as they pressed on her chest, trying to get her heart beating again. I don't remember much after that. I can't remember if they got her heart started or not. The last thing I remember for sure is the tormented scream that came from Whiskey when he saw the girl he's been in love with since he was a kid laying motionless, covered in blood. The look on Kellan's face when he pulled me into his arms, as he watched the mother of his child get carried from the room was heartbreaking.

I saw how torn he was between helping her and being with me. Obviously, I wanted to be in his arms, stealing his body heat, but I knew he needed to be with Shayla. She needed someone more than I did. Fuck, I really hope she survived. I can't deal with knowing she risked her life for me.

Squeezing Kellan's hand, his head instantly pops up. His beautiful face looks pale, and the bags under his eyes make him look even more exhausted than he normally is. There's a crease down his cheek from where the bedsheet rumpled up and pressed against him while he slept. Even with those little imperfections, when his gaze meets mine and his bright blue eyes glisten, he's never looked more fucking beautiful.

When he realises that my eyes are open, and I'm staring back at him, the smile that spreads across his face is blinding. He reaches up gently, his hand shaking slightly, like he's scared to physically touch me. He pushes a stray piece of hair away from my eyes, before leaning forward and pressing his lips to my forehead.

As he pulls back slowly, I reach up with my free hand, catching the back of his head, and pull him down to place his lips against mine. We've been apart for too long. I need to feel his lips on mine, and even though it's a small, almost innocent kiss, it speaks volumes.

"Fuck, Flower. You scared the shit out of me. Please don't ever do that again," Kellan croaks, his voice thick with emotion, as his eyes fill with unshed tears.

"Water." I reach out, trying to grab the glass of water that's just a little too far out of reach. Kellan moves quickly, reaching over to grab the glass, bringing it close enough that I could grab it. Instead, he helps guide the straw into my mouth, insisting on doing it all for me. I roll my eyes and then groan because I didn't expect such a harmless gesture to hurt so fucking much.

Taking some big gulps through the straw, I love the way the cold liquid feels against my incredibly dry mouth. After a couple of gulps, Kellan pulls the straw away, and I can't hide the evil glare I shoot his way.

"You need to take it easy, Flower. Do you need pain relief? I can grab the nurses to let them know you are awake." He starts to stand, but I tighten my hold on his hand.

"No, please don't go anywhere." I hate the terror that comes out of my mouth. Obviously, I'm in pain, and I wouldn't say no to some pain relief, but I can't bear to have him leave me when I've only just got him back.

Kellan sits back down and takes my other hand in his. "Okay, Flower. I'm not going anywhere. I just don't want you to be in pain."

I give him a small smile. "I will get them soon. I know they will make me drowsy, and I'm not ready to sleep again yet. I just want to stay with you for a bit. I need to know what happened. Is Shayla alive?"

Kellan's face scrunches and I want to reach out to straighten his face back to the beauty I love. He looks pained, like he isn't sure if he should talk about it with me or not. Letting go of his hand, I reach out to cup his cheek.

"Kellan, I'm not fragile and I'm not going to break. But I need to know."

Kellan shakes his head, and tears well up in his eyes. "That's just it, Mia. You are breakable because I saw you broken. I watched the paramedics shock your heart twice to try and get you back with us. You died, Mia, and it nearly killed me. They got you back, but rushed you into the operating theatre. You needed to have your spleen removed, and they gave you a couple of blood transfusions. You were in a medically induced coma for five days. They weaned you off the anaesthetic drugs two days ago, and I've been waiting for you to wake up ever since. Every minute of every day, I begged you to wake up. Every minute you didn't, I was forced to think about what life might be like without you. I can't even tell you how fucking painful that thought was."

My heart breaks for him as he bares his soul to me. "Kel...I'm so sorry. I've been out for seven days? What about Shay?" I mutter, shocked as it only seems like yesterday. He's gone through so much in the last week and I hate that I put him through that.

"Yeah. The longest fucking week of my life. I'm so sorry, Mia. I wish I could have saved you before you got so hurt. I tried. Shay was touch-and-go for a while, she needed a lot of surgery too. But surprisingly she woke up a couple of days ago. She has a long recovery ahead, the way you do, but I think she will be okay." His voice cracks at the end, and it breaks over what he's been through, but I'm over the moon about Shay. Knowing she risked her life for me is baffling. Yet I'm so incredibly fucking glad she did. I wouldn't be here without her.

"Kellan, of course I know that you tried your best. I would never think otherwise. I'm so sorry I put you through so much hell. Just know that every single day I fought to get back to you. I hate how we left things. I lied to you because I had to…or at least I thought I did. What Shay did…the way she broke us up, it was wrong. But I think she has more than made up for her mistakes."

Kellan leans forward and rests his forehead against mine as his thumb strokes the back of my hand. "I know that, Mia. I know everything, but the past is in the past. I will forever be grateful to Shayla for bringing you back to me. I won't put you on the spot because I know after everything you have been through you will need time, but just know that when you are ready, I'm right here."

I can't help but chuckle, only as I do that pain ricochets through the wound in my abdomen, and in my lungs too. Coughing, I try to catch my breath and Kellan pulls back, her brow furrowed in concern as my heart rate monitor beeps just for a second. Once I've caught my breath, the beeping goes back to normal and seems to fade into the background again. Kellan looks confused, and I know I have to explain myself.

"Kellan, I don't need time. I am not emotional. But I am done waiting. I love you. I think I have for a while, and if you really mean that you want to be with me, then I don't want to waste another moment."

I've barely managed to get the last word out before Kellan slams his lips against mine. This is the real kiss I feel like I've waited forever for. Bruising, dominating, and full of passion. I waste no time granting him access to my mouth, and as soon as I taste him, a moan rips from my throat. I wrap my arms around his neck, trying as best I can to pull him closer without pulling any of my IV lines out. I let him devour me, as I ignore all the aches and pains I feel and focus on the way my core heats up just for him. Pain stabs through me as I writhe around, trying to sate the delicious ache I feel in my pussy. I have never been so fucking turned on by just a kiss. One of his hands is on my cheek, the other at the back of my neck, but they don't even hint at moving. I want him to pull me closer, to touch me everywhere, but he doesn't.

I can feel my body heating up under his touch. A loud alarm rips through the room and we spring apart, like teenagers caught doing something we shouldn't. We are both panting, desperately trying to catch our breaths, which is something I'm struggling with. Each time I try, a shooting pain ripples through my lungs, and a ringing starts in my ears. Spots appear in my vision and I wonder if I'm about to pass out.

A nurse rushes into the room and appears to quickly assess the situation, looking at which monitor is beeping before looking at me. It's obvious that I'm struggling to catch my breath. What I hope isn't obvious is the way my lips are swollen after the best kiss of my life.

The nurse walks over to the wall behind me and reaches for the oxygen mask. As she starts talking to me, she moves to place the mask over my face. "Hi, Mia. I'm Rosa, and I'm your nurse. I'm very happy to see you awake. Just do me a favour please and take slow but deep breaths into the oxygen mask, as much as you can. You have had a slight dip in your oxygen levels and your heart was racing, and now we just need to get them back to normal. Clearly waking up was too much excitement."

With a small chuckle, I clutch the wound by my side when it feels as though someone is stabbing my side. I respond to her as best I can through my mask. "Waking up to him is what did it," I joke, nodding my head towards Kellan, and Rosa smiles.

Rosa doesn't appear to be much older than me, probably hasn't been qualified for too long. I see the way her eyes travel over Kellan's body, and she appreciates how fucking incredibly hot he is. Kellan barely even realises she's in the room, his eyes never leave mine.

As Rosa picks up my notes from the bottom of my bed, and begins to look them over, she replies, "You are a very lucky girl. Kellan has barely left your side since you arrived. No matter how much we tell him to go home, his answer is the same every time."

"I will go home when Mia does," Kellan says at the same time Rosa recalls his reply.

Fuck, my heart aches at how sweet this guy is, but I'm also concerned. "What about Hallie?" I can't believe he would leave his daughter for a whole week.

"They don't allow babies in the ICU, which is where you are now. Liam and Bree have been looking after her for us. Liam brings her to the cafeteria once a day and I sit with her for a bit while Bree visits you. It kills me to be away from her, but I know she understands. Getting you home with us is far more important," Kellan explains, and I'm sure Rosa swoons just as much as I do. This guy couldn't be any more fucking perfect.

"Your levels seem to be settling for now, Mia. But you need to take it easy. I can tell you're in pain, so I'm going to get you some pain killers. It'll probably send you back to sleep, but your body needs that. I'll be right back," Rosa explains as she puts some of the notes back into the folder at the bottom of the bed, keeping what I assume to be my prescription chart in her hand as she leaves the room.

"Kellan, I don't want to sleep. I want to stay awake, with you," I beg, as fear of what I might see when I close my eyes takes hold.

Kellan cups my face in his hands and pulls my gaze to him. "I'm not going anywhere. As I was trying to tell you before my kiss that set off the alarms…was I that good?" Kellan jokes, and I playfully slap him on the arm, trying not to laugh too hard because it hurts.

"Could you be any more big-headed?"

Kellan's face suddenly turns serious, his cocky grin that I love so much becomes stern. "Mia, I've never said this to another person and meant it the way I do with you. I love you, so fucking much it hurts. You asked before if I want you, and the truth is, I've always wanted you. For the longest time I was convinced I didn't know what love was, and that all women were just destined to hurt and leave me. Then I met you. Feisty, broken, but so incredibly beautiful. Your broken soul called out to mine. We're made for each other, Flower. I'm done waiting, and I'm done with all the obstacles getting in our way. I want to be with you. I want to build a life with you. I know I come with baggage in the shape of a beautiful little monster who loves to throw bananas at you and pull your hair. But, when we love, we do it with all our hearts, and I know I don't just speak for myself when I say this. Hallie feels the same, I'm more than sure of that. We love you, and we want you in our lives. If you will have us?"

Tears stream down my face and I have to wipe them from the

oxygen mask that's steaming up from all the emotion. My heart feels like it's swelling to twice its size, so I can make room for theirs. "I would be honoured to be in Hallie's life. You know I love her, and I love you. I guess today is the start of our forever."

I move the oxygen mask and lean towards Kellan, but he backs away and puts the mask back into place. "We have forever, Mia. I need you to get better and get off these monitors. Then I can kiss you as much as I want. Until then, you'll just have to imagine how good it will feel when I take you in my arms, and press my lips against yours. The feel of our bodies pressed together as I try to pull you closer, feeling all of you."

Fuck, I can feel my core starting to heat up, and the heartbeat that had been in the background starts to race again. If I don't calm down, I'm going to set off another fucking alarm. Kellan chuckles, loving the way the machines are telling him how I feel. His cocky grin says it all, and I can't hide the blush that spreads to my cheeks.

Thankfully, we are interrupted by Rosa, who gives me some pain meds. I know it won't be long before I'm out for the count. I know I'll sleep a bit easier, safe in the knowledge that not only will Kellan watch over me while I sleep, he'll be here when I wake up. He will always be here for me.

I spent almost two weeks in the hospital. After I first woke up, I had a couple of days in the ICU, where I think I slept more than I was awake, but the more I healed, the better I felt. That's when my care was downgraded and I was moved to the normal ward. Healing physically was surprisingly the easy part, it was my mental health that struggled the most. Every time I closed my eyes, without the help of medication, nightmares crippled me. I was forced to relive my worst moments in every painful detail, and after a while it became overwhelming. The darkness that has always lived on the outskirts of my life was slowly inching closer, consuming me.

I cried so much, and I retreated from the people that love me. I saw the hurt on Kellan's face the more I pushed him away during the day, refusing to talk to him. Yet, I still clung to him at night, desperate for him to never leave me.

After a while, the nurses began to notice the depression was slowly consuming me, and I wouldn't be surprised if Kellan didn't have a word with them. From then on, I started seeing a counsellor. At first, while I was in hospital, it was every day. Natalia, my counsellor, would come and just sit with me. She could see how terrified I was being alone. Ever since I woke up, I'd never been alone. While Kellan visits Hallie, Bree and Liam, or one of the Doughty siblings, or even Kian, comes to check on me. I've never dealt with being alone, until Natalia forced me to send Kellan out of the room. She wanted to take away my crutch. She said I had to learn to walk on my own, and yes, there will be times when I fall, but it's all about learning to pick myself back up again.

To start with, we didn't just talk about Kyle and the kidnapping, we talked about my whole life. All the pain, hurt, and abuse I've suffered for such a long time. Natalia said she was surprised I was as put together as I am. Most people who have suffered the way I have are so messed up, they don't know how to live normal lives. For a while, that was my biggest fear.

Here in the hospital, I'm in a little bubble. But the better I got, the closer I got to bursting that bubble. Then I would have to go back to everyday life. Don't get me wrong, the idea of going home with Kellan and Hallie, and living my life with them, that's exactly what I want, and I'm so fucking grateful I get that opportunity. What I worry about is if I'm capable of doing the norm.

After almost a month in hospital, healing both mentally and physically, Natalia decided I was fit enough to go home. I was on a stable regime of medications to get my anxiety and depression under control, and I would probably need a lot of therapy for a while, which luckily Natalia agreed to do. I suspect Bree and Liam had something to do with that, given Natalia is a hospital-based counsellor, and once I'm discharged from the hospital, I should have had my care transferred to the community support team. But the day I was due to leave, Natalia informed me she would be working with me on a private basis, and that I could ring her at any time. Having that crutch there, just in case, was just what I needed.

"Are you ready to go home?" Kellan asks from his position in the doorway. Hallie's in her pram, giggling away like this is the best thing she's seen all day. I love the fact that she's so happy all the time. She has a sweet innocence about her, and I sure as fuck am going to make sure she stays that way for as long as I can.

Looking around the room that has been my home for the last few weeks, Kellan has already taken all my things, including all the balloons and get-well-soon cards and gifts that I received. Taking a deep breath, there's still a slight ache, but it's nothing compared to what I felt before. Holding my head up high, I smile at my family. "You bet your ass I am. Let's get out of here," I say, as I walk over to him and press my lips to his.

I must've fallen asleep on the drive home, my body's still not completely healed and is struggling with the new meds I'm on. I should have known something was up when Bree and Liam didn't come to the door to greet me. I know them. Bree would normally have flung the door open and dived at me. Yet the house looks eerily silent.

Kel helps me out of the car, and ignores me completely when I tell him I can manage by myself. He just wants to help. Once I'm on my own two feet, he opens the door to the back seat and lifts Hallie out of her car seat. She gives a big yawn along with a bit of a grumble, before she rests her head on her daddy's chest, her big blue eyes wide awake, but her body too tired. Looks like someone else had a small nap on the short journey home too.

Kellan holds the baby in one arm and grabs my hand with the other. "What about the bags?" I ask, indicating that I'm more than capable of carrying my own bags. But he doesn't let go of my hand, and continues pulling me towards the front door.

"I'll come and get them later." Kellan pushes me towards the door, and I push on the handle, surprised and slightly concerned to find the door unlocked. Even though they knew we were coming, Kian would still have a mini fucking heart attack if he knew the door had been left open, even for a fraction of a second. He's a stickler for security, and I imagine now he's living with us, it'll be even worse.

The house is in darkness and it's so quiet, which is my first sign something isn't quite right. This house has never been quiet in all the time I've lived here. As I walk towards the living room door, the only noise is Hallie's occasional grumble from beside me. Kellan indicates for me to open the door, which confuses me, given he is standing right there and could do it.

As soon as the door is all the way open, the light goes on and cries of "Surprise" echo around the room. At first, I'm not going to lie, I jump so far out of my fucking skin. They fucking terrified me. But feeling Kellan squeeze my hand brings me back to the present and I realise there's no danger. Just a room full of people who are all gathered to see me.

Everyone rushed to greet me. Freya, Ryleigh, and Bree are the first to pull me in for hugs. I have grown so close to the girls while helping plan Bree's wedding, and I now class them as friends. Once Liam pulls the girls away, he steals a quick hug and tells me he's pleased I'm home. Kian, Shane, and Finn do the same. I'm even more surprised to see Desmond and Evan have been invited. The boys have been getting closer to Evan, and Liam is starting to rekindle a friendship he thought was lost a long time ago. But nobody ever expected that Desmond would want to be part of the family. From what Kellan was telling me, they are still all on edge, waiting for the other shoe to drop and for him to double-cross them, but I think they are wrong. I see the way Desmond looks at his children, including Kellan, a bright smile on his face as he takes them all in. I see the way he laughs and jokes with Hallie. He's enjoying being part of the family, and I'm not sure he would ever risk that.

We order pizza and the gathering drags on into the evening. Kellan is constantly checking on me, asking me if I need pills, or if I need to lay down. I love that he cares about me so much, but he is being far too overprotective at the moment. After the party, I will make sure he knows. He can love me, but he can't smother me. I don't need that.

The bell rings, and we all look around at each other in confusion. Kian jumps to his feet, and announces he will get the door. I guess being head of security, the job does fall to him. Particularly when everyone we know is already in the room with us.

Everyone listens, desperate to catch even just a glimpse of who it could be. There are raised voices, but not loud enough for us to hear what is being said. Until finally Kian comes stomping back in, an annoyed look on his face.

"Mia, you have a visitor. I have explained that as you only got out of hospital today, it would be better if he comes back another day, but he won't be told," Kian grinds out through gritted teeth, the cheeky smile he's famous for long gone.

"Who is it?" Kellan, Liam, and I ask, all at the same time. I tut at the overprotective men in my life, and I hear Bree giggle from beside me. I'm sure I hear her mumble something about me having to get used to it. It's how they are made. I know she's right. Liam's overbearing with Bree too. In fact, he's even worse now she's pregnant.

"Your dad." The voice floats through from behind Kian, and he opens the door wider to reveal Whitlock standing on the other side.

"No! Absolutely not. I told you in the hospital that you had to wait until she's better before you visit. In fact, I believe I said I would prefer you never visit at all," Kellan growls as he stands from the sofa, putting his body in between Whitlock and me.

There are so many people in the room, a few I would guess have some kind of weapon on their person, and I know of where a few weapons are close by, so I know I am in no danger, yet still Kellan wants to protect me. He knows how much my father has featured heavily in the therapy I've been having. He's to blame for the torture and turmoil I've endured, and Kellan is trying to save me from re-living that.

"Kel, it's okay." I grab hold of his hand and pull him to sit beside me, before I straighten my back, hold my head up high, and with a strength I didn't know I had, I face my abuser. "What do you want? You can say what you came here to say and then you can leave."

Whitlock walks into the room, and Kellan indicates he can sit in the spare armchair opposite. I hear Liam off to the side grumbling about how we now have more furniture we need to burn. It took a lot of convincing to stop him from burning the sofa after Kellan's mum's visit. Taking a seat, I'm actually shocked by how small my father looks.

All my life, I've seen him as this big, intimidating man. He stole my childhood and my innocence, and for years he terrorised my dreams. He was then replaced by new monsters, but I always seem to come back to him. He's the original abuser, the one who started it all. The one I won't ever be able to forgive, no matter how much therapy I have.

"I just wanted to apologise for all the hassle you had from Kyle. I genuinely believed when I arranged the match that you would be a good fit. I had no idea he was mentally unhinged. I am in the process of getting everything in place so I can wipe out the entire Fratacello clan. I believe I have located his father, and I will make them pay for the disrespect they have caused me," he spits, anger lacing every word, and I can't help but laugh.

"Fucking unbelievable," I mutter, more to myself than anyone.

"You will do no such thing, Mr. Whitlock. I know exactly where every member of the Fratacello family is, and they have my personal guarantee that they won't be harmed. They played no part in what Kyle did, and they hurt none of my people. He asked for forgiveness, and I granted him it. So, as your leader, I'm telling you to stand down. Failure to do so will be seen as a direct act of opposition against me and my leadership." Bree stands tall, her voice loud and strong, and I can't help but fucking admire her. She's talking to my father the way I always wished I could. She has the balls to stand up to him. There's no denying his face crumples into disgust, like he isn't happy about the fact that Bree's giving him orders, but my father isn't a stupid man. He holds his hands out in surrender, and lets Bree see that she has won.

"Fine. But I'm not happy about them getting away without being punished."

Bree simply shakes her head, her voice resigned. "They've paid a high price. They watched their only son get killed and allowed it to happen. They lost their house, their business, and their only son in one day. I think they've been punished."

My father turns from Bree, clearly no longer interested in what she has to say, and he addresses me instead. "Will you accept my apology? I will learn from this and the next suitor I find will be a much better match, I promise."

Holy fuck, did he just say what I think he said?

Kellan charges up from the sofa, and the collective gasp of breath from all the people watching the exchange confirms to me that he did in fact say that. He does intend on still selling me to the highest bidder. Marrying me off like I'm a piece of his property. Kellan, visibly shaking with rage, begins to pace before turning to face my father with fire in his voice. "I don't mean to sound disrespectful when I say this, but you can fuck right off. You will not be setting Mia up with anyone else ever again. You've already met the man she will marry. Me. This is not a proposal, because I can do so much better than this shitshow. But this is just me telling you that one day, I will marry your daughter. So you can stop looking for a suitor, because she has found one. We are happy together, and if your intention is to ruin that or cause trouble for us, then you can get the fuck out right now."

A smile spreads across my face and my heart races. Kellan just told the world that one day he wants to marry me, and I couldn't be happier. I know that Kellan and Hallie are my future, but hearing him confirm it is everything.

"You two?" my father asks, his gaze flitting between Kellan and me. His nose crinkled in that snobby look of disgust he's famous for.

I stand and walk to Kellan's side, before taking hold of his hand and clasping our fingers together. I give him the biggest smile I can manage before turning back to face my father.

"Yes. Kellan is the man I love, and who I'll be spending my life with. He knows everything. All about the horrors I endured as a kid, and he still loves me. He has seen all the skeletons in my closet, and he still chooses me. I don't want you in my life, and I won't have you in Hallie's life. So, I think it would be a good idea now if you left." My voice, for the first time in my entire life, stayed strong. It didn't waver, and my father knows I am serious.

Standing from where he was perched on the edge of the seat, he looks at us with barely disguised contempt. "Obviously I will have to be part of your life since I work with Mrs. Doughty here. I will keep my distance, but all I ask is that you don't go spreading lies brought on by that overactive imagination of yours, Mia." His voice has never sounded so small or belittling, and Kellan begins to yell at him, but I cut him off. He can deny the allegations all he wants, everyone that matters knows the truth and believes me. As far as I'm concerned, he just gave me the one thing I have wanted from him since I was a kid.

"I will keep my mouth shut, if you agree you have no claim on me. I am not your daughter, and I'm not a Whitlock that can be used as a business asset. I want to get away from you."

He laughs, no longer even trying to hide behind his professional businessman act. "You do realise if you do that you are cut off completely? No money, no trust fund, no nothing. You will lose it all."

A smile crosses my face, and that only serves to confuse him even more. "In your eyes I will have lost everything, but in reality, I have everything I have ever wanted right here," I say proudly, as I point to the family that has welcomed me in with open arms.

"Fine!" he snaps, but before he is able to continue and say anything further, Desmond, who up until a moment ago had been keeping quietly out of the way, steps forward.

"Come, Mortimer. I think it's time I showed you out." Desmond gently takes hold of Whitlock's arm and leads him to the door, Kian and Liam following closely behind to make sure nothing kicks off and that he actually leaves.

I don't wait for him to leave, I throw my arms around Kellan and press my lips to his, which he instantly deepens. His hand threads into my hair, while the other travels down my back before gripping my ass. I can hear the catcalls of our family, but I don't care. I just love the feel of being in Kellan's arms, and the taste of him on my tongue.

He pulls away, and I can't help but pout. "I'm so proud of you for standing up to him like that," Kellan says, the pride more than evident on his face.

"Did you really mean it when you said one day you would marry me?" I ask, suddenly wishing we weren't having this conversation with our whole family staring at us.

Kellan's cocky grin spreads across his face and just as he is about to answer, Hallie lets out a shriek, and holds her arms out from where she is on Ryleigh's knee and indicates she wants her dad to pick her up. Kellan leans down and as he picks her up, Hallie pulls on his hair, laughs, and says, "Dada."

The room goes silent, and Kellan and I look at each other with wonder and confusion. Did Hallie just say her first word?

"Dada! Dada!" she squeals, very much confirming that she did just say her first word. The look of wonder and joy on Kellan's face lights up the whole room, and I pull them both in for a hug.

After that the whole room erupts. People congratulate Hallie on her first word, others try to film her saying it again, while some—Kian—try to get her to say their name instead. The room is full of fun, laughter, and noise. Just the way it should be. I've never belonged to a family before, not a real one. But now I do, I can't imagine what life would be like without them.

Kellan leans in and whispers in my ear so the rest of my family can't hear. "There will come a time one day soon where we have to assassinate your dad, but first we need to find out how deep he is in all this bullshit. He has a reach much farther than we anticipated, and we need to know what he is capable of before we move against him. I just need to know that when the time is right, you will give us permission to end his life."

I pull away from him, so he can see how incredibly fucking serious I am. "I would pull the trigger if I could."

Kellan pulls me in, that cocky smile back on his face. "That right there is why I love you, Flower."

Kellan

From the day I brought Mia home, I never let her go. She practically moved into my bedroom, and it just felt so natural to have her in my space. Every night I fell asleep with her in my arms, and every morning I woke up looking at her beautiful face. But it wasn't smooth sailing. Every night Mia would wake up covered in sweat, screaming erratically. That, in turn, would wake up Hallie. So my sleep deteriorated rapidly. But I didn't care, I just wanted to help her. I hated seeing her in pain, and how fucking terrified she was.

At first I couldn't get her to open up, all I could do was hold her and let her know that she was safe. But, eventually she started talking to me, opening up about her nightmares. If I thought hearing her screaming in pain was bad, hearing all the gory details of what Mia has gone through in her life, my heart breaks for my beautiful girl. I never realised how strong my girl was until I heard all about what she survived. Because that's exactly what she did...she's a survivor, and I'm so fucking proud of her.

The more we started to talk, the more our relationship grew. I told her all about my past, and we both decided we should lay it all out on the table. No dirty little secrets in the closet that could come out to bite us in the ass, and the more we trusted each other, the closer we grew. The more I learn about her, the more I love her.

It's been around three months now since the horrific incident, and we're closer than we've ever been. But, I can tell Mia's getting frustrated with me. She thinks I'm deliberately withholding sex from her, and I am. I know by now she is pretty much healed, but whenever she takes her clothes off, all I can see is the fresh knife wound on her stomach, and flashes of that moment when she went into cardiac arrest floods my mind. Blood covers her whole body, and all I can think is, I don't want to break her. I know it's not logical, but that doesn't stop me from being terrified.

Mia's been getting more overt in her seduction, and fuck it kills me every time I deny her. Of course I want to fuck my very beautiful girlfriend. I'm hurting myself just as much as I am her. I don't even want to think about how fucking big and blue my bollocks are. I need to have sex with her, but I'm terrified.

"You all ready, babe?" Mia shouts from inside the en suite. She sticks her head around the corner and I catch a glimpse of her naked body. Fuck! Keeping my distance from her is getting harder and harder. Even with the new imperfections that litters her skin, it doesn't detract from her overwhelming beauty. In fact, when she smiles at me, shaking her hips, exposing her fucking glorious tits and ass, she looks perfect.

"Doesn't she look cute?" I reply, holding up my daughter who has the biggest scowl on her face.

Hallie isn't much of a morning person. She's grumpy as hell before she gets her breakfast, and this morning is even worse because I'm getting her all dressed up ready for our visitors. I stand her up on the bed, holding her under her arms since she can only stand if she's holding on to something or someone. She's getting much closer to being able to walk, though.

Hallie's dressed in a beautiful pink princess dress, with the skirt flowing out wide, thanks to the netting underneath. Her dark, jet-black hair that matches mine is curly and looks like it has a mind of its own. I've tried brushing it, but Hallie screams like I'm murdering her whenever she even see's the hairbrush. Mia's the one she will sit there for, like a little doll, while she styles her hair.

Once Mia has given me her approval, telling me how fucking cute Hallie looks, I grab a big, baggy T-shirt and I throw that over the top. I also add a bib, just in case. Hallie scarcely manages to go a whole meal without getting food on her, so this protects her outfit, and prevents me from having to change her again. Particularly since we're running late and our guests will be with us soon.

"I'm going to go and get breakfast started, Flower. See you downstairs."

When I enter the kitchen, Bree and Liam are already there, and they've started breakfast for everyone, which I couldn't be more fucking grateful for. Bree walks over and takes Hallie off me, putting her in her high chair and giving her the same breakfast she has every day. Hallie morphs into a happy baby, a big smile on her face as she squashes banana pieces in both hands before looking at the spoon Bree presents her with, with utter confusion. She isn't a fan of cutlery, preferring to use her hands.

"How are you feeling about today?" Liam asks, concern etched across his face as he hands me a mug of coffee.

Taking some big gulps of the delicious nectar that fuels me, I shrug my shoulders and give him a perplexed look. "Honestly, I'm not entirely sure how I feel. If you had told me a couple of months ago that Shayla would be coming around to visit, and that I'd be inviting her, I would've laughed at you. I would've thought you were off your tits. I hated her, and I never wanted her anywhere near Hallie. I'm not saying I completely forgive her, and I'm not sure how big of a part I want her to play in Hallie's life. Now that I know the truth, and after everything she did for Mia, I think she deserves today. Does that make sense?"

Liam and I sit down at the breakfast bar, drinking our coffee, while I keep an eye on Hallie, who's currently throwing banana at a very annoyed-looking Bree. Naturally that makes my daughter laugh even more.

Liam chuckles, but as Bree gives him the side-eye, he quickly turns his gaze to me. "No, I get it. I think you're doing a good thing. Don't get me wrong, I think there's too much water under the bridge for Shay to become a permanent fixture in Hallie's life. But she almost lost her life saving Mia. So, this is the least we can do for her."

We continue chattering on about random stuff, as I butter toast for us all. Bree comes to get some toast, and I can't help but laugh. She is covered in porridge and banana, and her scowl tells me she's not happy. "Your daughter is unruly. She doesn't listen."

Rolling my eyes, I stand up and grab a tea towel from the side. Walking over to Hallie, I grab hold of one of her little chubby hands, and I wipe it clean, before repeating the step on her other hand. She grumbles, but I just carry on. I duck down until I'm at her level, and use my hand to guide her chin until she makes eye contact with me. Her cute face is all scrunched up, and her button nose tilts up, like she is annoyed at something—or should I say someone.

"Hallie, unless you want me to take all the food away from you and feed it to you, then you have to stop throwing it about. It's naughty, and you know you aren't allowed to do that," I chastise her, whilst trying to keep the smile off my face.

Obviously, when I'm in bad cop mode, she has to know what she's doing is wrong, but at the same time she sure knows how to work an audience. Her bottom lip is pouting, and I watch as she tries to drag Liam into the mix with those puppy dog eyes that will win him over in seconds.

"Now, if I give you back your porridge, do you promise to eat it with a spoon and not to throw it at anyone?" I ask, holding her favourite elephant spoon up so she knows what I'm talking about.

Instantly she reaches forward, desperate to grab at the spoon I know she loves. "Dada," she coos, that beautiful smile spreading across her face, her dimples standing out on both cheeks. Fuck, that is me done.

Ever since she learnt to say her first word, I think she knew the effect it had on me, and how fucking proud I am every time I hear her say it. So much so that she has already started to manipulate me using it.

I hand over the spoon and give her a big kiss on the cheek before handing over the small amount of porridge she has left in the bowl. I'm giving her a poignant stare as she sinks the spoon in very deliberately, as if to prove she can behave if she chooses to.

"Oh, please say there's more coffee left," Mia pleads as she comes waltzing into the kitchen. Her dark skinny jeans cling to her legs, and as she walks past me to get to the coffee pot, I can't resist checking out how hot her ass looks in them. She's wearing a baggy black T-shirt that hangs off one shoulder, and stops just above her belly button, showing off that piercing I love so much. It's so innocent, just a small patch of skin across her stomach and the opposite shoulder, yet she still manages to have my cock standing to attention, straining hard against my jeans, desperate to get free.

As Mia reaches up into the cabinet above the sink to grab the coffee mug, her top lifts up even farther, only this time it exposes the bright pink scar that I hate so much. Don't get me wrong, it's not because I think it makes her look any less than perfect. This issue is all on me. I can't bear to look at it because I feel like I should have done more. I should have saved her before that monster even had a chance to scar her pretty body.

Mia catches me looking, and her brow furrows. Thankfully, before she can say anything, Bree speaks to her. "You look knackered, Mia. Long night?" she asks, wiggling her eyebrows seductively and I can't hold back the groan. Everyone knows we are together, but I don't want to be discussing my lack of sex life in front of the group over breakfast.

"I wish," Mia mutters, and Kian comes bouncing in. He walks over to Hallie like he does every morning and ruffles the hair on her head and she chuckles. He then heads straight for the coffee. He rarely talks until after his first mouthful, but the guy is always happy. No exaggeration, he has a ridiculous smile on his face all the time. Sometimes I really want to punch him for being too jolly.

"Were you about to say you wish you were in my bed rather than that grumpy asshole's?" Kian jokes, lifting his coffee cup in my direction, like he is toasting me. I grumble something about why the fuck we invited this wanker to live with us, but nobody seems to be listening to me.

Breakfast passes by in a blur, and it's not long until I hear the doorbell ring, and my heart starts to race. I haven't seen Shay since she was in hospital, and if I'm being entirely honest, I'm not sure how I feel. I genuinely meant it when I said I didn't want her to die, and that her risking her life to save Mia was something I wouldn't ever be able to repay her for. And even though Shayla has explained the past, and I get her reasons, that still doesn't erase the pain and hurt I felt. I still think she could have handled the whole situation better, if she had put her trust in me, I would've found a way to help her. Secretly, I don't think she would have ever left Jamieson. No matter how pissed she was at him, he was still the one she turned to whenever she was in trouble. He was…or should I say still is, her person, and I can't deny they are good together.

"Kellan. Snap out of it and go and get the door. I'll get Hallie ready, okay?" Mia snaps, pulling me out of the trance I appear to have fallen into.

"We will be outside on the patio, Kel. Just shout if you need us and I'll be in here in a flash," Liam adds, as we all disperse in different directions.

Kian grabs his mug of coffee and heads towards the stairs, before turning with that cheesy grin of his. "Yeah, I will be in my room. But just holla if I need to kick anyone's ass."

Bree tuts loudly before slapping Kian's arm. "There will be no ass-kicking. Now, get upstairs and clean all the gym stuff out of the room next to yours. Freya will be here in a few days, and if any of your stuff is in her room she will be pissed and you know it."

Stupid asshole is deliberately trying to wind Freya up. I think that's why he took the free room beside hers. When he started turning her room into a gym, she was far from impressed. It's already been decided that Freya is going to come stay with us for a while. I think she's been really lost in Ireland, just bouncing from one job to the next, not really knowing what to do with her life. So, Liam and Bree insisted she come here so we can help her decide what she wants to do. Luckily, Ryleigh and Shane are more settled, they've both got into Oxford University, so they are coming over to London to start university after the summer holiday. Well, they will if they pass their exams and get the grades they need.

Desmond has already promised them a house near to campus, which I think Liam's secretly pleased about. I think if Ryleigh lived in halls he would spend three years on the verge of a heart attack, worrying about her. He's obviously worried about them living together, but I'm not. Shane is good for her, he grounds her, which is exactly what a wild child like Ryleigh needs.

"Door! Now!" shouts Mia, breaking up our conversation as we all run to where we should be.

As I stand in front of the door, I take a few deep breaths before opening it. Shayla looks a whole lot better than the last time I saw her, and she's finally starting to get a bit of colour back to her cheeks. Her long blonde hair falls down her chest. She's dressed simply in jeans and a black tank top.

Whiskey has his cut on, since it's pretty much against MC rules to take it off. He's got a tight, dark T-shirt underneath with a pair of acid-wash jeans. He looks as brooding as always. Shay, on the other hand, looks down at the floor, averting her gaze like she's shy or afraid. I plaster a smile on my face and do my best to make them feel welcome.

"Hey, guys, come on in. We are just through here," I point, leading them through into the living room. Mia's already sitting on the sofa, Hallie on her knee.

"Hey, Shay, it's so lovely to see you," Mia says, giving her a small smile before pointing to the two empty chairs. "Have a seat. Kellan will get the drinks." She looks at me pointedly and I roll my eyes, taking in her very obvious hint.

"Of course, what can I get you both?"

Whiskey is the first to answer after they have both sat down. "Can I just get a Diet Coke, please?" he asks, and Shay asks for the same.

That's an easy order. I run into the kitchen and grab two cans from the fridge. For a moment I briefly consider offering them a glass, but I soon push that away. Only when we have older guests do we roll out the posh stuff. I can stretch to a straw and that's it.

Once everyone has a drink, I sit down on the sofa beside Mia, and she hands Hallie over to me. Hallie instantly reaches up and starts pulling on my hair with a giggle. I notice Shay is watching on with rapt amusement. Like my baby is the most interesting thing she's ever witnessed. I know that feeling. I get it all the time. It's pride knowing we created that.

For a while the silence doesn't seem too consuming, Hallie's giggles manage to cut through it, until Mia has clearly had enough and decides to break the ice.

"Shay, I'm so sorry I wasn't allowed to see you in the hospital. I really did try. I wanted to thank you for everything you did for me. I know the letter you sent after I wrote to you said not to worry about it, but I do. You risked your life for me, and I can't ever thank you enough for that." Mia's voice cracks at the end, emotion thick in her voice.

I'm a little taken aback. I had no idea they had been writing to each other. I thought we said no more secrets? I know what Mia will say, that she didn't want me to worry or overthink things. After all, she isn't the one with a history with Shayla, that's me. Mia has every reason in the world to be friendly with her, but I don't. I can't turn off the worries I have or the way I feel, and I know Mia wouldn't have ever stopped wanting to thank Shay for what she did. So, I guess, this is the best of both worlds.

"I meant what I said, Mia. It was my fault your life went to shit in the first place," Shay says, and Mia can't help but laugh. Both Shay and Whiskey look equal parts confused and offended, wondering why Mia would be laughing at them no doubt.

"Shayla, I can promise you, my life didn't go to shit because of you. It was in the crapper a long time before that. Yes, you broke up Kellan and me, and it hurt us both, but we've talked and we've got past it. You genuinely thought you were protecting this little one," Mia says, as she strokes Hallie's unruly hair. "My father is out of my life now, but even before that, I was trying to separate myself from him."

Shay shakes her head. "Whitlock is a dangerous man. He has

contacts everywhere. We already have intelligence saying he's trying to get guns to arm the Reapers, but sadly not on our side. A civil war will rip the Reapers in half, and hopefully the new generation will be successful. But, if your father backs the originals, like we suspect he will, that could be really dangerous for us. I don't tell you this to cause trouble. I don't know exactly which side he stands on, or what his true objective is, and that will always make him a danger to us all."

I look over at Mia, and she's looking back at me. This is something we are in agreement about. "Don't worry about Whitlock. We have a plan. We need to make sure we know what his plan is before we deal with him. But he's on our radar."

"Dada! Dada!" Hallie shouts trying to grab my attention, as she indicates she wants me to put her down. I hear a gasp from Shay and as I look at her, her hands are covering her mouth, but there's no denying the wonderment on her face.

"She can speak?" Her voice is quiet, almost choked up.

As I lower Hallie to the floor next to her box of toys, I turn to reply to Shay. "I wouldn't say she is talking. She babbles a load of nonsense words, and she can say the word dada. So naturally I have her pegged as a little genius."

Shay watches in amazement as Hallie shuffles around the room, crawling to each of the different toys, trying to decide which she wants to play with more. She has an annoyed look on her face because we tidied up since we had guests coming over. She clearly doesn't like having to work to find her toys.

"She looks so grown up," Whiskey mutters, the same look of amazement on his face too. They both can't take their eyes off my daughter, and to say my chest swells with pride is an understatement.

"I know, I can't believe she is one next month," Mia replies with a smile.

"Look, Shay. I have to be honest about this. I'm glad you are here, and that you get to see how happy Hallie is, but I'm not entirely sure how I feel about the whole thing. I got used to knowing you wouldn't be part of Hallie's life, and to start with, of course I was pissed, but I came around to it. Hallie's my daughter, and I'm more than happy raising her with just the help of my family, Mia included. I'm not sure if there's a place for you in that, and I'm not saying that to hurt you, I'm just trying to be honest." Fuck, I can't seem to stop mumbling. I don't want to upset anyone, but I also have to be completely honest.

Shay shakes her head, before getting up and coming to sit next to me on the sofa. She takes my hands in hers and looks me in the eye. For a second, I wonder if I should freak out. My body still remembers how much she hurt me, but then I feel Mia gently place her hand on the small of my back. It's like she knew I'd need her support.

"Kellan, I'm sorry if this has been confusing for you, but I want to make it very clear. When I signed those papers, giving Hallie to you, I meant them. I knew it would hurt, and I knew there would be times when I wanted to be back in her life, but I made a decision and I stick by it. You and Mia are all the parents she will ever need. Being in her life like this, just being able to see that she is growing up, is more than enough. Even if we never do this again, you've given me more than I ever expected. Hallie's your daughter, and I won't ever take her from you. You have my word on that. I won't even ask for more visits. They are a privilege, and something I won't ever take for granted. If I get more, that's a bonus. But they won't ever be expected, just appreciated. Does that make sense?" Her eyes are welling up with unshed tears, her voice thick with emotion. I know it hurts Shay not to be a regular fixture in Hallie's life, but I know I can't agree to that. I can, however, promise her the occasional friendly visit.

"I understand. I'm not making any promises, and we take each visit a step at a time, but if you would like to stay in her life, as a friend, I'm sure that would be okay."

A sob catches in Shay's throat and she pulls me in for a hug. "I think you just made my wife very happy," Whiskey jokes.

"I'm sure this doesn't really need to be said, but while the Reapers are at war, you will need to stay away," Liam says, from where he's leaning against the living room doorframe.

I shoot him a look. So much for not interfering. Bree isn't far behind. "Sorry, we didn't plan on interfering, but I think it's a good job we did. We have information that might be of use to you. The Reaper Pres has tasked Whitlock with arming them. I suspect he knows that you are planning a rebellion. He tried to get them off

Desmond, who came to us. We obviously haven't helped the Reapers. I'm sure you know my family doesn't do business with them. I met your dad once, Shayla, and to say he's a prick would be an understatement," Bree jokes, and Shay simply nods her head in agreement.

"Just because we didn't arm the Reapers, doesn't mean someone else didn't," Liam adds.

"If you are determined to get rid of the current Reapers and replace them with the new generation, then maybe we can come to some sort of arrangement. Like I said, I've never agreed to work with the Reapers before, for obvious reasons, but I think you will bring about a new age, and it's one I would be happy to support. You would have to recognise my leadership, the way everyone else who works for me has to, though," Bree adds with a shrug of her shoulders.

I see Shay and Whiskey looking at each other, they remain silent, but it's like they're having an unspoken conversation. I can see the way she pleads with her eyes. She has always craved safety, and there's no denying that having the Doughty family's protection would go a long way towards her finally feeling safe.

"I'll need to discuss it with my other Church members. It's a generous offer, and I will present it to them that way. Whatever we decide, I hope that won't change anything between Kellan and Shay," Whiskey says politely, showing Bree the respect she doesn't necessarily command, but gets anyway. It's like people can just tell she is a leader.

"No, of course it won't. But as I said before, I can't make any guarantees of when you can see Hallie, but I also won't have her in any danger," I explain.

Shay smiles. "Kellan, I think I have more than proved that everything I have ever done has been for the sole purpose of keeping her safe. I promise I won't step anywhere near her if I'm in any danger. I will always put her wellbeing first." Shay turns to me with that same shy smile that hooked me almost two years ago. "Can I give her a hug, please?" Her eyes widen, and I can see she's desperate for me not to turn her down.

"Of course you can." Before I've even finished my sentence she slides onto the floor and scoops Hallie into her arms. Hallie responds how she does to most people, by hitting her around the head and pulling on her hair, but Shay smiles through it.

Whiskey eventually joins Shay and Hallie on the floor, and they lay together for a while, talking to us about random things as the morning progresses. Liam and Bree soon disappear again, happy they've helped with the Reaper situation. I never thought I would see the day Bree got involved with the MC, but if she can help Whiskey rid the world of those original assholes, I'm all for that.

After a couple of hours, the time comes where they are reluctantly saying goodbye. Hallie's getting a little ratty, and no doubt hungry. I gather her up into my arms as we walk Shay and Whiskey to the door. The smile on their face tells me they have had a good time, and shockingly, so have I.

As they are leaving, I stop them, catching us all unawares as I say something I hadn't planned on saying. "Next month we're having a party for Hallie's birthday. We would love it if you could come."

Shay's eyes widen as big as saucers and she throws her arms around me and Hallie, thanking me continuously. "In case you didn't catch that, we would love to come," Whiskey jokes as he pulls Shay into his arms. She looks up at him, a big smile on her face. She's looking at him like he hung the moon, and I thought it would be hard for me to see them so happy, but it isn't. I'm happy for them. I don't have any reason to be jealous. I have the love of my life by my side already.

"Oh, before I forget, I want to give you this. You won't need it just yet, but one day soon, I know this man is going to propose to you. He hasn't told me, but I can see it in his eyes. He looks at you in a way I've never seen from him before. You are his world, second only to Hallie. When you take on Kellan, you get Hallie too, and I know you know that. I know you want that too. So, when that day comes and you agree to be Kellan's wife, then you open this envelope and sign the papers. They're already signed by me, so you won't have any trouble with them," Shay explains, and we both look confused.

"What is it?" Mia asks, looking inquisitively at the large Manila envelope.

"In there is the adoption paperwork you need. It's all signed by me, drawn up by my lawyer. Once you become Kellan's wife, you can sign this document, and Hallie will legally be your daughter."

Mia's breath hitches, and she looks at me with tears in her eyes. We've talked about one day getting married, and she's always said she wants to be in Hallie's life, but we never really talked about her becoming her mum.

"I don't know what to say," Mia says, tears rolling down her cheeks

"Just promise me you will love her enough for the both of us. You will be a great mum. She is lucky to have you," Shay says, as she pulls Mia in for a hug.

Shay then reaches out to me, and I let her hug me. "I hope you don't mind me doing that. I don't want to steal your thunder. But I have to say you are an idiot for not marrying her already."

Whiskey pulls Shay by his side, laughing at her. She leans forward and kisses Hallie on the cheek who giggles before reaching for Whiskey, indicating she wants him to kiss her too. Which of course he does. My daughter can wrap men around her little finger, even at such a young age. We say our goodbyes and watch them drive away.

As we turn to walk into the living room, Mia is a little quiet, and I ask her what's wrong. She looks at the Manila envelope and after I've placed Hallie in her play pen, she hands it to me. "This belongs to you. It was nice of Shayla to do this, but Hallie's your baby, that's a decision you should make, not her."

Fuck, could I love this woman any more? "Mia, the only reason I never brought it up before is because in my eyes you already are Hallie's mum. It never occurred to me that we could, or should make it official. But, I agree with Shayla. When the day comes that I ask you to be my wife, I will also ask you to be Hallie's mum because we are a pair. Then it's up to you what you want to do."

The smile on her face widens as she pulls me against her, and fuck does my dick respond instantly. "I will need a better proposal than that, for starters. But we both already know what my answer is. I love you both, so much, and I can't wait to spend forever with you both. Oh, and tonight, no more excuses. I want you to fuck me. I want to feel your cock going in deeper and deeper, until I can't feel any fuller.

I want you to make me scream your name. I'm done healing. Now I want you to fuck me."

"Well, it looks like I'm going to have to try to put Hallie in her own room from now on. Can't have her in the room while you are screaming my name now, can we?" I joke, and Mia chuckles before pressing her lips against mine, her hand reaching around to cup my ass, and fuck if that doesn't send an electric shock to my cock. I can't fucking wait until tonight. I have a feeling we night need a babysitter for in the morning because I plan on making up for lost time and fucking her as much as I can.

Mia may be broken, and she may have been through more trauma than most people can even imagine, yet she is still standing. She is a survivor who wants to take back ownership of her body. She wants to forget about all the pain she has had inflicted on her, and she wants to replace that with memories of us. I will teach her to love her body, and to be confident in her sexuality. No matter what, I will love her every single day of forever, and I promise to spend each day helping to piece back together her broken soul. She's put her trust in me, and I won't ever break it.

EPILOGUE
Kellan

"Are you awake too?" Mia mumbles, her head laying on my chest as her body tucks into my side. The feeling of having her pressed against my body just feels so natural, my body drawing heat and comfort from hers.

"Yeah, I'm awake. I can't believe she isn't," I grumble, and Mia chuckles, sitting up slightly as she turns her head so I can see her face. The small patch of sunlight streaming in through the little gap in the curtains is just enough to shadow our bodies with the right amount of light.

"It's not even five in the morning yet, Kellan. Be grateful she isn't awake yet," Mia laughs, and I take hold of her body, hands on her hips as I lift her and move her so that she is straddling my hips.

The duvet cover falls away from her, revealing her perfect curves. Her supple tits with pretty pink nipples are currently pebbled, showing me exactly how my girl's feeling. Her pale, smooth skin curves in all the right places and my hands fit perfectly along the curve of her hips. Her creamy thighs clamp beside mine, and I can feel the heat from her core against my abdomen.

Of course my dick is standing to attention. No matter how many times we have sex, I don't think I'll ever stop wanting this woman, or stop craving her. My cock's currently rubbing against her ass, and it won't take much manoeuvring to help my cock find its final destination.

"Well, I think I've just thought of a fun way we can kill time before our little monster wakes up. Today is a celebration, after all," I joke, as I rub my hand up her back, along her silky smooth skin, until I finally clasp my hand at the back of her neck. Using that hand, I pull her down until our lips meet, and as soon as we taste each other, our passion increases and we dive into each other.

Honestly, I can't even tell you how much I struggled getting Hallie into her own room. I think it's fair to say I found it harder than she did. The first few nights, she didn't settle, and we had a load of tears. It broke my heart, and I'm not even ashamed to admit that if it hadn't been for Mia, I would've caved. I would have let her stay in my room for as long as possible.

Mia, ever the resourceful woman, found a fucking fantastic way of distracting me from the anxiety I felt over Hallie being in a different room. It involves her very naked body, exploring my very naked body, and holy fuck I was so there for it. It's the perfect way to distract my brain.

As our lips explore each other, I move my hands across her body. Realising I need more access, I take hold of her hips and lift before rolling her until Mia's on her back and I'm lying above her. I barely break contact with her before my lips crash down against hers again.

Reaching between her creamy thighs, I pull her legs open more, so her knees are on either side of my body, pulled up to give me full access. I swipe my finger through her slit and I can't hold back the groan that rips from my throat when I feel how deliciously wet she is. Her hips tilt, begging me for more with her body, and when I slide two of my fingers in, giving her exactly what she asks for, her back arches from the bed as my lips swallow her moans.

Fuck! She's so wet, and her body is so responsive to my touch. As I slowly piston my fingers in and out, she moans, begging me for more. Something I'm only too happy to oblige.

"I need your cock, Kel. Please, fuck…I need more. I want more. Please," Mia moans as she tells me exactly what her body needs. It's something she's been working on, and over the last month, we've built her body confidence back up again. I've taught her how to listen to her body, to feel exactly what it is she needs, and to ask for it. Never again will she have to do anything she doesn't want to do.

"Since you asked so nicely, Flower. I guess I can help with that." Knowing how wet she already is, we don't need much more foreplay, and my cock sure as fuck can't get any harder.

Grasping the shaft in my hand, I move it up and down, getting him ready for the main event. Pre-cum beads on the tip, and I rub it in, dragging my pre-cum over my dick. Slowly, I swipe the tip through her slit, mixing my pre-cum with her juices, getting my cock wet and ready for her. I push the head against her clit, eliciting the sexiest groan from her as her back arches further and her hands fist the sheets. I move it to her entrance and slowly press into her pussy.

As soon as the first few inches are in, and I know Mia's accustomed to me, I slam the rest in quickly until I bottom out and Mia's cries of pleasure fill the room. I don't give her any time, knowing she can handle me. I pull back until just the head remains before pushing back into her hard.

Fuck, I can feel my balls start to tingle already. "Looks like this is going to have to be a quick, hard fuck," I whisper in Mia's ear, and I love the way her body shivers when my breath catches her ear.

"Fuck me hard then, babe." I don't think I will ever get over hearing my sweet, shy girl, flushed with pleasure, talking dirty to me. It turns me on so much, and I'm only too happy to give her what she wants.

Slamming my cock in and out of her pussy, her moans become more and more desperate and frantic as her hips thrust up to meet mine. Her fingers rake across my back, as her lips devour mine. It doesn't take long, as I pound my cock in harder and faster, and I feel Mia start to respond. Her moans are more frantic and desperate, as she claws to try and pull me closer. Her pussy grips my dick like the most perfect glove designed just for me.

"Oh fuck. Kellan, you're going to make me come. I can't..." Mia mutters against my mouth, and I can feel her muscles coil around me.

Fuck, she feels so good, and my balls are tightening to the point I know I won't be able to last much longer. "Come for me, Mia. Fall apart on my cock. I want to come with you." My voice is low, and deep, filled with so much passion as I try to hold off long enough for Mia to come first.

Luckily, all my girl needs is to hear my dirty words, and she falls apart in my arms, her body trembling beneath me as her cries of pleasure intermingle with her chanting my name. Her pussy clamps around my cock like a vice, and I have to hold still. Her pussy milks away at my dick, and within seconds I erupt alongside her. The moans of our joint orgasm fill the room, and as we both come down from that high, all that can be heard are our desperate pants as we try to fill our lungs with air.

Taking Mia's head in my hands, I slowly press my lips against her, our foreheads connecting. "Fuck, Flower. I don't think I will ever stop wanting you. It's like you are my own personal drug, and my body craves the high you give me."

"I don't want you to ever stop craving me. I'll always want you, Kel."

We stay like that, cuddled in each other's arms, until we hear crying coming from the baby monitor. Normally, I would wait a couple of minutes. It's something Mia's been teaching me. Apparently, there are times when Hallie wakes up, has a bit of a grumble, but ultimately she will soothe herself until he falls back to sleep for a bit. For a while, I hated leaving her to cry, but it got easier. She was seeking me, when she really just needed to go back to sleep for a bit longer.

But today, both Mia and I look at each other with excitement, and we know we aren't going to let Hallie fall back to sleep. Hell, we've been waiting for her to wake up today.

Rolling out of bed, I pull on some sweatpants, and I toss my baggy Liverpool football shirt in Mia's direction so she pulls it over her head. She runs into the bathroom, no doubt to clean up the mess we just made as I go into Hallie's room.

Picking my little girl out of her crib, I shoot her the biggest smile before giving her a kiss. "Good morning, my little Hallie Bear. I can't believe you are a whole year old today. My baby's getting so big," I sing, as she tucks her head into my shoulder and yawns.

I carry her back into my room and Mia has turned on the light to reveal the balloons we hid in the corner of the room. We spent fucking ages inflating them last night, and getting the last of her presents wrapped. Watching Hallie's eyes widen as she takes in all the big balloons—which we know she loves—I'm blown away by how fucking lucky I am.

Carrying her over to the bed, Mia joins us and as I sit Hallie on the bed, she instantly crawls until she's wrapped in Mia's arms. "Good morning, beautiful," Mia says as she plants a kiss on Hallie's cheek. She then begins to sing the happy birthday song, which I join in with, and that gets Hallie giggling like a loon.

We spend a short while just laughing together, opening the occasional present. Hallie looks overwhelmed by them all, and she can't decide whether to play with the actual presents, the wrapping paper, or the boxes. She also makes sure to chase some of the balloons around the bed in between opening presents.

Once we've opened the couple of presents we have for her, we get her ready to go down to breakfast. As Mia dresses in her usual jeans and cropped T-shirt, I dress Hallie in some jeans and a T-shirt that says 'I am one, so fear me!' and it suits her perfectly.

We are up earlier than we normally are, so I don't expect to see anyone else downstairs for at least another hour, but as we descend down the stairs, the lights are already on. It's clear someone else is stupid enough to be up at this hour. As we enter the kitchen area, Bree, Liam, Freya, and Kian are all sitting around the breakfast bar, nursing mugs of coffee. As soon as they see us walk in, they erupt with cheers.

"Happy birthday, Hallie," they shout in tandem, before rushing towards my very startled daughter.

Of course, as soon as she sees Liam, she wiggles in my arms, demanding to be put down. Over the last couple of weeks, she has been slowly finding her feet more and more, and has even managed a few steps while we're holding on to her. Liam and I utilise every opportunity to try to get her to walk, and this is perfect. I lower her onto the kitchen floor, keeping hold of her hands while she finds her feet. She hops up and down like a drunken sailor who hasn't quite found his sea legs yet. Once she's as stable as she's going to be, Liam sits just a couple of feet away from us, and holds his arms out.

"Come to me, Hallie Bear. Come and give Uncle Liam a big birthday cuddle," he coos, as she begins to take a couple of steps. When I'm sure she's found her footing, I slowly let go, one hand at a time. Her hips wiggle a bit, and at first it looks like that big baby booty that I love so much is going to bring her crashing down, but instead she takes a step. We all stay frozen on bated breath. She's managed one step before, but that's her maximum unaided, and we all stare, desperately hoping this will be the time.

I look over at Mia and Bree, who are both huddled behind Bree's phone, as she films, just in case. "Go on, baby girl. You can do it," I shout in encouragement, and she places her next foot down.

"Yes! Go Hallie," shouts Kian, as she surpasses anything she's managed before. For once, his big, cheesy smile doesn't make me want to punch him for being too chipper in the morning. Instead, it's infectious, and I know we all have matching expressions.

Hallie seems frozen, unsure of what to do next. At first it looks like she's going to sit down. She has, after all, exceeded her previous attempts and has gotten the praise she wants from us. Then she looks over at Liam, with his arms held out for her, and she gives him a big smile and a chuckle. She then surprises us all by taking the next few steps in rapid succession before falling into Liam's arms.

The kitchen erupts louder than a football stadium does when their favourite shooter scores in the last minute, giving their team the win. We are all thrilled and the more we celebrate and praise Hallie, the more she giggles.

The morning passes by in a blur, as we all eat breakfast together then open presents. Liam takes Hallie outside, saying he has a big surprise for her. We've all been banned from going to the bottom of the garden now for the last three weeks. Liam erected a massive tent to cover the area, and he wouldn't let any of us near. We all thought it was something for the party we are having here this afternoon, but no. Now the big tent has a bow attached to it, and Liam carries Hallie over to it.

We all gather in the middle of the garden, and he hands Hallie over to Bree so he can go to the tent ready for the big reveal. "Hallie Bear. I can't believe you have been in our lives for a whole year now. You are sweet, kind, and so incredibly funny. Even when you are causing chaos you enrich all our lives. So, as your favourite uncle, I wanted to make sure you got an extra special present."

Liam and Kian pull the tent down, revealing a massive children's play area. It's all made out of wood, and there's climbing frames, slides, swings, and a whole host of other games. There's a large sandpit with a little paddling pool beside it. Then over to the side there's a full-sized, adult trampoline, that I suspect is just as much for our use as it is Hallie's. The play area is designed to look like this magical palace, with boats and dragons, and even a big tower for her to climb into when she is older. It's the type of gift that she will be able to explore more the older she gets, and so it's no wonder that Hallie's face lights up brighter than a Christmas tree as she squirms in Bree's arms, desperate to go and play.

As I take in the beautiful area that Liam has created for my daughter, emotion clogs my throat. "You did this all for Hallie?" I mutter, already knowing he would do anything for her.

Nodding, Liam gives her a big smile before replying. "Well, she may have to share it, but that won't be for another few months at least." Liam looks over at the small bump that his wife now has on display. They are due to go for their main scan next week, and the baby is finally at that age where they can find out the gender. Which is something that's causing a lot of arguments in the house. Bree wants to know, she wants to be able to prepare and plan. Whereas Liam wants it to be a surprise. He doesn't care if it's a boy or a girl, they will be loved and adored no matter what. So that argument has been going on for a while. I keep my mouth shut. I know not to contradict a pregnant woman.

"I may have to move out when it comes time to teach her how to share," Kian jokes, pointing at Hallie, and I don't fucking blame him. Hallie's used to being the centre of attention, and is used to having Liam's full, undivided attention. So, I imagine when the time comes and she has to learn to share him, we will need to keep an eye on the baby. My girl can be ruthless.

While Ryleigh and Shane keep Hallie occupied in the play area, the rest of us work our asses off getting everything ready for Hallie's party. Kian and Freya blow up more balloons. Liam's in charge of helping the man set up the bouncy castle that we hired, as well as getting all the party bags put together. While Bree and Mia are in the kitchen preparing all the food, I put together a playlist that will both appeal to children, but won't make the adults attending want to blow their brains out.

As well as family and a few close friends, Mia has invited some of the mums and babies from the local playgroup they go to every week at the library. Hallie loves it there, and she's made some friends that she plays with really well. We decided to invite them because we didn't want it just to be an adult party. We want Hallie to play with other children her age. Besides, Kian and I have already vetted everyone who received an invite, and anyone who accepted were screened using a full security check. Nobody is entering this house without me knowing they aren't a threat.

The party's start time arrives quicker than we all expect, and we rush around making sure everything is perfect. Mia has taken Hallie to get her changed into the princess dress she picked out when we asked what she wanted to wear. As Mia walks down the stairs, holding my little princess in her arms, I'm so fucking blown away. Mia's changed into a short, white sundress with little flowers dotted across the bottom, and she looks so fucking perfect. The ball of pink in her arms is even wearing a matching princess gown, and the big smile on her face lets me know today is already a winner. No matter how the rest of the day goes, just seeing the smile my girl has is more than enough for me.

The guests begin to arrive. Obviously Liam, Bree, Freya, Kian, Ryleigh, and Shane are already here. The girls and Shane arrived yesterday. I'm pleased to see Finn and Evan have been able to travel over from Ireland for the party, claiming they wouldn't miss their niece's birthday for the world.

Annette also made the trip, and from the moment she arrived, she hustled into the kitchen, taking over from Mia and helping Bree. She insisted that Mia should be greeting guests with me. Declan and Belle arrive shortly after Annette. Belle remained close with the girls since they met on the hen night, and she came to visit Mia in hospital regularly. Liam and I have even spent some time getting to know Dec with Kian, and he's actually not a bad guy. He's a bit uptight at first, but he soon loosens up when you get to know him.

Paddy, Clodagh, Desmond, and Von are next to arrive, competing over which grandfather can shower Hallie with the most love. Even though Paddy isn't technically related to Hallie, it doesn't stop him doting on her. It's so weird to see Desmond behaving like a normal human. Although, something is going on with him and Evan. They appear to be in the middle of a fight, which is unusual for them as they are normally so in sync. Evan is like a mini version of Des, or he was, until he started to rebel. I make a mental note to find out what's going on with them, as it can't be anything good.

The tension rises when Whiskey and Shayla arrive, nobody quite knowing how to approach them being here. But as soon as Mia greets Shay with a hug, everyone seems to settle. Even Hallie shuffles her way across the garden to demand a cuddle from them both. I don't miss the way they smile as they both share a cuddle with her. Hallie has an incredible ability to cut through all the bullshit and tension, and draws everyone together and that's exactly how the party goes.

Everyone spends the afternoon talking to each other, and generally having fun. The Doughty's do their best to act normal in front of the baby club mums. Although, I don't miss the moment when one of the baby club mums, Jessie, walks over and begins hitting on Kian. The guy is a flirt, always has been, and normally everyone just ignores him. But this time, the more Jessie flirts with Kian, and he flirts back, the more it winds Freya up. At one point, when she stomps into the house in search of more wine, I catch the mischievous glint in Kian's eye. Asshole is flirting in front of her to deliberately make

Freya jealous, and surprisingly, it's working. In fact, it works so well that Liam smacks him around the back of his head and tells him to behave.

We all have a particular moment of shock when Desmond carries Hallie onto the bouncy castle, and he spends time jumping up and down, laughing with her, before shouting for his kids to join him. One by one they reluctantly climb onto the bouncy castle, and it doesn't take long until they are all laughing and having fun.

"Come on, Kellan. I said I want all my children on the bouncy castle," Desmond shouts, grabbing the attention of the whole party. I guess my paternity status is no longer a secret. At first I'm a bit lost for words, but as all the Doughty kids hold their arms out for me to join them, my heart starts to swell.

"Go on, Kel. They're your family," Mia mutters in my ear, as she pushes me towards the bouncy castle. I close the distance, and as I climb on, everyone begins to bounce, throwing me all over the place. We all end up cuddled together, each Doughty holding the shoulder of the next, as we bounce up and down in a circle, my daughter in the middle. She jumps up and lands on her bum, laughing her head off each time she does it, looking around at all her family as she does.

This is exactly what I wanted. All the people I love, all the people that love Hallie, all gathered together on a day that is just about her. It's one day where we all put our differences, or our personal shit, to one side, while we shower this beautiful girl with all the love we have. Seeing her happy, laughing, having the best day, that's all I could ever have wanted.

The event starts to die down after we cut the cake. The baby club mums leave, and it's just our family and friends that remain. The sun's starting to set in the distance, and everyone looks knackered from the fun of the day. Hallie's sitting on Shayla's knee, munching on some cake, while we all gather around the firepit to keep warm.

As soon as Hallie's finished eating, and Whiskey's helped clean the chocolate cake off her grubby little fingers, I know I'm not going to get any better moment than this. The sun is setting, bright pinks, purples, and oranges are flooding the sky. All our friends and family are surrounding the firepit, smiles on their faces. I take a big, deep breath, ignoring the nervous flips my stomach is doing, and the fact that I can hear my heart racing in my ears. No matter how nervous I am, I know it's just performance nerves. I have no hesitation over what I'm about to do.

As I get up to grab Hallie from Shayla's knee, I subtly slip my hand into my jeans pocket, to make sure it's still where I put it. Feeling the velvet box, I smile as I grab Hallie. I clear my throat, indicating I'm about to make a speech. My friends and family look confused, as they know I'm not much of a public speaker. But I know I can do this.

"First of all, I would like to thank each and every one of you for coming. For showering my daughter with presents and love. Today wouldn't have been anywhere near as amazing as it has been without you in it. Each and every one of you plays a special part in Hallie's life, and I hope to see you all at every one of her birthdays in the future." I make sure I look at Shay as I say that last part.

Mia and I have talked about it a lot over the last couple of weeks, and we've decided that Shay should be part of Hallie's life, as a friend. One day, when the time is right, we will tell her that Shay is her birth mother, but not until I decide. There won't be shared custody, set visiting days, or overnight stays. She can be part of Hallie's life, in the same way a friend might be. She can come to family events, come and see her for a play date, if it's okay with us, but it won't be a regular thing. That's the best I can do, and when I told Shay that, she said it was more than she ever expected or thought she deserved. Both she and Whiskey were very grateful, and if I'm honest, they've fit into the family dynamic well. Finn and Shay get on like a house on fire, and Whiskey is friendly to everyone, except me. He's still a brooding asshole to me, but I don't blame him.

Taking a big, deep breath to try and stabilise my nerves, I sit down next to Mia, with my daughter on one knee, while I reach out to grab Mia's hand. I try to block out the rest of my family and I speak just to Mia.

"Mia, I don't think there's ever going to be a better time to do this. I want to tell all the people that matter to us exactly how I feel. I love you. I think I've loved you from the moment I met you. Our shattered souls found each other, and we used our broken pieces to heal. We became one shared soul, and I can honestly say that my heart beats just for you. When Hallie was born, I didn't think it was possible to love someone as much as I love her. Then you came along, and it was a different kind of love. A slower one that crept up and bit me on the ass. I love you so much, and I truly believe I'd be lost without you. Hallie and I are so incredibly lucky to have you in our lives. So, we have one very important question to ask you." I let go of her hand, dig the ring out of my pocket, and flip the lid open before handing the box to Hallie. Obviously she attempts to put it in her mouth first, earning a laugh from all the people watching, until she lets me guide her hand to pass the box to Mia.

"Mia, would you do me the incredible honour of agreeing to be my wife and Hallie's mum?" I ask, and I watch as tears stream down Mia's face, hitting her beautiful, big smile. Thank fuck, they're tears of joy.

"Yes!" she chokes out, and I release the breath I didn't know I was holding.

Leaning down, I whisper in my daughter's ear, giving her the instructions we've spent the last two weeks practising. "Give the box to Mia, and what do you say?"

Hallie reaches over to pass the velvet box to Mia, and as she gives her the box, her voice rings loud all over the garden. "Momma."

Everyone gasps. Hallie says dada, and a whole lot of baby talk, but she's never said anything else. We've spent the last two weeks practising, and the closest I've ever gotten is a "Ma," which, to be honest, I would've taken. But, she manages to get the whole word out, I see the pure joy etched across Mia's face.

Taking the ring out of the box, she slides it onto her ring finger, and thankfully it's a perfect fit. You have no idea the amount of sneaking Liam and I had to do to make sure we got the right size. It's a simple white gold band, with a solitaire diamond in the middle. Understated but stunningly beautiful, just like its owner.

Once the ring is in place, she throws her arms around Hallie and me, before pressing her lips against mine. Just like every other time she's kissed me, we forget where we are, and that we are surrounded by people, and I want to deepen the kiss. Luckily, she has the good sense to pull away, and she plants a kiss on Hallie's nose, which gets

Hallie giggling in between her big yawns. My baby is exhausted, but she's determined to stay awake as long as possible, which I'm okay with. Today is a day I'd like to continue forever. I'm surrounded by my family, by the people I love, and Mia has just made me the happiest man alive.

If someone had told me a year ago that this is where I would be, I would have laughed. I never saw myself forgiving or being friends with Shayla. I never thought I'd be an actual Doughty, even if they did always treat me as one. Hell, a year ago, I didn't think I could be a dad. It's the best job in the world, and I couldn't be without my little monster. Now my family is bigger than ever, and I have Mia to share it all with.

If you'd told me I would be getting married, thinking about adding more kids into the mix, I would have wholeheartedly denied it. Thinking you had gone mad. Now, it's the only thought in my head. Imagining Mia carrying my baby. A little baby with mine and Hallie's eyes, but Mia's face. I see our future, and it's so fucking perfect. Who knew two people who were so broken could learn to trust and find happiness? I didn't, but I'm so fucking glad we have. I can't wait to spend forever with my girls!

If you enjoyed reading Kellan's story, you are going to love the rest of the books in the Beautifully Brutal Series. Keep reading to find out which book to start next…

THE *Beautifully Brutal* SERIES

Thank you so much for sticking with me while I told Kellan's story. After Dangerously Deceptive, I knew I'd made life really difficult for Kellan, and he had a whole heap of crap to overcome before he could get his happily ever after. But, never have I wanted to see a character find their happy as much as I did Kellan. He's quite literally the perfect imperfect man. He's real, honest, and incredibly sexy. The way he cares for his daughter is enough to burst your ovaries, but the way he manages his anxiety is what makes him so relatable. I have loved writing my lovable tech geek, Kellan, and I thank each and every one of you for taking a chance on his story.

Thank you for reading! I hope you enjoyed Trust In Me and if you did then you really need to read the other books in the Beautifully Brutal series.

THE BEAUTIFULLY BRUTAL SERIES BY EMMA LUNA

The Beautifully Brutal series follows the Doughty's, an Irish mafia family that are fighting to hold onto their power. Each of the main books in the series follows one sibling and the person they fall in love with. So while each couple will get their own HFN ending in their book, you will get more out of the series by reading the others. There are main plots and themes that run through all the main books, and the other characters feature heavily in all the books. So, you will get more out of reading all the books in the series. There's a recommended reading order below.

Please note - Dangerously Deceptive and The Ties We Break are prequels that are set before the events of Black Wedding. They do not have to be read in order to follow the main plot line. However, they do give back stories to some of the main characters, and reading them will give you extra info.

Dangerously Deceptive is Kellan's backstory and should be read after Black Wedding, but before Trust In Me.

The Ties We Break gives you an insight into Kian and Desmond's backstory, and should be read after Trust In Me, but before Fighting To Be Free.

To follow the main story line, this is the recommended reading order:

Black Wedding
Trust In Me
Fighting To Be Free
The Time Is Now
The Lies That Shatter
Together We Reign

HERE'S SOME MORE INFORMATION ON ALL THE BOOKS IN THE SERIES:

BLACK WEDDING - this is Bree and Liam's love story. When Liam kidnaps mafia princess, Bree, he bites off more than he can chew. She's not your typical princess, she has a plan and she wants to rule in a world dominated by men. So Bree comes up with a plan, she asks Liam to marry her, so she can get her title and together they can rule. But not everyone wants to see a female rule. With enemies around every corner, can Bree and Liam survive? And what happens when their marriage of convenience suddenly starts to feel real?

Buy ebook here: https://geni.us/BW-BB
Buy audiobook here: https://geni.us/BW-BB-Audio
Add to TBR: https://bit.ly/BW-BB-GR

DANGEROUSLY DECEPTIVE - this is Kellan's prequel and tells the story of how he became distrustful of women, and more broken than he was before. It's not a love story! This is an extra back story in the series, and does not have to be read in order to follow the series. If it's not for you, skip ahead to Trust In Me!

Buy here: http://Geni.us/DD-BB
Add to TBR: https://bit.ly/DD-BB-GR

TRUST IN ME - this is Kellan and Mia's story of how two damaged individuals learn to trust again and fall in love all over again. Trust in me is a single dad-nanny, enemies to lovers, forced proximity romance.

Buy here: http://Geni.us/TiM-BB

Add to TBR: https://bit.ly/TIM-BB-GR

THE TIES WE BREAK - this is a prequel set before Black Wedding. It tells the story of what happens to Belle when she is forced to auction her virginity, and Declan agrees to teach her. This is an extra book in the series, and does not have to be read in order to follow the series. If you want to follow the main storyline, you can skip ahead to Fighting To Be Free.

Buy here: http://Geni.us/TTWB-BB

Add to TBR: https://bit.ly/TTWB-BB-GR

FIGHTING TO BE FREE - this is Freya and Kian's love story. While Freya is fighting to be free of her Mafia Family, Kian is fighting for her. This is a friends to lovers, brothers best friend, forced proximity romance between an indie author and an MMA fighter who works for her mafia family.

Buy here: http://Geni.us/FTBF-BB

Add to TBR: https://bit.ly/FTBF-BB-GR

THE TIME IS NOW - this is Ryleigh and Shane's love story. When Shane is forced to return back to his mafia family to be the leader who was raised to be, his friendship with Raleigh is put to the test as they are forced to become enemies. When they are put on opposite sides, will Shane ever be able to tell her how he really feels? This is a friends to enemies to lovers romance.

Buy here: https://geni.us/TTIN-BB

Add to TBR: https://bit.ly/TTIN-BB-GR

THE LIES THAT SHATTER - this is Finn and McKenna's love story. When Finn is forced into his hardest honeytrap scam to date, he's forced to choose between finally finding love with McKenna, or following his father's rules.

Buy here: https://geni.us/TLTS-BB

Add to TBR: https://bit.ly/TLTS-BB-BB

TOGETHER WE REIGN - this is Evan and Teigan's love story, and it's the final book in the Beautifully Brutal Series. When enemies are exposed and the final battle is imminent, Evan must risk it all to save Teigan after she is sold to their enemy.
Buy here: https://geni.us/TWR-BB
Add to TBR: https://bit.ly/TWR-BB-BB

If you want to get a sneak peek at The Ties We Break, keep reading to find out what happens when Belle decides to auction off her virginity in a sex club, and manager Declan, has to help her learn what she like.

Please note - The Ties We Break is a prequel set before the events of Black Wedding. It doesn't have to be read to follow the main plot lines. If you'd rather stick to the main plot, skip ahead to Fighting To Be Free. Or, if you want to get some more back story on Kian and Desmond, and the sex club he runs, then this is the book for you. Keep reading for the first chapter...

Belle

"What do you mean all the money's gone?!" I yell at the pathetic excuse for a father standing in front of me.

"Don't yell at me, Issy. I didn't know how to tell you. I know both your grandma and Mum left the inheritance specifically for you, but I needed it. You don't understand," he whines, as I continue to pace around the shithole we call home.

"No, you're right. I don't understand. I don't understand how anyone could blow thirty thousand Euros in just two years. What the fuck have you spent it on? It sure as fuck isn't us because we still live in a shithole, and I'm the one putting food on the table, working all the hours I possibly can. This money was my way out, my chance to better myself. I have plans, Dad," I cry out as defeat spreads through my body, my muscles physically sagging.

Flopping down onto the old, ratty grey sofa, I pull my knees up to my chest, wrap my arms around them, and let my head flop onto my knees. I can't hold the tears back, they run freely down my face and I don't even try to stop them. This is the first time I have cried in years.

When I was younger, tears used to be a regular occurrence. I would cry for all the things I didn't have that other kids did; like money, food on the table that didn't come from a fast food restaurant or out of a bag, and a mum. I craved all the normal things everyone else took for granted. Every time I got bullied for having ratty clothes or had to miss out on a trip because Dad didn't have the money, I would cry. But then one day I asked myself why I was crying? What was I achieving by crying my eyes out every night? Sweet fuck all. That is when I decided I was going to do better, be better. I wanted to get out of Limerick, to go and see the world. But mostly, I wanted to get an education and train to do something I loved that would ensure I would always be financially stable.

I know that sounds weird and that most people would wish for riches, but unless you have been truly poor you won't know this feeling. You won't know what it's like to crave just enough money to buy food to last until the next payday. That is how I have been living. The week before my father gets paid his money from the state, if he has had a shit time or he's spent it before I got a chance to take it off him, then for at least a week, I know true hunger. I know what it's like to go to bed hungry and to wake up hungry, only getting something to eat because I qualified for a free school meal. How fucking sad is that? So, no, I have never craved riches, just stability.

"I'm sorry, Issy. I wanted to tell you, but I just never found the right time," he whimpers as he sits down on the edge of the sofa next to me. I feel him rest his hand on my knee, and I feel conflicted. I am so mad at him right now, I feel as though I could burst, but at the same time, he's still my dad.

"The right time would have been when I told you I got offered a place at Queen's College at the University of Oxford, and that I'd turned down any offer of funding and support because I knew I had Gran and Mum's money to use," I reply sarcastically, raising my head to look into his chocolate brown eyes. They're an exact replica of mine. In fact, they're the only thing I have in common with my dad, everything else is all Mum.

"I know, but you were so happy, I couldn't ruin that for you." His aged face wrinkles with sadness, and it occurs to me for the first time that my father really does look older than he actually is. I guess years of anxiety, depression, and booze will do that to a guy.

He didn't always used to look like this; grey, shaggy hair, wrinkled pale skin that sags from his bones, and a frame so thin he looks ill. He used to be strong, muscular, and proud of his appearance. I have seen pictures of him when he was younger, and I can see why my mum used to call him her Prince Charming. He really did look like all the Princes' from fairy tales. That all changed when Mum passed though. I was only eight years old, and even though ten years have passed, I remember it like it was yesterday. One day she wasn't feeling well, coughing a lot and struggling to catch her breath. Thinking she probably had a chest infection, we took her to the doctor. They diagnosed her with pneumonia and she went into hospital for treatment. Over the next couple of days, she became septic, and her organs started to fail. We watched her slip away right in front of our eyes. I've never felt so helpless or alone.

When Mum went, she took a piece of my dad with her. The romantic side of me wondered if that's what happens to soulmates when one dies. Do they take their partner's soul with them, to ensure they will meet again? I have no idea if I believe in that type of thing. All I know is that Mum and Dad met when they were fourteen and have been together ever since. Childhood sweethearts who fell in love and beat the odds. Everyone said they wouldn't make it, since Mum was from the rich side of town, and Dad was from the poor side, but they did, and then they had me.

My childhood was nothing compared to where I am now. I had a great house, good furniture, and food on the table. Mum was from a wealthy family, not like rolling in cash, but comfortable. She worked in a bookstore and spending my weekends lazing around the bookshop and reading everything in stock is what started my love of reading. Then when I lost Mum, I used these fantasy worlds to help me escape my own. I turned to books for support whereas Dad turned to alcohol and pills. I've tried to get him help. For ten years, I've tried to make him see that he's killing himself, but he never changes. Normally I would forgive my dad anything, but stealing the money left for me is unforgivable. Mum knew I wanted to do something with my life, and so the money she set aside when Gran died, was a good enough sum for me to go to a decent University. She wanted me to have a good education, and on her deathbed, that is what I promised her.

For the last ten years, I worked my ass off to get the grades I needed. When I finally got that acceptance letter for Queen's College at Oxford Medical School, I was over the fucking moon. I knew the thirty thousand Euros I inherited wouldn't pay for all four years, but I was happy to get a job. I just wanted to go to England and start over. A new life, a new me. Now, that's all gone. I'm supposed to leave in a month. I will never get the money in time.

"I-I'm s-sorry, Issy. P-please, forgive me. I-I have a little left. If you let me use that, I-I can go and t-try to make more," he stutters, as he pushes up off the sofa.

Rage courses through my body and I jump to stand in front of him. My dad isn't a tall man, maybe five-foot-eight, but compared to my five-foot-two frame, he looks bigger. Although, right now, he has never looked smaller to me. My voice is laced with anger as I place my hand firmly on his chest to stop him from moving. "Don't make the situation worse. We need that money for food. That is if you want to eat for the next week," I snarl.

He looks so deflated, but I can't bring myself to care. All I feel is rage for the loss of the future I promised Mum I would have. He starts to speak, no doubt to come up with more excuses, but I don't want to hear it. Walking towards me, as though to embrace me, I stop him, and before he can speak, I cut him off. "I am going out. I'll be back later, and for fuck's sake do not spend that money."

My threat hangs in the air as I grab my handbag and jacket off the sideboard where I left them. I throw on my well worn converse and storm out of the house. There's only one place to go to when I feel like this, Sian's house.

The walk to Sian's is short, thankfully, and having made it so many times before, I know all the shortcuts. I walk through the more deprived streets of Limerick, the ones I know so well that are littered with bin bags, random household items like mattresses, and even used needles. This area needs a lot of money invested into it, and some good paint jobs to get it looking anywhere near decent, but the town gave up on my neighbourhood a long time ago. Choosing instead to focus on the one nearby, the one Sian lives in.

Sian has been my best friend since I was five years old. She held my hand at my mum's funeral, she lets me stay at her house no questions asked when I need to escape from mine for a bit, and most importantly, she always has my back. We couldn't be more different, but that works for us. I'm a shy bookworm, who is quite happy going unnoticed in the background, whereas Sian loves to be centre stage. She's a party girl, making friends with everyone everywhere she goes.

I'm still wowed when I walk up the driveway, towards the house I think of as my second home. The house is grand with white bricks and beautiful bay windows. Sian's dad, Daryl, built the house just for his wife, Jill. I love watching them together, it's like seeing a love story play out in real life. Every time I say that, Sian rolls her eyes at me. She isn't at all a romantic like I am.

Daryl started with nothing, but he trained and worked hard to become an investment banker, which meant he was finally able to give his wife everything she ever wanted. But Jill isn't the meek housewife you would expect. She has fire, and puts her kids in their place the second they fall out of line, even now. She used to joke that she has a third eye, one that nobody can see, but it sees everything. Especially when her kids were naughty, she always knew, and growing up we had no idea how she did it. As adults, we now know it's simply because we live in a small neighbourhood, and Jill was friends with all the neighbours. But at the time, we really thought she magically knew whenever we were naughty.

I love hanging out at Sian's house, it always feels like a proper home. Sian and her two younger brothers are always arguing, and her mum is always pottering around the house doing some sort of hobby. Then, when it comes to dinnertime, they all sit down as a family and talk about their day. Even though I was always welcomed and treated like a family member, I still used to sit there and just watch them. I felt like the audience member of a show, watching Daryl and Jill. Even when they argue it's clear they love each other, like real love. The type that beats every hurdle and lasts for a lifetime. The love I dream about. The dream my parents had.

I don't bother to knock on the large wooden door, instead, I use the key I was given a few years ago and let myself in. As soon as I step foot in the entrance hall, I hear footsteps on the wooden floorboards heading my way. Jill appears in front of me, takes one look at me, and pity flashes through her eyes for just a fraction of a second before she pulls me into a giant hug. I embrace it, throwing my arms around my surrogate mum, and I let the floodgates open. As I rest my cheek against her chest, listening to the steadying rhythm of her heartbeat, my body is racked with sobs. Her hand rubs soothingly up and down my back, and I feel her guiding us into the living room. She breaks the hug for a second to sit us on the sofa before pulling me back into her arms. Her soft, gentle shushes soothe me, but she doesn't speak. This is one of the things I have always loved about Jill, she never forces me to talk. She always gives me time and space and just lets me talk when I'm ready. She doesn't question me or force me to talk when I don't want to. It's actually a brilliant tactic because I always tell her what's wrong eventually.

Finally, I pull back and look up into her deep, forest green eyes. Jill gives me a small smile that I try to return as she wipes stray tears from my cheeks. Some people were just made to be mothers, they can't help but mother people, and Jill is one of those. She loves her children fiercely, even when they don't deserve it. Her youngest, Tom, is a little terror, but she idolises him. Just like a mum should.

"Sweetheart, please don't cry. This is all new for me, I can't remember the last time you came to me crying. I'm used to the hugs, but this is new," she jokes, stroking my arm in comfort.

Slowly, I wipe the stray brown lock that's sweeping over my face back behind my ear before lounging back on the sofa to get comfortable. That's when I noticed my best friend, Sian, standing by the entrance to the living room. Her bright red hair is scrunched up on the top of her head in a messy knot, and even in baggy sweatpants and a hoodie, you can see how voluptuous Sian's body is. She is proud to call herself a curvy girl, and she embraces her body. Some people would call her fat, but they would be assholes. She is a healthy size, and given she is five-foot-seven, she is completely in proportion. Sian just likes to say she has an extra portion of everything, giving her curves. I've always admired her body confidence, it's something I've never had.

Once Sian knows I've spotted her, she gently walks in and sits down on my other side. As soon as her mum releases me, Sian pulls me in for a big hug. I hiccup and gulp down some big breaths, not sure I can manage any more tears. "Boo, what's the matter? I haven't seen you cry like this in years," Sian asks softly when she finally releases me.

Releasing a big sigh, I start to explain. Both mother and daughter sit transfixed, hanging on my every word, and I watch the anger rising in both of them the longer the story goes. When I finish, Sian hugs me but her mum leaps from the sofa and begins to pace across her beautiful, soft, grey rug.

"What fucking idiot gave that piss poor excuse for a father the ability to withdraw your money? Absolutely fucking crazy! I'm gonna give that eejit a piece of my mind!" she shouts, waving her clenched fist in the air. Her Irish accent gets a lot more pronounced when she yells, and it's funny to see such a usually quiet woman jumping to my defence. I want to hug her again and have her tell me it'll be alright, but she won't lie to me.

"Mum, sit down, will you, you're making me dizzy with all your pacing!" Sian yells towards her mother, who quickly flips her middle finger at Sian, letting her know she isn't happy about being told what to do. I chuckle to myself. Most of the time these two get on like a house on fire, but other times they bicker like an old married couple.

Jill starts her verbal comeback, so I decide I better step in. "Relax, Mrs O'Leary. I don't think he's worth your anger or my tears. I love my dad, but this is a step too far. I need to start calling the University, and anyone who can help me with grants or student loans. Once I've spoken to everyone and confirmed I'm screwed, then we can really worry. There may be someone who can help." I sigh, knowing it will be a pointless exercise. The cutoff to apply for financial aid was over a month ago, and I already sent the form back declining any help. I also have already confirmed my spot at Oxford, so it's not like I can go to a cheaper University I already turned down.

"Right, first, if you call me Mrs O'Leary one more time, I will tan your ass. You are like a child to me, Isabelle, and you know it. Call me Jill or don't call me at all, remember. Now that's out of the way, you get up to Sian's room and start making phone calls. Sian and I will be in the kitchen finishing supper. I've been slow-cooking a stew since this morning. I wanna do the finishing touches and bake some soda bread. We will shout you when it's ready," she instructs, cocking her hip as though she expects a challenge. She won't get one from me. I fucking love her stew. Sian, on the other hand, hates to cook and I see her start to protest, but her mother is having none of it and grabs hold of her hoodie covered arm, and begins dragging my feisty best friend towards the kitchen. Like mother, like daughter. They both have that typical Irish fire everyone talks about. I wish I had even just a spark.

I waste no time running upstairs to the room I think of as mine. I've been staying over so much that the O'Leary's put an extra bed in Sian's room so that I would know I always had somewhere to stay. I flop down on the grey bedspread I picked out, a massive contrast to the bright pink one that sits ruffled on Sian's bed. Taking a deep breath, trying to steady my racing heart, I let it out slowly as I begin my calls.

Over an hour later, I called every number I knew of, and then some that I found on Google. It's too late. All the scholarships and funding grants have already been allocated. I can apply again next year for any remaining years, but the first year is all on me. I asked admissions at the University of Oxford if I could defer my place by a year, that way I have a year to save up and also to apply for funding, but they made it clear this was a one-time offer. The snotty secretary I got through to spoke with the poshest English accent and delighted in telling me that places at Oxford Medical School are very prestigious and limited. There's a wait list snapping at my heels, like sharks waiting to take my place. Any other University I could have deferred my place, but not this one.

Tears begin to well up again, and I throw myself backwards until I'm lying on my bed staring up at the ceiling. I close my eyes and try to think of anything other than losing my dream.

I'm not entirely sure when it happened, but I must have fallen asleep, as the next thing I remember, Sian is sitting on the edge of my bed shaking me. I jump up from the sensation of being jolted awake. My heart skips a beat, racing to keep up.

"For fuck's sake, Sian! What have I told you about getting me up? You know I jump easily," I shout, as she laughs at my startled response. I'm the first to admit it's not difficult to scare or startle me, and Sian knows this.

"How did it go?" she mumbles, biting the corner of her lip.

"How I expected. If I turn down my place, I lose it for good. I can apply for support for year two onwards, but this year is all on me. I have a month to find almost thirty grand if I want to cover what I lost. So, unless I have some long lost rich uncle that pegs it and leaves everything to me, my only other option is to rob a bank." I hold my head in my hands, the despair quite evident in my voice. I'm not going to lie, robbing a bank isn't looking too bad right about now.

"You know I would make an amazing bank robber, but you are far too well-behaved for that shit," Sian jokes and I can't help but laugh. She's right, I'm not made for a life of crime. I hate any kind of attention, and would much rather curl up with a book. All the things a robber doth make.

"Look, Boo. I just talked to Mum about whether we can help you or not. Don't get mad at me, she was probably thinking it before I asked. But with me going off to University, and Terry needing to go to that special school, there just isn't enough extra to help out. We can give you some, but even I'm going to need extra cash as the money they're giving me is less than I expected," she huffs and I roll my eyes.

I love Sian, always have, but there's no denying she's an entitled princess. Her last comment just proved it. She is getting her fees and accommodation paid for and a regular allowance, but because it's a bit less than she was expecting she's in a mood. Then again, Sian has become accustomed to the spending lifestyle, and always seems to have cash to blow on things. I'm not sad by the comment itself though. I wouldn't expect them to help pay for me, that should be my own parents' responsibility. I'm also pleased they managed to get Terry into the school that specialises in kids on the autistic spectrum.

"I am grateful, but you know I'd never take your money. What's your plan to raise some cash?" I ask, and despite the layer of foundation she's wearing, I can see a slight blush spread across her cheeks and she looks sheepish.

"I don't know yet," she mumbles, obviously lying.

Staring with brows furrowed, I make it clear I'm not happy. "Don't lie to me. I can tell you have a plan, so what is it?"

"You won't approve." Her voice is firm and that just pisses me off more. I know I'm shy and reserved, but that doesn't mean I'm disapproving.

"Tell me!"

"Fine! So, you remember when I was with Ken?" she asks and I shudder. Fuck, that guy gave me the creeps, but she was infatuated with his slimy ass, so I stayed quiet. Luckily, they were a flash in the pan, over quickly.

"How can I forget?" My voice is laced with sarcasm and Sian's resulting eye roll makes me smile.

"He wasn't that bad. Anyway…Ken was into some really kinky shit, and he helped bring me out of my shell when it came to my sexuality. You know a bit, but there was a lot I didn't tell you. The main thing is that he liked to go to sex clubs… Well, just one, actually. Shades. It has a bit of a bad reputation given its owner, but we only ever went to the regular members' nights, not the underground scene." Her words register slowly. The more I take them in the more my mouth widens, and my eyes look like they're about to bug out of my head. As the shock spreads across my face, I see Sian roll her eyes as though what she just told me is no big deal. That there is nothing for me to be astounded by. When the fuck did my best friend start going to sex clubs? More importantly, why the fuck didn't she tell me?

"Shades, as in the members only club on the outskirts of town? I didn't even know it was dodgy," I ramble, circling around the real issues.

Everyone talks about the members only club, but nobody really talks about it being a sex club. Or if they do, I've never heard anything.

"It's owned by Desmond Doughty, and we all know how dodgy he is. Every time I've been there, and all that I've seen, they appear to be above board. I've heard rumours about more dodgy stuff happening behind the scenes, but that's just gossip."

A harsh laugh escapes my lips before she even has a chance to finish her sentence. "Yeah...because Desmond fucking Doughty is well known for his legal activities." Sarcasm drips off my every word, but my best friend ignores me with a roll of her eyes.

"Listen, Boo. Once a month, Shades organises an auction. I have only done one but I made a lot of money. Basically, you auction off a night with yourself. You set all the rules beforehand and everyone is securely vetted, so it's perfectly safe. You specify things you are willing to do, things you won't do, and anything that might raise the price tag a little more...things like that. Obviously, the more you are willing to do, the more money they are likely to pay," Sian calmly explains while I sit there looking at her like my long-term best friend just grew a second head I knew nothing about.

I wrack my brain looking for the signs, anything that I missed that would have shown me this side to her, but I can't find anything. My hands clench by my sides and my eyebrows draw together in annoyance. "Why the fuck is this the first time I'm hearing about this?" I spit out, louder than my usually calm tone.

"Because...and I mean this in the nicest possible way, Boo...you're a prude. We never talk about sex, not really. I'm not even sure if you're a virgin or not. Every time I've ever mentioned sex, and particularly with Ken, you go awkward as fuck. So, I avoid the topic of conversation and have just waited for you to bring up the topic. But, you never did. You're my best friend and I'd never want to make you uncomfortable, so I left it," Sian explains and I can't stop the flush of pink that spreads to my cheeks giving them a bright red glow.

Looking down at my now fidgeting hands, I'm embarrassed because everything she said is true. I have been so focused on my dream of becoming a doctor and getting out of this shithole, that I never really put much effort into other things. I've never had a serious boyfriend. Hell, I don't have any friends other than Sian. I'm much better alone in my room with a book in my hand. If we are talking about the literary world then I have loads of boyfriends, and I have experienced all manner of kinks, but sadly they're all in the fictional world where I spend most of my time. As a result, reality has suffered.

Don't get me wrong, I've kissed boys at parties, and done a bit of fooling about, but when Sian says she thinks I'm a virgin, of course I'm almost ashamed to confirm it. I'm about to go off to University, and I've never been on a fucking date.

"I'm not..."

Sian interrupts what I'm sure would be a very humiliating explanation, and I couldn't be more grateful. "Boo, you don't have to explain. Your private life is your own business, and if you want to keep it to yourself then I completely respect that. But in return, you have to respect that I don't tell you things."

"I can respect that, but I'd like to know more about Shades and how you made money. If you're okay telling me, that is?" I inquire whilst looking hopefully at my friend.

"Sure. So, I put myself on the lower end of the auction schedule, which basically means I'm only looking for light kink. I told them I'm submissive, looking for a Dom for the night. I gave a list of things I like and my hard limits. I told them I must have a safeword or I wouldn't take part. I'm happy to be bought by multiple people, including women, and am open to experimentation. I don't allow anything that leaves marks permanently, a sore ass for a day or two is encouraged. I just want to try new things and learn more about myself and my body. I explained I had subbed before and was trained to a certain level,"

Sian says, looking over at me to check if I'm still following along. My frozen expression has her pausing, and I nod for her to continue.

"I was bought by a man who gave me one hell of a fucking night, Is. He pushed me to places I've never even dreamt of going, and I loved it. I've met up with him again at the club to scene, but neither of us is looking for a long-term commitment. He paid the club ten thousand Euros for me, and I got nine thousand. They keep ten percent of the price for hosting. Oh, and when I say we met up to scene, that basically means that we act out a sexual fantasy that we have created together, meeting both of our sexual needs. As long as we follow each other's limits, we just let it evolve a little like a scene would in a film. So if someone says they want to scene with you, that's what it means."

I'm brought out of my bubble at the mention of the money she made, but also what they kept. "Isn't that a lot for them to keep?" I ask, hoping I don't sound too naive.

"They earn it, Boo. They make sure to screen all the applicants prior to the bidding, and if someone who bids on you is not a suitable match, they won't allow the bid to go through. I had a man bid on me, but he liked blood play, which is one of my hard limits, and so they refused his bid. Even if he promised not to do blood play with me, they can't take that risk. They want all their members to be safe. Everyone has a full sexual health screening before joining the auction or requesting a bidding plate. It's a really well-run process, Issy, but it's not for everyone."

Her words echo around my mind, as I try to take them in. There's so much in the statement that I don't understand. It makes me feel like a schoolgirl playing dress up at her mum's dressing table. Except, I don't have a mum, and I am a grown-up. So, I need to pull my big girl panties up and do what is needed to get me the money I need to get the hell out of here.

"I want to see the club," I state, hating how shaky my voice goes at the end. So much for sounding confident.

"Issy..."

"Look, Sian, I'm not saying I am going to sign up, but I do need to see what it's all about. I need money, and right now, this is my best option."

"Okay, Boo, have it your way. We may as well go tonight. Friday is a busy night, so there will be plenty to see, and I can sign you in as my companion. You will be given a black and gold wristband to wear, and you must have it visible at all times. The black basically means you're not available and are just watching, the gold means you aren't a full member yet. I will explain more when we're there because I can almost hear your brain ticking from over here." Standing, she walks over to the chest of drawers in the corner of the room as she explains the wristband system more.

"I have so many questions, I don't even know where to start." I sigh, beginning to feel overwhelmed, whereas Sian simply chuckles to herself.

Pulling her phone out, she types out a message while I wait, before finally looking up with a smile. "All will be revealed tonight, but it is much better to show you in person. I need to take a picture of your driving licence so they can do your background check before you get there tonight. Have you got it with you?" she asks, my eyes growing as wide as saucers. What kind of a place needs to conduct a background check?

Sian's laugh lets me know I said it out loud instead of in my head. "This is the type of place people come to if they want to try new things, or to explore their personal needs whilst maintaining their relationship. Or they just want to try things safely, and in some cases, away from the public eye. There are members in this club that are important people with high-ranking jobs, but when they put on their wristband they become nobody like everyone else in the room. When you become a full member, you will be asked to pick a club name. If you choose to tell people your real name, that is up to you, but most people don't. People pay a lot of money for anonymity, which is why you will be made to sign a Non-Disclosure Agreement before you can go in. I promise you that it's safe, and if at any point you want to leave then we will leave. Deal?"

Sian holds her hand out for me, like she always has since we were little. But not to shake hands. Instead, we link our pinky fingers together and shake on it. It's our version of a pinky promise, one we've stuck to all this time.

"Okay then, let's go and eat before Mum sends a search party. Then you can go home and get dressed. I will pick you up just before ten tonight. The live show starts at eleven, so we will have plenty of time to look around before then. Just for the record, I don't think this is a good idea, and I don't think it's the right way forward for you, Boo. But, I know your dad has put you in a terrible situation, which is why, against my better judgement, I'm taking you to the club. I don't think you are anywhere near prepared enough to join the auction, but I will let you judge for yourself," she explains, taking my driving licence off me and taking a picture of it. She also takes a snap of me sitting on the bed, but I don't question it. I have much bigger things to worry about right now. Like, what the fuck do you wear to a night out at a sex club?

If you enjoyed reading this sneak peek from The Ties We Break, then don't forget to pre-order it now:

https://geni.us/TTWB-BB

Acknowledgements

There's a massive amount of people I need to thank for getting this book ready, and apologies in advance if I miss anyone.

To my BETAs - Zoe-Amelia, Amanda, and Kerrie-Louise - thank you for all your hard work. For reading my rough version and helping me to make it better. Also, thank you for working on such a tight schedule for me. I couldn't do this without you!

To Rumi - My Amazing Editor - Thank you for doing such a great job, and for loving my characters. Also, thanks for working so quickly on my tight time frame. Your hard work is always much appreciated!

To Shaley at Pretty Little Images - thank you so much for working with me to get the teaser graphics as perfect as they are. I know I was super picky to start with, but we got there in the end.

To Dez at Pretty in Ink Creations - Thank you so much for creating this beautiful cover. This was the hardest one to get right, and I'm sure I annoyed the crap out of you while we were doing it. But I'm so pleased with the final result. You have got Kellan and Mia down perfectly!

To Ena and Amanda at Enticing Journey - thank you as always for your hard work and for getting my book into as many hands as possible. I couldn't do this without you.

To BL at Blurb Me Daddy - Girl, you helped me perfect these blurbs, and it was help that I really needed. You made my words shine and I'm grateful.

To Mr Luna - thank you for standing by my side while I'm on this crazy journey. You are always the first to believe in me, and I'm very lucky to have you.

To my LUNAtics - I have the best readers, and I cannot thank you enough for picking up my book and embracing the Doughty's. You love these guys as much as I do, and I'm so grateful for you throwing yourself in because it means I can keep writing them. I can't wait for you to see what is coming up!

Thank you to each and every one of you for helping make Trust in Me such a success. I'm so grateful and I can't wait for you to see what I have planned next.

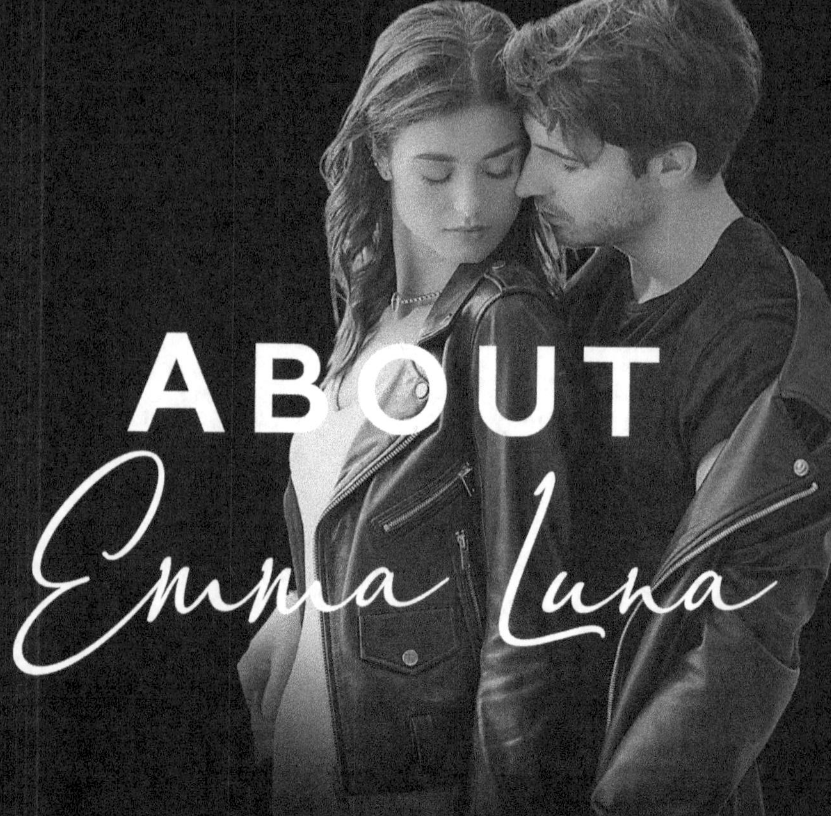

ABOUT
Emma Luna

Emma Luna is a USA Today Bestselling dark romance author from the UK. In a previous life she was a Midwife and a Lecturer, but now she listens to the voices in her head and puts pen to paper to bring their stories to life. In her spare time, when she should be sleeping, she also loves to edit, proofread, and format books for other amazing authors.

Emma's books are dark, dangerous, and devilishly sexy. She loves writing about strong, feisty, but underestimated women, and the cocky, dirty-mouthed men they bring to their knees.

When Emma isn't writing, promoting, or editing books she can be found napping, colouring in adult colouring books, and collecting novelty notebooks. She also enjoys coffee and gossiping with her mum, playing or having hugs with her gorgeous nephew, who is the light of her life, and curling up on the sofa to watch a film with Mr Luna. Oh and for those of you that don't know, Emma is a hardcore Harry Potter fan—Team Ravenclaw!!

Thank you for taking a chance on a crazy Brit and the voices inside her head. That makes you a true LUNAtic now too!

I love chatting and catching up with readers. I love letting you know what books I'm working on, what I have coming up next, and my new releases. So, don't be afraid to come and say hi, or drop me an email. If you love my characters, tell me!!

If you want to find out all things Emma Luna you can join my newsletter here:

https://www.emmalunaauthor.com

If you have facebook, you can join my reader group for exclusive news and giveaways:

https://www.facebook.com/groups/emmaslunatics

If you would like to check out any of Emma's other books or stalk her in more places, you can find everything you need here:

https://www.linktr.ee/emmaluna

facebook.com/EmmaLunaAuthor
instagram.com/emmalunaauthor
amazon.com/Emma--Luna/e/B082GNYLM4
bookbub.com/profile/emma-luna
goodreads.com/emmaluna
tiktok.com/@emmalunaauthor

MORE BOOKS
BY
Emma Luna

SINS OF OUR FATHERS SERIES

Broken

https://geni.us/SouF-Broken

.

MANAGING MISCHIEF

Piper

https://geni.us/MM-Piper

.

BEAUTIFULLY BRUTAL SERIES

Black Wedding - Bree and Liam's Story
https://geni.us/BW-BB

Dangerously Deceptive - Kellan's Prequel
https://geni.us/DD-BB

Trust In Me - Kellan and Mia's Story
https://geni.us/TiM-BB

The Ties We Break - Declan and Belle's Prequel
http://Geni.us/TTWB-BB

Fighting To Be Free - Kian and Freya's Story
http://Geni.us/FTBF-BB

The Time Is Now - Ryleigh and Shane's Story
https://geni.us/TTIN-BB

The Lies That Shatter - Finn and McKenna's Story
https://geni.us/TLTS-BB

Together We Reign - Evan and Teigan's Story
https://geni.us/TWR-BB

WILLOWMEAD ACADEMY - CO-WRITE WITH MADDISON
COLE

Life Lessons
https://geni.us/WA-LifeLessons

STANDALONES

Under the Cover of Darkness
https://geni.us/TL8-UtCoD

I Was Always Yours
http://Geni.us/IWasAlwaysYours

ANTHOLOGIES

Ours To Keep: A Why Choose (RH) Anthology
https://geni.us/OursToKeep

9 781916 531024